MEET ME
in
BARCELONA

Books by Mary Carter

SHE'LL TAKE IT

ACCIDENTALLY ENGAGED

SUNNYSIDE BLUES

MY SISTER'S VOICE

THE PUB ACROSS THE POND

THE THINGS I DO FOR YOU

THREE MONTHS IN FLORENCE

MEET ME IN BARCELONA

Published by Kensington Publishing Corporation

MEET ME
in
BARCELONA

MARY CARTER

KENSINGTON BOOKS
www.kensingtonbooks.com

KENSINGTON BOOKS are published by

Kensington Publishing Corp.
119 West 40th Street
New York, NY 10018

eISBN-13: 978-0-7582-8473-0
eISBN-10: 0-7582-8473-X
First Kensington Electronic Edition: August 2014

ISBN-13: 978-0-7582-8472-3 ˙
ISBN-10: 0-7582-8472-1
First Kensington Trade Paperback Printing: August 2014

10 9 8 7 6 5 4 3 2 1

Printed in the United States of America

I'd like to dedicate this book to: Dave France, who decided on a whim to go to Barcelona after seeing a piece on the Sagrada Família. Keep up your traveling spirit! And my three aunts: Carole Ranta, Dianne Hawley, and Donna Anservitz. They buy and read all of my books and even if they didn't, I love them dearly.

ACKNOWLEDGMENTS

I'd like to thank my editor, John Scognamiglio; my agent, Evan Marshall; my publicist, Vida Engstrand; my production editor, Paula Reedy; and all the other Kensington staff who work tirelessly to bring a book to the shelves and digital world. I once took a trip to Barcelona with a group of girls, and at times the dynamics were strained. As uncomfortable as it was, I'm thankful, for it inspired the idea of writing about a complex female relationship, a love/hate dynamic. I am grateful to be a writer, so that I can use and learn from all of life's little experiences, good and bad. I'd also like to thank my readers. May you, too, get to travel and see the world. But for the times when it's not feasible, I wish you grand journeys between the pages of a book.

CHAPTER 1

Grace Sawyer had never believed in magic, or miracles for that matter, but that didn't mean a girl couldn't pray for a little bit of both. She'd been praying a lot lately. She stepped into her mother's hospice room and crinkled her nose as the scent of SpaghettiOs and Lysol washed over her. She glanced at her mom's bedside table. Sure enough, sitting too close to the edge was a chipped brown bowl overflowing with SpaghettiOs, paired with an industrial-sized bottle of Lysol. Grace hesitated. Processed food in a can and industrial-sized cleaners were just the kind of things that could trigger an emotional avalanche inside her. This wasn't what life should come to in the end. It wasn't right. If replacing those bits with yellow roses and a nice roast dinner would have changed a single thing about this horrific situation, Grace would have done it lightning quick. This was her mother. The woman who had taken care of everybody else her entire life. Who had opened her heart to homeless, damaged children. She deserved more. But strangely, Lysol and SpaghettiOs were two items Jody Sawyer had insisted on lately. Grace had to fight her instincts, her primal desire to make everything nice, and instead keep each visit as pleasant as possible. She smiled even though neither of her parents had noticed her yet.

Her mother was wide-awake, eyes glued to the television in the corner, where a soap opera blared. Before she had moved into this facility, Jody had never watched a soap opera in her life. She wouldn't have been caught dead eating SpaghettiOs either. The Lysol, on the other hand, was familiar. Grace's mother had spent her entire life within an arm's reach of it. Most likely the product of having a revolving door of foster children. Where were they now? Not a single kid from the past had come to visit Grace's mother. After all she'd done for them. It made Grace rage inside, but her mother hadn't complained about it once.

Her father, Jim, sat next to the bed on his favorite recliner from home. Jim had put up quite a fuss to get them to allow it in the room, and he was extremely proud of the accomplishment. "I put up my dukes!" he'd say with a grin. Then he'd pump his fists in the air. He'd been practically living here since the doctor had given them the latest grim diagnosis. Grace couldn't help but think it was probably a welcome relief for her father's patients. Her father was a psychotherapist, and although he was insightful, Grace had always thought he was a tad too prying. Then again, maybe that was the whole point of going to a shrink. Baring your deepest, darkest secrets. It was Grace's idea of a worst nightmare. "Hi, Dad." Grace walked over and planted a kiss on her father's cheek. He looked almost as thin as her mother. He lowered his newspaper and took off his reading glasses. "Well, hello there, Graceful."

"How is she?"

"In and out."

Grace nodded and slowly approached her mother's bed. "Mom?"

Her mother's eyes didn't leave the television set. "Oh, hello," Jody Sawyer said. "Are you the cleaning lady?"

"Like I said," her father said. "In and out."

"It's me, Mom. I'm your daughter, Grace."

"My daughter doesn't clean," Jody said.

"She's got that right," Jim said.

Grace burst out laughing, then quickly tried to squelch it with a cough. Jody Sawyer pointed to the television and shook her head. She wanted them to be quiet. Grace looked at her father.

"Why don't you wait for a commercial?" he said. He patted the folding chair next to him. Grace sat. "How was your day, sweetheart?"

Grace reached into her bag and removed two McDonald's bags. She handed one to her father. He grasped the bag in one hand and squeezed her hand with the other like she'd brought him champagne and caviar. "Actually pretty wild," she said. "I have news."

"Do you mind?" her father said.

"Go right ahead."

He unwrapped his Big Mac and took a bite. "Mm-mmm," he said. He looked blissful. Grace wanted to bury her face in her sleeve and sob. SpaghettiOs and soap operas, and Mickey D's? Didn't they know they deserved better? They were from such a humble generation. Not like the entitled kids of today. Her parents were simple and good people. Let them enjoy what they enjoy. No use forcing kale or tofu burgers on her father now. Grace forced another smile, then reached into the second bag and handed him a napkin.

He winked at her and dabbed his mouth. Then his eyes went to her ring finger. "Did the boy finally pop the question?"

Grace laughed and stretched out her hand in front of her as if examining it for the first time. She hardly ever wore rings or bracelets; they got in the way of playing the guitar. Maybe now she would start. She would wear silver rings with semiprecious gems, like amber, and big chunky bracelets. Maybe even grow her nails and paint them pink. Was that a good enough trade for giving up on her dream? Grace slipped her hands under her legs as if she could shut out making any decisions by sitting on them. "Not yet. But you're never going to believe this—"

The soap opera went to commercial. A jingle for car insurance came on. "Gracie Ann!" her mother said. She smiled and opened her arms as if Grace had just walked into the room.

"Hi, Mom." Grace got up and hugged her mother. She felt so frail and tiny in Grace's arms. Grace could probably pick her up and carry her around the room without breaking a sweat. Not fair, God! Not fair. "You didn't eat your lunch," Grace said, glancing at the SpaghettiOs.

"She insisted on them," her father said.

"I ate ten Os," her mother said. "I couldn't possibly eat more than ten Os. I have to watch my figure."

"If you stuck her in the middle of a cornfield, crows would land on her," her father said with his mouth full of burger.

"You're not far behind, Dad," Grace said.

"Just how we wanted to spend our golden years. Hanging out in a farmer's field like a couple of straw men," her father mused in between bites.

Anything would be better than this place, Grace thought. She wished she could bring her parents to a beautiful field at the height of autumn. Give them trees with leaves on fire, and hay that shone like gold underneath an afternoon sun. Give them the smell of apples and the embrace of a warm wind.

"You look beautiful, Grace," her mother said. Jody Sawyer reached up with a trembling hand and touched the pearls around Grace's neck. "Is it your birthday?"

"In a few weeks, Mom."

"Happy birthday, darling."

"Thank you."

"How old are you now? Thirteen?"

"I'm turning thirty," Grace said. "How are you feeling?"

"I'm all better now, Gracie. I can go home now." Jody Sawyer looked at her husband Jim, as if expecting him to start packing up the room.

"I don't think today, Mom," Grace said. Or ever. As much as she tried to shut it out, Grace could hear the doctor's voice in her head in a constant loop. *Maybe a month, six months at the most, we can't say for sure. All we can do now is make her comfortable.*

Make her comfortable? Was there any comfort in knowing you had six months, maybe one?

"Gracie said she has some news," Jim said.

Her mother clasped her hands under her chin. "I love news," she said. "And fries," she called to her husband.

Grace nodded at her father. He picked up the second bag, then passed it up to Jody. It was odd. If Grace gave her the fries before she asked for them, her mother wouldn't touch them. If Grace waited until Jody voiced a desire for them, Jody ate every single one. Just one of the little mysteries of dementia. What a double whammy. The doctors weren't sure if fighting off the cancer had brought on the problems with her memory, or if she would've been hit with it anyway. There were just no two ways about it; life could be extremely cruel. "Give us the news," her father said. "Hurry before her show comes back. We're not allowed to talk during *Days of Our Lives*."

"Jake won an all-expense-paid trip to Barcelona," Grace said.

"Well, I'll be," Jim said. "How'd he do that?"

"The veterinarian group had some sort of a raffle," Grace said. "But Jake didn't even enter."

"He won a raffle he didn't even enter?"

"Dan went to one of the conferences without Jake and entered for him." Dan was Jake's partner at the animal hospital. He and Jake were like brothers.

"That was mighty nice of him."

"But we feel guilty. Dan could have taken the trip himself."

"I'm sure he filled out an entry for himself as well as Jake."

"True."

"And Jake won. Seems fair to me."

"But we would be leaving Dan to run the clinic all by himself, and he'd even have to watch Stella." Stella was the best English bulldog a couple could ever ask for. If she could, Grace would take Stella to Spain. Stella was a hit wherever they went due to her prowess on a skateboard.

"Well, isn't that special." Jim slapped his knee. "Jody, did you hear that? Gracie and Jake won a trip to Spain."

He had entirely missed the point that they felt guilty that

Dan would be getting the short end of the stick. It made her wonder how often he misunderstood his patients.

"That's wonderful, dear," Jody said. Her eyes traveled back to the television.

"I'm not going," Grace said.

"What do you mean?" her father said.

"There's a catch." There always was.

"You have to pay for your hotel?"

"No, it's all paid for."

"So what's the problem?"

"The dates are set in stone. We'd have to go at the end of next week."

"So?"

"It's a ten-day trip. I don't want to leave Mom for that long."

"Nonsense," her father said. "You have to go."

"I'd be gone for my birthday."

The soap opera was back. Jody snatched up the remote and aimed it at the television like she was holding it up at gunpoint. Grace's father patted her knee. "We'll celebrate with you when you get back, kiddo. Take it from me, kiddo—life's too short not to take free trips." Jody glared at Jim and pressed on the volume until it was almost deafening. A few seconds later, there was a series of soft knocks on the wall behind her bed.

"Sorry, Mrs. Maple," her father called out. "You have to turn it down, dear."

"That old bitch," her mother said. In all Grace's years growing up, with all the strange boys tearing through the house, and fighting, and even through the whole Carrie Ann ordeal, Grace had never heard her mother curse, let alone direct it at somebody. Jody turned the volume down a smidge and pointed at the television. "He's the one I like," she exclaimed. There was a tall man, visible only in silhouette behind a flimsy shower curtain. "They think he's Flo's long-lost brother, but actually he's just escaped from prison where he was convicted of murdering his second wife. Or is it his third? I can't remember. Second or third wife, take your pick. It'll come to me. Darn tootin' he's totally innocent, but I know that Flo. She's going to be sniffing around his tight buns like a hound dog short of a bone. Second. Definitely second wife."

Grace and her father looked at the television. The naked man stepped out of the shower, surrounded by steam. All you could see were his six-pack abs and bulging biceps. Grace supposed they wanted you to imagine something else bulging. This was definitely soft-core porn for women. Tan, and slick, and ripped, and glistening, he didn't seem to be in any hurry to pick up a towel. He walked up to the bathroom mirror, reached up, and wiped away the condensation. Soon, his gorgeous face came into view. Grace had to stifle a laugh as he began to touch his cheekbones like a blind man trying to see what he looked like. "Isn't it awful?" Jody said. "Pretending to be someone else? When all he wants to do is search for his wife's real killer."

Grace raised an eyebrow at her father. He looked down at his stomach, and in doing so dripped a thick glob of ketchup onto his fraying cardigan. "Didn't even look like that when we got married," Jim said.

"I think he must have had plastic surgery after his prison break," Jody continued. "That's why he doesn't recognize himself!"

Jim Sawyer watched his wife with a smile and a shake of the head. "You wouldn't leave her for ten days," Grace said to her father.

"They sure did a pretty good job on him though, don't you think?" Jody said. Based on where her mother was looking you'd think he'd had plastic surgery on his crotch.

"If Jake wants some old man tripping along with him, just say the word and I'll pack my bags," Jim said.

Jody glanced at Jim. He winked at her. She smiled back. Then she turned a smile on Grace. It was actually the first genuine smile Grace had seen out of her mother in a week. "You have to go, Carrie Ann."

Carrie Ann. The words felt like two gunshots to the chest. Just hearing that name come out of her mother's mouth made

Grace's heart start tripping. She almost shot out of her chair. "I'm Grace," she said. "Gracie Ann." Her voice cracked. "Dad?" she said.

"She's confused, honey. The past and the present, it's just one big, ugly glob." Pinpricks of shame began forming at the base of Grace's spine.

"I'm not confused," Jody said. "Carrie Ann came to visit me."

"My God," Grace said. This time she did shoot out of her chair. Carrie Ann was the only girl foster child the Sawyers had ever taken in. At first she had been like a sister to Grace.

"Who is she married to now?" Jody said. "I can't remember."

"Pay no attention to her, Gracie," Jim said.

"Why can't I remember?" Jody pressed on her temples with her index fingers, as if she could squeeze the memory out of her head.

Grace took a step toward her mother. "When did she come and visit you, Mom?"

"Grace, I told you she didn't," Jim said. "Don't egg your mother on."

"I'm not egging her on, Dad, but if Carrie Ann was here, I want to know about it."

Her father whacked his newspaper on the side of his chair. "I told you she wasn't! And I should know. I've been sitting right here!"

"She's still such a pretty girl," Jody said. "She asked about you, Grace. She asked me all sorts of questions about you."

Jim got up and threw up his arms. "She's out of her mind!" He began to pace.

"Dad," Grace said. "Hush." Her mother suddenly became very still, which meant she was listening. Grace took her father by his arm and led him back to his chair.

"I'm sorry. She won't remember me saying it."

"That's not the point."

"I can't help it. Carrie Ann this; Carrie Ann that. I thought we'd put that nuisance behind us for once and for all. Is this what it comes to? Reliving your worst nightmare?"

"I've never heard you speak so harshly about Carrie Ann,"

Grace said. Her mom was the one who used to say the worst things about Carrie Ann. She said Carrie Ann was evil. She said Carrie Ann was a curse that would follow all of them to their graves. Once she had even said there wasn't enough Lysol in the world to get rid of that stain. And each insult had cut into Grace like her mother was saying it about her. Her sister. Of sorts. Her own Dickens-like drama. Carrie Ann was the best thing that had ever happened to Grace, and she was the worst. She'd been out of their lives for nearly fifteen years. And Grace had spent every one of them trying, and failing, to put the past behind her. She turned to her father.

"Why didn't you tell me?"

"Tell you what?"

"That Mom's been talking about her."

"Because I don't want to dredge up all that nonsense. It's her damn medication. I keep telling the doctor it's making her worse, and he won't listen to me." Her father slammed his fist on the arm of the chair. "These people think just because we're old that we're stupid. She wouldn't be so forgetful if she cut down on some of those pills. How do I know that? Because she's my *wife*. Because I've been married to this woman for forty-four years. You know what he said to me?"

"Who?"

"That snot-nosed doctor, that's who!"

"What did he say?"

"Put me in my place. In front of my wife. 'You're a psychotherapist, correct? Not a psychiatrist? You don't prescribe medication?' That's what the snot-nosed so-called doctor actually said to me. Can you believe that? Some twenty-year-old who just started wiping his own ass. I'm telling you she's on too many pills! Makes her soupy. He won't listen to me!"

"It's okay, Dad. Calm down. It's okay."

"I can't bear hearing her talk about Carrie Ann. Your mother's the one who told us never to mention Carrie Ann's name again."

Forbid us. Forbid us to ever mention her name again. "I know, Dad. I'll talk to the doctor. Calm down."

"I always wanted to go to Spain," Jody said. She turned off the television and patted the side of the bed. So she'd heard and understood the conversation. God, the brain was a mysterious thing.

Grace went over and sat down. "You never told me that."

"I would hardly share that with a stranger."

I'm your daughter! she wanted to shout. But her mother couldn't help it.

"Just keep talking," her father said. "At least she's not dredging up ghosts, or drooling over naked stud muffins."

And now Grace couldn't believe her father had just said "naked stud muffins." Maybe getting away for a bit wasn't such a bad idea. Grace turned back to her mother. "Why did you always want to go to Spain?"

"My mother went to Spain. All by herself. When she was in her seventies."

"I know," Grace said. It had been just after Grace's grandfather had died. Her grandparents were supposed to take the trip together. Everyone thought Annette Jennings would cancel the trip. Instead, she buried her husband and packed her bags. Little Annette, who had never been outside of her home state. Grace had had many conversations with her grandmother about that trip. She was proud of her too.

"It was really something," Jim said. "Because in those days seventy wasn't the new fifty or whatever the kids say today. Seventy was *seventy*."

"Tell me about it," Grace said.

Jody Sawyer straightened up, and her eyes seemed to take in more light. "Well, it's not like it is now. Women didn't travel alone back then. Wasn't that brave? My mother sent me a postcard from Madrid of a beautiful tango dancer in a red dress. The dress was made of actual material—beautiful red silk right on the postcard. I'll never forget it. She'd only written one sentence on the back. 'Robert would've loved the landing.' My father was very picky with landings and always impressed when the pilot pulled off a smooth one. Anyway. As soon as I got that postcard I knew my mother was going to be all right. 'Robert would have loved the landing.' After she died I spent hours just touching that silky red dress with the tips of my fingers and imagining my mother dancing in the streets of Spain."

Jody Sawyer looked up and swayed her upper body slightly as if watching her faraway self dance. Then she looked down at her hands, twisting the bedsheet. "Look how ugly and wrinkled I am now."

"You're not ugly and wrinkled, Mom. You're beautiful."

"I wish I had that postcard now." Her mother looked up into space. "I lost it."

Grace hesitated. Did she, or didn't she? Grace opened the bedside drawer and took out the postcard. Her mother was right. The dress was silky. Grace handed it to her mother and watched her eyes light up. Next her mother gently outlined the edge of the dancer's dress with the trembling tip of her right index finger. Her fingernail was misshapen, the peach paint flaking. Grace would have to see if they could bring in a manicurist.

Jody looked at Grace, her eyes clear and bright. "Gracie Ann, you have to go. Film everything. I'm dying to see Barcelona through you." Grace must have looked stricken, for her mother laughed and then put her hand over her heart. "Sorry, no pun intended." Like antennas being manipulated for a clearer signal, sometimes her mother tuned in perfectly. Jody Sawyer laughed again, and Grace couldn't help but laugh with her.

"Mom."

"Make me feel like I'm there," Jody said, closing her eyes. "Help me shut out this hospice. Let me see beautiful Barcelona." She took Grace's hand and held it. "Do it for me. I'll feel like I'm with you. Bring a camera. And your guitar," she added. "You never know." When Grace still didn't answer, her mother opened her eyes, and lifted Grace's chin up with her hand like she used to do when Grace was a child. "Be brave, Gracie Ann. Just like my mother."

"Like my mother too," Grace whispered back.

CHAPTER 2

Barcelona. Just saying the name gave Grace a thrill, like a surfer riding the crest of a wave. Spain was a beautiful dream. The European city had a relaxed beach feel with a carnival-like atmosphere. Buzzing with activity, yet mellow at the same time.

Grace and Jake stepped underneath an archway and into the large town square that was just down the alley from their flat. Fifteenth century tan-stone buildings consisting of apartments on top and businesses on the bottom formed the outer edge of the square, while a round fountain with a statue of an angel took center stage. Her wings were spread, and in the palm of her stone hand she cradled a delicate bird. Wooden benches with faded green paint lined the perimeter, and potted plants positioned underneath awnings spilled their bright red and purple petals at meticulous intervals. With the ancient pavement and huge arches on all corners, it felt positively medieval. People adorned the square like well-placed decorations. A young girl with a backpack was sprawled on a bench with a sketchbook. A mother chased a toddler who was chasing a pigeon. A shopkeeper leaned on his broom and stared out at the hills. A group of schoolchildren scrambled around teachers who were trying to get them in line. Jake positioned his new state-of-the-art video camera in front of his face and eyed Grace through the lens.

"Film time," he said. "It's perfect here." It was true; strips of early afternoon sun streaked in through the gaps in the buildings and bathed everything around them in a comforting glow. There was a fresh smell in the air that Grace wished they could capture on film. Grace felt infused with hope, as if anything and everything was possible. Jake fiddled with his camera like a surgeon preparing his tools. She didn't ask how much he had spent on it, but she knew it had been in the thousands. So far he'd looked stricken any time Grace hinted that she wanted to give it a try. It took him a while to situate her just so, right in front of the center fountain, then a few steps to the right, then one step forward. Perfect. Wait—could she angle toward him just a smidge more?

"Recording," he said. He tried to say it with a Spanish accent, and it made her laugh. He grinned in return.

Grace stretched her arms open, looked directly at the camera, and did her best imitation of a genuine smile. "Hi, Mom. Hi, Dad. It's your daughter, Grace. I'm here with my boyfriend, Jake. As you can see, we arrived safely in Barcelona, Spain, and this town square is just a short stroll from our lovely apartment. Note all of the gorgeous stone buildings on the outer edge, and the arched entrances leading into cobblestone alleys. We don't see architecture like this in Nashville, do we?"

Jake lowered the camera and gave her a pained look.

"What?"

"You're stiff."

"You would be too if you had to constantly introduce yourself to your own mother."

"Aside from that," Jake said. He walked up to her, took her heavy handbag off her shoulder, and slung it around his own. He fluffed her hair. Then stepped back into filming position. Grace yawned. "No yawning."

"I'm jet-lagged."

"No complaining." She laughed. "That's better. Now relax. Just be yourself."

"I'm camera shy."

"You sing in front of hundreds of people."

Not anymore, Grace thought. Never again. But this wasn't the time or place to break it to Jake that her singing career was over. She was never going to sing in public again. Ever. "That's different." It was true. Instead of giving her stage fright, playing in front of large crowds had always comforted Grace. Country fans were always so supportive. She could disappear into the music, her voice, and blend into the collective audience. *But it wasn't long before I started to drift off. . . .*

"Stop thinking about that review."

Jake was reading her mind again. Spooky. "You started it."

"Are you carrying it on you?"

Jake was holding on to her purse. So, technically, at this moment she did not have it on her. Sometimes, in life, you had to rely on technicalities just to get by. "No." Just thinking about that awful review, just thinking about Marsh Everett made her want to smash and burn things. Childish. All artists had to deal with bad reviews. *Shallow doesn't quite cut it. . . . A dog bowl has more depth. . . .* How could he say such awful things about her? Even if he thought there was room for improvement, didn't he know she put her entire being into what she did? Didn't he know she was a flesh and blood person with feelings? Why didn't anyone warn her how much someone else's words could literally cut a person to the core? Grace had always thought she was strong, that she had confidence. But she wasn't. She was just a twig that could be snapped in two. Give her the sticks and stones any day. Words hurt. They burned.

Marsh Everett just didn't know her. Surely if he knew her, if he could see into her soul, he would like her. He would like her music. There had to be a way to get him to like her. This was everything she'd always wanted. And she had admired Marsh Everett. He was passionate about country music, and he had been the make or break of so many stars. She'd always imagined meeting him, maybe even becoming friends. She would have died of happiness a few years ago if she had known one day she was going to get his attention. Of course it would have been a good thing, because she would have wanted to be dead if she had known the horrible things he was going to say about her. *Stop it.* She had to let it go! She had to. This certainly wasn't the time or the place. But it hurt her to the quick, burned like a—

"Grace."

"Here," she said like a child who had just been called on in school. She should have ripped the review in half. She should have eviscerated every copy of *Country Weekly.* Jake looked as if he were trying to heal her with his mind. He looked so worried about her. "Take two," Grace said, as chipper as possible. "The show must go on!"

"Repeat after me," Jake said. "Marsh Everett is a turd." Grace laughed. Oh, if only the multimillionaire producer could hear them now. "Say it."

"Marsh Everett is a turd." *A turd who has been able to make and break many aspiring country singers. A turd who hates me.*

"Perfect," Jake said. "And scene." Jake gestured for Grace to start again.

"Hi, Mom and Dad. It's your daughter, Grace. Here we are in beautiful Barcelona. Robert would have loved the landing."

"What?" Jake said.

"Inside joke. I'll fill you in later." She gestured for him to keep filming. "Just look at this lovely town square." Boy, she felt foolish; she wasn't really cut out to be a tour guide. She swept her arm over the area. "Most of the buildings have businesses in the bottom—cafés mostly, even an Irish pub at the far end— and apartments up top." Jake panned up one of the buildings, taking in all the little windows where people lived. She pointed to the café straight ahead. "Jake and I had *jamón* and cheese sandwiches and a few glasses of sangria here yesterday." It had actually been a pitcher of sangria, but this wasn't a salacious, tell-all documentary.

"That's better. Chatty and personal."

"They'll be able to hear you too, you know."

"Sorry, Mr. and Mrs. Sawyer."

"He thinks he's Woody Allen," Grace said.

"There are no younger filmmakers you could reference?" Jake said.

"Not on the spot."

"Continue."

Grace pointed to the building behind her and gave Jake a moment to pan over. "I would love to live up there." She gestured to a window high up in a nearby building. "You could people watch all day long. In the afternoon groups of people come here to dance in a circle. Jake refrained yesterday, but he promises to do it before we leave."

Jake laughed. "I didn't promise anything of the sort, Mrs. Sawyer," he said.

"She wants you to call her Jody," Grace said. Although she might never remember making that request.

"Sorry, Jody," Jake said.

Grace wiggled her eyebrows and smiled at the camera, then continued. "At night the square fills with people, musicians, artists. And in the morning, there's hardly anyone but the pigeons and me. Well, yesterday morning anyway." Grace walked around the fountain. "We have a beautiful statue guarding this fountain." It was an angel; it had wings, of course it was an angel, but Grace didn't want to say the word *angel*, so she simply allowed the camera to take it in. Grace held up a Spanish penny. She'd actually brought it from home, from her childhood coin collection. She thought if she tossed it in a fountain in Spain it might bring extra luck. "I have the necessary accoutrements." She held the penny up and froze.

Oh, God. We all know what I would wish for, and we all know it isn't going to come true. What was the point? They couldn't film that. That was just cruel. She wanted to go home. She wanted to close her eyes and be home right now. She let the penny slip out of her fingers. It fell onto the ground, landed on its side, and rolled in a semicircle before plunking down on its face.

She smiled at the camera again, but this time she could feel her lips quivering. "Off," she said under her breath as she tried to hold the smile. Jake didn't hear her. "Look." She pointed at an apartment above them, to a pair of pink shorts hanging out the window to dry. "Adios for now," she said. Finally, Jake caught on. He shut down the recording session and turned to Grace. She was taking large, gulping breaths. Tears stayed at the brim of her eyes. She was determined not to cry. Jake reached for her. Grace put her hands up like a shield.

"Don't," she said. She felt horrible because Jake was being so nice to her, but she hated anyone touching her when she was upset. Try as she might, once her shields went up, it was hard to let anyone in. And kindness usually made it worse. She had too much hurt swirling around inside her. If she let it out, she might flood the entire city with her tears. And she did not want to break down. Not in front of all these Europeans. She turned her back on Jake and hummed to herself. She didn't care what anyone else thought. She liked her happy songs. They comforted her. It only took a few bars before she was calmer. "I shouldn't have done the fountain thing," she said.

"I liked it." He was still behind her, but made no further attempts to touch her. She wished she could just let herself open up, just let him hold her. The Sawyers—stoic to the end. Grace waited until the tide inside her eased. Then she turned back to Jake.

"Do you think she'll know I was going to cry?"

"I'll look at it later, okay? I won't upload anything sad. I promise."

"Good." Grace took another deep breath and wandered a few steps into the square.

"You'll do better with the next video," Jake said. "It's going to be all right."

"No. I won't. I think I should go home, Jake."

"Your mom wanted you to come."

"What if she sent me away just so she could let go?"

"First, I don't think that's the case. Second, if that's the way she wants it—and I'm not saying it is—wouldn't you want to respect her decision?"

"No. I'd want to be at her side. Holding her hand."

Jake held out his hand. This time, Grace took it. He gave her a reassuring squeeze. "How about a compromise?"

"I'm listening."

"We stay at least a few days. If in a few days you still want to go home, we'll be on the next plane."

God, he was the best boyfriend ever. Grace was afraid of breaking down again, so she simply nodded and squeezed his hand back. They walked. Grace tried to appreciate it, enjoy the moment. She was here in Barcelona the Beautiful, with Jake, on cobblestone streets with the smell of the ocean in the air, and tango dancers on street corners, and gorgeous architecture, and delicious food, and wine everywhere they looked, but all she wanted was to be in Tennessee in a hospice where the floors were linoleum and the place smelled like SpaghettiOs and Lysol.

"Xavier Gens," Jake said.

"What?"

"No offense to Woody. Gens is French. He directed *Hitman* and is also one of the directors involved with the much anticipated *Paris I'll Kill You.*"

Grace smiled. If Jake hadn't loved animals so much he probably would have gone on to become a famous director. "Shouldn't you pick a Spanish one?" Grace said.

"Can't think of one."

"Rodrigo Cortés. *Buried.*"

"Excellent!"

"Hitman, kill, buried," Grace mused. "Maybe we aren't really the vacationing type."

Jake laughed. "Don't worry. Ours will be the stuff dreams are made out of." He squeezed her. "I promise," he said softly.

Hopefully not the stuff her dreams were made of lately. Somebody was always dying. Not her mother, never once. But other people, ones she hadn't seen in a long time. A friend from school. A guy from her first after-school job. Even Robbie—the first foster kid her family took in—the one who had shoved her face in a pile of worms and tried to make her kiss them. In her dreams she didn't see any of them die—thank

God—but she'd hear about their deaths from someone else. In every dream she said the same thing. *But I just saw them!* As if that alone was enough to keep death away.

But never Carrie Ann. It was curious; Grace expected her subconscious to want to kill her off most of all.

Jake stopped, took Grace's hands. "I have a wild idea."

"What?"

"For the rest of today, and most of tomorrow." He stopped for dramatic effect.

"We should do as much filming and sightseeing as possible," Grace said.

"No. Really?"

"Absolutely. Let's get cracking. Miró, Picasso, Gaudí, or the beach?" She didn't want to do any of them. She wanted to go back to the apartment, crawl into bed, and pull the covers over her head. Spending every minute after work with her mother, and obsessing over Marsh Everett and his nasty review, had really taken a toll on her the past few weeks. But this was not the time to relax. Not if they were going to end this trip early.

"Oh."

"What. What were you going to say?"

"Nothing," Jake said.

"No. Tell me."

"I just did. For the rest of today, and most of tomorrow, I was going to say we should just do nothing."

Grace sighed, leaned into his shoulder, and almost started crying again. "I wish," she said.

"Your mom is going to be there when we get back. We'll be home before you know it."

You don't know that. But he certainly knew her. And he was probably right. She was just exhausted and worried. Besides, her father was right. Life was too short to turn down free trips. "I love you," Grace said. She didn't know what she would do without him, and she never intended to find out. Without his support, she would buckle.

"That's a wrap," he said. He tucked his video camera into its case and gave it a little pat. Grace laughed.

"What?"

"Are you going to kiss it good night?" Grace teased.

"No. I'm going to kiss it good afternoon."

Grace swatted him, and Jake pulled her in and kissed her instead. It was comforting at first, and then passionate. She used all her pent-up angst to kiss him back, and he responded by pulling her in tighter. She loved the feel of his back underneath her palms, the pressure of his lips on hers. She loved his smell. She loved his body pressed against hers. She desired him. She was so lucky; she must never forget how blessed she was. To have Jake. And wonderful parents. That was what life was all about. Love. Not letting a single moment slip by unnoticed. Grace and Jake had been dating three years, and she still wanted him all the time. When they finally parted, he grabbed her hand and picked up the pace. "Come on. Let's pick up some wine and chocolate and go back to bed." He sounded like a kid on Christmas. She felt like one. And later, that would be the real moment she wished they had captured on film.

CHAPTER 3

Jake opened the door to their flat and stepped in. Grace took a step forward and felt something underneath her right foot. She lifted her foot and saw a small black object resting on the yellow mat. Grace bent down and picked it up. It was a matchbook. The front showcased a pair of tango dancers. The woman was wearing a red dress. Her mother would love it. Grace flipped open the matchbook. In thick black ink, and tiny perfect letters, someone had written on the inside flap:

MEET ME IN BARCELONA

Some kind of spark zipped through Grace as she read the words. A mysterious invitation. Her very own message in a bottle. Grace stepped inside, and held the matchbook up to Jake. He had already kicked off his shoes and was on the sofa flipping through television stations. Grace wasn't fluent in Spanish, but she tried to guess what the content was by listening to the inflections. Happiness made a sound; so did anger, and so did fear. Most of the stations he had landed upon sounded very upbeat. Grace was beginning to like the Spanish. "Look what I found," Grace said. Jake glanced over and squinted. She dangled the matchbook. He held up his hand, and Grace tossed it to him. He caught it effortlessly and placed it in the palm of his hand.

"Cool," he said. "Where did that come from?"

"It was on the mat in front of our door."

"Huh." Jake flipped the matchbook open. " 'Meet me in Barcelona.' "

"Handwritten. What do you make of that?"

"Great advertising gimmick."

"But it doesn't say the name of the bar."

"Exactly. Piques our interest so we go looking for it."

"Do you want to go looking for it right now?"

"Are you kidding me?" Jake jumped off the sofa and advanced on Grace. He pressed her up against the door. Put his hand on her breast, kissed her neck. "Everything I've been looking for is right here. Always has been." Grace filled with warmth. She swatted him on the butt and then slipped the matchbook into her pocket. Something about it intrigued her.

Jake made a beeline for the bedroom, and Grace trailed behind, shaking her head and laughing. She stood in the doorway as he flopped down on the bed and made the come-here gesture with his index finger. "Meet *me* in Barcelona," he said. His hand fell to his jeans. He unbuttoned his top snap and pulled down his zipper. Just the sound of it made Grace tingle. He was such a goof. But she loved it, and he knew it. It had been forever since they could let loose like this. They should go on holiday more often. Jake slid down his jeans so she could see his underwear bulging at the top. He had a great penis. She had never thought she'd find herself thinking such a thing, but it was true. It was definitely one for the "Gratitude List."

"See what you've done to me?" Jake said, peeling his underwear down. The great penis saluted her.

"Looks like I'm going to have to do something about that," Grace said. She played with the top button of her shirt and deliberately slowed down her walk to the bed. Jake's eyes were glued to her body as she unbuttoned the rest of her top. She brushed her hand over her belly and started to slide it over her thigh. She felt the matchbook lying in her pocket.

Little Match Girl. The thought inexplicably leapt into her mind. Grace stopped in her tracks. The barefoot, bedraggled orphan. Begging for a single match. Her little body found frozen to death in the alley. *Thanks, Hans Christian Andersen, for scarring me for life.* Immediately, the image of the dead orphan was replaced by one of Carrie Ann. The first time Grace had ever laid eyes on her. Nine years old. Standing in the doorway of Grace's home. Blond curls in tangles. Dirt down the side of her face from dried tears. Lips pursed in defiance and chin tilted to the sky. Clutching a little flowered suitcase. Her knuckles were snow-white. Grace couldn't help but stare. The social worker's big, bright smile was jarring next to the little girl's scowl.

"I'd like you to meet Carrie Ann," the social worker had said. Grace remembered how the woman's voice had wobbled, as if she herself might cry. "Carrie Ann, I'd like you to meet the Sawyers." Something inside Grace had broken open. Something she hadn't even known was there. Just like with the dirty, starving kitten she'd found last winter and nursed back to health one eyedropper of milk at a time, a single glance at Carrie Ann's big blue eyes and Grace Ann Sawyer's heart had unfolded like an antique fan. She wanted to take every bit of sadness away from this strange girl, her same age, but so different it was as if an alien had just landed on her front stoop. A sense of destiny seized Grace in that moment, something she had never felt before. It was as if God himself had leaned down from the heavens and whispered in her ear: *Take care of her.* And right then and there, she had promised she would.

It was a promise she would break.

It haunted her to this day. Which was why something as simple as a matchbook could hurtle her back to the past. It was usually that moment that haunted her. The beginning. Not the end. She tried very hard not to think about the end.

"Stop," Grace said out loud. Carrie Ann was the last person

Grace needed to think about right now. Jake took his hands out of his pants and sat up.

"What's wrong?"

"Sorry. Sorry. I was just shooing someone else out of my head."

Jake sighed, flopped back down on the bed. "Repeat after me. Marsh Everett is a—" Grace jumped on the bed and straddled Jake. She bent over him and let her hair fall around his face as if she were capturing him in her net.

"Turd," she said, before placing her lips on his and crushing him with a kiss.

CHAPTER 4

Spain must have been working its magic, for the next afternoon, Grace's biggest problems were thus: The sun was a little too hot, and she had to scoot her chair a foot to the left to catch a bit of the shade; a fly landed on the rim of her wine glass, and she had to shoo it away (a Spanish fly, she thought; weren't all flies in Spain Spanish flies?); and a street performer tottering on stilts and draped in shredded black ribbons was staring at her as if *she* were about to put on a performance.

In contrast to the mass of black ribbons, his face was painted bright white. He looked like a shaggy mime. Or a giant eagle dipped in black and put through a shredder. As she watched, he held up his hands and made fists. Long, thin knives shot out of his knuckles. Grace jumped and let out a little scream. Her head darted left and right. Did anyone else catch that? No. People at neighboring tables were otherwise engaged. He had really startled her. She laughed at herself. Might as well have a neon sign above her head: TOURIST. Oh well, that was funny. Was he supposed to be Freddy Krueger, Edward Scissorhands, or Wolverine? It was like he had some kind of antihero identity disorder.

La Rambla teemed with street performers, all vying for attention and tips.

Situated a little to the right of the eagle-knife-man was a tin man on a bicycle. His bike was attached to two child-size bicycles on top of which were tiny skeletons, one in pants and a shirt with a baseball cap, the other in a dress with a ribbon tied to her skull. All three were painted to look as if they were made out of tin, and racing like demons. Where did he get those tiny skeletons? Grace hoped they were fake, purchased in a novelty shop catering to those who just couldn't live without tiny bones. The man's bike must have been rigged so that he was actually pedaling all three. Jake would study it until he knew exactly how the guy was doing it. He loved figuring out the mechanics of things, whereas Grace was always fascinated with the psychological underpinnings. Most likely the result of having a shrink for a dad. Or an endless stream of foster children as "siblings." If the tin man were to talk to them, Jake would ask him how he rides, and Grace would ask him why he rides.

After the tin man there was a headless body sitting in a folding chair next to a small dining table covered in a red-and-white-checkered tablecloth. The missing head was sticking up through the middle of the table, with a bottle of Jack Daniel's tantalizingly out of reach. Was he a little person? Or was he kneeling on the street underneath that table? That had to hurt. She hoped he at least had kneepads. Was the bottle of Jack Daniel's glued down? Barcelona attracted a lot of college kids out for mischief and mayhem. If some college kids snatched the bottle of booze, it would be pretty hard for the little person stuck under the table to chase after them. *We all have our crosses to bear,* Grace thought.

Farther down the street was an Indian chief with his bow drawn. He was letting tourists hold the bow if they paid to pose in pictures. Then, there was a man painted white, sitting on a toilet with his pants pulled down to his ankles, reading a magazine. Grace wondered if he left his bathroom door open at home. Imagine, carrying your toilet to work every morning. These people would make fascinating dinner guests. It was never-ending. Medusa, in a flowing red dress, with fake red snakes piled in her hair. A blue alien with gigantic hands. A robot made entirely out of recycled plastic bottles. Grace felt as if she had stepped into a book of twisted fairy tales. Except instead of being the ones in motion, all the characters were standing still, hoping to draw the crowds closer to them and their tip jars. It would be hard to stand so still all day. At least the street was lined with trees, blessing them all with a little shade. They certainly needed it today. All this stimulus, and yet the demented eagle-mime-Scissorhands was watching *her*.

Freaky. She didn't like being under a microscope. Didn't he realize he was staring?

Maybe he'd pegged her as a rich American and was trying to intimidate her into giving him money. The money part she didn't mind. But if he actually thought she was going to get up from her comfy chair and fat glass of wine, well, he had another think coming. Maybe he dressed like this just so he could stalk tourists. Maybe he was a Spanish serial killer. If things got too weird, she could run back to the room. If she ran screaming toward the building, maybe Jake would hear her. But not if his book was any good. When lost in a good book, Jake became deaf to the world. She couldn't remember what book he had picked up at the airport, just that it was a thriller. Jake ate them up. It would be ironic if she were slashed to death in the courtyard by a giant eagle-on-stilts while Jake obliviously read a less thrilling thriller six floors above.

The street performer was holding up his iPhone. She couldn't be sure, but it almost seemed as if he were aiming it at her. Was he taking *her* picture? Grace knew she was pretty in the "girl next door" kind of way, but this was Spain. The streets were paved with stunning women. Was there something wrong with her? How bad was it if she stood out amongst these characters?

Calm down, Grace. It's just a sales pitch. He wants you to pay him to have your picture taken with him. You're a young woman alone, and he's out to make a few euro. Just ignore him. Enjoy your holiday.

An English bulldog tottered by, tongue hanging down to the ground, squat body straining forward, ribs moving in and out like an accordion. Poor thing—this heat was something else. Grace had a sudden ache for Stella. *Please, Dan. Remember to take her out on the skateboard at least once.* Stella chewed electrical cords if she didn't get her skateboard fix. If she were here Stella would be splayed frog-legged under the table, tongue out, waiting to catch bits of falling tapas. Now that was the good life. Right here, right now was the good life.

Except for the heat. And the jet lag. And the street performer's odd interest in her. Definitely enough to make one feel slightly off-kilter. Drinking in the sun probably didn't help either, but she was on vacation, and it was practically required. She took another sip, and marveled at the taste. Spaniards really knew their grapes. Even the wine on the plane, delivered in little plastic cups, had been top-notch. She should know; she had three of them, and the flight attendant didn't even blink an eye. Welcome to Barcelona.

Grace stretched her legs and looked around. She loved how the outdoor cafés were smack in the middle of the street. Nobody made a fuss. Nobody said "Hey!" or *"¡Hola!* Why are you sitting in the middle of the street? Move to the side!" No, people adjusted to life. In this case, life buzzed around her. Tourists, and street artists, and locals occupied both sides of the mall. *Take that, cars. There are some places you just don't get to go.* Maybe she'd write a song about that.

But not today. No thoughts about songs, or orphans, or reviews today.

Then again.

Maybe if she read the review here, in Barcelona, while sipping wine in the middle of the street, it would lose its hold over her. Grace removed the article from her purse, smoothed it out on the linen tablecloth, and read it for the umpteenth time:

GRACE SAWYER DISAPPOINTS

How was that for an opening line? No matter how many times she read it, she still felt a hot flash of shame, as if she'd just stripped naked and run through town, as if singing were somehow a dirty and criminal act. The review didn't get much better.

> Last night at the Blue Moon Bar and Grill, Grace Sawyer didn't pop any guitar strings on her pricey Taylor Hummingbird. She sang in tune. And she always has a smile on that girl-next-door face. But it wasn't long before I started to drift off, and look forward to whoever was next— even if it was just the busboy. She never opened up and let any of us in. Shallow doesn't quite cut it. A dog bowl has more depth. If she wants to play at venues bigger than birthday parties, she'd better step it up. Sing from the heart. Sing her pain. Because if she doesn't do it soon, she'll be soon forgotten.

Grace folded the review, and then she folded it again, as if the creases could squeeze out his words, and when it was as tiny as she could get it, she shoved it back in her purse. Nope. It stung just as much in Spain. She'd toss it later. Or set fire to it.

A dog bowl! The busboy. Who does he think he is? Soon forgotten. Too bad she couldn't forget it herself. She was never, ever going to read it again. Ever. She would definitely burn it. She would take it to the town square and burn it.

Sing her pain . . .

What? Was he actually saying her songs didn't count if she didn't lose her dog, her truck, and her lover in the very first stanza?

But what if he was right? That's what really got up her grill. He was right. Her songs did have less depth than a dog bowl. Wait. Was he saying her songs had less depth than a dog bowl, or *she* had less depth than a dog bowl?

Don't listen to him, Gracie, her mom had said. She was having one of her "clear moments," and she had noticed Grace was upset. Grace had read her the review. Jody had taken her hand and looked her in the eye. *Your songs are wonderful. What does he know? Just be yourself.*

Thanks, Mom. But what if she wasn't good enough?

She shouldn't think like that. Especially not here, on a free holiday. Her mom was right. It was enough that her songs inspired a smile or two. People loved entertainment. All she had to do was look around her. This was the epicenter of having a good time. People tango danced on the streets here! Plopped their boom boxes down on the cobblestone streets, pushed PLAY, and danced while the crowds cheered them on. They weren't whining over lost dogs, or lovers, or trucks. If you dropped your gelato in Barcelona, you wouldn't cry. You'd go back for more. Life to the fullest. In the moment. That's it. Grace could *choose* not to let Marsh's criticism bother her.

She was on holiday, and she was going to soak up the pain.

Spain, she meant Spain. She was going to soak up Spain.

To hell with pain. She wasn't even going to think about it, let alone sing it. *Tell the truth, Grace.* She'd certainly had her share of pain. But she had no intention of using her mother's condition or ripping open wounds from the past in the name of art. Where was the beauty or truth in doing that? Besides, the past was the past was the past. She'd worked too hard to put it behind her. *Poor Little Match Girl.*

Stop it, Grace. Empty your mind of all your worries.

She drank some more wine and soon felt warm and floaty. The sound of Spanish guitar music drifted over her. She loved Spanish guitar. She'd never tell Jake this, but there were few things sexier than handsome men playing the Spanish guitar. Of course she couldn't see who was playing, so she didn't know for sure that he was handsome, but once notes like that came out of a guitar, the player instantly became beautiful to look at as well. Seduction at his fingertips. A male siren song if there was such a thing. And why shouldn't there be? *I'll crash on your rocks. . . .* Grace laughed again. Okay, probably time to lay off the wine. The entire day was stacked up in front of her like sweetly wrapped gifts. Which one would she open first?

She might stroll down the street and look at the artists' wares. She might make it all the way to the beach and dig her toes in the sand. The Miró Museum was down that way too, but she would go with Jake. She might meander the other direction and hit La Boqueria, the mesmerizing food market. Or, she might just sit here all day eating *jamón* and cheese sandwiches. In Nashville she'd be going to work just about now. Serving the drinks instead of drinking. She had never minded bartending on the side because she had known she wouldn't have to do it forever. Just until she was making real money from singing. And she had truly believed that day was just around the corner. That is, until Marsh Everett came along. He'd ripped her belief in herself right out from under her. She knew she shouldn't let him, couldn't let him, but she just didn't know how to repair the damage. He'd ripped open a gaping wound, and it was festering. No wonder she was thinking of Carrie Ann lately. Like her daddy used to say—"Bad news likes to hang out with worse news."

"Would you like another glass of wine?" The waiter stood politely over her and smiled. Grace smiled back.

"No thank you. Have to keep on my toes in case that eagle-thing follows me home." Grace pointed in the direction of the street performer, then noticed the waiter's puzzled look. Nothing there but a tree. The eagle-thing was gone. She looked in 360 degrees, but there was absolutely no sign of him. How did a stilt walker vanish into thin air?

"Have you lost your friend?" the waiter asked.

Or my mind. "No. Do you remember that eagle-thing that was right there?" Grace pointed to the tree. "On stilts?" She lifted her arms as if they were wings. Why did she do that? The waiter looked more confused than ever. It was hard to do "stilts" while sitting down. "Or is he supposed to be Wolverine? A flying Wolverine?"

"Señora, you are finished here?"

"Yes. *Gracias.*"

He picked up her empty wine glass, but stood staring at her for several seconds. "You are American? On holiday?"

"Yes. It's our third day." Not that the waiter cared about the details of their itinerary. He seemed more concerned about her mental health. He glanced at the empty chair beside her. Then, he shot another look at the lone tree. He thought she had invisible friends all over the place. She had never realized how swiftly one could be labeled as "off her rocker." Loco.

"He's in the room. Reading," Grace said. "We agreed to just do nothing today."

He looked at the empty chair and nodded. She held back a laugh; she didn't want him to think she was laughing at him.

"You are here in July," he said. "Very, very hot."

"*Sí. Muy calientes.*" She hoped she had said that right. Maybe he hated when tourists tried to speak Spanish. Especially since Catalan was the official language of this region, but she didn't understand the difference, and rudimentary Spanish was the best she could do.

"Too hot for your visit."

"I know. We didn't have a choice."

"You could choose September."

"Right, right. I just meant my boyfriend won this trip from work. In a raffle. The dates were set in stone." The look the waiter gave her was also set in stone.

"So, you are finished here?" he said again.

Finished. *Soon forgotten.* She almost missed the demented eagle. "Yes," Grace said. "*Finito.*" She picked up her purse and stood. "*Gracias,*" she said again.

"You are most welcome," he said. "Thank you for being finished."

CHAPTER 5

Grace headed down the alley and took a right under an arched walkway. From there it was a short stroll down a second cobblestone alley to the entrance of their apartment building. Grace was thrilled with the location and the accommodations. Knowing how cheap the veterinarian group could be, she and Jake had been expecting a low-budget hotel, or even a hostel. So they were completely surprised that it was a furnished two-bedroom, two-bath apartment. A full-time tenant of the building had greeted them upon arrival with the key and basic instructions. When Grace walked into the lobby now, she found him sitting at the same desk as when they had arrived. It seemed he was the doorman. Who didn't open any doors.

Grace gave him a smile, but his expression remained neutral. He was a short man in his early thirties, not much older than Grace and Jake. He had beautifully tanned skin and spikey black hair. His eyebrows were bushy, and his teeth crooked. He was half-beauty, half-beast.

"Hola," Grace said with a smile. She wanted to ask him about the deranged stilt walker, and she was curious about who owned

the apartment they were staying in, but the extent of her Spanish was saying "Hello" morning, noon, and night, and asking directions to restrooms, train stations, and libraries.

He openly stared at her. Just like the street performer. It was just cultural. She was a foreign object. *"Bona tarda,"* he said finally. God, everything about Spain was just so lazy and sexy. She loved it. She smiled and felt his eyes on her until she disappeared up the winding stairwell behind him. She opened the door quietly in case Jake was asleep. Instead, she found him pacing the living room, cell phone jammed in his ear. She couldn't catch what he was saying. He turned, saw her, and shoved the phone in his pocket.

"Hey," he said, wrapping her in a hug. "I missed you."

"I was only gone an hour."

He kissed her. "A lifetime," he said.

She flopped on the oversized sofa. The television was on in the background, tuned to the local news. She resisted the urge to lecture. They were in Spain and once again he was watching TV. But with all the other problems in Grace's life right now, she certainly didn't want to start a fight with Jake. Besides, at least it was foreign TV. It was always fascinating to watch the news in other countries. There was a beautiful female anchor in a red dress, and a handsome male co-anchor in a gray suit. They were smiling, so it must be the two-minute happy-news section of the program. The lull before the storm. That was the common denominator about news; it was usually bad.

"Who was that?" Grace asked. She propped her feet up on the coffee table. Jake took the seat next to the sofa, lifted her legs, and planted them in his lap.

"Dan," he said. She was surprised. Dan had assured them he wouldn't be constantly calling Jake while he was on vacation. Grace could tell from the look on Jake's face that it wasn't good news.

"What's wrong? Is it Stella?"

"Stella's fine. At least I assume she is. I didn't even talk to Dan. I was just leaving him a message."

"You called him?"

"I tried."

"Why?"

Jake sighed, patted Grace's leg. "Do you mind if I don't want to bring this up right now?"

"Is there a surgery scheduled today that you're worried about?" Jake and Dan were both skilled in emergency surgery, and it kept them both on their toes. But Jake could hardly help from here.

"No, it's nothing like that." Grace pulled her legs in and sat up straight. Jake was not the type to beat around the bush. "How was your adventure?" He was making an effort to sound upbeat.

"I drank Malbec in the middle of the street."

"Yes." He smiled and held out his fist. She bumped it.

"And was stalked by a shaggy mime on stilts. Or a deranged Wolverine-eagle."

"Wolverine-eagle?" Jake perked up. Men.

"I wasn't really sure who he was supposed to be."

"When in Spain." He tried to smile; it didn't reach his eyes. Jake was such a handsome guy. He had ash-blond hair—but it was dark, like sand when you finally dig to the bottom—and big hazel eyes, and obnoxiously long eyelashes. His face was strong and suited his six-foot frame. She intimately knew all of his looks. He was definitely worried about something.

"Tell me," Grace said.

Jake sighed, ran his hands through his hair. "I'm sure it's nothing. I really don't want to alarm you."

"Oh God. You just alarmed me." Was there another criticism about her in *Country Weekly*? Jake was almost more upset by that review than she was. She loved how protective he could be of her.

Jake strode over to a small desk against the wall, where his laptop was set up. "I shouldn't have read my e-mail."

Grace couldn't sit still. She approached his laptop. "You were supposed to be reading your novel."

"I know. I know." Jake gestured to his screen. His e-mail was open. "It's from Dan. Read it."

Grace leaned in as Jake enlarged the message.

Jake and Grace,

Just wanted to say hey. By now you realize I played
a part in the surprise ambush! Like the vet group
could actually raffle off a trip to Europe. You fell for
it, buddy! Who's getting married? Hope it's someone you like, ha ha. If not, dump them and enjoy
Spain with your gorgeous gal. Sorry about my part
in the deceit. Do the tango for me!
Adios!

Dan

"Surprise ambush?" Grace said.

"I knew there was something funny about that raffle. Didn't I
say it? Didn't I say I couldn't believe those cheap bastards paid
for a trip?"

"You did. Verbatim." *And I couldn't believe Dan would be so generous,* Grace thought. There was no use throwing that in Jake's
face right now.

"A surprise wedding. Can you believe it?"

It was hard to believe. Was this part of some elaborate proposal Jake was planning? Just last month, when they were at the
mall, he had stopped at the window of a jewelry store. "Would
you say you're more of a gold or a platinum girl?" he'd asked her.

"Are we talking records?" she teased. "Definitely platinum."

He had laughed, and that was all that was said on that matter.
Did he bring her here to marry him? In Spain? Grace felt a
rush of excitement.

"Why are you smiling?" Jake said. He seemed so serious. If
this was a surprise engagement, he was doing a good job of hiding it.

Yes, she thought. I'll marry you. Maybe outdoors? At Park
Güell? She'd seen pictures, and it was gorgeous. Or the beach?
Or in the middle of La Rambla? Could they get permission to
get married at Sagrada Família? Probably not. They weren't
even Catholic. And even if that didn't matter, the famous un-

finished cathedral would probably cost them a fortune. Heck, just about anywhere in Barcelona would be special.

They could get married in front of a gelato shop for all Grace cared. They could get married on stilts. Stick their betrothed heads up from dinner tables and collect money for the honeymoon. This was kind of like the honeymoon already. Situate themselves near tango dancers so they could double as the entertainment. Grace could even put fake snakes in her hair or wear a dress made out of recycled bottles. Something to really remember the day. Would she change her name? Maybe Grace Sawyer wasn't country but Grace Hart was. It would be a brand-new start.

Would she get a wedding dress here? Wait. Would her mother be well enough to fly out here? Maybe a wedding would give her a burst of energy. Grace couldn't imagine getting married without her parents. "A surprise wedding," Grace said. "Very exciting."

"It doesn't make any sense. Who do you think it is?"

"I don't have a clue." She hoped Dan would bring Stella. She could be the little ring bearer. Shoot up the aisle on her skateboard.

Jake opened his arms. "Is it wrong that I'm annoyed with this?"

"Oh," Grace said. Jake wasn't *that* good of an actor. Thoughts of her surprise Spanish wedding evaporated. "What did you say in your message?"

"I just told him to call me back ASAP."

"What time is it in the US?"

"I have no idea. I didn't even think before I called. It just—kind of freaked me out, you know?"

"Maybe it's a client."

"You think?"

"Some woman at work who is madly in love with you?" Grace said.

"And so they invite me and my girlfriend to Spain?"

"Good point. Still—could be someone from work. Someone grateful that you saved Fido—"

Jake laughed, and Grace was relieved to hear it. She always referred to every dog he worked with as Fido and every cat Fluffy. She loved that he still laughed at it after all this time. See? In life, it was the little things.

"I can't think of any clients who are engaged," Jake said.

"Maybe it's a canine wedding. That would be hilarious. Know any betrothed poodles?"

Jake wrapped his arms around her. Kissed the top of her head. "No, I don't know any betrothed poodles. Just a couple of lovesick beagles." They both laughed. They kissed again before Jake moved away. He was so good to her. He loved her. And boy, did she love him. She trusted him more than any man she'd ever met. She couldn't marry him when he didn't know the truth about her childhood. And maybe he wasn't going to ask her in Spain, but they would get married someday. She should get a jump on things by opening up to him. She should tell him about Carrie Ann. She should have told him a long time ago. She wasn't sure why she hadn't. Of course she didn't want to be judged. She didn't want to be pitied either. Not that Jake would judge or pity her. What was it then? Maybe the part of her that still wanted to keep Carrie Ann to herself. And of course, there was the shame. Shame had a way of silencing people. She would definitely tell him about Carrie Ann during this trip. But not this very minute. He was way too distracted. He went to the window, parted the curtain, and glanced out, as if he might be able to spot whoever summoned them here. "Besides—even if someone I know is engaged," Jake continued, "why would he or she pay all our expenses?"

Because they know we're broke? Grace's only paying job was bartending, and, even though Jake and Dan were doing well, most of the money went back into keeping their business going. "Maybe they're filthy rich."

"Well, that eliminates our clients, all family members, and my friends," Jake said.

"It's definitely weird," Grace said.

"So—what? We just wait around until we hear from this mysterious couple?" Jake said.

"No," Grace said. "It's their responsibility to get in touch. This is still our holiday, and I don't want to waste a second of it. Let's just go about it as we initially planned, and wait for the happy couple to reveal themselves. If it's someone we like, we'll go to the wedding."

"And if it's someone we don't like?"

"We'll disappear. This is Barcelona, baby. Plenty of places to run and hide." Run and hide. Just like she'd been doing most of her adult life. Just like Marsh Everett thought she was doing with her songs.

Jake rubbed his hands. "So much for our day of doing nothing. I'm energized now."

"Me too," Grace said.

Jake took Grace in his arms again. "I think we've no choice," he said. "Plan B. We're just going to have to go out and do something."

"Such a heavy burden," Grace said. "Gaudí, Miró, or Dalí?"

"How about the beach?" Jake said. "I want to see you in your bikini."

"Can we drink wine on the beach?" Grace said.

CHAPTER 6

After a lifetime of dreaming of tango dancers, and tapenades, and trendy shops, and sexy Spanish men on every corner turning to give her bedroom eyes, here she was, in the thick of it, and unable to enjoy any of it. Instead, Carrie Ann was virtually a prisoner in this flat. She couldn't even dream of doing anything until she saw Grace. She'd been pacing the flat, fanning herself with whatever was handy.

Spain was hot. Sticky hot. Heavy hot. Irritatingly hot. Coming in July was a definite error in judgment. Too late. *You made your bed, girls.* Jody Sawyer used to say that all the time. Was Grace going around saying it now? Carrie Ann hoped not. She would find out soon enough.

At least Rafael had a decent apartment spitting distance to La Rambla. Now that was cool. Not a bad place to disappear, now was it?

She went to the bedroom and changed into her bikini. She wasn't trying to get Rafael all riled up, but it was just too hot to wear anything else. Besides. She had paid dearly for tanning, and Pilates, and said bikini. Why do all that just to cover up?

But mostly it was because of the heat. Even her sundresses were too hot. How in the world could they call that swampy thing in the corner an air conditioner? It gurgled so much she was tempted to give it Pepto Bismol. It was probably a joke they played on the American tourists. She hadn't stopped sweating since she had arrived. If she had it to do over she would have picked Rome, or Paris. She'd always imagined herself as a Left Bank kind of girl. Less than a week away from her thirtieth birthday with Grace. What an adventure this was going to be. But had she gone too far?

No. Definitely not. All was fair in love and war, right? Besides, it was going to work. Carrie Ann was going to heal the rift between them if it killed her. Because Grace was family, and surely Grace wanted Carrie Ann back in her life; she was just too stubborn (as usual) to do anything about it. So Carrie Ann was going to step up, and she was going to give Grace a chance to redeem herself. And after that nasty review in *Country Weekly,* she was sure Grace needed redeeming. Nothing was more important in life than the ones you loved. Than family. It was because of Grace that Carrie Ann understood what it even meant to have a family. Even if Jody and Jim hated her, Grace made up for all of that.

"Don't let me down," she said, softly, aloud. Carrie Ann reached for her purse, took out the worn picture, and stared at it. Two Raggedy Anns and one Andy. Grace, Carrie Ann, and Stan. She and Grace looked pretty much the same. But boy, it was mind-blowing to look at Stan. He had been so unlucky as a kid. All that weight, and the acne, and the braces. Those greasy black bangs hanging in his face. Just one big pile of misery. He was lucky he had made it through that time without being on the evening news for going berserk. Carrie Ann liked to think that he had her to thank for that. She had done a good thing bringing him into the fold. Maybe even saved innocent lives.

But Grace. Oh, how she loved Grace. How long had it been since she'd seen her? (Not counting Facebook or from afar.) Too long. Way, way too long. She was flabbergasted that Grace had never reached out to her. Not once in all these years. Then again, Carrie Ann wouldn't have been easy to find. She never lived anywhere longer than a year. She didn't tweet, or Facebook, or put herself in the limelight. Maybe Grace had looked for her, but couldn't find her. Maybe Carrie Ann hadn't wanted to be found. But it was time. And it was the perfect time.

So it was decided. She would be the bigger person. She would make the first move. And she would do it with her usual flair. How far would she actually take things? Well, that would depend on Grace. But so far, if she did say so herself, she was nailing it.

She slipped the picture back in her purse. What would Carrie Ann do if her plan failed? She had to at least brace herself for the possibility that Grace would turn her back on her. Again. That couldn't happen. It just couldn't.

The front door suddenly swung open, and there stood Rafael in full costume. He slammed the door shut and glided across the floor as he slipped off his feathers. My God, how much did those things weigh? They were huge, black beasts, which looked capable of flight. After partially undressing, he turned and grinned at her with a face concealed under hideous white paint. He was also still wearing the eye mask. He continued to grin and balled his hands into fists. A swooshing sound cut through the air, and then the knives popped out. The silver gleamed as if he had just polished them, and he probably had. The freak.

"Are those real?" Carrie Ann asked. She took a step forward.

"I'll never tell," Rafael said. He thrust his hands up in the air.

"Weirdo," Carrie Ann said. More than once she had had second thoughts about involving him. But since it was too late to kick him off the team now, she was certainly glad he was on their side. She imagined he could be pretty scary under the best of circumstances.

Rafael arched his eyebrows and then took off the contraptions. He ambled over to his kitchen counter where he kept his stash and began to roll a joint. He lit it and rested it in the corner of his mouth. The place soon filled with the cloying scent of marijuana. He carried his stilts to a corner of the room, where he deposited them. Then, he threw himself on the sofa. Carrie Ann had just enough time to move her legs before he crushed them. The joint remained sealed between his lips. He reached Carrie Ann's legs and tried to put them over his lap. She pulled away and scooted to her corner of the sofa. He exhaled a gray cloud, and his eyes ran over her body.

"Are we going to the beach?" he said.

"No," Carrie Ann said.

"Come on. It is right at the end of the street. You are wearing the bikini. I am allowed to take you anywhere. This is Barcelona, baby."

Allowed to take her. What a misogynist. He offered her the joint. She shook her head no as she'd done each and every time he tried to get her to take it. Pot made her horny. Horny made her stupid. She was not hooking up with Rafael. "What are you going to do? Lie around all day like a dead fish?" Rafael said.

"Maybe." And maybe she'd slip out and do some exploring on her own. It had to cool down after dark. She'd always been more of a night owl anyway.

"You did not ask me about my morning work," Rafael said. "My Zero Zero Seven."

Double-O-Seven, you moron. "You're right. I didn't." Rafael was just too easy to bait, so she couldn't resist doing it.

"She's here."

So soon? Was he telling the truth? Carrie Ann sat up. It was everything she could do not to leap off the sofa and run down to their room. Grace was here. Just one floor below. Carrie Ann had to breathe. She had to take it slow. An ambush would only backfire. Despite herself, she could feel excitement thrumming in her, just at the thought of seeing Grace again. She needed her. She missed her. "Oh my God. Are you sure?"

"I don't like her," Rafael said.

Who cares if you like her, you egomaniac? Although it was an interesting statement. Everybody always liked Grace. Except maybe that guy who had slammed her in *Country Weekly.* Carrie Ann couldn't figure out what had possessed Grace to post that review on her own Facebook page. Why would you want people reading your bad reviews? Like those people who send annual anti-Christmas-cheer newsletters. *I have cancer. Steven is in rehab and we pray this will be the year he kicks cocaine. Happy Holidays, sorry I haven't been in touch since the tornado.* "You weren't supposed to talk to her. Did you talk to her?"

"I did not talk to her. But I was very near her. And she did not come up to take picture or tip me."

Why would she? You look deranged. Charles Manson would've steered clear of you. "You're sure it was her?"

Rafael set the joint on the edge of the coffee table and reached into his jeans. How could he wear jeans in this heat? Why didn't he have ashtrays? He pulled his iPhone out of his pocket, scrolled through it, and held the screen out to Carrie Ann. She took the phone and brought the screen in close. And there she was.

Her Grace. She looked just like she did on her Facebook fan page. Her sister. SBC. Sisters By Choice. She could still see the ten-year-old girl in the picture. And the eleven-, twelve-, and thirteen-year-old girl. She could see the two of them, sitting in Grace's tree house, pouring out their secrets in low, hot whispers. *I missed you, Gracie. I missed you so much.* She ran her finger over Grace's face. *My sister. I forgive you. Will you be happy to see me? Have you missed me at all? Will you be sorry when I suddenly disappear? Will you come looking for me?*

Rafael held his hand out for his phone.

Carrie Ann kept holding it. "Did she see you taking this?"

"Not even a tiny, tiny chance."

"She's here," Carrie Ann repeated. The first hurdle had been cleared. She thought she'd made a mistake recruiting that Dan guy. He had been so paranoid about the whole thing. And she had to be nice or he would've pulled out of it altogether. God, how he had gone on and on. *Why don't you just tell them you won a trip? He'll never believe the vet group is raffling off a trip. What are the odds of winning a trip? What if we're scheduled for surgery on those days? I don't know if I can get a replacement with this short a notice. I don't even know how many vacation days Jake has left.* On and on until Carrie Ann wanted to strangle him. At least she had finally gotten him to do it. *It's a free trip, and I'm practically family,* she had said.

Then why not go through Grace? Or her parents—

Because then Grace might figure it out. Carrie Ann didn't tell him the real reason—that Jody Sawyer had lost her mind. Actually, it was kind of nice to see her. Especially since Jody didn't remember how much she hated her. Carrie Ann didn't stay long enough to talk to Jim. When she realized how sick Jody was, she realized she couldn't drag them into this—not even unknowingly. So Dan was her only other option. But he just wouldn't quit.

A surprise wedding, huh? Does the groom even know?

They were here. Grace and Jake. Carrie Ann felt that familiar tug of jealousy that she felt when she saw all the pictures of the two of them. So in love. Laughing in almost every single picture. Nobody laughed like that all the time—did they? And there was some fat, drooling dog in almost every picture too. Grace was a cat person. Always had been. She'd loved that fat orange cat named Brady like it was her own child. "Our thirtieth in Spain. Just like we always said," Carrie Ann whispered to the picture. "It's going to be a doozy."

Rafael's phone rang. Carrie Ann jumped. He snatched it out of her hands, then picked up the joint and took a drag before answering. He spoke in rapid Spanish. When he hung up, he was grinning.

"What?" Carrie Ann said.

"Want to go to the beach?" he said.

"I said no," Carrie Ann said.

"That was Stefano. He said Grace and her *amigo* are off to the beach."

"Who is Stefano?"

"*Mi amigo,* he who sits in the lobby."

"Right." *He who sits in the lobby.* Who would she be? *She who lies on the sofa?* Rafael: *He who plays with knives.* "He's like the doorman or something?"

"It is the time of summer. When all the young foreign girls to come and stay." Rafael wiggled his eyebrows. Carrie Ann stood.

She raced to the window and glanced out. As usual, La Rambla was a mass of writhing bodies. She couldn't spot Grace or Jake.

"How does he know it's her?" Carrie Ann asked.

"I showed him the picture."

"How does he know they're going to the beach? Did he talk to them?"

"Why are you so worried about everyone talking to them? He says they come down, and they are carrying towels, and wearing swimming suits, and he says, 'Hola,' and they say, 'Hola.' And he says, *'Donde está,'* because all tourists understand *'Donde está,'* and they say, 'We are going to the beach,' in English, because they only know how to say 'where is library' in Spanish."

Sarcastic Spaniard.

Rafael took a last pull on the joint. He had smoked it down to the nub. When he looked up at her and smiled, even Carrie Ann had to concede there was something about his oddball personality that was a tiny bit sexy. Or she was getting a contact high? She'd have to watch herself. Another entanglement was the last thing she needed. "Would you like to go to the beach?" he said. "I wash my face and away we go?"

"*Sí,*" Carrie Ann said. "*Me gustaría ir a la playa.*"

Rafael clapped his hands like she was a seal who had just delighted him with a trick. She wanted to throw her head back, open her mouth, and bark for a fish. "Your Spanish is good. You are so surprising me."

"Yes," Carrie Ann said. "So is your English."

"You think?"

"Oh yes. You are so surprising me."

CHAPTER 7

Grace and Jake placed their matching towels so that Grace could catch a bit of shade from a neighboring umbrella while Jake took the full brunt of the sun. Despite working long hours at his veterinary clinic, Jake was always tan. Grace had a light toasting as well, but too much of it and she would burn. She wanted to warn Jake about skin cancer, but she never wanted to be one of those women who harped, or mothered. It was a slippery slope, and with Jake it was particularly tough to follow—he was impulsive; she was careful. Live and let live. She did, however, offer several times to help him put on sunscreen. He took one look at the giant bottle with SPF 50 in huge red letters and shook his head.

"You know they say there's no definitive proof that anything over SPF 30 offers much more protection," he said.

"Are you saying if I had SPF 30 you would wear it?" Grace asked.

"Nah. I'm fine, sweetie."

You're fine right now. Later you might turn into a lobster. I'll pay the price if you don't want to go dancing or make love because your back is on fire.

"If I let you put it on me will it make you stop staring at me as if I'm about to burst into flames?" Jake asked playfully.

"Yes, it will," Grace said, grabbing the bottle before he could change his mind. "It really will." Jake sat up, giving Grace access to his shoulders and back. His skin and muscles felt so nice and taut beneath her fingertips. Maybe she'd surprise him with Spanish guitar lessons one of these days. On his chest she outlined a little heart with her fingertips. She hoped it would work. Make theirs a love that lasted. She often indulged in little superstitions like that, just like the pancake pan she had bought, etched with little smiley faces. It was the simple things in life that got Grace through. She finished her artwork and handed him the sunscreen.

"Do me," she said.

"Again?" Jake said. "This *is* a vacation." She laughed, and he pulled her in and kissed her. In Spain, on the beach, kissing. See, Marsh Everett? Life didn't have to be baring your soul; sometimes it was baring your body. Then slathering it with SPF 50. "Is this waterproof?" Jake asked.

"You have to ask?" Grace said.

"Then let's go." Jake stood, reached for her hand, and pulled her to her feet.

"What about my purse?" Grace said. Jake glanced down at her little black satchel.

"Do you have a lot in there?"

"Fifty euros, a credit card, the key to the room, and my passport," Grace said. Jake looked around. The beach was crowded, and they were situated in the middle, about ten feet from the ocean.

"Tuck it under your towel. Then we'll pile our sandals and clothes on top. I'll keep an eye on it and run like hell if anyone goes near it."

"My hero," Grace said.

"You shouldn't carry your passport around. And maybe we'll get a little waterproof pouch so you can carry your money in here." He took his finger and slowly outlined her bikini top.

"You're going to drive me crazy if you keep doing that," Grace said.

"Good," Jake said. "You know how I like to drive." Grace swatted him away, then hid her purse under the towel and piled all of their things on top of it. Jake was right; she needed a better system. *Don't leave it,* her little voice told her. *Take turns swimming.* But she wanted to hold on to Jake in the ocean, feel the waves crash over their bodies, kiss in the Mediterranean. It would be fine, she told herself. Next time she'd have a better plan.

The water was warm and soft, like a relaxing bath. Grace spread her arms wide and paddled her legs in a lazy circular motion. After just a few minutes she felt lighter than she had in years. Jake wrapped his arms around her and scooped his hands under her legs, joyfully lifting her up in the water. She wrapped her arms around his neck, and they kissed. How long since they'd done this? The two of them working nonstop. Jake worked mostly days; Grace evenings and weekends. *Remember this. Take a snapshot in your mind; hold on to it when things get crazy again.*

"What are you thinking?" Jake said. His voice was a bedtime whisper.

"I don't care who gave us this trip. I'm just glad that they did."

"Me too." They kissed again. "Unless they want something in return," Jake added.

"Way to ruin it, Romeo." Grace wanted to get back to heaven. She dove into the waves and swam.

Grace ran for the towels, but Jake beat her to them. "It's still here," he whispered, holding up her purse with a dripping wet hand.

"Perfecto," Grace said, taking the purse.

"Will you remember to pick up some kind of fanny pack?" Jake said.

Grace swatted him in the butt. "For this fanny?" she said.

He reached around and grabbed her rear end. "I prefer this one."

"In Europe 'fanny' means something entirely different," Grace said.

"What?" Jake said with a smile that suggested he already knew.

"Let's go back to the room, and I'll show you," Grace said. They picked up their towels, wrapped them around their waists, and slid on their sandals. When they reached the street, a couple was coming toward them, their arms full with beach things. Grace and Jake parted so they could go through. The young woman lost her footing and bumped into Grace.

"Sorry," she said. Her voice was barely above a whisper. Her hair was tucked into a large, floppy hat, and she wore huge sunglasses. But her body was beach ready and tan. Grace felt a tiny bit jealous. Was Jake checking her out? That would be normal. The man she was with was tall, with dark skin. And a lot of hair. Grace wanted to buy him a razor. Just another slight cultural difference.

"No problem," Grace sang out. Grace continued on, but stopped a few feet later and turned around again. The woman had stopped too, and was watching Grace and Jake leave.

Grace slipped her hand into Jake's and whispered in his ear. "I think she likes you."

Jake squeezed her hand. "Or maybe she likes you," he said in a tone that suggested it wouldn't bother him in the least.

Carrie Ann couldn't believe someone could actually stomp through the sand, but when she announced she wasn't staying after all, Rafael sure managed to pull it off.

"They'll probably be back," he said. "We should stay."

"They won't be back."

"But we just got here."

"You can stay."

"I wanted to lie next to you on the beach."

No, you just wanted everyone to see you lying next to me. "We wouldn't have missed them if you hadn't spent so much time shaving your back."

"I wasn't shaving my back."

"I saw you."

"You are spying on me?" Rafael grabbed her wrist, and when she whirled around, she saw a huge grin plastered on his face. Carrie Ann glared at him, and he dropped her wrist. He stumbled back, ran his hand through his thick hair. He had hair everywhere. Another reason Carrie Ann wasn't attracted to him. "Why didn't you just talk to her? Why bump into her and then say nothing?"

"It's none of your business." Carrie Ann picked up the pace. She wished Rafael would just go back to the beach. Why was he following her home?

"If it's none of my business then why am I helping you?"

You're not helping me; you're helping him. "I don't know. Why are you?"

Rafael grabbed her hand and squeezed it. Carrie Ann pulled away. "Maybe it is because you are so beautiful. And feisty. I like feisty."

"And maybe it's because you are getting paid. To keep your eyes on me. Not your paws."

"I won't tell if you won't tell," Rafael said.

"Oh, I'd tell all right. So don't even think about it."

"How do you know this Grace?"

"You're not paid to ask questions."

"It is not much money, this pay. And you are staying in my home. So are your friends."

"And I appreciate it, Rafael. Thank you."

"Why don't we just take her right now?"

Carrie Ann felt a little jolt. Was he not on the same page? Ignorance was dangerous. "Take her? What do you mean, take her?"

"That is the plan."

She wanted to throttle him. His stupidity was going to cost her everything. "No." She didn't want to shout at him, but she had to set things straight. "We are going to take me. Not her. Me. That is the plan." God, he was dense! They never should have enlisted him.

"I don't understand what is the plan."

Carrie Ann squared her shoulders and stepped closer to

Rafael. "You're not to talk to her. Or even look at her anymore. Got it? That's the plan. Stick to it."

"It's all right if that means I get to stick to you."

"Gross," Carrie Ann muttered under her breath. But she was glad he was dropping the subject of Grace so quickly.

"If I were your boyfriend, I wouldn't let you out of my sight for one single second."

"That would make you a kidnapper."

"Ah, but I would be so nice to my captive. I would feed you wine and cheese. You would love it." He grabbed her hand again and tried to bring it up to his lips.

"Let go or I'll scream."

"Scream? Why do you say such things?"

"I do not like your hanging all over me."

"You are not any fun. You are—how do they say—party pooping."

"You're on your own, Wolfman," Carrie Ann said. She thrust the pile of beach things at him, and Rafael stumbled back as he tried to juggle them all.

"No, no, no," Rafael said. "Where I go, you go—remember?"

"It's supposed to be 'Where I go, you go,' and I am not going to the beach."

"You are upset about your friend."

Maybe he wasn't as shallow as she had first thought. Maybe she'd have to be a little more careful what she said and did around him. "Maybe a little."

"Do you want me to talk to her?"

"No. A hundred billion times no. Promise me you won't." He'd probably already freaked Grace out with that ridiculous costume. The last thing Carrie Ann needed was Rafael inserting himself on the scene.

"I promise if you come back to the beach."

Carrie Ann tried to smile. It wasn't easy. She just wanted to get rid of Grace's boyfriend and take her hands and jump and shout, "It's me! I'm here!"

Jake was even better looking than Carrie Ann had expected. From the looks of things they were headed back to have vacation sex. So strange. Little Grace. Having sex. Holding hands with a boy even. Singing country songs. She even had her own little following. She wasn't a child anymore. Walked right by Carrie Ann without recognizing her.

"Are you sure the microphones are in place?" Carrie Ann asked.

"*Sí, sí.* We will be able to hear everything they say."

"Okay, good."

"And do," he said, raising his eyebrows.

Pervert. She wasn't going to let him listen to any of it. "Thirty minutes, no more. I don't want wrinkles," Carrie Ann said.

"Deal." Rafael shouted it at the sky, as if he'd just made a bargain with God himself. Carrie Ann couldn't help but laugh. Hairy, yes, but still somewhat charming for a psycho. This time when Rafael forged ahead looking for the perfect spot, Carrie Ann followed.

She did, however, keep looking over her shoulder, wondering step for step where Grace was now. She was so near. Walked by Carrie Ann without so much as a second glance. Carrie Ann had expected more. Hell, she deserved more. She had always thought there was some kind of unbreakable bond between them. She would have bet her life on it. No matter how many years had passed, they should know each other like they knew their own shadows. If the roles had been reversed, Carrie Ann knew she would have recognized Grace. She would have *felt* her. God. Carrie Ann had really thought her foster-sister—slash blood-sister—would have recognized her. But Grace didn't even blink. Not one little flick of an eyelash. Huh. Carrie Ann was surprised at how much that hurt. Maybe Grace did recognize her and didn't want to see her. No, that wasn't possible. Grace was just too enamored with lover boy. It wasn't right. That wasn't the way it was supposed to be. Lovers were temporary. But sisters—how did the old saying go? *Sisters were sisters from cradle to grave.* Somebody, Carrie Ann thought, should have remembered that.

CHAPTER 8

Grace followed up their day of sloth by rising before the sun. She made coffee, retrieved her Barcelona guidebook, and sat at the counter with a highlighter. "Oh no," she heard Jake say. "Not the guidebook." Priceless given that he was in the other room. How long had he been lying there waiting to say it? Grace laughed. He'd appreciate her organizational skills when they started hitting the sites.

"You had your lazy day, animal man," Grace called out. "We're sightseeing today."

"But not until noon, right? Spain comes to life at night, babe. Right after a long siesta. Don't forget to pencil in our siesta."

"I was thinking Casa Batlló," Grace said. Antoni Gaudí's house was high on her list. She loved all the pictures of the modernist façade. Balconies with masked faces, endless curved walls, glittering mosaic tiles, spirals, and mini-domes stretching above an expansive rooftop terrace. The back of the house was supposed to be patterned after a dragon's spine. Located along Passeig de Gràcia, Grace's first pick wasn't far from La Rambla. There were also plenty of shops nearby, so they could sneak in some of that as well. Even though he'd never admit it, Jake loved clothes shopping almost as much as she did. Then, after touring the house they could stop in at La Boqueria, pick up some tasty morsels for lunch, and head back to the apartment. Siesta, then dinner, and maybe even a little dancing. It sure was generous of someone to pay for their flights and living expenses. *Unless he or she wants something.*

Jake's words came back to her as she poured two cups of coffee. He was right. Most people they knew could barely afford their own vacations, let alone pay for someone else's. And why hadn't the "surprise" been revealed yet? They should have been informed the minute they checked into the apartment. It wasn't fair to keep people waiting until the very last second. What if Grace and Jake missed the wedding because they were off sightseeing?

They were going to have to stick with their earlier conviction. It was hardly their problem. Grace didn't mean to sound ungrateful, but they were here and they were going to sightsee. If an invitation was coming, it had better come soon. Grace figured tomorrow they would go to the Dalí and Miró museums, and if Jake was up to it, Park Güell. The next day would be reserved for the Sagrada Família. And music. Grace wanted to check out the little jazz clubs and tango places she'd read about. Even though she sang country, Grace loved all kinds of music. She never understood why so many people limited themselves. It was as if it were against the law to like country, and classical, and jazz, and hip-hop, and rock and roll. She loved it all. Too bad she was done playing and singing it herself. Every time she even thought of playing she broke out in a cold sweat.

She brought Jake's coffee cup to his bedside and set it on the little table. He was already back asleep and lightly snoring. Grace loved that sound. She wanted to kiss his head, but she didn't want to wake him. The coffee might be cold by the time he woke up, but he'd appreciate the gesture nonetheless. There were no clocks in the apartment. He had all the shades down. It was seven a.m. The Gaudí house opened at nine. La Boqueria, nine-thirty. Some of the cafés might be open, but then again, maybe not just yet. Jake was right. She was starting too early. But she was wide-awake, dressed, and showered. Maybe she'd take her cup of coffee outside and wander around. That's it; she'd go back to the town square. She could relax there, enjoy her coffee, watch pigeons. She'd probably be back before Jake woke up again.

It was odd to see the lobby empty of the non-door-opening doorman. Did she expect he'd be sleeping there? She was just about to exit when she noticed a book lying on the desk. Curiosity drove her to go near it. She always had to know what people were reading, or listening to. She hadn't pegged the desk guy as a reader. Of course someone else could have left it. She reached for it before she even registered the title.

A TREE GROWS IN BROOKLYN

Grace stood still and stared at the book as if it might make a sudden move, strike out like a snake. It was so random, so wild. Her all-time favorite book. One of Grace's presents for her twelfth birthday. Grace had carried that book around so much that summer she had almost ruined it. It went in the bathtub, the car, under her pillow. She ate breakfast, lunch, and dinner with it clutched in her hand. What was it about a story about a girl living in Brooklyn that touched her all the way in Tennessee? Ironically, Grace used to read it in her tree house. What were the odds that the book would be right here, in the lobby in Barcelona?

Grace stared at the book, almost afraid to touch it. Obviously, it was a famous novel. And this building catered to tourists. Another American, maybe even a young girl, must have brought the book with her to Barcelona, and was leaving it for someone else to read. How could anyone abandon this book though? Although with the invention of eBooks, paperbacks were hardly cherished anymore. Grace picked up the book and hugged it to her chest. Well, she'd take it. Or was that selfish? Should she leave it for someone who'd never had the chance to read it?

No, it was meant for her. One of life's little surprises, or happy ironies. Since she didn't have her purse, she tucked the book under her armpit and headed outside.

It was a mild morning, still warm but a lull before the brutal heat of the day. As predicted, the square was quiet. The benches were empty, and the small fountain in the middle was indeed occupied by pigeons. A single shopkeeper was sweeping outside. It was a pizza place at night, but they served breakfast, and most important to Grace, cappuccinos. She wished she hadn't brought her coffee, but even so, she had left her money in the room. She couldn't win. Either she had too much with her, or not enough. Maybe in the future, all financial transactions would be completed through some kind of microchip implanted in one's finger. Grace would be drinking an espresso by now.

Grace sat on a bench and set the book next to her. She took in a few deep breaths and gazed at all the apartments above her. Several had clothing hanging out the windows, one a potted plant, and Grace could make out curtains or blinds on most as well. Jake was right. Everyone was sleeping. She was surprised there were no homeless people sleeping in the square. It was where she would go if she were homeless. She sipped her coffee, stretched out on the bench, and picked up the book. How great was this, to sit and read her favorite book in a square in Spain. Maybe there was a song in there somewhere.

> *There was a square in Spain*
> *Where you can feel no pain*
> *You can read your book*
> *Without a single look. . . .*

Marsh Everett would hate it. So what. Grace opened her book. It wasn't as beat-up as her original copy, but it was old. She flipped through the first few pages, curious if anyone had signed his or her name. She used to always sign her books. THIS BOOK BELONGS TO: GRACE ANN SAWYER. She always had to write out her full name because her initials spelled GAS. Her parents definitely didn't think that one through.

Sure enough, she caught handwriting as she flipped through. Instead of a name, there was simply a quote:

THERE, BUT FOR GRACE, GO I

Grace immediately righted herself from her sprawled position on the bench, as if sitting at attention would clarify the mystery. The message was written in capital letters in black ink. What was this? Grace knew what quote was being paraphrased. *There, but for the grace of God, go I.* This had to be some kind of joke. Was it from whoever had paid for their trip? Were they going to leave Grace and Jake little clues until they figured out who the mysterious couple was? Grace wanted to drop the book, but she couldn't seem to let it go. She looked around the square. Breathe. Sit up. Think of everyone who might know this was her favorite book.

Her parents, of course. But they certainly had nothing to do with this trip. It would be sweet as hell if they were renewing their vows, but it just wasn't possible. Not with her mother's condition. Jody had probably forgotten a dozen times where Grace was, let alone who she was.

Then there was Dan. He didn't know this was Grace's favorite book, but he could at least tell them something about the person who had called him. Grace wondered if Jake had tried calling Dan again, or if he'd called back. Darn the time change. Grace wanted to call him right now, but she was pretty sure it was like three a.m. in Tennessee.

Who else knew about this book? Had she mentioned it in any interviews or on her Facebook page? She had. She'd mentioned it on her Facebook page. It was on her "About" page. You had to go looking for it, but it was there.

So much for relaxing. Grace would drive herself crazy going through this alone. She needed to get Jake's take on it. The shopkeeper waved at her as she passed by.

"*Hola,*" he said. "Good morning."

"*Hola.*" She waved back, really wishing she could go in and buy an espresso. Next time. That was the great thing about life.

Every day was a do-over. She hurried back to the apartment, half looking behind her every few steps. She was being ridiculous. Whoever was surprising them had thought this through. They would all laugh at the fact that it was spooking her a little. *There, But For Grace, Go I. . . .*

Wait. Was it someone who had a crush on Jake? Oh, God. But they were getting married, right? So maybe this was kind of tongue in cheek—*I never would have fallen in love with my husband if you hadn't been with Jake—*

Jake was going to have to come clean. He probably knew exactly how many women had crushes on him. There were probably a lot. Was this one a psycho? Or just trying to be funny? Well, it wasn't funny. Free trip or no, it was just plain dense to freak someone out like this. At least they left the book on the desk downstairs and not at her doorstep. Still, Grace found herself hurrying past the desk and up the stairs, ready to scream if anyone was following her. She fumbled with the key. God, she was shaking. Jake would calm her down. She closed the door a little harder than she meant to. It slammed shut. She was still trembling when she locked it.

"Grace?" Jake emerged from the bedroom in his boxers. She loved how his hair stuck straight up in the mornings. Grace held the book up. Jake just looked at it and waited. It didn't register with him. But now of all times was not the time to get her feelings hurt over the fact that he couldn't remember the name of her favorite book.

"Someone left this for me at the desk," Grace said.

"What desk?"

"In the lobby." Grace opened to the page and showed it to Jake. He read it aloud. "Start talking, Jake," Grace said.

"What?"

"Someone at work, or one of your clients, or God knows who else—someone is in love with you. That's who lured us here."

"Wait, wait." Jake headed for the stool at the counter and sat down. Grace followed. "*Lured* us here?"

"Yes. Someone is in love with you, and she lured us here to get rid of me so she could have you all to herself."

"Flattering."

"Jake."

"I'm kidding. Relax. Besides, it's *your* favorite book. Why do you think this has anything to do with me?"

Grace opened up to the page with the writing. "There, but for Grace, go I," she read.

"Weird. Let me see that." Jake took the book, read it again, shook his head.

"It's a clue. Someone left it for me to find."

Jake ran his hand through his hair. "Is there any coffee for me?"

"I left a cup by your bed." Jake gave her a kiss on the nose, then slid off the stool. He padded into the bedroom. A minute later he poked his head out the doorway.

"Where?" he said.

"On the table."

"It's not there."

"It has to be." Grace walked into the bedroom and headed for the table. She was fully prepared to say, "If it were a snake, it would have bit you." Instead, she found herself staring at an empty space. Not even a coffee ring. "You must have moved it," Grace said.

"I've been asleep."

Grace glanced at the other bedside table. Besides Jake's thriller, there was nothing there. "Maybe you took it into the bathroom," she said. She started to turn. Jake gently caught her arm.

"I've been sleeping. I haven't moved from this bed until just now when you slammed the door."

"I didn't slam the door." Grace headed for the kitchen. Maybe it was on the counter. But she knew she had put it on his table. There wasn't a single doubt. Jake must have moved it. People were known to do stranger things in their sleep. Eat, walk, fight. Why not move a coffee cup? Still, it was just another strange thing on top of an already strange morning. Had someone been in the apartment? Watching Jake? "Jake. Think. Is there anyone slightly crazy who is madly in love with you?"

"Of course not. Wait." Jake stopped. He looked up and to the right and then frowned.

"What?"

"There is one girl."

"Who?"

"She's about this tall." Jake held out his hand to Grace's height. "Gorgeous brunette hair. Hazel eyes. When she sings—"

"Har har." Grace whacked Jake on the shoulder; he pulled her in to him.

"You really think someone was here?"

"I put that coffee cup near your bed. I swear to it, Jake. I swear to it."

"So you think, what? Someone came in here just to steal a cup of coffee?"

"Maybe he or she was watching you sleep. The same person who left me this book. And then—I don't know—he or she took the coffee to let us know he or she was here. Someone is messing with us."

Wait, Grace thought. She came home rather quickly. Someone could still be in the apartment. Hiding. Jake watched Grace looking around the room. He stepped forward.

"You think he or she is still here?" he whispered. Grace nodded, grateful he was no longer hinting that she was losing her mind. Jake turned and surveyed the apartment. Grace was silently listing all the places one could hide. Under the bed. In the closet, or in the bathroom. There weren't any windows open. But technically could someone have gone out the fire escape and closed the window behind himself or herself?

She followed Jake back to the bedroom. He crouched on the floor and peered under the bed. Maybe this wasn't such a good idea. What did she expect Jake to do if he found someone? Fight? Jake wasn't a fighter, and she didn't want him to be. "Jake," Grace whispered. "Let's just go."

Jake stood up from the bed. "It's clear."

Grace grabbed his sleeve. He looked at her. *Let's go,* she mouthed, pointing to the door. Jake shook his head no, held up his hand. He opened the closet, and disappeared inside for a moment. Grace covered her mouth with her hands. She couldn't take this.

"Please, Jake," she said.

"No one," he said. He was no longer whispering. He headed for the bathroom. Grace followed. Unlike in the horror movies, their shower didn't have a curtain to dramatically pull open. It had a clear door. The minute they turned on the light they could see it was empty.

"You shouldn't have done that," Grace said. "What if he or she is armed?"

"Shit," Jake said. He pointed. There, on the bathroom sink, was the cup of coffee. It was still full. Grace slumped against the doorframe. Jake pointed at it. "I did not put that there," he said. "Is there any chance you did?"

"No. No chance."

Jake wiped his brow with his forearm. He was covered in sweat. "Okay. Now I'm kind of getting freaked out."

"Call Dan," Grace said. "Now."

"I think it's like four a.m.," Jake said.

"Do it," Grace said. "If he allowed some stalker to use him to lure us here under false pretenses, I can deal with disrupting his beauty sleep."

"Good point." Jake said. He picked up the coffee cup. He smelled it. "Do you think someone poisoned it?" he half-joked. Grace snatched it and dumped it in the sink.

"That could've been evidence," Jake said.

"Shit," Grace said. "I didn't think of that."

"We suck at this."

"Maybe this is why nobody gets up early."

"Agreed. Let's go back to bed." Jake wrapped his arms around Grace and maneuvered her back into the bedroom.

"Jake?"

"Yes, my love?"

"I want to go home."

Jake sat on the edge of the bed and brushed a strand of hair out of Grace's face. "Someone is just playing a bit of a game," he said. "Don't let that person get to you."

"I don't care who it is or what he or she has paid for. I'm not going to the wedding."

"I agree."

"You do?"

"I don't like being played with either. Screw their wedding. But that doesn't mean we should run home. In fact, the best revenge would be to have the holiday of our lives."

"At least call Dan. We can figure it out from there."

Jake nodded and kissed Grace. She put her arms around him and kissed him back. "I'll protect you," he said.

"My hero," Grace said. "Now call Dan."

"Yes, ma'am." He planted a kiss on her nose and dug his phone out of a pair of jeans on the floor. Grace lay in bed as he made the call. She closed her eyes. *Answer,* she pleaded. She wanted to get these paranoid thoughts out of her head so they could thoroughly enjoy Barcelona. *Please just answer.* She headed to the front door of the apartment to double-check that it was locked. An envelope had been slid underneath the door. There in elegant calligraphy were their names:

GRACE AND JAKE

Grace swiped the envelope and held it at arm's length. Grace and Jake. Her name came first.

"Still no answer," Jake said from behind her. Grace shoved the envelope down her shorts.

"What's that?" Jake said. Grace whirled around, conscious that the tip of the envelope was peeking out at her waist. She casually covered it with her hand. "Did you just stick something down your pants?"

"They're shorts." Cut-offs actually, but she was already on a slippery slope.

"What is that?" He reached for it.

'Wait," she said, for the first time ever blocking his hand from that region. "I'll do it."

"What is that?"

"Someone slipped it under the door."

"Why are you hiding it?"

Shoot. He was angry. Why was she hiding it? It was really hard to come up with convincing lies. How did people do it? "Some girl is stalking you, and I think you know exactly who it is," Grace said. That was certainly one way. Put the innocent bystander on the defensive. Pick a fight with the man you love. Good going, Grace.

"Bring it to the counter," Jake said. She set it on the counter, and the two of them just looked at it. "Why are you so sure this has to do with me?"

Grace couldn't swear to it, but Jake sounded just a tad thrilled with the prospect. "Because whoever is doing this used your work to launder the trip."

"Launder the trip? If you're just working your way through the alphabet, then 'lured' should come after 'launder.' "

"Enough with the jokes. You know what I mean."

"Are you jealous?"

"If some psycho is after my man? You bet I am."

"Really?"

"Yes. Really." She took his face in her hands. It was true. Sometimes she did get jealous. She kissed him. "I just wanted to read it first. I'm sorry."

"Should we place a bet?"

Yes, Grace thought. *I bet we're not going to like it.* The feeling was so strong, not based on fact, just an uneasy gnawing churning in her. The same sick feeling she got whenever she thought about Stan Gale.

"You look as if you think it's laced with anthrax," Jake said.

"I was not thinking that. Until now."

"You can look for gloves if you want, but I say let's live dangerously and just open it."

Grace opened the envelope before Jake could beat her to it. A card slipped out. On the front was a photo of Casa Batlló at night. The colorful mosaic tiles glowed under a full moon.

MAGIC BY NIGHT

As the sun dips into the Mediterranean and darkness descends on Barcelona, Casa Batlló is hosting an

exclusive musical event on its rooftop terrace. You are
cordially invited to mingle with the magic of Antoni
Gaudí and engage every sense in this exquisite
nocturnal drama.

A pair of tickets was tucked into the envelope. Grace pulled them out and held them up. "It's for tonight," she said.

"Exquisite nocturnal drama?" Jake said. He took the card. "You missed this part." He pointed to some writing on the bottom of the invitation. It was true. Grace had overlooked it entirely. "Who do we know with the initials SBC?"

"What?" Please, God. He did not just say SBC. Hearing Jake speak the initials sounded so wrong. As if he'd just picked up a hand grenade and said, "Hey, what's this pin?" just before pulling it. Grace snatched the card back. She had heard right. It was there in the corner, in capital letters. SBC. Sisters by Choice.

Carrie Ann.

Oh, God. It couldn't be. It couldn't be. Could it? Was she here? Grace wanted to see her. It had been so, so long. She'd tried searching for Carrie Ann on the Internet but had never found a single, solitary thing. What was her life like? What was she like? The thought of seeing her again gripped Grace like the thrill of a roller coaster. Yet she was terrified. They were connected. That's why Grace had been thinking about her lately. They were connected. She should have listened to her instincts. She should have told Jake. She should tell him now. Grace felt charged, as if she were going to explode. Why couldn't she ever control her emotions? Should she sing now? Sing her pain?

"Does SBC mean anything to you?" Jake asked.

Yes. Carrie Ann was my sister. She's nearby, and I knew it. I've felt her. We are connected. Like radio waves. Like handcuffs.

"Grace?" Jake said again. "Does SBC mean anything to you?"

Sisters. Sisters by choice. Or by force. "No," Grace said. "It doesn't mean a thing."

CHAPTER 9

Grace's mother had been telling the truth after all. Carrie Ann had gone to the hospice to see her. *She asked me all sorts of questions about you.* Grace held the invitation and studied it while Jake showered.

Magic by Night. Carrie Ann used to practice magic. She was wicked at pulling a quarter from your ear, she could seemingly swallow a scarf whole, never to be seen again, and she stumped Grace time and again on a card game in which she always, every single time, guessed Grace's card correctly. All this in a freckled, fair-haired package. Some of the happiest "family" moments had come when Carrie Ann was willing to do her tricks in the den for everyone, even the boys. Grace almost laughed— it sounded horrible; did Carrie Ann twist those words around like she did everything? *The Sawyers made me do tricks in the den for the boys. . . .*

Carrie Ann had planned to grow up to be the first famous female magician. Grace had always expected she would. Expected to open the *New York Times* or turn on the television to see Carrie Ann with her long blond hair and knockout figure in a glittering skintight dress performing a death-defying trick.

SBC. Instantly, Grace was back in the tree house on their twelfth birthday. Carrie Ann didn't know when her real birthday was, so she decided it was the same as Grace's. July twenty-ninth. Carrie Ann had held up the paring knife with the pearl handle. Its blade gleamed in a stray beam of sun sneaking in through the gaps in the tree.

"Swear." With her usual flair for dramatics, Carrie Ann had thrust the knife up. Grace had followed it with her eyes. "On our thirtieth birthday, we will celebrate in Rome." For the briefest second, Grace had imagined being thrown into the Colosseum with a roaring lion, while Carrie Ann watched gleefully. The loser would be dinner.

"Thirty?" Grace had said. It had sounded ancient. "Rome?" It had sounded far.

"Or Paris," Carrie Ann had said, running the tip of the knife softly across Grace's upper lip. "But I prefer Rome." Grace had blinked, waited a few seconds and then cautiously pushed on Carrie Ann's arm until the knife was no longer touching her face. Then, she had nodded.

"Rome," she had repeated in a raspy whisper. Carrie Ann had scraped the tip of the knife across her index finger until it sprouted bright red blood. Then, she had handed it to Grace to do the same. Grace had flinched and shut her eyes as she swiped it as fast as she could.

"Well done," Carrie Ann had said. Grace had swelled with pride at the compliment. Carrie Ann had quickly pressed her finger to Grace's, and their blood had mixed.

"Now we're sisters by choice," Carrie Ann had said. "Aren't we?"

"Yes," Grace had repeated. "Sisters." Although she hadn't been so sure about the choice. Sometimes she had felt a little trapped by Carrie Ann. It made her feel so guilty; what was wrong with her? She'd always wanted a sister. But did they all scare you a little bit the way Carrie Ann did? Just a little. She'd even prayed for someone like Carrie Ann long before she showed up at their doorstep with her little flowered suitcase.

"Sisters by choice," Carrie Ann had said. "SBC. Forever."

A Tree Grows in Brooklyn. "Why do you carry that stupid book wherever you go? How many times have you read it? You do know there are other books in the world, don't you?" Carrie Ann had been jealous of a book. She had grabbed it and ripped a corner off of the cover. "Do you like it now?" Carrie Ann had asked. "Or does it have to be perfect?" Grace had known it was some kind of test, some kind of trap.

"I still like it," she had said.

"Just as much?"

"Yes. Just as much." But she hadn't. God help her, she hadn't. She had taped the corner back on, but it never felt quite the same.

There, but for Grace, go I. . . .

Oh, God. Grace thought of the very last time she had seen Carrie Ann. At Lionel Gale's funeral. Standing tall underneath that willow tree in a long black dress. Wearing black to Lionel's funeral. That was Carrie Ann, all right. Grace hadn't dared. She had worn navy blue instead. She had been so afraid to look at Carrie Ann, and when their eyes did accidentally meet and lock, Carrie Ann had seemed to be silently screaming at her. *You betrayed me. I hate you. This is just as much your fault as it is mine.* Every time Grace thought of that, that a man might be alive if she had just done things a little bit differently, her chest constricted, and she'd find herself gasping for breath. Sing your pain? A man's life in our careless hands—how's that for pain?

Carrie Ann had cornered Grace as she was exiting the funeral home. At first Grace had thought Carrie Ann was going to hurt her. She had backed all the way up into a corner of the vestibule. She had eyed umbrellas in case she needed to protect herself. That was the other strange thing. It had been raining nonstop since Grace found Lionel Gale hanging by the neck in his barn. It had been as if the skies were crying out, punishing Grace.

"You'll be sorry," Carrie Ann had said. Strange, it hadn't been said like a threat. In fact Carrie Ann had sounded almost sad for Grace. *You'll be sorry.* As if Grace weren't sorry already. Stan's father was dead. Lydia's husband. A man was lying in a casket just a few feet away. Because of them. Why was Carrie Ann saying, "You'll be sorry" as if it were some future event and not the anchor that had just been lodged in Grace's gut? For the first time in the five years since Carrie Ann had swept into her life, Grace had stood her ground.

"I never want to see you again," Grace had told her.

Carrie Ann had given her a sad little smile. "But you will," she had said. "But you will."

Now, here they were, all grown up and in Spain. In five days it would be their thirtieth birthday. Grace held her breath. This could not be happening.

"Grace?" Jake said. He stood behind her with a towel wrapped around his waist. Grace had no idea how long he'd been standing there. "What's wrong?"

"Nothing."

"Liar." Jake rested his hands on her shoulders and gently brushed his lips against her cheek. "Tell me."

Grace jerked away. "You're wet," she said, hoping he'd believe that was the reason. The truth was, she just didn't want him near that part of her. The girl she used to be. The lengths she'd gone to, to please Carrie Ann. She didn't want to talk about Stan Gale, or Lionel. She definitely didn't want to talk or think about Lionel. "Are you sure there's no one at work who's in love with you?" It came out harsher than Grace meant it. She would give anything if it were some woman from Jake's work. Anything if it weren't Carrie Ann. Why would Carrie Ann go through Dan? How would she even know about Jake or where he worked?

She's been stalking me. The truth hit Grace, hard and cold. Carrie Ann was close. As close as a strange set of fingerprints on Jake's morning coffee.

"This can't be anyone from work," Jake said. "I mean—the receptionist flirts with me a bit—"

Grace slid off her stool. "Lyndsey?" Dyed blond, big boobs, straight white teeth, skinny rest of her.

"Don't go Glenn Close on me," Jake said. "It's harmless flirting."

"Do you flirt back?" In the moment Grace didn't really care. She just needed to keep talking. She needed to make this some- one other than Carrie Ann. If this was Carrie Ann, Grace was booking the next flight back to Tennessee.

"I joke back. I guess you could call it flirting. But there's no undercurrent."

"What does that mean?"

"It's not hidden. There's no agenda or desire behind it. Everyone at work knows how crazy I am about you." He took her in his arms again. "Besides. If it was someone who had a crush on me—why did they invite the two of us?"

"Maybe she lured me here to kill me off. Have you all to her- self."

Jake placed his hand over his heart and lowered his voice. "I'm going to need a mourning period."

"You jerk." Grace bumped him on the shoulder, and Jake leaned in and kissed her.

Jake held up the tickets to Casa Batlló. "Well, you were just saying you wanted to go."

"Oh my God. You're right. Do you think they're listening to us?"

"Who?"

Carrie Ann. "The mysterious bride and groom."

"You're joking, right?"

"No. I think we should sweep for bugs."

"The only bugs we know how to sweep for are the creepy, crawly kind. Even then—they usually get away."

"You're the one who insists we scoop them up and take them outside."

"I'm a vet. First, do no harm. Or first—do not squash."

Grace lowered her voice to a whisper. "I think someone is lis- tening to us."

"Did anybody ever tell you you're adorable when you're paranoid?"

"No."

"That's because you're not." He said it in a normal voice. Grace made a grab for his towel. Jake pinned her hand to his hip with one hand and waved the tickets with his other. "What do you say?" he asked. "I'm up for an exquisite nocturnal drama. You?"

CHAPTER 10

From the moment Grace and Jake entered Casa Batlló, she felt as if they were underwater. Curved, smooth-domed ceilings, cool blue tiles, porthole windows, and walls evoking undulating waves adorned every corner of the house. Grace wanted to take her time and yet race to the roof terrace at the same time. She was sure that was where Carrie Ann would plant her proverbial flag, surveying her territory from above. Grace flipped through the brochure they had handed her upon entering. It was still daylight; the sky would darken in about an hour. Grace wanted to be early. She wanted to see Carrie Ann first, ease into it, try and control the damage.

The entire back of the house was indeed built to resemble a dragon, with its prehistoric tiled spine arching to an apex on the roof and dropping down the back wall of the house. There was also a room on the roof terrace where you could go inside, close the door, and be treated to shadows lit by the illuminated fountain in the floor. The Dragon's Belly. It was supposed to induce a meditative state. Grace could use all the meditation she could get right now.

"It's like we're in a giant conch shell," Jake said as they passed through the Noble Floor. Besides mosaic tiles and marble, the woodwork was so rich and smooth that it too almost looked like it belonged under the sea. Wood was also used above numerous doorways, showcasing ornate patterns of interspersed glass and tile, arranged in irregular oval shapes, like seashells. Dripping chandeliers hung in every main room, and stairways curved upward in a sensuous S. It was a drunkard's delight, not a straight line in sight. Some of the ceilings actually swirled in, like mini tidal waves. It was almost impossible to comprehend the mind behind this masterpiece. Suddenly, it made Grace feel very small, and yet emboldened at the same time. This genius wasn't designing from a place of pain; the marvels around her, down to the tiniest fixtures, could only have been created from an overwhelming outpouring of joy. Imagine a Marsh Everett equivalent saying that Gaudí would be "soon forgotten." How foolish.

Not that she was comparing herself to the genius. But still. There was a place where joy existed, and she was standing in it. Although ironically the street on which the house sat was known as the "block of discord." Manzana de la Discordia. One of the wealthiest streets in Spain. Homeowners used to pull out all the stops to outdo each other. Each one hired a better architect until it all ended with Gaudí's pulling off the transformation of Casa Batlló. Nobody dared to outdo this one. Resistance is futile, Grace thought. She linked arms with Jake. "Maybe the mystery couple is waiting on the roof," he said.

Great minds think alike. Except there's no mystery, and there's no couple. "Ready to jump off after they say their vows?" Grace said. And just like that, she imagined Carrie Ann's body falling off the roof.

"Fire-breathing start to a life together," Jake said.

Grace twirled his words around in her head. They would make nice song lyrics. *I'd slay a fire-breathing dragon for you. . . .*

"You're composing in your head," Jake said.

"How did you know that?"

"You get this certain look on your face." Jake smiled. He

leaned in and kissed Grace on the nose. "I love that look." Grace made a faint roaring noise. "Was that supposed to be a dragon?" Jake said.

"You do know me."

"Don't do it again." Grace laughed, and her voice echoed down the cavernous hall. He was holding on to her, and not lagging behind, or racing up ahead. She was going to have to lose him on the roof.

The minute they opened the doors to the terrace, Grace was hit with a rush of air. As cool as the interior of the house was, there was something slightly claustrophobic about it, like being inside a submarine. But the roof terrace was expansive, and the sky was just starting to tint orange overhead, and the mosaic tiles glittered in the drowsy remains of the sun. Tables were being set up for the evening extravaganza, and a small orchestra was warming up. Waiters bustled around with vases of blood-red roses and crisp white-linen tablecloths. Visitors without tickets for Magic by Night were politely being told it was time to leave. Grace was relieved that those with tickets were allowed to stay and watch the sun set. Soon all the little lights around the roof would be lit, and the dragon house would indeed become a thing of magic.

Ahead, just to the left, people were filing in and out of a small door. Otherwise, Grace would have missed it, for the doorway blended into the wall like a chameleon. Hidden in plain sight. "That must be the meditation room," Grace said. The Dragon's Belly. Ironic. Grace's insides felt just like a dragon's belly. *Carrie Ann, are you here?* Grace wouldn't miss finding out for anything in the world, although a very big part of her was desperate to flee.

"It's surreal, isn't it? Hard to imagine someone with this much talent and imagination."

As soon as Jake said "imagination," an image popped into Grace's head. Carrie Ann had once hung a hundred red ballet slippers from the branches of the tree house. It was the prettiest thing Grace had ever seen. She had thought Carrie Ann was

a genius. She had been a thief too; apparently she'd been stealing them from a local ballet class and hoarding them away for
the past year while she dyed them red. The things she pulled
off really did seem like magic.

Where are you, Carrie Ann? Are you here?

"Jake. Don't hate me."

"What's wrong? You look sick. Are you sick?"

"Yes. No. I have to tell you something."

Jake's cell phone rang, slicing through her words. Jake
glanced at the screen. "It's Dan."

Grace nodded. She should have told him he didn't need to
answer. She should have told him exactly who was doing this.
And she definitely should have told him she was probably very,
very near.

"I'll meet you back here." Jake walked to a private corner of
the terrace. Interesting, he wanted to be alone for the call. Now
who had something to hide? Grace had probably made him
paranoid that some woman from work was obsessed with him.
She shouldn't have led him to believe that. She'd made mistake
after mistake. Just like she had always done when Carrie Ann
was around.

Grace stood for a moment watching him. Part of her wanted
to stay glued to Jake's side and to the conversation. Instead, she
turned and headed for the Dragon's Belly. Jake would tell her
everything soon enough. She filed in past several people and
soon found herself in a concrete room with shadows playing
along the walls and ceiling. When they were full to capacity, the
door shut. The faint sound of dripping water and classical
music accompanied the light and shadow show. Grace took a
few deep breaths. It was damp inside, like a cave. Soon, between the wisps of light dancing along the walls, and the low,
soothing sounds, Grace began to feel lighter and lighter. She
started paying attention to her breaths, purposefully making
them deep and slow.

But just when she thought she was going to actually relax all
the way, Grace felt a swoosh of air along the back of her head,
and suddenly a hand was pressing into the small of her back,

nudging her forward. One by one the little hairs on her arm stood up. She would not be afraid. She would not let Carrie Ann make her come unglued. Grace whirled around and was just about to grab on to whoever had touched her, when she saw a stricken young Spanish woman in front of her. *"¡Despensi! ¡Perdoni!"* she said, and pointed to a little girl who was hanging on to her hand, straining to get to the door, tears dripping down her cheeks. Grace knew exactly how she felt.

"Sorry, sorry," Grace said. She backed out of the way. The walls felt like they were closing in. Like that scene in *Star Wars* she could never watch, where the garbage compactor or elevator or whatever they were in was getting smaller and smaller, while the drip grew louder and louder. She had to get out. Just like the little girl, Grace had to get out.

Grace scooted to the door, determined to appear helpful. She turned the doorknob and pulled. The door didn't open. She pulled harder. It was stuck. She twisted the knob, leaning her entire body into it to give it weight. Then she pulled again.

"It's stuck," she yelled.

"Shhhh," echoed through the room. The mother reached around her, turned the knob, and easily pulled the door open. She gestured for Grace to go out first. Feeling ashamed that she was getting out before the crying child, but not wanting to prolong the ordeal, Grace stumbled onto the roof, then bent over and took short breaths. The child stared at her as the mother dragged her away, tears gone, now straining to keep looking back at Grace. Claustrophobia. She hadn't had it in years. She had thought she was over it. Letting in thoughts about Carrie Ann must have stirred something in her subconscious. Carrie Ann had once locked Grace in their hall closet. It had only been for an hour, but it had felt like all day. By the time Carrie Ann had let her out, Grace had broken into hives and thrown up in a pair of polka-dotted rain boots.

Grace lifted her head and immediately scanned the terrace for Jake. This trip wasn't going to work out. They would be on the first plane home. He was no longer in the corner where he had taken the phone call. She didn't see him anywhere. Had he come into the little room without her knowing? Had he left the roof without telling her? No. He would never do that. Unless reception had been bad on the roof and he had to go somewhere else?

The orchestra began to play. Laughter and clinking glasses echoed throughout the terrace. Grace took a deep breath and smoothed her hair. She couldn't look panicked. Everyone was so well dressed. Beautiful fabrics, and heels, and men in tuxedos and soft gray suits, and women with gorgeous legs. Grace had worn her best dress, a tight blue number, and although she was in no danger of being kicked out, she was well outfashioned.

She dug through her purse. She had left her cell phone at home. Wait. Did she even have her own key? She was starting to regret following Jake's advice on leaving her valuables at home. She combed through her purse once more. No key. Jake had to be here. He would never just leave her here. Had he somehow been lured away? Before she could tell him about Carrie Ann?

Grace traversed the roof all the way back to the door leading into the house. She turned just as a waiter paused in front of her with a full tray of champagne. At his nod, she took a glass. Just as she moved away, she saw a tall, blond woman standing in the middle of the roof deck. She stood out like a beacon in a stunning red dress. Her hair flowed just past her shoulders in soft waves. She was scanning the crowd. Grace couldn't move; she couldn't breathe. Carrie Ann's eyes finally landed on Grace and locked in. Grace stilled as she took in her estranged friend. She would have recognized her anywhere. She was an older version of the coltish blond hellion Grace had known, but Carrie Ann still had the same freckles on her nose, the same long blond hair, the same look in her eye that suggested she was the keeper of everyone's secrets. The sun had set; the lights were twinkling all around the roof. It was her. It was Carrie Ann.

She did not make a move toward Grace, but a smile lit up her face. If the sky had opened up and struck Grace with a bolt of lightning, she wouldn't have been half as shocked. It was as if Carrie Ann had sent a surge of electricity through the rooftop terrace. Grace wanted to launch into Carrie Ann's arms, and she equally wanted to turn and flee. The ambivalence rendered her immobile. A hand touched her waist. She jumped.

"Hey." It was Jake. Grace still couldn't move. She couldn't take her eyes off Carrie Ann. "Grace?" He turned her around. Concern flooded his eyes as he searched her face. "What's wrong?" Reluctantly, Grace took her eyes off Carrie Ann. She should never have lied to Jake. It was too late now.

"I—I was looking for you," Grace said. Her voice was barely a whisper.

"I just spoke with Dan."

"And?"

"He said it was a girl who called him." Jake waited. Grace made a conscious effort not to allow any emotion to show on her face. She was getting a second chance to tell the truth. "Any idea who that might be?"

Carrie Ann was here. Just a few feet away, staring at her. A sister of sorts. Whom Jake knew nothing about. Grace couldn't get the words out. It was too late. Too late. "What?" Grace said.

"Is there any reason—any reason at all—that some woman would say she was your *sister?*"

"Not a real sister," Grace said. She whispered it, because for all she knew Carrie Ann was moving closer. Grace didn't want to look. *Act normal. Say hello to Carrie Ann. Greet her like you would greet any old childhood friend.*

"So who is she?" Jake said. And then, he seemed to sense Carrie Ann's presence, or maybe like Grace he felt her, and he turned and he saw her. She had moved closer. Just a few feet, but close enough to see her clearly. She looked eerily beautiful—an ethereal angel in a devil's dress. There was almost a pleading in her eyes. Grace had hurt her feelings by not acknowledging her. *Think,* Grace thought. *Think.* How could she make any of this right? Even better—how could she make any of this go away? Jake stared at Carrie Ann, who flashed him one of the biggest smiles Grace had ever seen. Oh, how Carrie Ann used to get away with murder whenever she used that smile.

You haven't changed, Grace thought. *And you still have some kind of hold over me.* Grace didn't like it, and she could literally feel Carrie Ann's presence weighing her down. But then, just like that, Carrie Ann's face softened, almost as if she were afraid of Grace, and instantly Carrie Ann was that wounded little girl standing in Grace's doorway, scowling and clutching her vinyl flowered suitcase. Grace's heart broke open. She stumbled forward. "Carrie Ann," she said. She still couldn't raise her voice above a whisper.

"Hi, Gracie," Carrie Ann whispered back. Without warning, Grace felt a lump in her throat, and tears invade her eyes. She bit the side of her mouth to keep from crying. Carrie Ann noticed it though, swooped up the information, and then threw her arms around Grace. Jake took the champagne glass out of Grace's hand seconds before it would have smashed on the ground. Carrie Ann smelled good, like vanilla and lemon, and she held Grace tight. "Finally," Carrie Ann was saying over and over again. "Finally."

Grace opened her eyes and saw Jake standing behind Carrie Ann. He was totally confused. And dare she say—hurt? Grace pulled away. "Jake," she said, turning to him. "This is Carrie Ann." Jake held out his hand, but instead Carrie Ann threw herself into his arms and hugged him the same way she'd just hugged Grace. Claiming everyone around her, just like she always did. Jake soon pulled away and looked at Grace.

"I'm her sister," Carrie Ann said. She looked at Grace. *Your turn.* Challenging Grace. Was she going to refute it?

"Carrie Ann was my foster sister," Grace said.

"I thought you said your parents took in all boys," Jake said.

Carrie Ann grabbed Jake's hand and put it on her breast. "They're real," she said. Jake removed his hand as quickly as possible and threw Grace another look.

"This trip?" he said to Carrie Ann. "Was this you?"

"Surprise," Carrie Ann said. "Not just foster sister, Grace."

Grace opened her mouth to speak, but nothing came out.

"How so?" Jake said.

"Blood," Grace said. It came out in a whisper.

"Sisters by Choice," Carrie Ann said. "We cut our fingers with a knife. We pressed our blood together. We took a vow. SBC forever."

"We're not twelve anymore," Grace said. She surprised herself by saying it out loud, carried by a flash of anger.

"SBC," Jake said. "The card." He looked at Grace. She looked back without blinking. "You knew?" he said. *You lied*, he meant.

"I wondered," Grace said. *I lied.*

"Are you getting married?" Jake asked Carrie Ann.

"Are you proposing?" Carrie Ann shot back. Grace took Jake's hand and gave it an I'll-tell-you-everything-later squeeze. He didn't squeeze back. Carrie Ann reached out and took Grace's other hand. Carrie Ann used to do this with Stan. She would grab his hand and then Grace's hand, as if sealing the three of them together forever. Grace used to absolutely loathe feeling his clammy, chubby hand in hers. The thought made Grace drop both hands. Her temple began to throb along with the pulse of the crowd.

"Are you okay, Grace?" Jake said.

"She's claustrophobic," Carrie Ann said.

"No, she's not," Jake said.

"Are you kidding? She's always hated small spaces. Don't you see how shallow her breathing is? The sweat breaking out on her forehead?"

"Grace?" Jake said.

"I need to get off this roof," Grace said. She imagined going to the edge and hurling herself over.

"I've got you," Carrie Ann said. She looped arms with Grace. "I know this great Irish pub where we can get cozy and catch up." Grace glanced at Jake.

"By all means," he said, pointing to the door. "I would love for somebody to catch me up." He was looking at Carrie Ann. But he was talking to Grace. The exquisite, nocturnal drama had just begun.

CHAPTER 11

Carrie Ann ushered them into a taxi and rattled something off in what sounded like fluent Spanish. The taxi sped off. For a split second Grace wondered if she should be paying attention to markers so she could figure out how to get home. How had this even happened? Just like when they were kids, Carrie Ann was taking the reins. At least this time Grace had Jake with her. He wasn't going to cave to Carrie Ann's every whim like poor Stan. Grace was going to have one drink with Carrie Ann and then make an excuse to go home. Book the next tickets back to Nashville. As the taxi zoomed through the streets of Spain, Carrie Ann chattered about local sights. Did she live here? If Grace didn't know better, she would have said that Carrie Ann was nervous about something. About seeing her. And here Grace was planning her escape. A familiar curtain of guilt descended on Grace. Carrie Ann had gone to a lot of trouble. Grace should be thrilled to see her. They weren't kids anymore. Surely Grace could handle her now. How was it that Grace was always immobilized by ambivalence when it came to her SBC?

"Do you live here?" Grace said.

"No. But I have a friend who does."

Suddenly, Grace saw it. The couple who had bumped into them on the beach. Had that been Carrie Ann? With the hairy guy? Did she purposefully bump into Grace and then not say anything?

"Why all the mystery?" Jake said. *Good for you,* Grace thought.

"Let's just have a few drinks first," Carrie Ann said with a laugh.

The Irish pub was tucked into an alley, making patrons feel as if they had been invited to a secret and hidden club. Even though the cab driver had gone in a circle to get here, Grace recognized the area. It wasn't far off of La Rambla. At the least, she would know how to get home. "We could've walked here," Grace said. That's when something else hit her. "Are you staying in the same apartment building we are?"

Jake paid the taxi fare as Carrie Ann forged ahead without answering. Grace had an urge to push Jake back into the taxi and leave Carrie Ann here on her own. "Carrie Ann," Grace said. Carrie Ann stopped. She turned around. A streetlight lit the back of her hair and cast a soft glow. "This feels a bit like a game."

"An adventure," Carrie Ann said.

"Aren't we a little old for adventures?"

"On the contrary. We become old when we stop having adventures." Jake slipped his hand into Grace's. She was grateful. She squeezed, and Jake squeezed back.

"We're only staying for one drink," Grace said. "We have a lot to do in the morning." Carrie Ann didn't answer, she simply watched Grace, and then nodded. Soon the three of them were situated at a little table in the pub, all with a full pint in front of them. Carrie Ann fixed her eyes on Grace, and once again it felt like volts of electricity were ping-ponging through her body. She had a million questions, and she couldn't even get one of them out of her mouth.

"How long did you live with the Sawyers?" Jake said.

Five years, Grace thought. Enough to completely alter Grace's life. Enough to end a life.

"Oh, since I was nine years old," Carrie Ann said. She made it sound like she had never left.

"Five years," Grace said. "We haven't seen each other since we were—" Grace stopped. Carrie Ann had left—had been forced to leave—when she was fifteen. So that was six years. And then Grace had seen her again. The last time was at Lionel's funeral. Grace certainly didn't want to think about that. "It's been a long time," Grace finished lamely.

Carrie Ann nodded as if Grace had finally gotten something right. Then she lifted her chin, and her eyes flashed in familiar defiance. "All boys? That's what you tell people?"

Grace felt her cheeks grow hot. Carrie Ann always did know how to nail you to the wall when you were least expecting it.

"I have a terrible memory," Jake said. "I'm sure she mentioned it."

Carrie Ann let out a laugh that sounded more like a bark. "Your boyfriend is a terrible liar," she said. She winked at Jake. "You're lucky, Grace. There's nothing worse than living with a man who is a consummate one."

From the look on Carrie Ann's face there was a story there. Grace couldn't imagine any man living up to the larger-than-life Carrie Ann. But Grace didn't take the bait. "How did you find me?" Grace asked. Carrie Ann stared as if trying to read the intent behind the question. Grace felt her confidence draining. "It's just, I tried looking you up a few times. There was nothing." It was true. Not a trace of the girl Grace once knew. What she didn't say was that she probably wouldn't have actually reached out if she had found her. Grace had just been curious what she would find. She'd tried Facebook, Google searches, everything. She'd been too petrified to try and look Stan up. She doubted very much if Carrie Ann had stayed in touch with them, but she didn't dare ask her either. Not in front of Jake. "Is your last name still Gilbert?"

"That was never my real last name anyway," Carrie Ann said.

Grace nodded. She remembered the story. Gilbert was the name given to Carrie Ann at the orphanage. Gilbert was the name of the police officer who had found her abandoned on the steps of the precinct. Later, a caretaker had named her Carrie Ann because as an infant she had wailed so much the staff started saying to her, "Baby, why are you carrying on?" "Carry on" became Carrie Ann. Grace didn't know if the stories were true, but she had no way to check them, and they sounded somewhat plausible.

My mother must have really loved me, Carrie Ann used to say. *She could have put me in a Dumpster. But she didn't. She left me with the police. They probably would have thrown her in jail if they had caught her. But she was willing to risk it. Because of how much she loved me.* It always gave Grace a stomachache, listening to Carrie Ann say this with such conviction. *Mother of the year—thanks for not dumping me in the trash.* Grace for one hated whoever Carrie Ann's mother was. She hated her. She used to dream of the things she'd say to her if she ever met her.

Carrie Ann grabbed onto Grace's hands and held them, grinning as she stared at her.

"We look just the same," Carrie Ann said. "You're still skinny and brunette and an inch shorter than me."

"You haven't changed either," Grace said.

"There is a difference with you," Carrie Ann said.

"What's that?"

"Duh! You're a big famous singer now. I don't remember you singing when we were kids."

"I was always singing. Making up songs on the spot."

"You were? I never noticed."

"Dragging my guitar around?"

"That sounds vaguely familiar."

Carrie Ann had always had a way of making Grace feel as if she were losing her mind. She knew Carrie Ann remembered that she sang and played guitar. Carrie Ann used to complain about it all the time. "You once told me that only old, drunk men played the guitar."

Carrie Ann belted out a laugh. Jake laughed too. "I did?"

Carrie Ann said. Grace finally joined in the laughter. Carrie Ann always did have a way with words. Grace hated to think what Carrie Ann had seen in her other foster homes that made her think only old, drunk men played the guitar. Maybe Grace should write a song—"Old, Drunk Men"—

Jake held his beer toward Grace and looked at Carrie Ann. "She's composing in her head," he said. Grace blushed.

"That's so sweet. Sing it for us."

"Too soon," Grace said. For a lot of things. Too late for others.

"How are your mom and dad?"

"Great," Grace said quickly. Then she curled her hands into fists under the table. Carrie Ann had gone to see Grace's mother. Was she going to admit that?

"What are they up to these days?"

Grace didn't flinch. So Carrie Ann was still a liar. "Same old." Just the thought that Carrie Ann knew what was happening to Grace's mother, that Carrie Ann had sat by her bedside and smiled, when Carrie Ann knew, she knew how much Jody had once hated her—

But that wasn't fair either. Grace had always felt her mother had never given Carrie Ann a real chance. She had been too worried that Carrie Ann was a bad influence on Grace. Of course, Grace's mother had been right about that—

"Is your father still shrinking heads?"

"Yep." Grace could feel Jake watching her again, taking in the fact that she was uncomfortable talking about her parents with Carrie Ann.

"So," Jake said, setting down his pint. "I'm still dying to hear what led to this reunion when you haven't seen each other in so long. And is there going to be a wedding? I didn't exactly bring a suit."

"No wedding," Carrie Ann said. She dipped her hand into her purse, and it came out holding a diamond ring. "Already married," she said, twirling it in the light.

"You are?" Grace was truly shocked. It almost hurt. She'd missed out on so much of Carrie Ann's life. Grace didn't know her at all, and yet in some ways Grace knew her like she knew herself. There had been a time she couldn't imagine not being there to watch Carrie Ann walk down the aisle or vice versa. Whom had she married? Where was he? Was he good to her? Carrie Ann dangled the ring over her pint glass, then dropped it in. Beer fizzed over the side as the diamond bobbed at the surface. Carrie Ann pushed the glass away. Well, that was one question answered. Grace wondered what was wrong. She hated him, whoever he was, for hurting Carrie Ann. Grace waited for Carrie Ann to retrieve the ring. Instead, she stood up. "I'm going to the little girls' room." Grace waited for her to ask if Grace wanted to join her. She didn't.

"Carrie Ann," Grace said.

"I don't want it," Carrie Ann called over her shoulder. "You keep it." Grace and Jake stared at the glass.

"She's joking, right?" Jake said.

"That's the thing about Carrie Ann. You just never know." Grace didn't even know if Carrie Ann was going to come back to the table. The thought of her walking out now made Grace feel as if someone had punched her in the stomach.

"I'm not much of an expert, but it looks like the real thing to me," Jake said, looking at the diamond ring. "And it ain't small."

Go big or go home. Grace plucked her hand in the drink and brought it out. She wiped it with a linen napkin and stopped short of putting it on her finger. Then she put it in her purse.

"Grace," Jake said.

"I'm not keeping it. Just keeping it safe."

"What if she accuses you of stealing it?"

"What do you want me to do? Leave it for a Spanish busboy?"

"Don't get upset with me."

"I'm sorry. It's just she always does this!"

Carrie Ann returned to the table and didn't even glance at the glass. "I don't like this place," she said. "Let's boogey." Grace stood, wobbled a bit. She hadn't even finished her beer.

"Are you okay?" Jake was up like a shot.

Grace took Carrie Ann's hand. She looked at Jake. "I'm so sorry. Do you mind if we have just one minute?"

Jake was hurt. Grace could tell. He covered it with a quick smile. Always the Southern gentleman. "Of course."

"We'll be right back." Grace pulled Carrie Ann through the crowd. She realized, as they bumped against other patrons, that she didn't know where they were going or even what she was going to say. They found themselves in a narrow hall. To the left was a door. Grace pushed it open, still clinging to Carrie Ann's hand, and soon they were out in the hot night air, in the alley. Drunk kids stumbled along, and a few older couples held hands and smiled and shook their heads at the young partiers. Carrie Ann pulled a pack of cigarettes from her purse and held it out to Grace.

"No thank you."

"Figured." There was disapproval in the remark. For a split second Grace wanted to grab a cigarette and wipe the smirk off Carrie Ann's face. Carrie Ann lit hers and smiled as a couple of young men passed by. It was returned tenfold. One of them threw open his arms and said something to Carrie Ann in Spanish. She laughed and flirted back in their native tongue. But when they started to approach, Carrie Ann held out her arm and spoke to them again, this time sounding stern. They glanced at Grace, then shrugged and shuffled off.

"What was that?" Grace said.

"Boys will be boys," Carrie Ann said.

"What did you say to make them leave?"

"I told them you were having a nervous breakdown, and if they came any closer you would start screaming your head off." She held Grace's gaze, as if challenging her not to believe it.

Grace wasn't going to play games. "Why this trip, Carrie Ann? Why not just pick up the phone and call me?"

Carrie Ann blew out a plume of smoke and walked in a little circle. Her high heels clacked on the cobblestones. "Would you have answered, Gracie?"

"I—I—"

"You—you."

"Don't do that. I have a right to be upset."

"Why? Because you got a free trip to Spain?"

There's no such thing as a free trip. "You went to see my mother, and then you lied to my face about it."

Carrie Ann turned, her face softening. "I'm sorry about Jody. I really am."

"That doesn't answer my question." Grace put her arms around herself even though the night air was soft and warm. The music had followed them outside and joined in with the other noises of the night.

Carrie Ann's head tilted to one side as she stared through Grace. "You didn't ask me a question."

"Why did you visit my mother and then lie about it?"

"I had a right to visit her. Was she or was she not my mother at one time too?"

And here it was again, another loaded one. Carrie Ann was playing Russian roulette, Twenty Questions–style. "It's not a matter of 'rights.' My mom isn't well. You should have talked to me first."

"I didn't upset her, and I didn't stay long."

"Did you see my father too?" Grace wasn't sure where the question came from; she'd never worried about her father lying to her. His reaction when Jody had brought up Carrie Ann was not that of a man who had seen her. What was happening to Grace? It was a dangerous world when you stopped trusting everyone you loved.

"I saw him, but he didn't see me. He was coming down the hall as I was leaving."

"Why all of this sneaking around?"

Carrie Ann threw out her cigarette and crushed it into the pavement. "I told you. I'm in trouble."

Here we go, thought Grace. Here comes a portion of the truth. "What kind of trouble?"

"God. Give me a chance to breathe, would you? This isn't easy for me. In fact seeing you again is the hardest thing I've ever had to do. I was terrified."

"Of what?"

"Afraid you wouldn't want anything to do with me. Afraid you'd see that I was still a nothing—"

"You were never a nothing."

"Tell that to everyone else."

Grace took a few steps toward Carrie Ann. Grace was handling this all wrong. No matter what, she didn't want the girl she used to know, used to love, to feel defensive. Nor did Grace want Carrie Ann to think Grace's heart was made of stone. "I've thought about you all these years. I had always hoped that you found a new family, had one of your own, or became a famous magician—"

"All those things are true."

"Really?"

"Yes. And I have a pet unicorn. Her name is Horny." Carrie Ann's tone changed again; this was the same Carrie Ann, moods like Mother Nature, sweeping in at a moment's notice with either a torrential flood, or nuclear sunshine.

"You can't fault me for hoping," Grace said.

"Maybe they should have named you Hope," Carrie Ann said.

"There, but for Grace, go I," Grace said. "What did you mean by that?"

Carrie Ann clapped her hands and grinned like she had just won a prize. "You got the book. I was worried somebody else might have snatched it."

"What did you mean?"

"It was a clue. I was trying to tell you I was here."

"As opposed to just—telling me you were here." Carrie Ann looked at Grace. "I just don't understand all the secrecy. And I still don't get why we're here. In Spain. And how you could afford—"

Carrie Ann touched Grace's arm. "We used to be able to communicate through clues, remember?"

"We played games—"

"Scavenger hunts," Carrie Ann said. "I loved them."

"Where are you going with this?"

"Sometimes people have to read between the lines, Grace."

"I'm not thirteen anymore. I have no idea what you're really trying to say, or why you're not just saying it."

"Jake is very nice," Carrie Ann said.

"Yes. He is."

"Is he the type who will stand by you? Do anything for you?" Carrie Ann whispered it. There she went again, trying to be dramatic.

What was that supposed to mean? Grace was about to ask when she stopped. "How did you know about Jake? And Dan? And why go through him?"

"You put your whole life on Facebook, Grace. I'm not knocking it. I'm just saying. You should be more careful."

"Right." Grace took a deep breath and turned around. She didn't want to lash out. She didn't want a fight. "So. You're married?" Something darkened over Carrie Ann's face, and she gave a curt nod. "Kids?"

Carrie Ann looked away. Then took a drag of her cigarette and shook her head as she watched the smoke blow out. "Can you imagine me? A mom?" Actually, Grace could. She wouldn't be perfect, but Grace could see Carrie Ann being a cool mom. "Hello, Mommy Dearest Two," Carrie Ann said.

"That's not true."

"I didn't exactly have role models. Unless you count *your* parents." The look Carrie Ann flicked Grace's way was a definite challenge. Grace let it go. "Do you have children, Gracie? A family of your own?"

"Not yet."

"But you will. And you would be such a good mother, much better than me."

"That's not true—"

"I wouldn't screw it up on purpose; in fact, I would fight to the death for my kids. But you—you probably wouldn't have to fight at all. You would just know what to do." Carrie Ann fumbled with her cigarette pack, withdrew a second, and lit it.

"You just finished a cigarette," Grace said. Normally she didn't lecture people. But she suddenly felt a surge of resentment over all the times she hadn't spoken up for herself with Carrie Ann. The things she had been intimidated into doing.

"It's Europe; I'm an adult; I can chain-smoke if I want to chain-smoke."

"Who books such an expensive trip for someone she hasn't said two words to in fifteen years?"

"It's not my fault we haven't talked." Carrie Ann's voice rose above the din. "I was the one cast out of the family."

"That's not entirely fair."

"I knew I was taking a gamble. But the money—who cares. And the apartment belongs to my friend Rafael's parents, so that didn't cost me anything. I thought the price of two plane tickets was worth the chance to heal my deepest childhood wound."

It was out there, in the open. Childhood, and wound. Big, festering, still-infected wound.

"I just feel a little ambushed," Grace said. "And there's a lot of water under the bridge."

"Enough to drown," Carrie Ann said. She threw the rest of her cigarette to the ground, and they both stared at the orange ember for a few seconds before Carrie Ann crushed this one out too. "Maybe I could have gone about this in a better way. But I had to see you. I need you, Grace. I'm in trouble. I'm in really, really big trouble. Believe me. Hear me. I really need you to hear me. I didn't have any other choice."

CHAPTER 12

I didn't have any other choice. Carrie Ann's words echoed down the alley.

Of course you did, Grace thought. *You've always had a choice. And you always make the wrong one. You haven't changed. You thrive on trouble. Drama is like oxygen to you, Carrie Ann. You aren't allowed to need someone you haven't seen in fifteen years.* On the other hand, now that Carrie Ann was here in front of her, it didn't seem like fifteen years at all. It had been yesterday, and this was her sister.

"It's getting lonely in there." Jake stepped out into the alley. Grace wondered if he had heard Carrie Ann's last comment. She was happy to see him either way.

"It's getting late," Carrie Ann said. "We should go." Was she kidding? She just said that she was in big trouble, and now she was acting like nothing was wrong. Typical. "We can walk," Carrie Ann said. "I'll just leave money for the—"

"It's paid," Jake said.

"Thank you."

"Hardly a dent when you consider what you've paid for," Jake said.

Grace couldn't tell whether he was being facetious or not. She wondered if he liked Carrie Ann. Did she even want him to like Carrie Ann? The thought of mixing her past with her present was jarring. "Jake," Grace said. "I hate to do this to you, but Carrie Ann and I were right in the middle of discussing something—"

"Nonsense," Carrie Ann said. She put her hand on Grace's arm. "We'll talk tomorrow."

"But you said you were in—"

"Tomorrow," Carrie Ann said, a little more insistent. "It just hit me how exhausted I am. I wouldn't even be able to hold up a conversation."

Just like old times. Turning on a dime. How could she still be like this? A part of Grace wanted to push back, get everything out in the open tonight, but a larger part of her didn't want to hear whatever tale Carrie Ann was about to spin. Grace looped her arm through Jake's, and they began the walk back in silence, although there was plenty of noise from others on the street. It was comforting, in a way, to allow others to do the celebrating. A good night's sleep. Maybe that's all Grace needed. Whatever drama Carrie Ann was stirring up could wait.

"Where is your apartment?" Jake said. Grace was seized with instant, irrational jealousy as she imagined Jake sneaking into Carrie Ann's apartment at night, slipping into her bed. God, where did this come from? She'd never distrusted Jake.

"One floor above you," Carrie Ann said.

Grace thought of the coffee cup. Had Carrie Ann actually been in their room? She wondered if Jake was thinking the same thing. When they reached the building, Grace took Jake's hand. "We're going to take our nightly stroll in the square," she said.

"Breakfast? Tomorrow?" Carrie Ann asked. "We have so much to catch up on."

"Sure. There's a great outdoor café. The first one as you exit the walkway from our building—"

"With the red umbrellas?"

"That's the one."

"Perfect." She glanced at Jake. "I hate to be rude, but can we keep it just us girls?"

"Sure," Jake said.

"But I've been dying for you to see this outdoor café," Grace said to Jake. "With all the street performers? I want Jake to come." Maybe she was afraid to be alone with Carrie Ann. Afraid it would be so easy to slip into their old roles. Grace, submissive, squashing her own instincts just to please Carrie Ann. But this was also her romantic holiday with Jake—no matter who had paid for it—and she wanted him by her side.

"I'm sorry. I'm not trying to exclude you to be hurtful, Jake. It's just Grace and I have some extremely personal things to talk about—"

"It's no problem," Jake said. "Really. You know me, Grace. I like my beauty sleep."

"Say ten? I like my beauty sleep too." Carrie Ann looked at Jake when she said that. As if they were kids and Carrie Ann was still the center of attention. Trying to manipulate him like he was Stan. Or was Grace reading too much into it?

"See you at ten," Grace said. Then, without looking back, she took Jake's hand and walked as quickly as she could away from Carrie Ann.

Jake stopped the minute they turned down an alley and were out of earshot. He just looked at her and shook his head.

"It's a long story," Grace said.

"Three years, Grace. We live together. We've talked marriage."

You've talked marriage, Grace thought. *But no proposal.* "I'm sorry. But every single bad memory I have of childhood revolves around that girl." Grace pointed in the direction where she had last seen Carrie Ann, although with any luck she would be long gone.

"We're supposed to share the good and the bad. Especially the bad."

"It's really bad, Jake. It's really, really bad."

Jake sighed, ran his fingers through his hair. "Well, let's sit down, and you can start at the beginning."

"No." Grace grabbed Jake's arm as if to keep him in place. "Not tonight. Please. Please don't make me relive all this tonight."

"You have to tell me something."

Grace knew he was right, but it was just too long and complicated a story. "We kind of bullied this kid named Stan, okay? I mean—bullied is the wrong word—it's not what you're thinking—"

"I'm not thinking anything yet."

"She bullied him by being nice to him, okay?"

"She bullied him by being nice to him," Jake repeated slowly.

"Yes. Because he thought she really liked him. But she didn't. She couldn't have."

"Because?"

"Because Carrie Ann just liked to stir up trouble. She didn't care what people were saying as long as they were talking about her. And he was the number one kid in school everyone made fun of. He was overweight, and his face was full of pimples, and he smelled, and he had greasy hair—but honestly none of that bothered me as much as how he used to stare at me. . . . He was so awkward and strange."

"I was awkward and strange too," Jake said.

Oh, God. He thought she was a jerk. Stan had given her the creeps. She shouldn't have mentioned how he looked. "I sound horrible, I know. But there was something really off about him, Jake. He made me so uncomfortable."

"So what did you do?"

"I didn't do anything—I mean besides not looking him in the eye. I swear I didn't do anything."

Jake was silent. He was probably thinking he didn't know her at all. That the Grace Sawyer he knew was too nice to be a mean girl. But with Stan Gale she had felt something akin to repulsion-at-first-sight. The more she had expressed how she felt, the more Carrie Ann had brought him around. Like he was her new pet.

It still made Grace shudder. Grace should have stood her ground, told Carrie Ann that she was not going to go along with Carrie Ann's little game. The worst bit was—Stan had known it. He had known Grace was repulsed by him. She couldn't hide it any more than he could hide his sad blue eyes.

"So I went along with it. I let him up in my tree house. I let him follow me home from school most days. And I tried to pretend we were his friends. And it just led to some pretty awful stuff, and I know you deserve to hear all the gory details—but I'm begging you. Not tonight."

"But why didn't you at least tell me the basics?" Jake said. "Like—oh, we did take in a girl once. Her name was Carrie Ann."

"Because I've spent the rest of my life trying to pretend she doesn't exist."

"That makes the story sound really bad, Grace."

Jake wasn't going to settle for no explanation. Grace started to walk, not wanting to look at him while she talked. Jake followed her. When they got to a corner, they could hear tango music coming from below. They were standing in front of a set of stairs going down to a basement. A sign with the name of the club and a painting of tango dancers sat discreetly in a window halfway down. "Come on," Jake said. "Let's see if we can have a seat and get a drink."

They descended into the little club. After entering through a screen door and then a beaded curtain, they were bathed in a glowing red light. It was a pretty tight room jammed with tables and a small bar in the back. It was halfway full. On the back wall was what barely passed for a stage. A pair of tango dancers gracefully danced back and forth on the allotted space. Grace and Jake took a minute to watch them. They made it seem easy. As if the nights were made for seduction. Grace wished she could feel so carefree. She and Jake quickly took a booth as far away from the music as possible. A few seconds later they had a pitcher of sangria and Jake had ordered some tapas off the menu. For a brief moment Grace felt as if they were on holiday again.

"You were talking about Stan," Jake said.

Grace sighed, and absentmindedly picked up a matchbook on the table. "Speaking of Carrie Ann," Jake said. Grace's head shot up. Had she followed them here? "Relax," Jake said. He pointed to the matchbook. Grace looked at it. It was the same one Grace had found on their mat. She flipped it open.

"Empty," Grace said. "Carrie Ann wrote the message."

"Surprise, surprise," Jake said. "So. Continue."

Grace knew there was no getting out of it. At least she had sangria and dramatic background music. Maybe every bad memory should be accompanied by the tango. "My mom didn't like what Carrie Ann was doing to Stan. She wasn't as worried when we were younger, but once we got to be teenagers. Well. She didn't like how close Carrie Ann, Stan, and I were getting. She said it wasn't healthy. To the point where she was even willing to let Carrie Ann go back into the foster system."

"How close you were getting? Like. Romantically?"

"No, God, no. Just thick as thieves I guess you'd say."

"I still don't get why your mother would want to put Carrie Ann back in the foster system. That doesn't sound like her."

"Well, she did. I didn't get it either. I was devastated. I broke down crying in art class."

"Sorry."

"Not as sorry as I would later be."

"Huh?"

"My art teacher was Lydia Gale. Stan's mother."

"Wait. Your favorite teacher in the whole world? That Lydia? The one with the flowered skirts?"

Grace was flattered at how much Jake remembered. "That Lydia." She had told Jake all about her. Well, everything except about her son, and her husband, and Carrie Ann. She had told him all the important parts; she had given him the cut-and-paste history. She had told him how exotic Lydia Gale had seemed to her, how she had loved her homemade flowered skirts and rebellious attitude. There was no right and wrong in her class, just "creating." Most days they could work on absolutely any project they liked, and Lydia was a hundred percent supportive. On top of that the kids were told to call her

"Lydia" unless a grown-up was around, at which point they had to call her "Mrs. Gale," but only until the other adult was gone. Then, she was just Lydia again. Grace didn't think there had ever been a single day that Lydia wasn't smiling. It was for this reason that later, when Grace had found out Stan was Lydia's son, Grace had almost refused to believe it. Had he been adopted? How could this surly child come from such a sunny woman?

"The next thing I knew, Lydia and her husband were offering to take Carrie Ann."

"That was good news, right?"

"It seemed like the perfect solution." Except that it bound them even tighter to Stan. Grace didn't say that part because Jake seemed on guard about the whole Stan business. Jake wouldn't feel sorry for Stan if he'd ever met him. "Carrie Ann could stay at the same school, and I could sneak through the woods and down the road to see her."

"Over the river and through the woods?" Jake said.

"No river," Grace said. "Just woods."

"Why did you have to sneak?"

"My mother didn't want me seeing Carrie Ann any more at all."

"That doesn't sound like your mom."

"I thought she was totally overreacting. And of course it made me want to go over there even more."

Jake nodded, offered her some tapas. Grace shook her head. She'd lost her appetite for everything but sangria.

"Can I stop you for a second?" Jake asked.

"Please do," Grace said.

"If Carrie Ann hadn't shown up, do you think you would have told me any of this?"

"You mean on this trip?"

"I mean *ever*, Grace. Would you have ever told me any of this?"

Grace hesitated. She didn't want to lie to Jake anymore. "No. Probably not."

"My God." Jake stared out the window for a moment, even though there was nothing beyond it but a dark stairwell. When he turned his eyes on her again, she could see she had really hurt him. "Do I really know you?"

"Of course you do." Jake didn't look convinced. "Do I know all of your childhood secrets?"

"Yes."

"Oh. Okay. Like the time you killed a bird with a stone? That's it? That's all you got?"

"I wasn't a serial bird-killer if that's what you mean. And that haunted me forever. I told you that. It's because of that poor bird and my guilt that I decided to become a veterinarian."

"Well, how about grown-up secrets? You didn't tell me Lyndsey wanted to jump your bones until this trip. Were you ever going to tell me about that?"

"If I thought it was important."

"Well, there you go."

"Having a sister is important, Grace."

"You're really stuck on that sister thing, aren't you? She wasn't actually related to me. Did you miss that part?"

"You're getting angry. That's not my intention. I just don't want us to have secrets from each other."

"Okay. No more secrets. A few weeks after Carrie Ann started staying with the Gales, she sent me a clue to come see her—"

"A clue?"

"Writing in the book? The matchbook? It's classic Carrie Ann. I guess she's always fancied herself a spy."

"Got it. Go on."

But Grace didn't want to go on. She was tired. Drained. Seeing Carrie Ann again had been such a shock. Jake already hated Grace a little bit, and that's because she hadn't known how to describe how creepy and intense Stan had been. If she told the story tonight she might actually ruin their relationship. "I don't want to keep secrets from you, Jake. I swear on my life. But I'm going to get too upset if I tell this tonight, and I won't be able to sleep."

"Well, maybe I won't be able to sleep if you don't tell it."

"I started the story. Isn't that enough?"

Jake took out his wallet and threw money down on the table.

"Let's go," he said. They left the bar and started to walk again, this time toward the apartment without even discussing it. As if they knew there was nowhere else to go from here.

"Carrie Ann didn't like living with the Gales," Grace started to say when they were almost home. Jake put his hand up.

"No," he said. "You're right. You've said enough for one night. I don't want to force you to tell me anything. I'm tired too, Gracie. I don't want to fight." Jake pulled Grace in to him and kissed the top of her head.

"You probably think Marsh Everett is right," she said.

"What?"

"I guess I don't sing my pain because I can't even bring myself to talk about it. I think there's something wrong with me. I think there's something inside me that's broken."

Jake turned around, then before she knew what was happening he was on one knee in front of her. He took her hand, kissed it. "I'm sorry," he said. "I don't need to know every little secret to know who you are." He touched her heart. "You're the woman I love. And the woman I love is not broken. She is real, and she is good, and she is whole."

Grace felt tears in her eyes. "Jake."

"I love you, Grace Ann Sawyer."

Tears slipped silently down Grace's face. "I love you too."

He reached into his pocket. He was going to propose. This was it. He was going to ask her to marry him on the streets of Spain. Yes, yes, yes. Grace's breath caught. But when his hand was visible again, he wasn't holding a ring box. It was a flyer of some sort. He rose to his feet.

Did he forget the ring? Grace thought. *Or am I just crazy?*

"I was going to save this as a big surprise," Jake said. "But maybe you need to know about this now." He handed the flyer to Grace. She stared at it.

GREC FESTIVAL de BARCELONA

An international theater of dance, music, and circus.

She looked up at Jake.

"It's one of the most outstanding cultural events in Barcelona," Jake said. "It's at an open-air theater—Teatre Grec on Montjuïc. Over a hundred thousand people will be in attendance, Grace."

"Fabulous," Grace said. She hugged Jake, then pulled back. "It sounds great." *Maybe not as great as a ring.*

"You don't understand," Jake said. "I'm attending. You're performing."

"Excuse me?"

"You can sing anything you want—up to three original songs—"

"How did this even come about?"

"The flyer was in our mailbox back home. They were looking for talent to sing, and the dates just happened to correspond with our trip—"

"Wait. Wait. This flyer was in our mailbox? In Nashville?"

"Yes. And then I called your manager—"

"You didn't think it was odd that this flyer just happened to get delivered to our mailbox right after we won a trip to Spain?"

"Yes, I did think it was odd, but crazier things have happened. Hell, for all I knew, everyone who books a trip to Spain gets this flyer—"

"But we didn't book this trip, we thought we won it in a raffle."

"Look. I figured the flyer was related to our winning the trip, but did I stop and research the who, what, where, when, and why of how it ended up in our mailbox? No, I did not. But I did look the festival up on the Internet, and it's a really big deal, and so I called your manager and—"

"You actually called my manager?"

"And he thought it was a great idea. And then he called the venue, and I think they even saw the demo on your Web site, and you were in."

"No," Grace said. "No." This was Carrie Ann again. Using Jake to get to her. Grace should never have felt sorry for her again, never given her the benefit of the doubt.

"Grace, Grace. I'm sorry I didn't tell you. And granted

maybe the venues you've played haven't been this big, but you can do this in your sleep—"

"It's not for real, Jake. This is part of a game."

"Is that what you really think? Or are you just afraid to sing?"

"Don't you see it?"

"See what?"

"Carrie Ann is behind the flyer like she's behind everything else."

"What is 'everything else'? It's a free trip to Spain, Grace. Not a prison sentence."

"You don't understand."

"Explain it to me. A few months ago you would have been dancing with joy at this opportunity."

"A lot can happen in a few months."

"You're seriously telling me you don't want to sing anymore?"

"That's right. My singing career is over, Jake. It's over."

"Why?"

"Because I don't want to do it anymore."

"Are you really that insecure?"

"Excuse me?"

"All artists get bad reviews, Grace. It's part of being an artist in the first place."

"It's not just that. Every time I even think about playing again, I get these panic attacks."

"Every performer gets butterflies—"

"These aren't butterflies. They're attacks."

"I feel like you're attacking me."

"I'm not. I'm just so frustrated right now. I don't know what her game is—but it isn't good. I don't feel good."

Jake stared at her. He was just trying to help. "Are you sure, Grace? Are you sure you're not jumping to conclusions?"

"You think all of Barcelona wants to hear me sing? That's sweet, Jake. But it's not for real." Grace tried to lighten her tone. She didn't want to fight.

"You're a songwriter. You can't shut it off even if you say you want to."

Jake looked so intense. Grace didn't like upsetting him. She reached up and caressed his face. "What about you, babe? Can I shut you off?"

"There are ways," he said. He pulled her in and kissed her neck. "Take me home, and I'll show you the ways."

It was a relief to crawl into bed. Except, of course, Grace couldn't sleep. From Carrie Ann's making Jake believe Grace had a spot in a Barcelona concert to the possible aborted proposal, there were too many things swimming around in her head. Long after they had made love and Jake was snoring peacefully beside her, Grace was still wide-awake, trying not to look at the shadow on the ceiling. It looked exactly like a noose. She used to see them everywhere she went, like shapes in the clouds, except back then everything had turned into a cloud.

Lionel Gale. He was the real reason Grace couldn't handle seeing Carrie Ann. He was what the two of them needed to talk about. Get it in the open. Tell the truth, both of them, for once in their lives. Would it help? Or would it make it worse?

Did Carrie Ann ever think about him? Did she think about Stan and Lydia? Did she hope, from time to time, pray, actually, every night, that the two somehow went on to have an okay life? A yearning to call her mother hit Grace like a sledgehammer. Not the mother in hospice who went in and out of remembering things. But the mother who knew and remembered it all. The mother who more than once had tried to warn her about Carrie Ann.

Grace got up, padded over to the window, and looked out. For the most part La Rambla was quiet, although streetlamps glittered down the promenade and the occasional couple or individual strolled by. Grace thought about her upcoming birthday. She remembered the day Carrie Ann had decided she was going to have the same exact birthday. Grace had actually been pretty excited at the prospect and had run to tell her mother. She was in the kitchen, bowls spread out on the counter, Betty Crocker cookbook open. It was always a challenge feeding so many kids, so she cooked in bulk. Whatever she made on Mondays they ate until Thursday.

"Carrie Ann and I are going to have the same birthday," Grace had announced. Jody had turned, wiped her hands on her apron, and then pointed to the stool at the counter. Grace had sat. Jody had slowly returned to stirring as she talked to Grace.

"She picked the exact same birthday, Gracie?"

"Yes. Both of us are now July twenty-ninth."

"But that's *your* special day. We can give Carrie Ann one of her own."

"Carrie Ann wants us to have the same birthday," Grace had said. To this day she could recall the clawing panic she had felt at the prospect of upsetting Carrie Ann.

"I heard you, honey-pie," her mother had said. "But what do you want?"

"I want Carrie Ann to be happy," Grace had whispered. She had stopped short of admitting she'd promised the skies she would take care of Carrie Ann. And it was true, too. Grace had wanted her to be so happy.

Jody had come over to Grace, put her hands on her arms, and looked her in the eye. "I know you like her, Gracie. But some people won't ever be happy, no matter what good comes their way. And mark my words, that little girl is one of them."

"She's not. She's very happy here."

"Maybe to an extent. But she's been through too much. There's nothing you, or me, or Daddy, or anyone else will ever be able to do to fill the holes inside her." The holes inside her, Grace had thought. As if Carrie Ann were a piece of Swiss cheese or a sinking ship. "You can't save her, Gracie, do you hear me?"

"But I made Brady all better."

"Honey. Brady was a kitten. People are much more complicated than kittens."

"But maybe they're not. Maybe she just needs a lot of love."

"You can love her all you want, Gracie. You can be her friend. But you have to love yourself more. Be your own friend more."

"I don't mind sharing my birthday."

"Gracie Ann, you aren't listening to me. Share your birthday if you want. Just don't think you can save her, all right?"

"Save her from what?" Grace had said.

"Herself," her mother had said. Grace had been thoroughly confused, and it must have shown on her face. Her mother had actually stopped cooking and sat across from her. "You will never be able to do enough to make up for all the bad things she's gone through. Carrie Ann was nine years old when she came to us. The world can do a lot of damage in nine years."

"But she's already better. I make her happy."

"At what expense?"

"Huh?"

"Oh, Gracie. I just hate to see you turning yourself inside out trying to please her. She's damaged, sweetheart. Believe me. You can't fix her."

Now, wide-awake in Barcelona, Grace understood what her mother had been trying to say. She had been right. Grace couldn't fix Carrie Ann. But a kind of clawing guilt had dug into Grace, and she couldn't let it go, and all these years she had pushed back on a single horrendous thought, covered it up as quickly as she could. The question reared up at her now, and she was too worried and too weary to fight it off. *You can always run, but you can never hide.* It came to her now, and sat heavy and wet in her lap. What if, in spite of all her good intentions, and heart full of love, what if the choices Grace Sawyer had made had actually made Carrie Ann's life much, much worse?

CHAPTER 13

Carrie Ann was dreaming about Grace when her blanket was violently ripped away. Her eyes flew open. Rafael towered over her, glaring.

"Hey," she said. "Jerk." God, he could have given her a heart attack. She wanted to get back to her dream; she hadn't been there in so long. The tree house. Stan. For a few seconds they were kids again. Before everything changed. When they were happy. Playing Go Fish, drinking Bud Light, smoking Camel cigarettes.

Rafael screamed at her in Spanish, and, when she didn't respond, he switched to English. He was furious that she had snuck off to meet Grace last night. Carrie Ann grabbed her blanket back and held it up to her chin. "I am to be by your side, always," Rafael said. "He isn't going to like this."

Carrie Ann didn't like the look Rafael got in his eyes sometimes. She got up and brushed past him, and headed for the coffee pot. "I think you need to get a few things straight, Rafael. I know he is your friend and all, but this was my idea. He is going along with *my* plan, and you are not my shadow nor my bodyguard."

"He said to stay with you until he is here. That is why he is paying me for."

"That is *what* he is paying you for."

"*Sí, sí.* Now you agree."

"Your English *sucks.*"

"*¿Qué?*"

"You heard me."

"From now on, you go everywhere I go."

"You can't treat me like a prisoner. This is my show. I'm the director."

"I am to be with you always."

"English isn't that literal. When he said that . . . he just meant . . . most of the time. Do you understand?"

"No, he not say, 'most of the time.' He say, 'always.' "

"I'll talk to him. I'll make sure he explains it—*muy bueno*—so you can comprehend-o."

"We go everywhere together."

"Good lord, you're annoying. Call him."

Rafael eyed her. Then, he took out his mobile and dialed. He spoke briefly, then handed her the phone.

Carrie Ann didn't even say hello. "Did you tell him to breathe down my neck every freaking second?"

"I just want to make sure you have backup."

"Why would I need backup?"

"We don't know anything about this Jake."

"He plays with puppy dogs for a living."

"Are we ready to get the show on the road?"

"Not yet. I wasn't able to get into it with Jake there."

"Time is going to run out."

"I'm meeting with her this morning. I'll set the stage." Rafael was staring at her. Carrie Ann walked away and didn't speak again until she was near a window. Then she lowered her voice. "I don't think Rafael is the best choice."

"He's harmless."

"He's aggressive."

"You'll thank me later."

"What's that supposed to mean?" Carrie Ann didn't like his tone. She should have never told him about her plan. She had just thought it would be even more spectacular if he was involved. As usual, she had made a mistake. "If you don't talk to him, he might wind up with my knee in his balls."

He laughed. "He's doing what I told him to do."

"Well, un-tell him. This is my reunion first and foremost."

"I'll handle Rafael. Now when are you meeting with Grace alone?"

"I already told you. This morning," Carrie Ann said. "Grace and I are meeting for breakfast at ten." Carrie Ann glanced up at Rafael. "And I don't want a shadow."

"Fine. Hand him the phone." Carrie Ann smiled. "Hey," she said. Rafael looked up. She tossed him the phone.

He listened, and murmured. "Got it," Rafael said. He hung up, looked at Carrie Ann.

"Told you," Carrie Ann said.

Rafael called him back from outside, in front of the building. His *amigo* spoke without even saying *hola*. "Did you get that? He'll be alone this morning."

"*Sí. Sí.* I will get him."

"But not until I text you it's time. Got it?"

"*Sí, sí.* I wait for you. Then I get Jake."

"Don't let him make any noise."

"He will not see me coming."

"Don't even look at Carrie Ann again before she leaves. She'll see it in your face."

"She know nothing. I am so very good."

"The place is ready?"

"*Sí, sí.* It's ready."

"Call me when he's there." The phone went dead. Rafael grinned. He couldn't wait. He needed the release. And he hated American men. Rafael would be on the ledge and through the window before Jake was even awake.

* * *

Carrie Ann took her time getting ready. She wore a pretty green dress that flared just above the knees. She brushed out her long blond hair. She put on just enough makeup but not too much. She grabbed the stack of letters. All tied together with string. She tucked them into her purse, knowing she would have to say just the right thing when she brought them out. Grace would actually be doing herself a big favor if she ever got around to reading them.

Rafael stood in front of the door. "What are those?" he said, pointing to the purse.

"They're private," Carrie Ann said.

"Let me see." He held out his hand.

"You'd better watch your step," Carrie Ann said. "One more phone call and you're out of this for good."

"He needs me," Rafael said. "I am supplying everything."

"What the hell does that mean?"

But Rafael just grinned. Damn him. Damn both of them. There was definitely a screw loose with Rafael. The sooner she got away from him the better. He stood in front of the door, but she wasn't going to let him intimidate her. She tried to push him out of the way. Then she tried to pull him out of the way. He remained with his back to the door, arms crossed, grin slathered across his face.

"If you want to go out, I want a kiss," he said.

"You're disgusting." He shrugged, smiled. "Get out of my way before I knee you in the balls."

He looked down at her knee. When he looked up, he was no longer smiling. Carrie Ann held his gaze. Finally, he broke off with a huff. "Blondes are not more fun," he said.

"Probably not," she said. "But we at least know how to get things done."

Grace would be at breakfast, wouldn't she? Carrie Ann had this awful feeling that Grace was going to run. Grace had been terrified to see her. Terrified. Carrie Ann's phone buzzed. It was him.

Are you with her?

God, he was so controlling. So exacting. What was with these guys? He was turning out to be just as much of a minefield as Rafael.

Not yet.

She should have listened to the age-old adage *If you want something done right, you have to do it yourself.* This was about her and Grace, period. This was supposed to be fun. They were barely into it, and the boys were acting so weird that she was definitely not having fun. Once she reached the outdoor café, she situated herself so that she would be able to see Grace coming down the alley. Normally Carrie Ann hated to eat outdoors. Flies and beggars and everything in between. But this way Grace wouldn't be able to give her the slip. Carrie Ann would chase her down the street and tackle her if she had to. Maybe Grace wasn't going to show. Maybe she and Jake were on a plane back to Nashville. Maybe all this preparation had been for naught.

Ten minutes past the time they were supposed to meet, Grace came walking down the alley. Her head was down, and she moved quickly. She was such a different girl when she was on stage. Carrie Ann had seen her several times in Nashville. Carrie Ann usually came late, sat in the very back, and slipped out while people were applauding. She hadn't been ready to actually confront Grace face-to-face. Sitting there, watching her on stage, Carrie Ann was filled with a sense of awe, and fierce pride. *She still feels like family,* Carrie Ann thought. *She's still my sister.*

Boy, did Grace come to life on stage. Her eyes sparkled. She was confident and witty. And she was good. Damn good. What a gift. Carrie Ann felt that familiar tug of jealousy. She had always thought she'd be the one to make it. She would be the first female magician to rival the big boys. Carrie Ann Gilbert—CAG probably would be her stage name. Not the pretty assistant, but the mastermind. She'd have hot young men as her assistants, and she'd probably bed all of them. A wild child. Presto chango! Except Carrie Ann would never change. Why should she? She liked who she was. Unlike some people.

Except Carrie Ann never had become famous. Grace, on the other hand, was on the verge. At least she had been. Was she really going to let that scumbag producer shame her? Carrie Ann wanted to knock some sense into Grace, then do something about the producer. Grace had a gift. It was a crime to walk away from talent like that. Carrie Ann hoped Grace and Jake had followed through with the festival. Singing in front of a huge crowd in Barcelona would do Grace a world of good. But Grace hadn't mentioned it, and there was just no subtle way of bringing it up. Grace probably suspected Carrie Ann had something to do with it, but she wouldn't know for sure. If Carrie Ann was going to sew up the perfect adventure, she was hardly going to point out the seams.

Carrie Ann sat up straight, put on her best smile, and threw her hand in the air and waved it around. "Here, Gracie." Grace's head snapped up, and once again she didn't look happy to see Carrie Ann. Grace approached slowly, a frown on her face.

"Good morning," Carrie Ann said.

"Morning." Grace sat down, spine straight, stiff. She looked around as if expecting someone to jump out at her.

"How did you guys sleep?"

"Fine, thanks. You?"

"Oh. Well. I was a little wound up. Excited from seeing you, I guess. It was hard to sleep."

"I'm surprised you wanted to meet so early."

"Why? You pictured me as some sloth who doesn't get up before noon?" Carrie Ann kept a smile on her face, but she didn't feel it. Was it going to be like this the whole time? Pulling teeth to get Grace to talk to her? And normally, Carrie Ann didn't get up before noon. She was making a real effort here. Couldn't Grace see that? They would have a drink, loosen up. "Do you want a mimosa?"

"No. Just coffee."

"You have to wave to the waiters here like you're trying to

bring in an airplane." Carrie Ann once again put her arm up, and when the waiter arrived she ordered two mimosas and two coffees.

"I didn't want a mimosa," Grace said.

"No worries. I'll drink for the both of us."

Grace smiled, a pitiful attempt, and looked around her. "The street performers are something here, aren't they?"

Finally. Some conversation. "They're totally nuts!" Carrie Ann said. She almost told her about Rafael, but stopped herself. Carrie Ann wanted to reach across the table and touch Grace. She wanted to take her hands in hers. She wanted to get on her knees and beg Grace to be nice to her. "It's so good to see you."

Grace looked her in the eye. Grace had changed. She wasn't the shy little girl she once had been. "Is it?"

"How can you ask that? Of course it is." This time Carrie Ann did reach across the table. And even though Grace didn't squeeze her hand back, she allowed Carrie Ann to touch her for a moment. "I've never stopped thinking of you."

"The last time I saw you, it wasn't under the best circumstances, Carrie Ann."

"Oh, God, I know. It was awful. Just awful. But the past is the past. I totally forgive you."

The waiter came just then with their drinks. Grace's mouth was hanging open. Okay, Carrie Ann had been pushing it with the "I forgive you," but really Grace was the one who had betrayed her. Grace should be sorry. Carrie Ann was being the bigger person, and Grace couldn't even be grateful.

Grace picked up her coffee, then put it down. "I have to ask you something."

"Anything."

"Did you come into our apartment the other day and move a coffee cup?"

"You're joking, right?"

"No. Someone came in while I was in the square with the book you left me—and he or she moved Jake's coffee cup."

"Seriously?"

"Yes. Seriously."

"Weird."

"Was it you?"

"I think I already answered that."

"Whose apartment is it?"

"Belongs to the parents of a friend of mine."

"Do you think this friend could have come into our apartment?"

"Grace. You sound totally paranoid. You know that, right?" Damn Rafael. She was going to pluck his feathers out one by one.

"By your own admission you've been cyber-stalking me. You strung me along with this whole mystery trip. It's within the realm of possibility."

Carrie Ann leaned back, downed her mimosa, and felt tears threatening. She finished the second mimosa and stood up. She threw twenty euros on the table and started to walk away. Screw Grace. It took about fifteen steps. Just when Carrie Ann thought it was never going to happen, she heard someone running behind her.

"Carrie Ann. Carrie Ann." She stopped, turned. Grace was out of breath, and finally there was a little bit of kindness in her eyes. It made Carrie Ann furious. She reached in her purse and pulled out the stack of letters.

"What's that?" Grace said.

"Tell me again how you never lie," Carrie Ann said. Grace just looked at her. "I thought so. These are letters. All addressed to Grace Sawyer. All marked 'Return to Sender.' " Carrie Ann held the pile out accusingly. "I wouldn't have had to stalk you if you had answered even one of my letters."

"Letters?" Carrie Ann let them drop with a thud. She watched Grace bend and pick them up. "You sent them to my parents," Grace said after a moment.

Carrie Ann pointed to RETURN TO SENDER. "That's your handwriting, Grace."

CHAPTER 14

Grace clutched the letters and searched her mind for an excuse. "My mom and I have near-identical handwriting."

"You want to stick with that, little Miss Truth-teller? So I guess you're saying your mom doesn't even let you think for yourself?"

Grace held up her finger. "One rule. Do not talk about my mother."

"I suppose there are other topics that are off-limits too," Carrie Ann said.

"What am I doing here, Carrie Ann? What do you want?"

"Read them, Grace. I want you to read them." Carrie Ann wanted to walk away for real now. It was bad enough that Grace had rejected one hundred of her letters, flat out rejected them in bold, black ink, but how dare she not even admit to it? Carrie Ann had expected more. Tears. Excuses. Stammers. *Explanations.* That old familiar fury, her constant friend, churned within her.

Grace had told Jake that her parents had taken in all boys! As if she could erase Carrie Ann. After all Carrie Ann had done for Grace. Grace had said she loved her too. She had said they were family. Carrie Ann felt as if she had a giant claw tearing at her heart.

This had been a colossal mistake. She felt that now. She would tell the boys the plan was off. "Good-bye, Grace." Carrie Ann started walking away.

"I'm not chasing you anymore," Grace said. Carrie Ann stopped and turned around. They stood, facing each other in the middle of La Rambla. Tourists, and street performers, and impatient locals rushed by and around them, but the two only saw each other, cocooned in their own little bubble of pain.

"Of course not," Carrie Ann said. "Why should you? You have Jake. You have your family. Of which I'm obviously not a part." How could she have been so stupid? An icy-hot feeling of shame invaded her. How she'd always clung to the idea that no matter what else happened to her in this world, she had Grace. That family was the one you chose and someone had chosen her. Why did everyone always walk away from her?

"I'm sorry you haven't had a good life—"

"Me too," Carrie Ann said.

"I—I didn't mean to hurt you, Carrie Ann."

"But you did, Grace. You really did."

"And you hurt me. But neither of us can change the past. So why am I here, Carrie Ann?"

"Because I have no one else. And I had to give it a shot."

"What's going on?"

"I'm in trouble. I told you that."

"What kind of trouble, exactly?"

For a second, Carrie Ann focused on the hills in the distance. Then she looked Grace in the eye. "I think he's going to kill me." This was it. Carrie Ann had Grace's attention now.

"Who?"

Hadn't Grace been listening the other night? "My husband. My psycho husband."

"Why?"

"Because I tried to leave him. Because that's what psychos do."

"Have you gone to the police?"

Carrie Ann scoffed. "I have a restraining order, but most of the women who are killed by boyfriends or husbands are killed *after* they get the restraining order. The lady at the court office told me that. Can you believe that?"

"Carrie Ann."

"It's true. I'm worried it's only a matter of time before he finds me here."

"And so you invited Jake and me to be a part of your drama?"

"It was a mistake. I see that now. But I thought I should warn you."

"Warn me? About your husband?"

"Yes."

"Why would you—"

"I married Stan Gale." The words had the exact impact Carrie Ann had expected. Grace froze. Her face paled. And her mouth literally dropped open. Carrie Ann had to admit that it was totally satisfying. It took Grace a moment before she spoke.

"Stan?" Grace said. "You married Stan?"

"I know what you're thinking."

"I'm guessing he's changed quite a bit?"

"Why, Grace, I didn't realize you were so superficial."

"Carrie Ann. He was overweight. He had acne. He had braces. He had a profuse sweating problem. He had those greasy bangs that were constantly covering his eyes—"

"He lost weight, his skin cleared up, the braces are gone, his hair no longer hangs in his eyes, and for all I know he got Botox in his armpits because he smells just fine!"

"But."

"But, but, but."

"But he was just plain creepy!"

"I'm surprised you remember anything about him at all. As I recall you couldn't even make eye contact with him."

"Because he was creepy!"

"And you really hurt him."

"Me?"

"Do you honestly think he didn't know how you felt? That you were repulsed by him?"

"It wasn't just because of his looks."

"You could have fooled me."

"Carrie Ann. He was—"

"Creepy. I know. You've said it." A woman with a million shopping bags slammed into Carrie Ann. Grace immediately caught her arm. She pointed to a nearby bench. They walked over and sat, each looking anywhere but at each other for a few minutes.

"You are not married to Stan Gale." Grace said it as if it were a fact.

"I'm done talking about this." Carrie Ann brought out her pack of cigarettes, even though for once, she didn't feel like a smoke. Instead, she took one out and simply rolled it between her fingers.

"Come on. Just admit it. You're putting me on."

"Swear to God, hope to die."

"After everything that happened? After what happened with Lionel—"

"We are not going to talk about that." Now Carrie Ann did light her cigarette. She could never talk about Lionel without smoking.

"My point exactly. You actually want me to believe you married Stan Gale?"

"You don't understand. It's different now. At least I thought it was."

"I don't believe you. I just can't believe you."

"Frankly, my dear, I don't give a damn. Just don't say I didn't warn you."

"Warn me? Why do you have to warn me?"

Carrie Ann blew smoke out, then offered the pack to Grace. This time, after a slight pause, Grace took one. "Because his looks might have changed, but his personality hasn't. And I might have told him a certain version of the truth when it came to you."

"A version of the truth?" Grace placed the cigarette in her mouth and let Carrie Ann light it. "What version would that be?"

"I told him that you were the one who spread the rumors about Lionel."

A coughing fit ensued. Carrie Ann waited. Grace crushed the cigarette out on the bench, then threw it to the ground, and covered it with her foot. "That's a lie." She sprang from the bench. "You know I didn't. I didn't say a word to anyone!"

Carrie Ann rose slowly and squared off with Grace once again. "Oh, I know that, Gracie Ann. More than anyone else on earth I know that."

"And you've hated me ever since." Grace said it slowly as if she were just now working it out.

"You were supposed to be the one person who believed in me." Carrie Ann stepped as close to Grace as she dared. "But I'll forgive you. I'll forgive everything if you just help me now."

"You married Stan. I can't—I don't even know how that could have possibly come about."

"Why? Because he was always so in love with you?"

"What? Oh my God. No. No."

"Don't tell me you didn't know. The more you hated him, the more he loved you."

"I have to go. This is crazy. This is all crazy." Grace stepped forward, and Carrie Ann grabbed her hand.

"You can't walk away now, Grace. You're in this too."

Grace yanked her hand away. "How am I in this?"

"Have you ever walked through a swamp, Grace?"

"I feel like I'm in one now," Grace said.

"So you should know. It doesn't matter how prepared you think you are. The long boots. Maybe a stick. A rope in case you sink. But even if you make it across, and manage to lift your foot onto dry land, you still have all this muck clinging to your boots. Muck, and weeds, and mud, and sticks, and all sorts of *gunk*, clinging to your boots. Weighing you down with every step you take."

"For once in your life, Carrie Ann, stop talking in riddles, and tell me what's going on," Grace said.

"You can't walk away from the past. It still clings to you."

"What do you want?"

"I want you to acknowledge what you did to me." A few people were looking at them now, as if they were putting on a theatrical experience. *Let them*, Carrie Ann thought. *Let the whole world hear.*

"I didn't do anything."

"Exactly. Exactly, Grace. Except that doing nothing was certainly doing something. And saying something."

"What was I doing, Carrie Ann? What was I saying?"

"You were leaving me in danger! You were saying I was a liar. How could you? I really want to know. How *could* you?" Carrie Ann was screaming now. She'd better be careful or she was going to physically attack Grace. The need for release scraped at her insides. The only thing that stopped her was the totally stunned look on Grace's face.

"I didn't believe you." Grace's voice was barely a whisper. "That's how. Is that what you want me to say?"

"Yes," Carrie Ann said. "That's what I wanted you to say." Carrie Ann started to walk. Grace followed at a distance.

"You were always telling tales, Carrie Ann."

"Not always."

"Pretty much always."

"You've changed, Grace." Carrie Ann picked up her pace, and Grace had to run to catch up with her again.

"I've grown up." Grace grabbed Carrie Ann's arm, forcing her to stop.

"I'm happy for you," Carrie Ann said. "I guess that makes me Peter Pan."

"Please," Grace said. "Don't be like this."

"Like what? I just thought you should know. About Stan."

"That—he blames me?"

"For the record. I tried to take it back. I tried to tell him it wasn't you—"

"It was you!"

"Me? My God, Grace. Use your head. Why would I want to spread that rumor?"

"Because I wouldn't."

"I wanted you to tell *one* person, Grace. Just one." Carrie Ann poked her finger at Grace as she spoke, wanting desperately to make contact, poke Grace in the chest until she cracked.

"My mother wouldn't have changed her mind."

"We'll never know, will we?"

"Just admit it, Carrie Ann. You started the rumors."

"No, Grace. If you believe nothing else that I've ever said or ever will say, hear this loud and clear. I swear on my own grave. You were the only person I told."

"Then who did?"

"I don't know."

Grace was entirely off balance now. She didn't know where to put her hands. They played with her hair, then covered her mouth, then folded across her chest. She looked as if she were drowning in air. "I can't do this. I won't. I won't fall for your lies again. My father was right. You're the girl who cried wolf."

Carrie Ann took a step back, swallowed the lump in her throat. "Your father?" she said. *Him too.* "I see." Grace hadn't believed her. Still didn't believe her. Wouldn't believe her for the rest of her life. "Sounds like it's been a while since you've heard that story, Grace."

"What does that mean?"

"It means you've forgotten the end." Grace just stood. And stared. "Do you remember the end?"

"I remember."

"Then say it."

"I don't want—"

"SAY IT."

"The end?"

"Yes, Grace. The end."

"The boy cries wolf again, and this time there really is a wolf, but nobody comes running."

"Exactly, Grace. Exactly."

"Exactly, what?"

"Maybe your dad is right. Maybe I am the girl who cried wolf. But if that's true, then this is the end. Because, I'm telling you, this time—there really is a wolf."

CHAPTER 15

Twenty minutes after Grace left for her breakfast with Carrie Ann, Jake was still lying in bed. If he wanted to get to the market, he was going to have to get his ass in gear. He'd get all of her favorite foods, some candles, and a nice bouquet of flowers. And this time, he wouldn't forget the ring. Boy, he'd almost blown it. Had actually gotten down on one knee in the middle of the street, only to discover he had left the ring back in the apartment. At least he had the flyer for the concert in his pocket, although that had turned into a fiasco.

But he was actually glad the proposal hadn't worked out; he wanted to at least try to set up the camera and film it for Jody and Jim. Not to mention posterity. He and Grace could watch it when they were eighty. The biggest problem was, he no longer had the element of surprise. Now Grace suspected something, and her birthday was too obvious of a day—plus he hated when people tried to usurp one celebration by piling another one on top of it. *Tell the truth, Jake. You're all nerves.* He wasn't sure when exactly he was going to pop the question, but he should at least gather supplies while Grace was out.

Engaged. To be married. It was exhilarating. And terrifying. He hated seeing her so upset over her past. He'd really pushed her to tell him everything too, and he felt bad about that. He wanted to help her through it, whatever it was, but he certainly didn't need her to explain herself or her past to him. He loved Grace unconditionally. And he knew her. She was a good person. So whatever she'd done, whatever peer pressure had made her do, she had been just a kid. And it seemed like she'd been punishing herself enough. In the past singing was what had always made her thrive. He couldn't bear the thought of her losing that. He was glad Marsh Everett wasn't here. Jake wasn't a violent man at all—had never even been in a real fight, nothing beyond schoolyard shoving. But if that man were here, Jake would be tempted to throw a punch. Heck, he might even enjoy it.

What he couldn't quite figure out was what exactly he thought of Carrie Ann. There was actually something quite mesmerizing about her, and it was obvious she and Grace had a strong connection. At times Carrie Ann seemed like someone who would fight to the death over Grace. It was beyond bizarre to witness another person this protective of his girl, especially considering he hadn't even known she existed a few days ago. She was beautiful too, strong, yet somehow had that damsel-in-distress thing going on. But he'd take a genuine girl like Grace any day.

He sprung up and pulled his jeans on. Normally he showered first thing, but this morning he was anxious to get out of the house. Grace had said she wouldn't be long, and given her ambivalence toward her childhood friend, he might not even have enough time to beat her back to the apartment. He threw on a T-shirt, grabbed his wallet and keys, and headed out the door. He stopped, feeling like he was forgetting something. He stood frozen on the stairs, debating whether or not to go back inside.

Finally, laughing at his inertia, he moved on, taking the stairs two at a time. He was tempted to shout his good news to all of Spain. He didn't know exactly when, but he was going to propose sometime on this trip. He would know the perfect moment when he saw it. He gave a wave to the doorman, who just stared back, and soon was out on La Rambla. A small crowd was gathered on the side of his apartment building, all huddled together and pointing up at the roof. Jake followed their gazes and then stopped in his tracks. A man in a black bird costume was on the ledge of the building one floor above Jake and Grace's flat. My God. This was the creature Grace had seen on the street. One of La Rambla's eccentric performers. And this one was a ledge-walker. Jake wished he had his camera, but of course in his hurry he'd left it on the counter. Did he have time to go back for it? He started back, then stopped. No. He had to get everything ready for the proposal. The performer probably did this every day; he would get a picture another time. *There are all kinds of crazy people in the world,* Jake thought to himself as he headed for the market. All kinds of crazy.

Rafael paced while he made the call. "He wasn't in the apartment," he blurted out when the irritated voice on the other end of the phone picked up.

"Are you alone?"

"Yes."

"So Carrie Ann has no idea?"

"I tell her nothing."

"Good."

"He was not in the apartment." Rafael wasn't going to admit that he'd totally blown it. He had thought it would be fun to wear the costume; instead it had attracted a crowd. It would have been impossible not to entertain them a little; that's who he was.

"I know. You said that."

"What do you want me to do now?"

"Nothing. Just have Carrie Ann call me." Like magic, the door opened, and she walked in. "She's here now," Rafael said.

"I thought you said you were alone!"

"She just walked into the door. Just, just now," Rafael said.

"What now?" Carrie Ann said. Rafael held out the phone. "He wants to talk to you."

Carrie Ann took the phone into her bedroom and shut the door. She threw herself on the bed and stared at the ceiling. "Listen to me, Stan. You can't keep calling me every five seconds."

"I didn't. Rafael called me."

"Why?"

"Just to tell me you weren't back yet."

"I told you. He's psycho!"

"How did it go with Grace?"

"Well, I certainly have her attention. I think this might actually work."

"What exactly did you say?"

"Oh, just that you were a psycho and I was afraid for my life and that you might be after her as well."

"Is she scared?"

"On guard."

"Good."

"You know, I had no idea you were going to get so into this."

"You're not the only one who wants to clear out the cobwebs, Carrie Ann."

"Fair enough. So when will you be here? When will you abduct me?"

"You'll know me when you see me."

"I still think we should dump Rafael."

"We can't. He's giving us and them a place to stay."

"You have money. Find us another place to stay."

"Don't push it." He hung up. Carrie Ann couldn't believe it. It was as if he'd forgotten this was *her* adventure. What cobwebs did he want to clear out? Was he still obsessed with Grace? Sure sounded like it. She went back into the living room to face Rafael. He was wearing his ridiculous bird costume.

"Well?" Rafael said.

"Well, what?"

"What is next on the plan?"

"Just relax. We wait for him to arrive."

"*Sí.* We wait."

"And no more breaking into their apartment and moving things around."

"¿Perdoni?"

"Don't go into their place again!"

"It's my place too."

"Not while they're staying there. You're going to leave something behind and screw everything up."

"Like what?" Rafael said.

"Like one of your stupid little feathers."

"I do not like you speaking to me like that." Rafael flapped his wings. "These feathers are strong. Go ahead. Pull one."

Carrie Ann shook her head. "I'll pass."

Rafael strode over to the window and stood like a king surveying his territory. He swore in Spanish. "There he is. He's carrying groceries. He went to the market." Each statement was said as if he had just unraveled the mysteries of the universe.

Carrie Ann joined him at the window, and they both watched until Jake disappeared under the arch. "Why do you care where he goes?" Carrie Ann headed for the door.

"Where are you going?" Rafael said.

"None of your business."

"Maybe you should just disappear now," Rafael said.

Carrie Ann pointed at Rafael. "You work for me," she said. "And I'll disappear when I want to disappear."

Once out of Rafael's literal eagle eye, she hurried down the steps, hoping to catch Jake before he went into the apartment. Luckily, he was just coming up as she was going down. She stopped and waited.

"Hey," she called.

"Hey." Jake stopped. Carrie Ann was fascinated with the way he watched her. As if vetting her for Grace. "How was your breakfast?" he asked.

"Honestly, Jake, I screwed up."

"How so?"

"I was wrong not to include you. I'm really sorry."

"Nah. I wanted to go out to the market anyway."

"Listen. I know you don't know me, and you don't owe me anything, but—I'd really like another chance to hang out. Just the three of us."

"Why don't you talk to Grace about that?"

"I really don't want to get into the gory details, but I don't think she'd say yes if I asked. She's upset that I excluded you."

"I think we worked through that."

Carrie Ann shrugged. "I just thought it would be nice if I extended the invitation to you first this time. I'd like you and Grace to go to the Sagrada Família with me. Have you been there yet?"

"No."

"Great. It's a must-see."

"When are you going?"

"Tomorrow morning. We can go early and beat the crowd."

"I'll mention it to Grace."

"Okay. If you decide to go I'll be waiting in the lobby at ten." Carrie Ann hurried across the lobby and out the door before Jake could say another word.

Carrie Ann wandered around the town square near the apartment building. Was she doing the right thing? Or was she going too far? Once again she had a really bad feeling about involving Rafael. And Stan was acting kind of weird too. She should call him and tell him not to come. Would he freak out? This was her game. Her magic trick. She'd been practicing all her life.

By the time she was thirteen years old, Carrie Ann could impress most everyone with her tricks. First, she was simply drawn to the titles. Magician. Illusionist. Conjurer. Mentalist. Escape Artist. She also liked the names of certain tricks: Assistant's Revenge. Burning Alive. Crusher. Devil's Torture Chamber. Dismemberment. Guillotine. Impalement. Table of Death. The Mismade Girl. She particularly liked a definition she ran across:

Magicians are capable of doing seemingly impossible
or supernatural feats using natural means.

And so she had set her mind to doing just that. First, and
foremost, she had taken the Magician's Oath:

> *"As a magician I promise never to reveal the secret of*
> *any illusion to a non-magician, unless that one*
> *swears to uphold the Magician's Oath in turn. I*
> *promise never to perform any illusion for any non-*
> *magician without first practicing the effect until I*
> *can perform it well enough to maintain the illusion*
> *of magic."*

"The illusion of magic." She liked that. She counted on it
most days. Within a few months she could whip a quarter out of
an unsuspecting adult's ear. If she was in the company of kids
only, she would more often than not pretend to pull the quarter out of their behinds. Already at her full height of five feet,
seven inches and with long blond locks, she looked more the
part of the magician's assistant. No matter how hard anyone
begged, Carrie Ann would never give away her secrets. If there
was one thing a tossed-around foster child knew how to do, it
was keep secrets.

She could do The Four Robbers card trick, turn a multicol-
ored scarf into solid black, pull a quarter from whichever ori-
fice she chose, and she was well on her way to pulling a stuffed
rabbit out of a hat. She frequently fantasized about sawing a
very good-looking man in half. "Someday," Carrie Ann used to
say, flashing her teeth, "I'm going to make someone disappear."

CHAPTER 16

The Basílica de la Sagrada Família is a church for the people, funded by the people. Antoni Gaudí accepted the commission and in 1883 began his remarkable construction with the crypt. Next he started on the apse, and then the cloister. It was to be an enormous church with a Latin-cross ground plan and soaring towers. He wanted the architecture to speak of spirituality from a sculptural perspective. He housed nativity scenes in specific corners so that people would step back and stare in sheer wonder. In 1914, Gaudí abandoned all other works and dedicated the last years of his life to the Sagrada Família. He even lived his last few months in his workshop in the church, surrounded by plans, and sketches, and photographs.

One of his main plans for the building, carried out after his death, was the Passion façade. It is made up of symmetrical parts: the great portico and the bell towers, rising sternly into the heavens.

In the ensuing years the Sagrada Família was subjected to various acts of destruction in addition to the crypt's burning down, and new architects taking over where others left off, but despite the challenges, people worked to preserve the dreams Antoni Gaudí had for the Sagrada Família. With its soaring spirals, and concave and convex shapes, and statues, and Glory façade with magnificent stained glass windows that truly make you stop and drop your jaw, the Sagrada Família felt instantly comforting to Grace, and she needed comfort, for tagging along with them, at Jake's invitation, was Carrie Ann.

Grace walked ahead, trying to calm down and lose herself in the sheer size and beauty of the architectural masterpiece. It almost made her want to pray. Spirals rising into the sky. Stained glass twenty feet high. Enormous. Incomplete. Just like life. Their footsteps echoed through the cavernous chapel. They climbed to the very tip of the cathedral towers, where through the gaps in the stone windows the city of Barcelona unfurled below them.

"Makes our problems seem so small, doesn't it, Grace?" Carrie Ann said.

"Actually I was thinking it makes my goals seem small," Grace said. Her problems, since Carrie Ann had arrived, were bigger than ever. *This time there really is a wolf.* Who says that to someone? And really, what had Grace ever done to Stan except have a very normal creeped-out reaction around him? She had even tried to be nice to him at Lionel's funeral. That had been excruciating for her. The last person she had wanted to look at and offer condolences to was Stan Gale. So if he had it out for Grace, then Carrie Ann was to blame. Now Grace was supposed to stand in a high tower with her and not fantasize about throwing her off of it?

"It's a gorgeous view," Jake said.

"It's important to change your perspective now and again," Carrie Ann said. "Look at life from a new angle."

There she went again, trying to absolve *herself* of the sins of the past. *I forgive you,* she had said at breakfast. Grace had almost choked on that one. Forgive her? Forgive *her?*

"Look this way," Jake said. He held up his camera. "Carrie Ann—say hi to Jody and Jim—"

"No," Grace shouted. Her voice echoed through the tower.

Her mother and father could not find out about Carrie Ann. Grace lunged for the camera. She tripped and fell into Jake, slamming her hands into the camera. It flew through one of the open gaps and hovered in the air for the briefest of seconds before plummeting to the ground. Jake let out a yell. Grace cried out too, then slapped her hand over her mouth.

"Hello, Jody, hello, Jim," Carrie Ann called over the edge with a laugh.

Grace whirled on her. "That was worth thousands of dollars."

"Don't look at me, darling. You're the one who tackled him."

Grace turned to Jake. His face was red. He too was staring over the edge. "Jake, I am so, so sorry."

"Why? Why did you do that?"

"I just—I didn't want you to record us—"

"Why didn't you just say stop?"

"I wasn't thinking." It was a lie. She had been thinking. About Carrie Ann. God, this just wasn't going to work out.

"I could have just erased it." He was really upset.

"Sylvester and the Magic Pebble," Carrie Ann said.

"Not the time," Grace said.

"What?" Jake said.

"Another one of Grace's favorite childhood books. Sylvester is a donkey who finds a magic pebble. He sees a lion and is so frightened he wishes he were a rock. Later, he's like—why didn't I wish the lion would disappear? Or that I was safe in my home, or a million other things. Instead, he was stuck being a rock."

"Thanks for that lovely rendition," Grace said. Carrie Ann took a bow.

Jake glanced at Grace, who mouthed, "I'm sorry." He put his hands on top of his head. "I didn't get it insured," he said. "It was the whole reason for this trip—"

"How's that?" Carrie Ann said.

"Never mind," Grace said. "I'll pay for it, Jake. I'll buy you a brand-new one."

"You don't have that kind of money. I barely had that kind of money." In the small outlook, Jake began to pace.

"I have credit cards."

"It will max them out, Grace."

"I have money," Carrie Ann said. "Lots of it." Grace and Jake just looked at her. "At least my soon-to-be ex-husband does." She dug through her purse and held up a credit card. "Might as well max this out before he gets to me." Grace glanced at Jake. When she had filled him in on her meeting with Carrie Ann, she had left out the bit about Carrie Ann's being married to Stan. And that supposedly he had it out for Grace because Carrie Ann had lied and told him Grace was the one who had spread rumors about his father. Rumors that had led Lionel Gale to hang himself from the highest rafter of his barn. Grace had sworn she was going to tell Jake everything. She had agreed that there shouldn't be any more secrets. And here was her past, ready to explode like a shaken soda can. No wonder he hadn't asked her to marry him. She was a mess.

Carrie Ann thrust the credit card at Jake again.

"No thank you," Jake said. "Grace, I need some space. I'll see you back at the apartment." Before Grace could say a word, they were watching the back of his head recede. It took a lot to upset Jake, so it hurt all the more that she'd pushed him to that point. Why was Carrie Ann back? Why couldn't she just leave them alone? Grace didn't want to think about Stan, or Carrie Ann, or the past. She'd paid her penance. Maybe she, like Gaudi before her, should live out the rest of her days in this church. Or at least the rest of the trip.

"He's testy," Carrie Ann said.

"Really? *Sylvester and the Magic Pebble?*"

Carrie Ann shrugged. "It popped into my head."

Grace hated herself. Jake had been so excited to film their trip. And her mother had looked forward to seeing the film clips, getting a bit of escape from her reality. Grace had really blown it. It was hard not to blame Carrie Ann. Grace closed her eyes and concentrated on her breath. She tried to count to ten in Spanish. When she opened her eyes, Carrie Ann waved the credit card again.

"I meant it. Stan is loaded. We'll just get another."

"Do you hear yourself?"

"What?"

"You said you're afraid of him. That he's a wolf."

"So?"

"Yet you're willing to charge up his credit card?"

"We're married. It's our money."

"If what you're saying is true—"

"If what I'm saying is true? If?"

"I don't want any of Stan's money."

"You probably think it has cooties on it."

"We're not twelve anymore, Carrie Ann." Grace tried to sound haughty, but Carrie Ann was right. It made her shudder to think about touching anything of Stan's.

"Are you sure about that?"

"I'm leaving."

"Look." Carrie Ann reached out and touched Grace's arm. "I'm really sorry about his video camera, all right? I just wanted to have a nice time with you and Jake."

"I think I'm under a Spanish curse."

"Well, you know the cure for that, don't you?" Grace just looked at her. "A little retail therapy? I won't even use Stan's credit card."

Grace hesitated. She really wanted to follow Jake home. But she knew him. He was going to need a little bit of time to clear his head. She could make things worse if she went home now. "I'm not going to buy anything, but I'll go with you," Grace said. Carrie Ann grinned and linked arms with Grace. It startled her. They used to do this all the time as kids. Her father used to joke about them being Siamese twins. The Grace of back then could have never imagined a time when Carrie Ann wouldn't be just an arm's length away.

Grace didn't think she'd ever shake her bad mood, especially with what happened with Jake, but soon she found herself actually enjoying shopping with Carrie Ann. Part of Grace still felt like a little girl around Carrie Ann, so realizing they could shop and go places without her parents' permission was a heady experience. They had used to sneak into Grace's mother's closet and try things on, take turns being the shopkeeper and the movie star. Now here they were, all grown up, shopping in Barcelona. Carrie Ann knew of a great cosmetic store, and as soon as they entered, they came to a dead halt and looked at each other.

"Are you thinking what I'm thinking?" Carrie Ann said.

"Coral Bliss," they both said at the same time. And then they laughed. It had been close to Easter time. They had been following Grace's parents at breakneck speed through the mall, when Carrie Ann had suddenly shoved something in Grace's raincoat. Grace remembered reaching down and feeling the sleek tube of lipstick. "Don't stop," Carrie Ann had whispered in her ear.

"My heart was hammering so loud I thought the whole store could hear it," Grace said. "I still have nightmares." It was true; for years she had been guilt-stricken, sure that she would be punished, or worse, not allowed into heaven. Who risks eternal life for a tube of Coral Bliss? Even after crushing the lipstick, and throwing it into the trash at the curb, and watching the garbage men take it away, she had still been haunted.

"I wanted to see how you would handle it," Carrie Ann said. "You always seemed so afraid of everything."

And big tough Carrie Ann wasn't afraid of anything, Grace thought. She probably hadn't given a second thought to taking it.

"I don't need any makeup," Grace said. "Do you?"

"All you need in Spain is the kiss of the sun," Carrie Ann said. "Let's go to Miss Sixty." Carrie Ann seemed to know exactly where they were going, and Grace was content enough to tag along, feeling more and more relaxed around her long-lost friend. Every once in a while she would steal a look at Carrie Ann, catch a wisp of her white-blond hair in the sun, or her full lips spread in a smile, and Grace would think: *She is family. She's feisty and beautiful, and she came here to be with me again.* And for a few minutes Grace could cocoon herself in the moment, without letting in any of the stagnant water pooled underneath the very old and very long bridge.

134 • *Mary Carter*

"European stores are so much nicer, don't you think?" Carrie Ann said after stepping into the clothing store and within seconds finding a perfect lace top. "This is absolutely made for you, Gracie." It was a soft pink. An innocent color. Carrie Ann held it out to Grace, and then insisted Grace try it on, even though Grace knew she wasn't going to let Carrie Ann pay for it. Carrie Ann was right though. It did look good on Grace. Then at Carrie Ann's insistence they tried on the exact same dress, short and white with big red flower petals, and stood side-by-side looking into the full-length mirror in the open area of the dressing room.

"If you colored your hair blond and wore heels, we could be twins," Carrie Ann said.

"You have blue eyes," Grace said. Like Stan. She still couldn't believe Carrie Ann and Stan were married. Carrie Ann had married the boy she had bullied. Poor Stan. Grace had a hard time believing that he was now the one threatening Carrie Ann. How much was Carrie Ann distorting the truth? She had definitely always lived in the fun house–mirror version of the world. Truth is what you believe it to be, Grace mused. That was a scary thought when it came to Carrie Ann.

Carrie Ann waved her hand. "Contacts could hide blue eyes."

"Well, I seriously doubt you would want to look like me, and even though you supposedly have more fun, I've never harbored a secret desire to be a blonde."

"Don't you ever get tired of your life? Don't you ever just want to be someone else?"

Sometimes Grace wanted things to be different. But you could never be someone else. Grace's practical side just didn't allow her to indulge in this kind of thinking. She wished to be someone else as much as she wished to be a giant oak tree. "No," Grace said.

"I'd become someone else like that." Carrie Ann snapped her fingers. "And I'd trade places with you in an instant."

"Me?"

"Don't pretend you don't have it made."

"I'm a struggling country singer," Grace said. *And my mother has between one and six months to live.*

"Mostly I just want out of my marriage."

Grace couldn't believe she'd married Stan in the first place, and Grace couldn't help but go there again. "How long have you two been married?"

"Four years."

"How did it even happen?"

"Do you really want to know?"

The words thumped in Grace's ears. She was instantly back in the hayloft, Carrie Ann leaning intensely into her, practically breathing down her neck, asking her the same question. *Do you really want to know?*

Grace should have run. She should have shouted, *No! I do not really want to know.* She hated how Carrie Ann did that, how swiftly she could make you feel as if you were the one to blame, as if that one loaded question was a legally binding contract—*Do you really want to know?*—and that in answering yes, you, solely, were responsible for whatever came out of Carrie Ann's mouth next.

"Only if you really want to tell me," Grace said, hoping to sound as if she didn't care. There. That felt better. Why hadn't she said that back then? Because she was never prepared enough to deal with Carrie Ann. Grace couldn't believe how quickly she was regressing into a little kid again. *I'm an adult,* she reminded herself. Almost thirty. *I am an adult almost thirty, and I am in Spain with my boyfriend.* How many times did she have to say it before she felt it?

"My therapist thought it would be a good idea if I went back to some of the old places. The ones that haunted me." Grace felt her chest start to constrict. This store was so small. She wanted out. "So I started with the Gales. Lydia still lives in the same house," Carrie Ann said. "But she tore the barn and the tire swing down."

Grace wanted her to stop talking. She didn't want to hear

any of it. Except maybe how poor Lydia was doing. She'd changed so much with the whole incident. Was she all right now? Was she still an artist? Did she still believe that it was a child's birthright to draw outside the lines?

It was partly Grace's fault. All the hideous things that had happened to one of her favorite people in the world. Even if it wasn't *entirely* her fault, she had to take some of the blame. And it killed her. The guilt was poison running through her veins. But she didn't dare probe into Lydia's wellbeing any further. No matter how well they were getting along, information was Carrie Ann's weapon of choice. Grace could never let herself forget that.

"And you—fell in love with Stan?" Grace just had to ask. Carrie Ann turned on her with a disappointed look. "Stan's right," she said. "You've never been able to see the real him through your goggles of disgust."

"Stan said that? About me?"

"Of course. He knew you abhorred him."

"That's a little strong."

"Is it, Grace? Is it?" Carrie Ann left Grace standing dumfounded and headed back into her private dressing room. Grace reluctantly went back into hers. Which didn't mean she had any real privacy. The rooms were side-by-side and they could hear every zip and breath each other took. After a few minutes Carrie Ann started talking again as if she'd never stopped. "I had no idea about his temper—until last year."

"What happened?"

"He got crazy jealous, that's what. Of everything. If I talked too long to the female cashier at the grocery store, he would go nuts."

"Did he—was he violent?" Grace looked at herself in the mirror. She didn't look anything like Carrie Ann. The dress hung on her, whereas it hugged Carrie Ann's curves.

"I have pictures of all my bruises, every one of them, if you ever want to see them."

Grace didn't answer at first. What did you say to that? Wimpy, whiny, Stan Gale an intimidating abuser? It was unfathomable on so many levels. She felt better when she slipped back into her jeans, and top, and cowboy boots. Now that felt like her. "That's horrible, Carrie Ann. Nobody deserves that." She couldn't imagine Carrie Ann's putting up with that. "You didn't leave after the first time? I'm not trying to blame you—"

"No, I get it." Grace heard the curtain open, and then another one, and soon Carrie Ann was standing in Grace's little room in her bra and panties. Carrie Ann turned and looked at Grace through the mirror. "I used to think that of battered women," she said. "That they were weak. And stupid."

"Carrie Ann. I didn't mean—"

"I never thought I'd let a man hit me. Every time I said, 'next time I'm going to leave.' But he was always so sorry. I'd think— he's different. He has a temper. He didn't mean it. We'll get through this. All that bullshit I used to judge other women for thinking."

"I'm so sorry. I'm glad you got out." Speaking of out, Grace wanted out of this tiny dressing room. She draped the dress over her arm and tried to step out. Carrie Ann grabbed Grace's wrist.

"You're so lucky to have Jake."

Grace looked at her wrist. Carrie Ann let go. "I know," Grace said. She stepped out of the dressing room.

Carrie Ann walked back into her own dressing room and without bothering to shut the curtain again pulled her green dress over her head. "Is he going to stay mad at you for a long time?"

"No," Grace said. "He's not like that. He'll probably call me any minute now."

"I hope so, Grace," Carrie Ann said. "I'd really hate to be the one to come between you."

CHAPTER 17

Grace wanted to walk back to the apartment, but Carrie Ann insisted on a taxi. As they bumped along, Carrie Ann reached over and took Grace's hand. "I knew we'd get back in touch," she said. "We're sisters. Signed in blood." Grace wanted to remove her hand, but didn't know the proper amount of time to wait so that Carrie Ann wouldn't be upset. Ten seconds? "Listen," Carrie Ann said when Grace finally pulled free. "I have enough of Stan's money to travel for a few months. What do you think?"

"That sounds great. I'm happy for you."

"Not just me. You and me."

"Not going to happen." Grace didn't mean for it to come out so harsh, at least she didn't think she did, but the stress over her mom, and the camera, and Jake, and the heat made it impossible to be diplomatic.

"I see. Not even going to pretend to think about it."

"I have things going on at home. I don't even think we're going to stay here the full ten days."

"Because of your mom?"

"I told you not to talk about my mom," Grace said.

"So much for thinking you would care."

Grace wasn't going to rise to the bait. "Just because I can't drop my other obligations, doesn't mean I don't care." Grace's cell phone rang. She jumped. Her heart lifted when she saw the screen: **JAKE**. She snapped it open. "Jake?"

"I'm sorry," Jake said. "I didn't mean to storm off."

"It's okay. It's okay. I'm so, so sorry about your camera." Next to her, Carrie Ann rolled her eyes. Grace scooted closer to the passenger door.

"Don't be. I'm going to buy another one," Jake said.

"I'll pay for it."

"Nah. This trip is about your mother, remember? It's on me."

"Really I want to—"

"Shhh. We'll worry about it later. I'm not getting anything too fancy—just something that will do the trick. And guess what?"

"What?"

"I already uploaded all the videos we took, so those aren't lost."

"That's great."

"We still have some catching up to do."

Yes, Grace definitely had some catching up to do. She was going to come clean with Jake, tell him the whole tale. Then maybe they'd get all their sightseeing in and head back to Nashville. She wanted to end things on a good note with Carrie Ann, and the longer they hung around together, the less chance there was of that happening. "I'll be ready when you are."

"Where are you now?"

"In a taxi. I'm on the way back to the apartment."

"I'll be there in a little bit myself. What do you say we hit the Miró museum, just the two of us?"

"I'd love to."

"Good. You going to have any trouble from Carrie Ann?"

"Of course not."

"Okay. See ya in about an hour."

"I love you."

"I love you too." Grace hung up and snuck a glance at Carrie Ann. She was looking out the window. Grace heard an intake of breath. Carrie Ann was crying. "Carrie Ann?" Grace felt a physical pain in her chest, a visceral ache. Her insides literally churned at the sound of Carrie Ann crying. By the time Carrie Ann had come to live with them, she had already been in ten foster homes. She had refused to even unpack her suitcase for the first three months. Had slept with it at the foot of her bed, as if they were going to spirit her away in the middle of the night. Grace's first feeling of real pride, of accomplishment that made her heart feel as if it were going to burst in her chest, had been the day Carrie Ann let Grace help her unpack her little suitcase. That hadn't been easy for that tough little girl; she had to soften a part of herself just to let Grace in. And somewhere along the line, Grace had lost sight of that. After all, wasn't that the point of having a family? People who would love you through it all, warts and all? Grace had forgotten that too.

Carrie Ann was right. They were sisters. Grace had promised her that all those years ago. That was something else she'd forgotten about families; you were stuck with them. A hundred unopened letters. Grace had lied about her mother's hiding them from her. She was the one who had written RETURN TO SENDER across every single one and stuck it back in the mailbox. Grace reached over and took Carrie Ann's hand. "Don't cry," she said.

"I don't think I can get through this alone."

"You're not alone. I'm here. I'm right here."

"You're not. I've lost you."

"You haven't."

"You're not even staying the full ten days."

"We'll stay a few more days. And maybe you can come to Nashville sometime."

Carrie Ann turned to look at Grace. "Do you mean it?"

"I do."

"Thank you." Carrie Ann squeezed Grace's hand. She leaned her head on Grace's shoulder. "Are you and Jake going somewhere by yourselves?"

"We're going to a museum. I wasn't sure it would be your style."

"I'll go anywhere. I just don't want to be alone."

"Okay," Grace said.

"Do you think I can squeeze in a nap first?" The cab pulled up to the stop closest to their apartment.

"Jake said he'd be about an hour."

"Perfect." By the time they were back in the building and Grace had disappeared into her apartment, doubts were already creeping back in. What had she done? Not only had she promised Jake they'd be alone at the museum, but now she'd just invited Carrie Ann to come to Nashville sometime. Most people wouldn't think twice about it, but Carrie Ann would. That invitation was like another cut to Grace's finger, another vow in blood. She leaned against the door and softly banged her head. *What were you thinking, Grace?* Her mother's words came back to her. *You can't save her.*

Grace flopped down in the bed and buried her face in the pillow. *Come home, Jake.* He would help her figure this out. She would tell him everything, and then together they would figure it out.

An hour later, Jake still wasn't home, and he hadn't called again. She wondered if Carrie Ann was still sleeping. Grace wished she could sleep, but she felt strangely energized. She also felt like she was forgetting something. Did she have her purse? It was on the counter. Grace began to empty it out. Something clinked on the counter. Carrie Ann's diamond ring. Grace had forgotten all about it. She slipped it on her finger. It fit. The diamond was huge. Better not get too attached. Grace took the ring off and tucked it into her purse. Then she pulled out a credit card and driver's license. They weren't hers—hers were always tucked in her wallet. The license belonged to Carrie Ann Gilbert.

How did those get in there? Carrie Ann must have slipped them in without Grace's noticing. Why would she do that? It was just as disconcerting to find something added to your purse as it was to discover something missing. She studied the driver's license. Carrie Ann looked like a pretty all-American blonde. Her address was in Atlanta, Georgia. Had Carrie Ann mentioned that? Was she living there with Stan or had they separated? Maybe with this new info Grace could find something on the Internet.

Grace took the license over to Jake's laptop. But when she went to log in, a little box popped up asking for a password. Jake had never locked his computer before. They brought the laptop primarily for video chats with her parents, so Jake wouldn't deliberately shut her out of it. Would he? Maybe that little assistant of his had sent him naked pictures and Jake didn't want her to see them. Grace was reaching now. Jake wasn't the type to hide things on his computer. But if he hadn't locked it, then who had?

Heavy footsteps echoed above her. It sounded like more than one person was traipsing around upstairs. The hairy guy from the beach? Grace would have to ask Carrie Ann about him. Or she could casually ask the doorman who didn't open any doors.

Grace went into the hall and tried to peer all the way down to the lobby. The staircases curved so that you could actually see a good ways down but she couldn't make out the desk from this angle. She texted Jake as she headed down the stairs.

Wandering nearby. Let me know when you're home.

The guy was back at the desk. Perfect. Even though he simply looked at her without a word or a smile, Grace walked up to him. *"Hola,"* she said. "I'm Grace."

"Hola, Grace," he said. "I am Stefano."

"Do you work here?"

"I am here to help." Now he was smiling, as if she had just offered him her escort services.

"I'm just wondering, have you met my friend Carrie Ann? Blonde. Also American. She's one floor above me?"

"Yes, but don't worry. I can love two girls just as much."

"Lovely. Do you happen to know the guy she's staying with? Tall—uh—dark hair?" *And a lot of it.*

"Rafael. My good friend. *Amigos.*"

"That's right. Rafael. I just wanted to thank him for letting us stay here."

"He is at work."

"Oh. I thought I heard him up there." Grace glanced up at the apartment. She swore she had heard a man's voice up there.

"Your boyfriend is with her."

At first Grace didn't quite understand him. "Jake? You saw Jake go up there?"

"*Sí.*"

He must have been confused, but Grace kept asking questions. "How long ago?"

He shrugged. "Thirty minutes ago."

Grace leaned forward and lowered her voice. "Listen. Have you ever seen Rafael or Carrie Ann go into our apartment?"

"I see nothing."

"Okay."

"That's why I am good at my job." The smile was back.

Wait. So was he saying he had seen someone go into their apartment, but he was going to turn a blind eye? "What is your job?"

He put his hand on his heart. "Security. You feel safe with me. *¿Sí?*"

About as safe as a baby with a rattlesnake. "*Gracias,*" she said, although she really had no reason to be thanking him. She headed back up to Carrie Ann's room. Jake couldn't be in there, could he? When she got to the door she stopped and listened. She could no longer hear voices. Had she just imagined things? And what about Stefano? Had he out and out lied? Grace knocked. No response. She knocked louder. "Carrie Ann?" she called. "Jake?"

She stood in the hall and texted Jake.

Where are you?

Half a minute later he responded.

Got caught up. Meet you at Miró at 3:00?

"Jake?" Grace called again. And again, there was no answer.

Call me ASAP.

Phone dying. Sorry babe. C u @ 3.

Grace realized she didn't even have a cell phone number for Carrie Ann. She went back to her apartment and scrawled a note on an envelope.

Miró Museum 3 p.m. See you there. Grace.

She slipped it underneath Carrie Ann's door and was halfway down the stairs when she was hit with a strong feeling that she was forgetting something. Video call her mother. That's what she was forgetting. And now she couldn't even do it because Jake had password protected his computer. The afternoon was getting more frustrating by the minute. She continued down the stairs, wondering if she should buy a calling card instead.

It was slightly cooler outside than it had been for the past few days, but Grace was hot from running up and down the stairs. It was an easy walk to the Miró Museum, first toward the beach, then up the massive hill to the right. Maybe she'd look at some artwork on her way to the museum or grab something cold to drink and just sit on the beach. She certainly could stand to calm down.

She bought a calling card at a small shop at the end of the street and called her mother. Her father answered. "Finally, Gracie. Your mother was worried sick." Grace cringed, although this was an expression they used all the time.

"Jake's laptop isn't working," Grace said. "I had to go out and buy a calling card."

"Well, how goes it?"

"It's lovely, really. But we also broke our video camera."

"That's terrible."

"We were at the top of the spiral in Sagrada Família, and Jake dropped it while trying to get a panoramic sweep."

"That was an expensive piece of equipment," her father said.

"He was insured." Grace had no idea the lie was going to pop out of her mouth until it was too late. At some point she had started protecting her parents from the truth.

"Ah, thatta boy."

"Listen. How is Mom?"

"She's fine, Gracie."

"Is she awake?"

"No, she's pretty far under or I'd give her a jostle for you."

"Oh. Is she . . . ?"

"About the same, darling. About the same."

"How are you holding up?"

"Fair to middling. I'll tell you—we both enjoyed that video. You and Jake have a nice chemistry together. We can tell you're really having fun. So as soon as you replace your camera, keep those rolling in. It does your mother good."

"I wish I were there."

"No, you don't. And she doesn't either. She wants you two to have a good time."

"You'd tell me if I needed to come home."

"Of course. I'm telling you to stay."

"Because it wouldn't be any trouble—"

"The doctors are going to lower your mother's dose of medication. I think her memory will start to improve."

"I should come home and talk to them—"

"Believe me, I gave them an earful."

"I bet you did."

"Once she starts remembering things I'm going to take her on a few outings a week."

"That's really great, Dad. I'm so happy she has you."

"She has you too, pumpkin. And you promised her Barcelona."

"Okay." A familiar lump was lodged in her throat. She did not want her father to hear her crying.

"What are you lovebirds up to today?"

"We're going to go to the Miró Museum."

"Excellent."

With Carrie Ann. He had enough to worry about. Considering how upset he had gotten when he thought Jody was simply imagining Carrie Ann, Grace definitely didn't want to give him the news long distance. "Give Mom a kiss for me."

"I'll give her two. And you just enjoy every minute you can."

There was a Spanish guitar player at the base of the hill leading up to the Miró Museum. The delicate notes immediately lifted Grace's mood. She sat on the edge of a concrete wall and closed her eyes. The sun felt good on her eyelids, and she let the music wash over her.

"I wish I had my camera." It was a male voice, and, unless he had learned how to pull off a foreign accent in the past few hours, it wasn't Jake. Grace opened one eye. Standing very near, to her right, was a man staring at her with a slightly crooked smile. He was a foot taller than her, had wavy brown hair, eyes the lightest brown she had ever seen, a dark tan, and stubble. He didn't look Spanish, and his accent sounded slightly French but not quite.

"He's good, no?" he said. Grace nodded and looked away. She had always been shy about being hit on, and relieved when she had met Jake, thinking that part of her life was over. She could already feel her cheeks heating up. Jake was always comparing her openness while playing onstage to her shyness in everyday life, but in her mind they were totally separate things. When she was on stage she had an entire audience to hide behind. One-on-one was much more intimidating. Still, as a performer, it was something she should probably learn to get over. Carrie Ann certainly never had a problem around people.

"Do you play?" the foreigner said, gesturing to the guitar.

"Not Spanish guitar," Grace said. "Not like that anyway."

"But the guitar you play. No?"

"How did you know?"

"You are strumming the air." Grace looked at her hands, and sure enough they were in guitar position. It startled her, and then she laughed. The foreigner laughed with her and then edged closer. "I have always admired musicians. They can play what they feel. Me? I must always keep it inside."

Grace smiled and nodded. It was the best gig in the world. *Sing her pain—*

"How long have you been in Barcelona?" He too sat on the concrete wall, although he gave her plenty of space.

"I'm losing track," Grace said. "I think it's our sixth day." There. She brought up Jake by the use of the word "our." If this man was hitting on her, he'd probably say "Are you with your boyfriend?" or some such, and he could soon be on his way. Otherwise, maybe he was just being friendly. Music had a way of opening people up, allowing them to let down their guards. "How long have you been here?" Grace asked.

"Sixteen days."

"Wow." She wondered what he did that allowed him so much time off. Then again, he was European, and they always had more vacation days. "Where are you from?"

"I am from Belgium," he said.

"Cool."

"But I have been traveling for the past year."

"For the past year?"

"Yes. I write a travel blog."

"Wow." She was suddenly very conscious of using the word "wow" twice in close proximity; she probably sounded very American. And that, as every American learned while traveling in Europe, was never a good thing. Grace looked at her phone. Jake should be along in twenty minutes. The stranger was indicating the musician.

"Maybe he would let you play," he said. "If I ask nicely."

"Oh, no. No. I couldn't. I wouldn't."

"Why not? I would love to hear you play." He kept his eyes on her and continued even when she broke eye contact. She felt a chemical attraction to him, and it was making her feel a little guilty. He was very attractive. It was normal, she supposed, to have this reaction to a handsome man, but it still jarred her. She hadn't felt any sexual feelings toward any other man since she had met Jake.

"Where all have you been?" Grace wanted to get the focus off of her.

148 • *Mary Carter*

"I have been all over Europe of course, and some to the States, but in my last job I was living in the Congo."

Grace watched him to see if he was putting her on, but his light brown eyes remained steady. Would he think she was hitting on him if she told him how unique his eyes were? And even more startling, *would* she be hitting on him?

The only things she knew about the Congo were from Barbara Kingsolver's *The Poisonwood Bible*. She figured it was a very beautiful but very dangerous place. "What took you to the Congo?" Something told her this man was the type to go exactly where no one else would.

"I was the director of an international rescue agency." Once again, no trace of joking.

"Wow." Oh, God, there she went again. "I'm sure you have a ton of stories."

"You could say that." He smiled at her as if he had a ton of juicy ones that he was never going to tell.

"It must be a pretty tough place to live though?"

"Of course. Our building was surrounded by a stone wall and armed guards. My house was guarded as well. Plus I had three dogs. The people, they have it rough, but they are survivors. But do not feel sorry for me. I had good pay and a beautiful house on a lake. I would kayak every morning. I also had a lot of friends. You have to put the tough times in perspective."

Grace stopped herself from saying "wow" again. They were sitting pretty close, just staring at each other, when a female voice sliced through the air.

"Up to no good, we see!" Grace and the man turned to see Carrie Ann waving and shouting from a few feet away. Jake was next to her. She was wearing the shortest red dress Grace had ever seen, and it looked fantastic on her. Jake at first looked sheepish, until he glanced at the man sitting so close to Grace. Then he looked annoyed. Carrie Ann on the other hand, eyed the foreigner up and down like she was going to bid on him at auction.

"Jake," Grace said. "I'm so glad to see you." It was true too.

An overwhelming feeling of relief flooded Grace, as if she had feared she would never see him again. Not caring who was watching, she launched herself into his arms. "Where were you?" she said when she finally pulled away.

"I got caught up with a few things," Jake said.

"I overslept," Carrie Ann said.

"Stefano said he saw you go into Carrie Ann's apartment," Grace said to Jake. "I knocked on the door for like fifteen minutes and tried calling both of you."

"Stefano?" Jake said.

"The guy who sits at the desk," Grace said.

"Lovers," Carrie Ann said. She elbowed her way between them and looped arms with each. "Let's not fight in front of our new friend." She gave the Belgian man the once-over, her smile widening as she took him in. She held out her hand. "I'm Carrie Ann," she said. "And you are?"

"I am Jean Sebastian," the man said.

"Of course you are," Jake mumbled. Grace snuck a glance at him. Was he jealous? He was the one walking around with Carrie Ann in that dress. Grace should be jealous. And why did she get the feeling that he was lying about being in Carrie Ann's apartment? Jake wasn't a liar. She couldn't let her imagination run away with her.

"We both just happened to be listening to the guitar player," Grace said. She gestured to where the guitar player had been, just a few minutes ago. He was gone. Why, every time Grace turned around, did somebody in this city disappear?

"We ready?" Jake said. He took Grace's hand with barely a nod to Jean Sebastian and headed toward the hill leading to the museum.

"We're going to the Miró Museum," Carrie Ann said to the newcomer. "Would you like to join us?"

Jake stopped abruptly. Grace stumbled forward. "Is she serious?" he said.

"She's like that," Grace said. Always dragging in strays from the periphery. Like poor Stan. Although if Carrie Ann was telling the truth it wasn't "poor Stan" anymore. Either way, this poor Belgian traveler had no idea what he was getting into. *Run, Jean Sebastian, run,* Grace wanted to shout.

"I will let you on your own," Jean Sebastian said.

"Then do give us your number," Carrie Ann said. "We can meet later for a drink."

"Unbelievable," Jake said. Carrie Ann was rummaging around in her purse, presumably for pen and paper.

"We'll meet you at the entrance," Grace said. Carrie Ann barely waved her hand.

Jean Sebastian looked at Grace and held her glance. Wow, was he attractive. "Nice to meet you," he said. "Good luck with your guitar."

"Thank you. Good luck with your travel blog." *I hope I never run into him again,* Grace thought to herself. She was horrified at how quickly she had lusted over a complete stranger. Lust at first sight. That was normal. She couldn't help that. But hanging around with him when she knew that's how she felt—now that would be wrong. Somehow she was going to have to get the message to Carrie Ann, without her figuring out how to use it against her, that under no circumstances was Jean Sebastian going to be tagging along.

CHAPTER 18

At the top of Montjuïc, Grace and Jake were treated to a fabulous panoramic view of the city. The building housing the museum was made of smooth white stone and was done in traditional Mediterranean style. In accordance with Joan Miró's wishes, exhibits were always from a variety of contemporary artists. That was a man with a true love of art, just like Grace's philosophy of musicians embracing, encouraging, and sharing the works of others. True artists, once they reached a certain level of acclaim and satisfaction, were not solely focused on themselves; instead they welcomed and encouraged others. Grace liked Miró's whimsical works and primary colors. It was amazing what he could do playing with the basics. Like Gaudí, Miró didn't seem to be baring his pain; he was playing; he was creating joy.

"Isn't this gorgeous?" Grace said as they stood outside taking in the view.

"Good luck with your guitar?" Jake said.

"Oh my God," Grace said. "You are a little jealous."

"My name is Jean Sebastian," Jake imitated in a horrible

French accent. "But you can call me Jean Sebastian." Grace laughed. "I think your friend Carrie Ann likes to stir up trouble," Jake said.

Grace didn't answer. What a Pandora's box her acknowledgment would open. "I still don't get why Stefano told me he saw you go into Carrie Ann's apartment," Grace said.

"How does Stefano even know what I look like?" Jake said.

"He's been watching us come and go," Grace said.

"Great. Stefano and Jean Sebastian. I'd better never leave your side." Jake looped his arm around Grace's shoulder.

"Speaking of leaving my side—why didn't you come back to the apartment?"

"Because you texted me and told me to meet you here instead," Jake said.

"No, I didn't," Grace said. "You texted me and told me to meet you here instead."

"You're trying to make me think I'm going crazy, aren't you?" Jake said.

"Are you sure the text was from my number?"

"It's a new phone, babe. I didn't memorize your number."

"Oh." That made sense. They'd each bought disposables in Spain. She didn't have Jake's number memorized either. "Let's make a pact to memorize each other's number."

"Agreed," Jake said. Grace looked in her purse for her cell phone. She brought it out. She opened her messages and held them out to Jake. He read through them, shaking his head.

"I didn't send any of these."

"But you responded to some," Grace said. She showed him.

He read them aloud. " 'Got caught up. Meet you at Miró . . . Phone dying.' Oh my God. These aren't from me—none of them."

"And you weren't in Carrie Ann's apartment?"

"Why do you keep going back to that?"

"Because if you were at Carrie Ann's apartment, then she had access to your cell phone and she could have sent the messages."

"My phone is always in my back pocket," Jake said.

"Wait," Grace said. "So you were in Carrie Ann's apartment?"

Jake sighed, looked away. "Someone who has a big birthday coming up shouldn't ask too many questions."

"Oh, God," Grace said. "Don't tell me you're letting Carrie Ann use that as an excuse to get you in cahoots with her?"

"Cahoots?"

"You know what I mean."

"I'm sorry, Grace. But secrets are allowed when you have a big birthday coming—"

"Stop saying 'big.' "

"Good-bye, youth; hello, thirties."

"Enough."

"Dirty thirties? I like the sound of that one." Jake grabbed her and kissed her hard. Grace pulled back. God, she wanted him right here and right now. He wasn't usually this passionate in public. He was doing this out of jealousy. Grace could live with that. But first she had to make sure he stayed far away from Carrie Ann. She had worn that little red dress just to rile Jake up. Grace had to admit, Jake wasn't the only one who was jealous.

"Apparently I haven't done enough to convince you that you cannot trust a single thing Carrie Ann says." Grace was suddenly furious. Here she was, extending herself to Carrie Ann again, and what was Carrie Ann doing? Luring Jake into her apartment for God knows what reason, using Grace's "birthday" as an excuse, and then getting ahold of his cell phone.

"There's no way she could have taken my phone out of my back pocket without my knowing."

"I told you Carrie Ann used to be a magician?"

"You're saying she slipped it out of my pocket?"

"That's exactly what I'm saying."

"Not possible."

"She was really, really good. Even for a little kid. Incredible slight of hand."

"No. Not a chance."

"Was she ever standing really, really close to you?"

Jake blushed; it was all the answer Grace needed. "It's okay. She's like that."

"Let's just say I believe you. Why would she do that? What does she have to gain?"

"I don't quite know yet." *Tell him. Tell him who she married. Then tell him everything about the past.*

"You were right. You don't owe her anything. We'll say our good-byes after the museum." Jake sounded determined. Grace should tell him about her mistake, how she had accidentally kind of invited Carrie Ann to come to Nashville sometime. And then tell him how someone like Carrie Ann would take that to heart. "Hey—did you talk to your mom?"

"I couldn't call from the computer. You password protected your laptop."

"No, I didn't."

"Well, someone did."

"Are you serious?" Jake had graduated to angry. "Let's go," he said. He took her hand and started to pull her away from the entrance.

"It's okay. I talked to my dad. Mom is fine. She was resting. I didn't mention you-know-who."

"I want to go see my laptop."

"But we're right here. You've been wanting to see this museum."

"Well, now all I want is to get us away from your psycho friend." As if summoned, Carrie Ann appeared at the top of the hill. Jake looked at Grace. She squeezed his hand.

"Let's just get through this," she said. "Please?" Jake didn't look happy, but he didn't say anything to Carrie Ann, and he willingly entered the museum.

They walked through the exhibits in silence, each lost in their own thoughts. One of the first things Grace saw was a small room painted red. A grand piano sat in the center of the room. Above it was the most magnificent chandelier Grace had ever seen, hovering and glittering over the piano. Black, white, and red. The effect was arresting, almost violent in nature. The image lingered long after she moved on.

She found she loved the sculptures better than the paintings. One was of a man doing a backflip. He seemed to hover midair,

•

and, despite staring and walking around it, Grace couldn't figure out how they were holding it up. Carrie Ann was smiling as
if she knew, but Grace wasn't about to ask her. She should pull
Carrie Ann aside and confront her with what Jake had told her,
but Grace just didn't have an argument in her at the moment.
She wanted to shut everything off. She was going to stop letting
Carrie Ann kidnap them.

The roof had a garden with more Miró sculptures and a view
of Barcelona. The people who lived here were so lucky to have
all this in their backyard. There weren't too many places in
America, if any, that had this much culture with a beach feel.
The sun felt even hotter on the roof, and Grace leaned against
a barrier and closed her eyes.

"Somebody has an admirer." Grace opened her eyes. Carrie
Ann stood in front of her, that smile on her face again. In her
left hand she was holding a folded piece of paper.

Grace eyed the offering, but didn't take it. "What's that?"

"Jean Sebastian's phone number. He wanted me to give it to
you." Grace glanced around. "Jake's downstairs, staring at lines
and circles."

"I don't want it," Grace said.

"You don't even want to know what he said?" Before Grace
could answer, Carrie Ann opened the piece of paper and showed
it to Grace.

Hola, Grace.

IT WAS A PLEASURE

I'd very much like to meet again.

And, indeed, underneath he had left his phone number.
Grace couldn't help but feel a tingle of flattery, and she prayed
Carrie Ann didn't see the blush working its way up her face.
"He's hot," Carrie Ann said. "I flirted my ass off, but he kept
asking about you." Carrie Ann shook the piece of paper in her
hand as if she were ringing a bell. "He's going to meet us for
drinks and dancing tonight," she announced.

156 • *Mary Carter*

"What?" Grace said. "No."

"No?" Carrie Ann said. "Why not?"

"Well, just . . . I mean. Because." *We're not going!* Tongue-tied around Carrie Ann again. Grace hated that about herself. The more things changed, the more they stayed the same. "Jake has a headache," Grace said. "I'm not sure if we'll go."

Carrie Ann eyed her. "Did you tell him you invited me to Nashville?"

And, there it was. Proof that Carrie Ann had not only taken Grace quite literally, but here she was acting like she was going to book a seat on their flight back. "Not yet."

"Why not? The sooner the better, don't you think?"

"So—you're planning on coming soon?"

"Isn't that what you meant?"

"I just . . . wanted you to know . . . you weren't alone."

"So you didn't really mean it."

"Of course I did. I just didn't know you were thinking about visiting so soon."

"I can't be anywhere near Stan. And I don't want to travel Europe alone."

"Maybe you'll meet a handsome stranger who likes to travel and run off with him," Grace said. "Did Jean Sebastian tell you he travels for a living?"

"You want me to travel Europe with a guy who fell in love at first sight with you?"

"That's ridiculous." Grace felt her face heat up again. Had he really said that to Carrie Ann? She was pretty sure he had to have felt the same instant attraction. Which didn't mean anything. She wasn't going to see him again. Carrie Ann could find another boy toy.

"He didn't write me a note," Carrie Ann said. She thrust the note at Grace.

Grace looked up to see Jake approaching. "Let's talk about this later," she said. She shoved the note back at Carrie Ann. Carrie Ann gave a knowing smile. Jake joined them, and Carrie Ann immediately looped arms with him like he was one of her many accessories. Then, as if in slow motion, the note from Jean Sebastian fluttered to the ground.

"Whoops," Carrie Ann said. Grace lunged to pick it up, but Jake got to it first. He handed it to Carrie Ann. Carrie Ann smiled and took her sweet old time taking the note back from him. Gone were the tears, the fear of the psycho husband, the "I'm all alone" lament. Grace had a sinking feeling that she'd been played. Hook, line, and sinker. "How's the head?" Carrie Ann said to Jake as she rubbed the piece of paper between her fingers. When Jake frowned she reached up and ruffled his hair. Grace wanted to kill her. Jake raised an eyebrow and looked at Grace.

"I told her about your headache," Grace said. "And how we might not be able to go dancing with her and Jean Sebastian tonight."

"I'm afraid it's turning into a migraine," Jake said. "In fact I'd like to go back to the room and lie down. Will you go with me?"

"Nonsense," Carrie Ann said. "Don't you two know the best thing about vacationing in Europe?" She waited, but neither Grace nor Jake replied. "Foreign drugstores! Spain has some great medications. We're going to one right now, and I won't take no for an answer."

The pharmacy was in a stone building that looked like it was from the 1500s. On the outside a neon green circle with a plus sign was the only clue what the building was. Grace hated to admit it, but she agreed with Carrie Ann. It was fun to check out medications in a new country. The pharmacist handed Jake some tablets that he said would cure a migraine. Grace wondered if he had anything to cure a frenemy from the past.

Jake leaned over and whispered in Grace's ear. "As soon as we buy this, we'll say we have to go back to the apartment so I can take it."

"Agreed."

"Get what you needed?" Carrie Ann sailed up the aisle, her arms full of bottles. "I fucking love it. I think there's codeine in all of this."

Grace couldn't help but laugh. Sometimes she had really missed Carrie Ann. "Don't worry. When I come to Nashville I won't take up your entire medicine cabinet," Carrie Ann said.

"What?" Jake said. "When you what?"

"Come to Nashville," Carrie Ann said.

"You're coming to Nashville?"

"Of course. Grace invited me."

"We have to get back to the apartment right now," Grace said.

"We're going out at nine o'clock," Carrie Ann said. "I'll come by."

"We'll let you know," Jake said.

"Even if you're still down for the count, you're not going to keep Grace in, are you?"

"Grace always makes her own decisions."

"Of course she does. So, Gracie, you're coming tonight, aren't you?"

Carrie Ann stared at Grace. Jake stared at Grace. She was going to have to take some of Jake's headache tablets. Grace headed for the door. "We'll let you know," she called over her shoulder. What she hated more than anything at the moment was that she really did feel like going out, and drinking, and dancing, and just letting loose. One big dance-off, and then she and Jake could go home. The only thing she had to figure out was how to keep Carrie Ann from following her. Maybe the Jean Sebastian angle was still viable. He'd only met Grace for a few seconds. Carrie Ann was hot. A few drinks, some close dancing—this might just solve all of Grace's problems. And all she had to do was get Jake to see it the same way.

Once outside Grace started in the direction of their apartment building. She was grateful that for once Carrie Ann took a hint and let them off on their own. She was still in the drugstore trying on sunglasses. For all Grace knew she was going to try to charm the pharmacist out of the really good stuff. Suddenly, Jake grabbed her arm and swung her around. "Where do you think you're going?" Jake said. Grace stopped. Jake was smiling.

"Oh God," she said. "I totally forgot you don't actually have a migraine." Grace tensed, expecting Jake to confront her with inviting Carrie Ann to Nashville. Instead, he laughed and pulled out a small device, the size of an iPhone. "What's that?"

"My new video camera."

"It's tiny."

"It will do the trick. What do you say we stroll through the food market. Then we can go to the downtown park. The one with the fountain and the giant elephant tusks. We'll take silly videos to send to your mom."

"Perfect." Hand in hand they now walked in the opposite direction of the apartment. "What if we run into her?" Grace said. She really didn't want to hurt Carrie Ann's feelings again. Carrie Ann's manipulative side could be tamed with kindness, but inflamed when she felt slighted.

Jake looped his arm around Grace's shoulders and kissed her cheek. "We'll tell her she was right—European drugs work fast."

Mercat St. Joseph de la Boqueria welcomed shoppers with a triangular entrance sign made of stained glass and iron rods. The enormous food market was alive with people and produce. Pig heads. Fruits and vegetables. Seafood. One stand had jars of honey and spices, the next succulent crabs on ice, and the next colorful premade juices in tall plastic cups with long straws. You could find just about anything here, and it was where all the Catalan chefs came to buy produce, meat, or seafood for the numerous top restaurants in Barcelona. It was a parade of food, the Mardi Gras for foodies. Grace decided to keep her eyes feasted on the arrays of fruits and vegetables rather than on the animal heads, or in some cases entire bodies, glass eyes staring at you forever. Poor little piggies and goat heads, all hacked off and lying on one side, eye staring up at the rafters of the market. Grace crossed herself and murmured, "Circle of life." Jake filmed nonstop, slowly panning his new camera over every gross item.

A case full of delicate eggs resting on straw had a sign: NO TOCAR; don't touch. Another bin had mushroom caps as big as Grace's head. And more eggs, ones that looked as if they'd been laid by a dinosaur, probably ostrich. A candy stall beckoned. Jake loved licorice. She bought a pound of it, then faced Jake.

"Carrie Ann is married to Stan Gale," she said.

"The kid you used to bully?"

"I shouldn't have put it that way. I didn't bully him. I just didn't like him, but I still let him think he was our friend."

"So—wait—didn't she say her husband was an abusive psycho?"

"Yep."

"This gets weirder and weirder."

"She said she wants to get away from him. So she asked me to travel Europe with her for the next couple of months—"

"No, Grace. You didn't."

"Of course I didn't."

Jake looked like he was about to read her the riot act. "Good. Because I could barely get you to enjoy ten days, so it would really—"

"I just told you I wouldn't. You know I couldn't leave my mom for that long."

"But you'd leave me for that long?"

"I didn't say that." Grace heard her voice rise in frustration. Several heads turned. Great. They were becoming one of those couples who immediately unraveled while traveling together. Although she could see how easily it could happen. She was tired and stressed, and even the fun parts felt strained because of the energy you had to expend when everything was so new and exciting. Having an out-and-out brawl was almost tempting. Especially since they were in a food court. So many things to throw. There was probably a song in there somewhere: *I threw some grapes in Spain because my man was a pain. . . .*

"Really?" Jake said. "Now?"

"Shit." She couldn't believe it was that obvious when she was mentally composing. How could she possibly leave any mystery in the relationship when he knew her inside and out? "I'm just trying to explain why I told Carrie Ann that she could visit us in Nashville."

"I think I have officially talked myself into a migraine," Jake said. He rattled the pills in his bag. "I'm actually going to go home, take these, and lie down." He started to walk away.

"I'm sorry. I didn't mean to do it. I just didn't want to see her cry."

"I didn't even bring it up, Grace," Jake said as he walked. "Because I wanted one minute where we actually felt like we were on vacation again."

"Okay, okay. I do too. But I also don't want us to hold things in." Jake stopped abruptly, and Grace almost barreled into him.

"Now that's rich," he said. His face was set in anger. Grace really hated herself for thinking it, but he was so damn sexy when he was angry.

"We were in the cab, and she said she had no one, and she started crying—"

"Crocodile tears no doubt," Jake said.

"How can you say that?" Jake started walking again. Grace had to speed up to keep pace with him. He knew she hated when he did this. She was five foot four; he was six foot two. Even his leisurely pace seemed like speed walking compared to hers. "You don't even know her."

Jake turned and waited for her to meet his eyes. "Exactly," he said. He was calm again. Calm and reasonable. If she wasn't careful it was going to make her furious. "This girl shows up after fifteen years. A girl you didn't even tell me about."

"We're back to this?" They were outside now, past the arch. They stopped underneath a tree.

"Yes, we're back to this. Think about it, Grace. What does that say about her that you wanted to pretend she didn't even exist?"

"I never forgot she existed," Grace said quietly. But she had tried.

"I no longer even want to know what happened back then.

Believe me. Now that I've had a dose of her, I know it can't be good."

Without speaking they headed down La Rambla. The street performers were back in force. Grace wanted this to be a happy moment, when she and Jake could share in the wonder and discuss each one of them. Instead he walked straight ahead as if he saw nothing but red. The minute Grace had seen SBC on the invitation, she should have booked the next flight home.

"Jake, are you going to stop?" She had to say it again, but Jake finally stopped. "Thank you." So much for telling him everything right now. And this probably wasn't the time to point out that he was the one who had invited Carrie Ann to the Sagrada Família. He was right. They needed to get back to having a proper holiday. "Why don't we shoot some video at the park like you said?"

"So where are we leaving this? Is she coming to Nashville with us?"

"I'm working on that. Right now she doesn't want to be alone. But she's also the type of woman who always has to have a man. I thought maybe we should let Jean Sebastian come dancing tonight."

"No. Definitely not."

"He travels for a living, Jake."

"Good for him."

"If he and Carrie Ann hit it off, they might just ride off into the sunset together."

"And if they don't?"

"Look. She was family. Once. What if I tell her I didn't mean it and something horrible happens? I don't think I could live with that." Not again. Once was certainly enough for a lifetime.

"You're going to have to tell your parents."

"I realize this." Jake looked off into the distance. "Are you mad at me?"

Jake looked at her. It only took a few seconds for his face to soften. He shook his head and then pulled her in to him and wrapped his arms around her. He kissed the top of her head.

"You have a big heart; I have a big penis. Neither of us can help that."

Grace laughed. Jake's eyes sparkled. She kissed him. "Thank you."

"For what? Having a big—"

"For everything. And if Carrie Ann does come to Nashville it won't be for long. I promise."

Jake touched her cheek. "Okay. But if I find out she's been playing us—playing you—she's gone. I promise that."

"I'll kick her out myself," Grace said.

CHAPTER 19

Jake and Grace held hands as they walked around the Gothic Quarter. They tilted their heads back and stared up at the old cathedrals, posed with statues, and took in the fountain at Plaza Catalunya before strolling along Passeig de Gràcia. Finally they arrived at Parc de la Ciutadella in the Ribera district. Barcelona's "Central Park" was an oasis in the middle of the city. A passerby told them the park contained a zoo, a lake, several museums, and a large fountain. The fountain, or as they learned, the Cascada, was easy to spot. Loosely based on the Trevi Fountain in Rome, it had both a raised and lowered part, each marked by their own statues, and a waterfall. The upper part boasted a triumphal arch, complete with a chariot and four horses. The lower portion was guarded by a large winged dragon. It was done in Baroque style, and the architects, Josep Fontserè and Elies Rogent, had been helped by a young student Gaudí. It was thrilling for Grace to see it in person after reading about it in her guidebook.

Grace loved statues. Every city should have them. Large

winged dragons and rearing horses. Patches of green grass and flowering trees. They found the giant elephant statues, and Grace sat on the tusks as Jake filmed. Then she took the camera and filmed Jake on the tusks. At least with this cheap camera he wasn't so afraid of her touching it, and he was way more re laxed. She loved the walkways and arches, and the palm trees that hung out in the periphery, offering shade to nearby benches. Jake and Grace went back to the fountain, where they recorded a video for her parents. Grace knew she sounded stiff again, and she was downright lying by not mentioning Carrie Ann, but this time Jake didn't even try to direct, nor did he comment on her obvious omission. They were now partners in crime.

"Let's get gelato and go back to the room," Jake said, nuzzling her neck. It was starting to resemble the holiday they were meant to have.

The gelato did not disappoint. There were so many flavors and stands offering it in Barcelona, it might as well have been considered a national pastime. Back in the room, Grace and Jake eagerly fell into bed. Grace reached for him. He was as soft as the gelato. This was not like Jake.

"I'm sorry," he said.

"It's okay."

Jake removed her hand, sat up, ran his fingers through his hair. "I'm pretty stressed. It's normal."

Grace snuggled up and kissed his neck. "I don't care about that. I just wish you weren't stressed."

"I just keep seeing her face."

"Carrie Ann? Gee, thanks." Grace pulled her knees up to her chest and scooted to the headboard. She wrapped her hands around her knees.

"Don't cocoon on me. I didn't mean it like that. If I meant it in a sexual way—don't you think Mr. Rogers here would be standing at attention?"

"Mr. Rogers?" Despite herself, Grace burst out in laughter. "Is it a beautiful day in the neighborhood?"

"I don't know why I called him that."

"Should I buy him a sweater for Christmas?"

"All right, you." Jake laughed. "No wonder he's soft. Sorry, buddy. You're not Mr. Rogers. You're The Rock."

I wish, Grace thought. It must be hard to be a guy. "I can't believe she's only been here a few days and she's already ruining our sex life."

"Ouch," Jake said. "One incident and our entire sex life is ruined?"

"Of course not, sweetie. But Carrie Ann is the black cat of luck."

"Don't let her get to you."

"My parents thought I was too easily manipulated by Carrie Ann," Grace said. "She had—almost a kind of spell over me, I guess. In a way I thought my sole purpose in life was to be the one person who would love Carrie Ann no matter what."

"I agree with your parents. That she's a master manipulator."

"But she's also had a horrible life, Jake. You should have seen her the first day. Standing in our doorway with her little flowered suitcase. Looking lost, and so alone, and yet tough at the same time. I'll never forget that image."

"But you guys took her in. Gave her a home."

"We tried."

"What happened?"

"Carrie Ann started to get jealous if I spent time with anyone else. Little by little I gave up my other friends. Quit swim class. Stopped pretty much everything but hanging out in my tree house with Carrie Ann. It really wasn't healthy. Heck, she was even jealous of Brady."

"Your cat?"

"Yes. I loved that cat."

"I remember. Brady, you told me about."

"Once Carrie Ann realized how much I loved Brady, she seemed to hate him. I think she was even glad when he died."

"Ouch."

"Anyway. It was just the two of us. Except for Stan." Stan was always right there, but Grace usually filtered him out. She wasn't proud of it, but it was almost as if Stan had become part of the scenery. Sometimes Grace thought that the only reason Carrie Ann had wanted him around was because Grace did not.

"Just don't tell me you lost your virginity to Stan." Jake got out of bed, picked up his boxers from the floor, and pulled them on. Then he crawled back in bed.

"What? No. God, no." Grace shuddered at the thought. "A couple of days after Brady died—" An unpleasant image rose in her mind. Brady, lying on their front step, neck lolled to the side, eyes glassy and staring up at the sky. "Was when my mother—"

A loud clang reverberated through the room. It sounded like a thousand cymbals had come crashing down. It came from the direction of the window. Grace started. Jake sprang out of bed. "What the fuck?" He headed for the window. Grace scrambled out of bed, picked her sundress up off the floor, and hastily put it on. "Someone's out there," he said. "Jesus." Grace caught a glimpse of a large, black wing. "Jesus. What is that?" The creature seemed to now be climbing up the trellis.

"The demented eagle from the street," Grace said.

"Again?" Jake said. "He was out on the ledge yesterday too." A window creaked from somewhere above them, and then a thud shook the chandelier in the kitchen. They looked to the ceiling. "Do you think he was trying to come in *our* window?"

"Oh my God," Grace said. "It's the hairy guy." What did Stefano say his name was? "From the beach with Carrie Ann. The hairy guy is the demented eagle."

"When did we see Carrie Ann at the beach?"

"I forgot to tell you. That woman who bumped into me, and I said she liked you and you said she liked me?"

"Carrie Ann?" Jake said.

"Yep."

"And yet another thing you didn't tell me."

"I forgot. I swear. I just forgot." Jake headed for the door. "You're in your boxers," Grace pointed out.

"He's in an eagle costume," Jake said.

"Good point," Grace said. She scrambled after Jake, who was

already halfway up the stairs. By the time Grace caught up, Jake was already knocking on Carrie Ann's door. Rafael. That was it. "Rafael?" Grace called out. Jake looked at her.

"Stefano told me his name," she said.

"Who's Stefano?"

"The doorman who doesn't open any doors." Jake looked as if he wanted to hear more about it, but turned his attention back to the door. He put his ear against it slightly. All was quiet. Grace imagined Rafael standing still in the middle of his apartment, waiting them out.

"He stands like a statue for a living," Grace whispered. "He's going to win this game."

"Say something else," Jake said. He pressed his ear closer to the door.

"Rafael? It's Grace. Carrie Ann's friend? We've been wanting to meet you. Thank you for letting us stay here." Grace paused. There was some shuffling from within the apartment.

"I thought we were going to confront him about breaking in," Jake whispered.

"I think Carrie Ann put him up to this," Grace whispered back. "You catch more flies with honey."

"Probably. But who the hell wants to catch flies?" Grace gave Jake a look. He shrugged, then gestured for her to keep going. "Anyway, Carrie Ann said she wanted us all to go out for drinks and dinner and dancing tonight. So we just wanted to say hello." More shuffling and definite sounds of footsteps coming toward the door. Grace pulled Jake back just in time for the door to swing open. Rafael stood in jeans and nothing else. Grace had never seen so much hair on anyone's chest in her life. But it didn't seem to bother him a bit. A long, black feather stuck to his bicep.

"*Hola,*" he said with a grin inappropriate for someone who had just been caught trying to sneak in through their window. "Did you say drinks and dancing?" He grinned, mimed taking a drink, and then gyrated his hips. The feather didn't budge. "My club," he said. "We go to my club."

* * *

There was a line at Rafael's dance club by the ocean. It was far away from La Rambla and totally secluded. Grace supposed that was ideal for a club; they could blast their music as loud as they wanted—no neighbors to complain. Rafael said he was part owner along with three other street performers. He said they had gone in on the investment in order to support the dream. Grace had thought that the street performing was what they were doing to reach the dream. Turned out it was the dream. There was something sad and beautiful about that.

From the looks of the crowd waiting to get in, the club was a good investment. It was a white squat building, winding around in a Z shape, with two levels and various dance rooms with the side facing the ocean wide-open. The sun was just starting to set. Carrie Ann had taken so long getting ready that when they headed out at ten p.m., they decided to skip dinner and go right to the drinking and dancing.

When Carrie Ann had heard about the change in plans, she had thrown a fit.

"Rafael's club? You invited Rafael?"

Carrie Ann was at it again, acting dramatic. It was as if she were terrified of Rafael. "You invited Jean Sebastian," Grace had said.

So far Grace had made a point of not looking at Jean Sebastian or talking to him beyond saying hello. He looked hot in his jeans and blue dress shirt. It was aqua, and it made his light brown eyes seem almost blue. "She brought him to cause trouble," Jake whispered in Grace's ear.

"Please," Grace whispered back. "Let's just have fun tonight." They needed it. Who cared anymore what Carrie Ann did or didn't do? They needed to let loose and just enjoy themselves. Grace was the last one up to the bouncer. He held out his hand for her ID while eyeing a younger girl in the line. Grace reached in her purse and handed him her license. He glanced at it, then glanced at Grace.

"*Entre*," he said.

"*Gracias*," Grace said. He frowned, and she quickly moved

on. *"Grassy-ass,"* her dad had said before she left. *Isn't that what they all say in Spain?*

The minute they were in the door, Carrie Ann grabbed Grace's arm and squealed. "I knew it!" she said. "I told you!"

"What?" Grace said. The men immediately wanted to make their way to the bar. Jake touched Grace's arm. They looked at each other, and she nodded. He was asking if she wanted her usual. She loved how well he knew her.

"Actually we should all get sangrias," Rafael said. "The sangria is the bomb. It's dance club–style, *mis amigos*—with a little zing."

"I'm in," Carrie Ann said. "I do like to zing."

"Might as well try new things," Grace said to Jake. He nodded and headed off with the boys. "You told me what?" Grace said the minute he was gone.

"That we could pass for each other. And you're not even a blonde or wearing high heels."

As usual, Grace had no idea what Carrie Ann was talking about. And, also as usual, she wasn't sure she wanted to know.

"Take out your ID," Carrie Ann said. They'd already been through this once, but Grace sighed and took out her driver's license. She held it out to Carrie Ann. "Look at it, silly." Carrie Ann turned her hand around. Grace looked at the ID. It wasn't hers. Grace read the name in disbelief. Carrie Ann Gilbert. Her blond hair, her smile.

"What?" Grace was flummoxed. She dug through her purse. She had showed the bouncer Carrie Ann's ID? She remembered now, finding it in her purse with the diamond ring. But she had showed the bouncer the ID from her wallet, which should have been hers. "Where's my ID?"

"I left it back in the apartment." Carrie Ann grinned like she was expecting some kind of medal.

"You went in my purse?"

"I switched them right in front of you. I wanted to see if I could still do magic."

"What else did you do?"

"What do you mean?"

"I don't know. Your hands were in my purse. Did you switch or take anything else?"

"It was a joke. Don't be this way. I totally forgot I'd done it until I saw the bouncer asking for ID. But I was right. You got away with it."

"Because bouncers don't give a shit about ID—"

"Why are you so worked up? It was just a little joke."

"The way you texted me from Jake's phone the other day?"

"What?"

"He told me he was at your apartment. And we both received texts that we didn't send."

"I didn't—"

"This is why people don't trust you."

"People? Or you?" Carrie Ann's eyes were huge and lit with anger. Jake approached carrying two humongous sangrias. "Just in time," Carrie Ann said, taking the glasses from him and offering one to Grace as if she were the one who had just purchased them.

"Thank you," Grace said to Jake. Jean Sebastian and Rafael brought up the rear, each carrying two drinks.

"It's a special," Rafael said at their looks. "Two for price of one."

"Let's find a table," Jean Sebastian said. They pushed through the writhing bodies and headed for the second story, where they commandeered a table that looked down onto the dance floor. It was just as crowded upstairs as it was on the dance floor, and there were only two seats available. The men all let Grace and Carrie Ann sit down. Carrie Ann twirled her straw in the drink, then looked at Jake.

"I hear you thought I took your cell phone the other day," she said.

"Carrie Ann," Grace said. "This is between you and me."

"I didn't take your cell phone. I didn't send texts as if they were from you."

"Let's forget about it," Grace said.

"Well, somebody did," Jake said. "And it was while I was with you."

"The two of you are perfect for each other. Paranoid thing

one, and paranoid thing two," Carrie Ann said. "Did it ever occur to you, Grace, that Jake was lying to you?"

"No," Grace said. "Of course not."

"Of course not," Carrie Ann mimicked. She turned to Jake. "Have you ever lied to Grace?"

"No," Jake said.

"Give me a break," Carrie Ann said. "You lied about being in my apartment."

"And then I told her the truth," Jake said.

"So it's okay to lie, as long as you follow it up with the truth?"

"Jake lied because you guys were planning to surprise me for my birthday," Grace said. "That's a different kind of lie."

"So lying is a matter of degrees," Carrie Ann said.

"I don't want to have this conversation," Grace said.

"You should," Carrie Ann said. "It's important."

"I can't seem to drink this fast enough," Grace said.

"We know you've lied, Gracie. Your parents took in *only boys*. Your mother sent those letters back. Have you read them yet?"

Of the two of us, you're the pathological liar. Your lies destroy lives. All Grace had to do was finish the drink, and she'd finally be able to speak her mind. "I haven't had time," Grace said.

"You should have made time," Carrie Ann said.

Jake leaned down and whispered in Grace's ear, "I don't want to stay."

"Me neither," Grace whispered back. "Let's finish these, dance to a few songs, and slip out." Jake nodded.

"Why don't you boys find a place to hang. We'll hit the dance floor soon," Carrie Ann said. She was smiling again, as if she hadn't just started a big fight.

None of the guys needed any convincing, and they went to lean against a wall not far away. Grace was glad Rafael was here to keep Jake company—as strange as she had thought he was at first, he was actually kind of nice and funny. Not to mention they were staying in his parents' apartment for free.

"Speaking of Rafael," Grace said, as if she'd been thinking out loud, "do you have any idea why we caught him trying to sneak in our window?" Grace also thought of the way he had stared at her when he had seen her at the outdoor café that morning. Grace realized now that couldn't have been a coincidence. Carrie Ann had had her little spies out and about.

"It's all part of his eagle act," Carrie Ann said. "He wasn't trying to sneak in your window; he just walks along the edge."

"He also took my picture my first morning here," Grace said.

"Look," Carrie Ann said. "You won't have to worry about him much longer."

"What does that mean?"

Carrie Ann didn't answer; she was surveying the room. Her eyes landed on Jean Sebastian. From the way she was looking at him, she had a little crush on him herself. Grace told herself it didn't bother her in the least. She wanted the two of them to get together.

"Why won't we have to worry about Rafael much longer?" Grace asked again.

"God. Can we stop talking about this? I just want one night of fun."

Grace held herself back. Carrie Ann was the one who had started it. But the truth was, Grace just wanted to have fun too. And the sangria was finally working. Grace suddenly had a very nice buzz. Carrie Ann was checking out Jean Sebastian again.

"I think Jake is jealous of Jean Sebastian," Carrie Ann said. "That should spice things up."

Grace squirmed. "We don't need spicing up. I hope you brought Jean Sebastian here for you and not to cause problems in my relationship."

"Relax. My God." Carrie Ann took Grace's hands. She pulled her up and the two hurried down the steps to the dance floor. Grace couldn't believe how good it felt to just let go, move her body to the music. When Rafael came by with two drinks and handed her another one, she didn't even hesitate. She took it and winked at him. He grinned and handed the other drink to Carrie Ann. Grace wasn't going to let a single serious thought enter her head for the rest of the night. They had the ocean, and a DJ playing great music, and sangria. They were in Barcelona, baby! By this time the boys had wandered downstairs too, and

Grace found Jake, pulled him out for a dance, and kissed him as passionately as she could. When Jake tried to maneuver her into the hallway for more kissing, she laughed and pushed him away and took Carrie Ann's hand, and pulled her out to the dance floor.

"My God, what is in those sangrias?" she said as she twirled around. She wasn't sure if she was spinning or if it was the room.

An memory instantly assailed her. Twirling in the rain just three days after Carrie Ann had come to live with them. Grace had twirled, while Carrie Ann had stood just a foot away, staring, bangs sticking to her forehead with each drop of water. Carrie Ann had never twirled, had never felt enough of the joy required to make the movement, at least that's how Grace had interpreted it later. At the time she had wondered why her twirling seemed to be making Carrie Ann angry. At least Carrie Ann was twirling now, commanding the dance floor in a little black dress, blond hair whipping behind her, a smile plastered on her face. *See,* Grace thought. *We've made it. We came through. Through the fights, through Lionel's death, through the lies. Right here, right now, we are happy. I am happy. Carrie Ann is happy.*

Jean Sebastian and Carrie Ann had been staring at each other all night. Maybe the two would go off together after all.

"Another drink!" Carrie Ann said, pulling Grace toward the bar in the middle of a song she liked.

"No," Grace said. "Three is enough for me." Where were Jake, and Rafael, and Jean Sebastian? Grace looked around, but it was too crowded. There were so many people. The lights were pulsing and bright. And then, as if out of nowhere, Jake appeared in front of her. He was smiling. She smiled back. They were both feeling good. She didn't remember him wearing that shirt. She wanted to ask him about it, but her tongue felt a little swollen. He wrapped her arms around his waist, pulled her in to him, and kissed her.

Oh, God, what a kiss. She felt brazen, and a little bit like an exhibitionist. She held him as tight as she could and kissed him with abandon. It felt exciting and new. She didn't stop his hands when they brushed over her breasts and her ass. She was in Spain; she could let her hair down a little.

He pulled away and gazed at her lovingly. "I'll be right back." Grace could only smile as he disappeared again. She felt so good one second, and so bad the next. She was lost in bodies, strangers' bodies everywhere she turned. Her chest began to constrict a little. She suddenly wanted nothing more than to be in bed with Jake, listening to each other breathe.

"One more," Rafael said, popping up next to her with a drink. Grace shook her head. He thrust it at her, and she pushed back on his arm. Carrie Ann stepped in and put her hand on the side of Grace's face. "Are you okay?"

"I need to lie down," Grace said. When did everything start spinning? "Where's Jake?"

"Lean on me. I've got you."

"I feel funny. Do you feel funny?"

"No, Grace. I feel wonderful."

Grace's head pulsed. Something was wrong. Somebody had put something in her drink. She knew it. "Jake," she screamed while she still had the voice to do it. It was too loud in the club.

"I've got you," Carrie Ann said again. "Shit," Grace heard her say. That wasn't good, Grace thought. Carrie Ann sounded worried. She was the queen of not worrying. From somewhere she heard a phone ring. She thought she heard Carrie Ann say, "Oh my God. It's Stan." Or did she say, "Oh my God—this isn't part of the plan"? Or both? Grace wanted to laugh, but she was feeling too sick. Carrie Ann still had one arm around Grace's waist. Grace felt fuzz behind her eyes. Seriously? Did Carrie Ann just say plan—or Stan?

"I don't want to see him," Grace said. "I don't like Stan. I *never* liked Stan." Thick, soft fuzz surrounded her. And then she dove into it.

CHAPTER 20

A dark presence hovered in Grace's peripheral vision. The next thing she knew a mass of black ribbons descended on her, completely covering her and obscuring her vision. Was she at a car wash? She hadn't brought her car to Spain, had she? Was she home? Did she dream Spain? No. She was sitting in the middle of La Rambla. "Rafael, quit it." Instead of going away, the thing danced on its stilts. Grace scooted her chair back, and the thing, for she wasn't sure it was Rafael after all, stepped forward. Long black ribbons brushed against her thighs.

"Please go," Grace said. "I don't have any change." It was a lie; she had change, but she was not going to reward this thing for scaring her like this.

"I'm not scared." But she was—scared silly. Grace stood, sending her chair clanking to the ground behind her. She looked around for a waiter. There was no one. No one but the creature, dancing on stilts.

Grace turned and ran. Clack, clack, clack, the thing behind her could run too, even on stilts.

"Hey," Grace yelled. Help. Grace could feel it directly behind her, but before she could whirl around and give it a shove, it slammed into her back, sending her hurtling to the pavement. Palms out, Grace landed, her hands scraped and stinging, her breath knocked out of her as the thing lay on her back. Grace began to scream. The thing on her back began to laugh. Grace rolled to her side, struggling to right herself. The thing leaned down; its face was one inch away from her face. Its black-rimmed eyes stared into hers; its large red mouth opened in a grin. Screaming, Grace reached up and ripped off the mask. Blond hair fell over her face. Red lips grinned at her. Carrie Ann. Grace shrieked even more. Carrie Ann laughed, loud and long, her head tilted back, her blond hair glowing in the Spanish sun.

"I hate you!" Grace yelled. "I hate you!" Something jarred; the scene shifted. Grace wasn't lying on La Rambla with Carrie Ann on top of her. It was a dream. But now she was awake, or at least she thought she was, and she was lying down on something cold and hard. The ground. And although she couldn't be sure, it felt as if something was on top of her. But she couldn't move. She'd had this condition before. Where her mind would wake up before her body. She was paralyzed. Panicking would make it worse. She would have to relax, fall back to sleep, and wake naturally. Hard to do when you had this awful feeling you were lying on the cold, hard ground somewhere. Where was everyone? What had happened? Grace remembered dancing. She remembered a club by the ocean. Carrie Ann. Jake. Jean Sebastian. Rafael. Where were they? She wanted to scream. Panic flooded her. Her mind raced, but her body remained cold and very, very still.

CHAPTER 21

Grace lifted her head. Images, rather than thoughts, swam before her eyes. Cold, hard, white, gray. She was on a cold, hard floor. Saw a sink and a mirror, then the toilet. A bathroom floor. Passed out. Lovely. As bathrooms went, it was small and dank, and lit by a single bulb emitting a slight buzzing sound. Graffiti was sprayed on the walls. Musings in Spanish and a few choice drawings. Penis and breasts, the usual public restroom fare. The club. Was she in the club? She slowly lifted herself into a sitting position. Her head thumped something awful. She immediately wanted to cry. Homesickness, deeper than she'd ever felt in her life, hit her in the gut. She wanted to be back in her living room, with Stella at her feet and Jake whistling in the kitchen as he made coffee.

She had a stark feeling of terror as she got to her feet and looked in the mirror. Her dance club outfit. Blue dress. Her hair, previously straightened, was frizzed out. Her mascara ran underneath her eyes, giving her the raccoon look. She felt nauseous, and waited a moment to see if she was going to throw up, but it seemed to pass. She turned on the faucet and splashed cold water over her face. Besides the buzzing, there was silence. Why couldn't she hear the music from the dance floor? How long had she been here? Where was Jake?

She reached for the door. It was locked. Panic joined hands with the thudding in her head. "Hello?" She rattled the door. "Hello?" She pounded on the door. "Hey. I'm locked in. Open!" How did you say *open* in Spanish? She tried to dredge up ancient lessons from *Sesame Street,* but all she could hear was *agua, agua, agua.* Shit. She knew they had taught *open* on one of those episodes. Open sesame.

Jake would never have left her here. The thought slammed into her. If she was here alone, then something was wrong with Jake. Was he also passed out in the club? She had been drugged; she knew that for sure. She remembered the fuzzy feeling in her head. Carrie Ann. *This wasn't part of the plan.* Oh, God. What plan? Did this have something to do with Stan?

Grace had to get out of this freaking bathroom and find out where everyone else was. So much for staying calm. Sometimes you just had to panic. She hurled herself against the door and screamed. "Open. Help! Help! Help!" She yelled until the back of her throat burned. Okay, okay. *The club is obviously closed, Grace.* And nobody had noticed a girl passed out on the floor. Didn't they have security and cleaning personnel? Not a very nice thing to do to an American tourist. She wasn't even in the stall; she had been sprawled out in front of the sink. Unless she'd somehow moved in the middle of the night. Regardless, they should check the stalls too. Rafael had said he was part owner. Maybe they'd all stayed late. The owners probably let their friends stay after-hours all the time. For all Grace knew, maybe people were always passing out in the bathroom and in Europe it was just considered a successful night out. Grace slid back down the wall and crumpled on the floor. She was exhausted.

Jake. Please be okay, Jake. Please, God, let him be okay. This was all her fault. Well, she'd learned her lesson. As soon as she found Jake, they were out of here. Sans Carrie Ann. And this time Grace didn't care how much it hurt Carrie Ann's feelings. *Way to go, Grace. It only took being drugged and abandoned in a public bathroom to stick up for yourself.*

"Grace?" It was a male voice. But it didn't sound like Jake. Grace got up a little too quickly, and her knees buckled.

"Help," she said.

"Hold on." She heard a wrenching noise, and the door opened. Grace put her hand on the sink to help herself up.

"I've got you." Hands gripped her underneath her armpits and helped her up. It was Jean Sebastian. He too was wearing the same clothes from last night and also looked as if he'd been through the wringer. When she was upright, his hands fell to her waist. He kept them there and looked at her with concern. "Are you okay?"

"My head."

"Mine too."

"We were drugged?"

"I woke up in the middle of the dance floor. I only had one drink."

"I was locked in," Grace said.

Jean Sebastian pointed to a chair lying sideways on the floor. "Somebody propped it under the doorknob."

Not a chance of its being an accident. "Jake? Where's Jake?" Grace gently pulled away from Jean Sebastian and headed out of the bathroom. Her head swam. She reached out to steady herself. Jean Sebastian was right there, offering his arm.

"Easy, easy. The others aren't here."

"Jake wouldn't leave me." The club was dim. Only a little light was streaming in from a skylight. The side that had been open to the ocean last night was now walled and gated. It was impossible to tell what time it was. Grace spotted a familiar black shape on top of the bar. "My purse?" She approached it, almost not believing it. She reached for it. It felt just as heavy as before. She went through it. Her wallet, with Carrie Ann's ID. Carrie Ann's engagement ring. The keys to the apartment. No cell phone. The cash she had left. Someone had left the ring and the cash, but had taken her cell phone? Someone who didn't want her calling anyone.

"Is everything there?"

"My phone is gone."

Jean Sebastian felt his pockets. "Mine too. And my wallet. Your wallet is there?"

"Even my money." She had seventy euro in her purse. "We have to search this entire place. Carrie Ann, Jake, Rafael. They have to be here. The men's room?"

"I've been in there. Empty," Jean Sebastian said.

"You look down here. Yell if you find anyone or a phone. I'll search upstairs."

"You're not too steady on your feet," Jean Sebastian said. "Why don't I go up and you look down here?"

Grace nodded. "Please. Find Jake." Grace looked behind the bar. No phone. The cash register was locked tight. Once again she wondered how in the world the employees had left at least two of them in here unnoticed. And Jean Sebastian had said he woke up in the middle of the dance floor. It didn't seem possible that anyone could miss that. "Jake?" she called. "Carrie Ann? Rafael?" She heard Jean Sebastian call out the names upstairs. In less than ten minutes she had searched every nook and cranny. There was nobody here. Jean Sebastian came downstairs with the same news.

"We have to find an exit," Grace said. "Maybe somehow they're back at the apartment." Jake would be out of his mind with worry. And he certainly wouldn't like her being locked in here with Jean Sebastian, but now wasn't the time to worry about that.

"There's a window upstairs. It opens. But we have to walk a pretty tight ledge and jump onto the first floor balcony, and then to the ground."

"You're joking, right?"

"The rest of the place is locked and chained. Our only other option is to wait until this evening. I don't think they open until after seven p.m."

"We can't wait that long. I have to find Jake."

"Come on. I'll show you." Grace followed Jean Sebastian up the stairs. She couldn't believe she was contemplating skirting a ledge and jumping onto a balcony. That was for the movies, not real life. But there was no way she was going to stay cooped up here until seven p.m. while Jake was God knows where. Maybe the others were passed out on the grounds just outside.

Grace looked out the window that Jean Sebastian had managed to open. She was relieved to see that the building wasn't that high at all. Even if she fell, it meant breaking an ankle, not plunging to her death. Still, she had a feeling she was going to need her ankles intact. "Let's just yell for help," Grace said.

"Go ahead," Jean Sebastian said. "Although I doubt anyone will hear you but the seagulls." Grace stuck her head out and yelled for help. She could hear her voice echo in the morning air.

"Hello?" Jean Sebastian yelled. "Anybody there?" After a few more attempts, Grace resigned herself to what had to be done. She wondered what Marsh Everett would think of her now. Climbing out on ledges in Spain. She'd have to write about this one day. Use it all for her art. What a crock of shit. Whoever came up with that deserved to be beaten. If Jake were here right now, he'd know she was on the verge of composing in her head. It was the thought of finding him that made her climb out the window and stand on the ledge. It was about three inches wide, and she'd have to scoot along the wall about six feet. She was petite, and as long as she didn't look down, or panic, it was within the realm of possibility. Jean Sebastian was right beside her. "Don't stop," he said. "Don't think."

"But where are we going?"

"When you get to the edge, you'll see. Right below is a first-floor little balcony. I was out for a smoke on it last night."

"I didn't know you smoked."

"Once in a while. When I drink. I hope you are not choosing this moment to lecture me."

"Definitely not." Grace's heart was pounding. She was in danger of hyperventilating. Jean Sebastian was right. Nike was right. Just do it. She scooted a little to the left.

"That's it."

"It's not that high."

"Two stories."

"Even if I fell, I'd probably just break my ankle."

"As long as you protect your head and neck." Great. She shouldn't have opened her mouth. She felt frozen with panic. "You're right; you're right," Jean Sebastian said. "You would only sprain an ankle."

"I can't do it. I can't move."

"You're a singer, right?"

"Yes. But it's hardly the time for a concert."

"It's a perfect time. You sing, and you move. You sing, and you move."

"What do you want me to sing?"

"Whatever song you like. Whatever makes you feel good."

See, Marsh Everett. See? Grace glanced out. The sun was low on the ocean. It was a beautiful and peaceful morning. Where were the locals? Why couldn't somebody be out walking his or her dog? They could call the fire department and bring ladders. But the club was out of the way, probably so they could party as loud and as long as they wanted. Grace picked a popular country song; she wasn't going to sing one of her own right now—a critique was the last thing she could take at the moment.

"Take your cat and leave my sweater"—Grace scooted a few more inches than the last time. "We've got nothing left to weather"—scoot, scoot.

"I thought it was take your cap," Jean Sebastian said.

"That's a common misconception," Grace said. Scoot, scoot, scoot. "It's definitely cat."

"Take your cat and leave my sweater," Jean Sebastian said.

It sounded funny in his accent. Grace laughed. Then she was in danger of getting the giggles. When Grace got the giggles, her whole body shook. It used to happen all the time with Carrie Ann. One of Carrie Ann's favorite pastimes back then had been giving Grace the giggles in all the wrong places, like church. She needed to think of something serious. Lionel Gale.

184 • *Mary Carter*

She saw him dangling from the noose in the barn. His black leather shoes were level with her eyes. Shining from a recent coat of polish. Before he had crawled up to the hayloft, attached the rope from Stan's tire swing to the rafters, and slipped the noose around his neck, he had polished his shoes. Just thinking about it made Grace cry out.

"Easy, easy," Jean Sebastian said.

She was going to have a breakdown. Calm down. *Calm down. Sing a few bars of the song you wrote for Stan. You won't crack up. Singing does help you calm down. Just do it. Jean Sebastian won't know.* Grace took a deep breath.

"It was a Tuesday night, he was a working man, he had a son named Stan." It was strange at first to hear her own singing voice. God, she'd kind of missed it. Grace scooted and scooted and scooted. "She was a foster child, she was a girl gone wild, her name was Carrie Ann." Grace was focused and calm. "We shared my tree house, she was a friend in need, but not a friend in deed." She stopped.

"Keep going," Jean Sebastian said. "Keep singing." He sounded strained. Grace needed to listen to him. She needed to shut out everything else and just sing.

> *Stan had a tire swing,*
> *He liked everything,*
> *He was a boy with hope*
> *His feet could touch the sky,*
> *He could really fly*
> *It was a long, thick rope. . . .*

Finally she was at the edge.

"That song," Jean Sebastian said. "You wrote it?"

"Yes."

"It's beautiful. Sounds sad."

You have no idea. "I've never sung it for anyone."

"Why not?"

"It's personal."

"I want to hear the rest sometime."

"Now what?" Grace said.

"The balcony is just around the corner. You'll have to scoot, then either bend down, or just jump. From there, it's only another short jump to the ground."

"Oh, God."

"Don't think, just sing and go."

"It was a Tuesday night, he was a working man, he had a son named Stan." Grace stepped out farther and planted her foot. She rounded the corner and lost her balance. Jean Sebastian's arm was on her chest in an instant, and he held her back against the building. She could feel his arm atop her breasts, and she could feel her heart beating against his forearm like a one-woman drum circle.

"Easy," Jean Sebastian said. "Easy." He sounded so in control. It dawned on her that his experience in the Congo had probably prepared him for much worse than this. "If you stay still, I think I can make it around you. I'll jump onto the balcony first and then I'm there to catch you. Okay?"

"Okay." Grace hated that she was so afraid. But she was immobile again, and no amount of singing was going to help this time.

"Don't move."

No problema, she thought, but she couldn't even say the words. She pressed her back hard against the building. Jean Sebastian scooted close to her. He put one hand on either side of her, one foot on either side of her feet. They were face-to-face, close enough to kiss, and she had the most inappropriate urge to do just that. Jake would not like this one bit. Jean Sebastian scooted his left hand out farther, then brought his right to her other side and finally swung his last foot over. He was now on the other side of her. From there he jumped. She heard a bang as he landed on a chair on the balcony and knocked over a cigarette bucket that clanged to the ground. He landed with the chair on top of him and his top leg bent.

"Are you okay?"

"Un momento." Jean Sebastian moaned and held his leg. He thrashed out and kicked the cigarette bucket away. "Maybe I will quit," he said, flicking butts off him. "Fuckers." Grace guessed the word worked no matter what your native language was. She wondered what the Belgian word for fuckers was. Jean Sebastian soon righted himself. He held out his arms. "Nothing broken." He moved close to the edge and kept his arms open. "I'll catch you. I promise."

He was tall. And seemed pretty sturdy.

"Can you move the chair? And get rid of the cigarettes?"

"You're pretty picky for a damsel in distress."

"Sorry."

Jean Sebastian shook his head and smiled, but moved the chair and kicked cigarettes out of the way. "Good?"

"Better."

"Jump."

"Oh, God."

"I've got you." Grace jumped. Jean Sebastian's arms wrapped around her, but the force of her coming into him sent him stumbling back a few steps. Their bodies slammed into the rail of the balcony, and for a moment Grace was sure they were going over. Jean Sebastian was definitely in a back bend. If the railing gave, they wouldn't even have time to protect their heads and necks. Jean Sebastian grunted, then curled forward, and the two of them hit the deck of the balcony with a thud. Grace felt all the air go out of her lungs as Jean Sebastian fell on top of her. This was the moment when being petite certainly didn't help. "Sorry, sorry." Jean Sebastian immediately removed himself from her. "Are you all right?"

"I'm okay."

"You can talk. Good. Means you can breathe."

We're setting the bar pretty low here, aren't we? Jean Sebastian held out his hand. Grace took it, and he hauled her up. They looked over the balcony rail. It was still a good six-foot drop. Jean Sebastian was already lowering himself over the edge. Maybe compared to the Congo, this was like recess. He hung for a minute and then dropped. He landed on his feet. Stan used to drop out of the tree house like that. Funny how seeing Carrie Ann was bringing back all these memories, a tidal wave of little moments.

"Your turn," Jean Sebastian said. "I'll catch you if I can."

"Catch me if you can," said the Belgian man. She really was a girl out of Nashville.

CHAPTER 22

Grace couldn't get to the apartment fast enough. She and Jean Sebastian walked for a short while and then encountered a taxi-cab driver snoozing in his car on the side of the road. They startled him by pounding on the window, but got a smile out of him when Grace flashed the cash. He was then as chipper as could be, as he raced around the streets of Barcelona toward La Rambla. He didn't even seem to notice that Grace didn't speak Spanish. Jean Sebastian knew enough to keep up a conversation, and after he told her they were discussing sports, she could not have cared less. The world could be ending and men would still be talking sports. She just wanted to get to the apartment and find Jake. She had this horrible feeling that he wasn't there. Again, there was no way he would have ever left her on a bathroom floor. If he too had been drugged, where did he end up? They were going to have to call the cops, but the apartment was the first step. The cops. Probably not the slang used for Spanish police. What a nightmare it was going to be, working with police from a different country. Would they care about a missing American tourist? Well, Grace would make them care. Oh, God. She was going to miss another call with her mother. This was just a nightmare. Her mom might be out of it, but her dad would probably catch on that something was wrong.

When the cab drew up as close as it could get, Grace threw the money at Jean Sebastian and started to run to the apartment.

"Wait," Jean Sebastian yelled. "I don't know where it is."

Right. Grace stopped, already breathing heavy, and waited for Jean Sebastian to catch up. Luckily, he was smart enough to make it fast. "Sorry."

"What if they're not there?" he said as they ran toward the building. They. He was worried about Carrie Ann too. Possibly Rafael. All she could think about was Jake. Was it wrong to blame Carrie Ann? She was just a magnet for trouble. Could Stan have pulled this off all by himself? She supposed it was easy enough to drug a bunch of drinks, but wouldn't he have needed help in getting the others wherever he had taken them? Wait. Hadn't Carrie Ann said something about Stan's being friends with Rafael? Her memory of last night was too fuzzy for Grace to be sure. If only she'd warned Jake! This is what she deserved for keeping things from him.

"These are nice," Jean Sebastian said as they went under the archway leading to the apartment building's entrance.

"Rafael's parents own it, I guess," Grace said.

"You guess?"

"Well, it's not like I've ever met them." *And I take everything Carrie Ann says with a boatload of salt.* Grace raced into the lobby. Stefano wasn't at the desk. Great. The one time he could actually be useful, and he was gone. Grace flew up the stairs, taking them two steps at a time. Her hands shook as she inserted the key and threw the door open. "Jake?" She was immediately hit by a feeling of stillness. Emptiness. "Jake." She tore through the place, looking for any signs that he'd at least come home after the club. As far as she remembered, things looked exactly the way they had when they'd left for the evening. Jake's comb and toothbrush were even in the same spot in the bathroom. He'd never made it home from the club. That reality was like a slap to the face. Where were they? What was happening to them?

"Anything?" Jean Sebastian stood in the doorway. Tears invading, Grace shook her head.

"Carrie Ann's apartment is directly above," Grace said. Jean Sebastian nodded and turned toward the stairs. Grace was about to follow when the computer began to ring. She stopped. Her mother. She turned to Jake's laptop, expecting to find it password protected as before. Instead, the screen was open and available. Had Jake been able to get in and remove the password requirement? She knew her mother would be anxious to hear from her. And Grace didn't want to miss out on a single conversation with her mother. Not a single one! She had to bite down hard on the side of her mouth to stop the flow of tears. She sat in the chair in front of the computer and answered the call.

"Gracie?" There was always a few-second delay until the picture came in. But she could tell just from her mother's voice that Jody was coherent. These rare times were little gifts. Actually getting to speak to her mother, the one that remembered.

"Hi, Mom. Hi there. How are you?"

"Oh honey, it's so good to hear your voice. Can you see me?"

"Not yet." And then the picture came in. Jody Sawyer was sitting up in her bed. Her hair looked like it had recently been done, and she was wearing makeup and a regular top. In other words, she had dressed up for this phone call. "There you are," Grace said. "Oh, Mom. You look beautiful."

"So do you, darling. Although you look a bit tired."

"We went to a dance club last night."

Jody clasped her hands together and opened her mouth in an O. "A dance club. I love it."

"It was really fun." *You know. Except for being drugged and left overnight on the bathroom floor and waking up to find that Jake has probably been kidnapped.* "It was right on the ocean." Grace could feel someone in the doorway. Jean Sebastian was standing there. Grace held her index finger up. "Can you hold one sec, Ma? There's a neighbor at the door."

"A neighbor," Jody said. "How intriguing."

"Hold on." Grace ran to the door. "Sorry—my mom."

"You have to talk now?" Jean Sebastian said.

"Yes. I have to. It's a long story." Grace glanced upstairs. "Anything?"

"I knocked. Over and over. No answer, and I couldn't hear anything coming from inside," Jean Sebastian said.

"Okay. You can sit at the counter, but don't make a peep, okay?" Jean Sebastian nodded. Grace went back to the call. "Sorry about that, Mom. So tell me how it's going."

"Oh, fair to middling. My tumor shrunk a little bit, honey. Isn't that great?"

"Oh my God. That's so great. And you're feeling better?"

"I think your adventure is reviving me. So tell me. What else have you lovebirds been doing?" Grace managed to tell her about Casa Batlló and Sagrada Família and the Miró Museum without giving away that anything was wrong. "Where's my future son-in-law?" Jody asked.

"He's actually out at the market," Grace said. "Getting a little something for our lunch."

"That sounds wonderful. Will you drink wine with it?"

"Oh, yes." *No. I'm never drinking ever again.*

"Hey, Graceful." Her father's head popped onto the screen.

"Hi, Dad."

"How's our traveler today?"

"I'm good, Dad."

"You look tired."

"She was out dancing, James. All night long. Remember when we used to do that?" It had been a long time since Grace had heard her mother call him James. Grace bit her lip to keep from crying.

"Did we ever do that?" Jody swatted Jim and smiled at Grace. *All the time,* she mouthed. Grace smiled.

"Have you seen Stella, Dad?"

192 • *Mary Carter*

"As a matter of fact, Dan brought her by just the other day."

Dan. It was partly his fault they were in this mess. Grace was going to strangle him when they got back. "How is she?"

"Feisty. She's a hoot on that skateboard."

"Cats don't skateboard," Jody said.

"Stella's a dog, Mom. Our bulldog."

"We don't have a dog," Jody said. She sounded irritated. "We had a cat, Brady."

"Yes, we had a cat. But that was a long time ago. I have a dog now." Grace knew better, but sometimes she just wanted to puncture that veneer of forgetting.

"Brady," Jody said. She looked at the camera. She looked frail and vulnerable. Then her face hardened; her lips pursed. "Carrie Ann strangled Brady," she said.

Grace heard the squeal of a chair behind her. Jean Sebastian had almost fallen off it. "What?" Grace said. "No. Brady just died. I found him on the steps."

"I found him on the steps," Jody said. "I had just enough time to remove the scarf wrapped around his poor neck before you saw him."

"Dad?" Grace said. This had to be her mother forgetting things again. "Dad?"

"That's when I knew Carrie Ann had to go," Jody said. "She strangled Brady. That's when she had to go."

"Dad?" Grace said.

"Gracie, let's not keep this conversation going," her father said. "You two just have a good time."

"Is she telling the truth?"

"Who are you?" Jody said.

"We'd better go," Jim said.

"Dad. Answer me. What about Brady?"

"We didn't have any proof, darling," Jim said. "But we had to play it safe. It was your pink scarf."

Grace's hand flew up to her mouth. "Couldn't it have been one of the boys?" she said.

"They weren't allowed in your room," Jim said.

"That didn't mean they wouldn't go in."

"It was just—the way Carrie Ann reacted when we told her Brady was dead. I can't explain it, honey. But I saw her eyes. She already knew. And she wasn't sorry. Not one bit. I'm telling you, sweetie, I think your mother was right about that girl."

"Oh my God. Oh my God."

"Honey, that was a long time ago, okay? The last person we need to ever think about is Carrie Ann."

"I'm sorry, Dad. I have to go."

"No problem, darling. Tell that handsome boy we said hello."

"I will." *As soon as I find him.* "Bye, Mom. I love you."

"Who are you?"

"Wait," Jim said. "Jake's mother called me."

"She did?"

"It seems her boy isn't as good at keeping in touch. She wanted me to tell you to give him a swift kick in the behind next time I talked to you. Make sure he calls his mama now, darling."

"No problem!" Grace and her father said their good-byes. Grace felt a pang as he disappeared from her computer screen. Oh, no. Just what she needed. Barbara Hart's getting a whiff of something wrong. That woman was an alarm-puller in the best of times. She had to find Jake ASAP.

"Is your mom okay?" Jean Sebastian said.

"She's fine," Grace said. She didn't want to talk about her mother with just anyone. Jean Sebastian kept his eyes on hers. "She has cancer," Grace said. "The doctors give her one to six months. Her memory comes and goes."

"I'm so sorry."

"Jake and I are supposed to be videotaping this trip, sending her little movies of our wonderful time."

"I couldn't help but overhear," Jean Sebastian said. "Did she say Carrie Ann strangled your cat?"

"I don't know. I mean that's what she said—but the medicine makes my mom confused at times."

Although it certainly explained everything. Why her mom had suddenly announced that Carrie Ann had to go. Grace had thrown a horrendous fit that day. She'd screamed at her mother. "I hate you! I hate you! I hate you!" Not once did her mother tell her the real reason Carrie Ann had to go. Would Grace have believed her? Did Carrie Ann kill Brady? Had her mom warned the Gales?

That girl is evil, her mother had once said. It all made sense now. Brady, lying on the steps, his neck drooped down the step. Oh, God. She did it. She did it. *You know she did,* a little voice inside Grace said. *You know she did.* That's why Carrie Ann had gone to live with Stan. And Lydia. And Lionel Gale.

"Stop," Grace said out loud.

"What?" Jean Sebastian said. "What's happening?"

"Nothing. I just can't think about the past right now. We have to find them." If Carrie Ann had killed Brady, it had been because she was jealous. Because of how much Grace loved Brady. And it wasn't near as much as Grace loved Jake. This was insane. "Let's see if Stefano is back."

Jean Sebastian looked flummoxed. "Stefano?"

"The guy at the desk."

"Right."

Grace sailed down the steps. Stefano was just walking out the front door. Grace ran after him. "Hey," she yelled. He didn't turn around. "Hey," she yelled louder. He must have headphones on. Grace sprinted after him and touched his shoulder from behind. He spun around, crouched, and threw up his hands. Even after he saw it was her, it took him a few minutes to recover.

"Sorry I—" He had lowered his hands. He had a fresh black eye. "Oh my God," she said.

"It's no thing." He spoke like they were in the Bronx instead of Barcelona. He'd been watching too many American movies.

She briefly wondered if one of the females in the building had gotten sick of his leering and let him have it. "What happened?"

"What do you want? Are you following me now?" He glanced up and saw Jean Sebastian coming out of the building and threw his hands up again.

"He's with me," Grace said. "What happened to you?"

"Looks recent," Jean Sebastian said. He gestured to the black eye.

"Do not worry. It's no—"

"Thing," Grace finished for him. "If you say so. Listen. We had some trouble of our own last night. Have you seen Rafael, Carrie Ann, or my boyfriend, Jake, since last night?"

Stefano threw his arms up and began ranting in Spanish. The only words she understood were Carrie Ann and American. She wished she hadn't taken French all four years in high school. She turned to Jean Sebastian.

"He said an American man claiming to be Carrie Ann's husband did that to him."

"Oh my God."

"Then he stormed up to the room. Stefano called Rafael to warn him. But no one answered. When the guy came back down, he thought Stefano had sent him to the wrong room on purpose. They fought. He said—basically the Spanish equivalent of 'You should see the other guy.' "

Jean Sebastian held out money to Stefano. He snatched it up and walked away. "Wait," Grace said. Jean Sebastian held out his arm to stop her. "I have more questions."

"Give him some space."

"You paid him?"

"We might need to ask him more later."

"I thought your wallet was stolen."

"It was. I keep cash in my pocket too just in case."

"We need to find out everything he knows."

"He said the American guy beat him up and then left. For right now that's all we know." He turned, crossed his arms, stared at Grace.

"What?"

"Carrie Ann is married?" He sounded upset.

So Grace was right. Jean Sebastian did have a thing for Carrie Ann. So much for thinking he liked her. Not that any of that mattered—then or now. "Was. They're separated—I think she even filed for divorce. She said she came here because she was afraid he was going to kill her."

"And you're just telling me this now?"

"I wasn't even sure if I believed her. I'm still not sure."

"After what Stefano just said?"

"He could've been paid to lie. I wouldn't put it past her."

"I have a feeling there is a lot more to this story."

"And I don't have time to tell it. We have to go to the police."

"Police? So soon? Are you sure?"

"Jake is in trouble. I have to find him."

"What is this American husband's name?"

"Stan," Grace said. "His name is Stan Gale."

CHAPTER 23

Grace put her hands on her hips and looked up and down La Rambla. As usual, it was swarming with activity. She had filled Jean Sebastian in on Stan with as few details as possible. She just wanted to get to the police station. Jean Sebastian told her there was one nearby.

"Lead the way," Grace said.

"But they could be up in Carrie Ann's flat." Jean Sebastian gestured back toward the apartment. "If their drugs have not worn off, they might not have heard me knocking." Shoot. That was a good point. She wasn't thinking. And did Spain have that missing-twenty-four-hour rule? She hoped not. That was way too long to wait. Either way, they needed to gather as much information as possible. Once at the police station, they were going to have to know exactly how many people were missing. It was so strange. Grace knew she had passed out—that was her last memory. Just before that she had been making out with Jake on the dance floor. No wonder she'd felt so free to be so intimate in public—the drugs had been working their way through her system. She remembered Carrie Ann's saying "Stan" or "plan," and then she remembered falling and Carrie Ann's trying to hold her up. Did Grace regain consciousness after that but she couldn't remember? Carrie Ann wouldn't have just left her in a crowded bathroom. Then again, maybe she would have. But the club had still been packed at that point. Somebody would have helped her. Oh, why couldn't she remember? Grace turned back toward the building. "We need to get into their apartment. And a phone—we need to get to a phone. We'll call Jake, Carrie Ann, Rafael—we have to know if their cell phones are on."

"You have all their numbers?"

"Just Jake's. The others were in my phone."

"Carrie Ann's was in my phone too."

"Okay. Well, we have to get to a phone and call Jake. Maybe he is somewhere and he's been trying to call me. He must be worried to death."

"I sure would be." Grace glanced at Jean Sebastian. He was looking at her intensely. She didn't know what to make of the comment, and even if he was hitting on her at this totally inappropriate time, she didn't have time to analyze it. "I'll bet Stefano has the key to Rafael's apartment. Wait. Rafael is a street performer. We can look for him out on La Rambla."

"Okay. Try to get in the apartment. Find a phone and try calling Jake. Look for Rafael."

Grace and Jean Sebastian hurried back to the apartment building, dashed through the lobby, and headed up the stairs. It did feel good to have some sort of plan. "And then go to the police," Grace said.

"And tell Jake to call his mother," Jean Sebastian said.

They banged on the door. No answer. Grace tried the knob. She even tried ramming the door with her body while turning the knob. It was locked, and if anyone was inside, he or she was still too heavily drugged to answer. Grace remembered that Rafael had climbed down to their window, so it was within the realm of possibility that they could climb upstairs. But she'd had enough of that with the dance club ledge, so she kept her mouth shut. "I have to find someone's phone," Grace said.

"Why don't we just buy a disposable?"

"I need more money," Grace said. "I'll check the room and meet you downstairs."

"Why don't you send Jake an e-mail?" Jean Sebastian said.

"An e-mail?"

"E-mail, Facebook—whatever he might be able to check."

"Okay," Grace said. She didn't think Jake would stop to check his e-mail, but she guessed it didn't hurt to cover all bases. She ran into the apartment. Her money was still in the drawer near the bed. But her debit card was gone. Instead, there it was, Carrie Ann's credit card. Damn it. Carrie Ann's ID, her ring, her credit card. Was this all another Carrie Ann plot? If she was messing with Jake, she was going to be sorry. Grace left Jake a quick e-mail.

> I'm home from the dance club. Looking for you. My phone is gone. Where are you?

She didn't want to waste time saying much more. Jake never checked Facebook anyway, and she had resisted posting their every step on her own page, so Grace skipped that part. A hundred euro would be enough for a disposable phone and then some. She still had Jake's warning in her ear about carrying all her ID. Not that it had done her much good—

Her passport. Oh, God. She hadn't seen her passport in the drawer. She ran to the drawer and pawed through it. Gone. Her passport was gone. Jake's was too. Did Jake move them? She was going to have to toss the apartment. But all she wanted to do right now was get a phone and call Jake. There was a kiosk right on La Rambla.

"Anything?" Jean Sebastian asked when she came down to the lobby.

"No. Except my passport is gone. Jake's too."

"My God," Jean Sebastian said. "This is a thought-out plan."

This wasn't part of the plan. . . .

"Let's go get a phone." They found the nearest kiosk, and Jean Sebastian helped her negotiate. They paid forty euro. Grace called as fast as she could. Thank God they'd had that conversation about memorizing each other's numbers. Jake's phone immediately went to voice mail. That wasn't good. Usually there were a few rings before voice mail kicked in. Did it mean the phone was turned off? "Jake. Jake. It's me. Where are you? I have a phone." Grace left the number, twice, in a clear voice. "Call me. I'm going to the police." By the time she hung up, tears were streaming down her face. Jean Sebastian pulled her in and hugged her, and she didn't stop him. She thought of her second day in the square, how Jake had gone to hug her and she wouldn't let him. Now here she was hugging a total stranger. Who, she'd already admitted to herself, she had a chemical attraction to. She'd been a selfish girlfriend, and she was a selfish girlfriend. She pulled out of the embrace. *Please, God. Help me find Jake. I'll never hold anything back from him again as long as I live.*

"We'll find them," Jean Sebastian said, rubbing her back. "Try Carrie Ann."

"Right." Grace stared at the phone. "Her number is in my other phone," she said. "I don't have it memorized."

"We have to get into that apartment."

"Let's look for Rafael. He dresses like some kind of black bird with a white face."

"Really?"

"It's totally creepy." Grace suddenly remembered her drug-induced dream. The thing chasing her down the street, knocking her over, pulling off its mask to reveal a laughing Carrie Ann. Maybe Grace knew deep down inside this was a Carrie Ann game she was playing. She almost hoped it was. Carrie Ann certainly might scheme and manipulate, but she wouldn't physically harm anyone. Stan, on the other hand—

That was only if Carrie Ann was to be believed. Grace was going to have to try and look up Stan's number. Call him. She had no choice. But not now, and not in front of Jean Sebastian. She appreciated his help, but that didn't mean he needed to know every dirty detail. Grace and Jean Sebastian took opposite sides of La Rambla. Grace moved down the line of street performers. Medusa with the snakes. The white man was back on the toilet. She wondered if he changed his newspaper every day or pretended to read the same one. The head was sticking out of the table. She no longer cared whether or not it had kneepads. She just wanted to find Jake and get out of Spain. She wanted to go home. She reached the end of the line on her side. From here there were art dealers and musicians lining the rest of the way to the beach. She tried Jake again. Voice mail kicked in immediately. "This voice mail is full. Please try your call again later."

No. No. No. Grace wanted to hurl the phone down the street. Would texts go through if voice mail was full? She texted him.

Call me ASAP.

She left the number for the new phone even though it probably would show up with her text. She kept doing things that didn't really matter, but she had to do something. The police. She had to go to the police. She crossed over and began to scan the street for Jean Sebastian. God, what if she lost him too? What would she tell the police? *I don't know why, but everyone who hangs around me seems to disappear.*

Grace wiped her brow. It was slick. The sun was brutal. She was still wearing the clothes she had worn to the dance club, slept on a bathroom floor in. She was going to have to shower and wear something presentable. Otherwise the police might think she was some kind of drug addict; they might not take her claims seriously enough. And she wouldn't blame them. Grace wouldn't have believed any of this either if it weren't for the fact that she knew Carrie Ann. And Carrie Ann was capable of almost anything.

CHAPTER 24

Just as Grace was about to turn into the alley to go back to the apartment, she saw Jean Sebastian waving at her from across the way. She waited for him to catch up.

"Hey," he said. "I thought we were going to meet up."

"Sorry. I didn't see you, and I have to shower and get to the police station." She looked at him. "Unless?" Had he spotted them? He shook his head. "So we're missing Rafael, Carrie Ann, and Jake."

Jean Sebastian put his hand on her arm. "I need to get my things," he said. "I think I should stay with you." Grace hesitated. Jake probably wouldn't like it if less than twelve hours after he went missing she was already shacked up with another guy. A very good-looking guy from Belgium who used to be the director of an international rescue agency in the Congo. Then again, Jean Sebastian probably had some skills that would come in handy. Plus he spoke Spanish. Lastly, she was terrified of being alone. What if the psycho husband did exist and decided to go after her?

"Okay," she said. "I'll take a shower, get dressed, and wait for you at the apartment."

"You won't go anywhere else. You promise?"

"I promise. You should shower too."

"I am European." At her look, he laughed. "I will shower," he said. "But it won't take long. I am going to buy a phone too—let me write down your number." Neither of them had a pen, so he borrowed one from a passerby and wrote the number on his forearm. His muscles bulged. Strong. He was definitely an asset. That was the only reason she wanted him along. Jake wouldn't want her to face this all alone, would he?

"Check your e-mail, check your Facebook, everything," Jean Sebastian said. "Any way someone might use to communicate."

"Okay. But we're going straight to the police, right?"

"I don't like it. But I guess we don't have a choice."

"See you soon."

"Lock the doors," Jean Sebastian said. She hesitated. Should she ask him to come up now and check the apartment to make sure no one was in there? After all, someone, Rafael most likely, had climbed in before just to move things around. No. She wasn't going to start sounding like someone who was afraid of her own shadow. Besides, she would be thrilled to see Rafael climbing around her apartment right now. But what if it was Stan? She wouldn't be thrilled to be alone and in the shower with him roaming about the apartment.

"Jean Sebastian?" He had only gotten a few steps away. He stopped, waited.

"Someone broke into our apartment before. Moved things around."

"So maybe it is this husband?"

"Can you just give a sweep of the apartment before you go? Make sure I'm alone?"

Jean Sebastian hit his forehead. "Of course. God, I'm in such a hurry." He stopped, grabbed her hand. "This is why we have to take our time," he said. "We have to be able to think." She nodded. Together they headed back to the apartment. They had gone a few steps before Grace realized they were still holding hands. She pulled away. "Sorry," he said. "I didn't even realize."

Grace gave a nervous laugh. "I didn't either."

"Felt natural," Jean Sebastian said very softly. Grace didn't acknowledge it. What was happening? Cheese and crackers. Jake wouldn't like this one bit. But her safety came first; they would both agree on that. The sweep of the apartment showed no one was hiding in closets or under the bed or in the shower. Jean Sebastian locked every single window and pulled all the shades.

"I'm not leaving," Jean Sebastian said. "I'll wait out here while you shower. Then we'll go to my place."

"No. I feel better now that you've checked."

"I don't. Three of your friends are missing. Until we find them, I'm with you."

Grace opened her mouth to argue. He was right. She really didn't want to be alone. "I won't be long."

She had an awful, guilty feeling while she showered, and she didn't know why. Maybe just the thought of being naked while another man was just outside the door. A man she was attracted to. Was he thinking about her in here? Imagining her naked body in the shower? She was the girl next door according to Marsh Everett. She certainly wasn't having a girl-next-door experience. Did lusting for someone else in your fantasies count as cheating? Surely Jake fantasized about other women. Including Carrie Ann. He wouldn't have been human if that little red dress of hers hadn't prompted some sort of secret fantasy. Although there had to be a special room in hell for a girl who was having lustful fantasies about another man while her boyfriend was missing. Bad, Grace. Bad, bad, bad. To think, just a few days ago she was ready to spontaneously marry Jake in Spain. Maybe all of these thoughts were some sort of side effect of the drug's wearing off. It made her feel less guilty to think so anyway.

She ran the water as cold as she could stand it. She cupped her hands and gathered water and splashed it on her face. A memory flashed into her mind. Last night. Carrie Ann propping Grace up, bringing her into the bathroom.

"I think you drank mine," she had said. "I think he was trying to drug me." Carrie Ann had sounded truly panicked.

"Who?" Grace had said. She had begun to slip down the wall. "Where's Jake?"

"Oh, God." Carrie Ann had pulled her up. She had turned the water on. Splashed some on Grace's face. "I have to get you home."

"I feel funny."

"I'm sorry. I'm sure it was meant for me."

"Are you lying? You were always such a liar." Had she really said that to Carrie Ann? "You even lied about library books." Oh, God. She had said it. Carrie Ann's eyes, kind a few seconds before, had flashed.

"Library books?"

"I let you have my library card," Grace had slurred. Why wasn't the wall holding her up? "You took out like ten books. And then weeks later the librarian was calling me, asking where they were. What did you say? 'I took them back, Grace. I swear I took them back.' And where did I find them?"

Under her bed, where Carrie Ann stashed everything.

Grace had been on the floor again. Carrie Ann had squatted down so that they were eye-to-eye. "Is that why you thought I was lying about Mr. Gale?"

"How many times do I have to tell you? I didn't tell! I didn't tell!"

"I know you didn't tell, Grace. My question is—why? Why wouldn't you tell something like that?" If Grace could trust her memory, Carrie Ann had been leaning over her.

"Because you're a liar!"

"You have no idea how much you hurt me," Carrie Ann had said.

What happened then? Grace couldn't remember. Had Carrie Ann stormed off? Had she just left her there?

Did you strangle Brady, Carrie Ann?

Grace turned off the shower even though she was still soapy. "Stop," she said out loud.

There was a knock on the bathroom door. "You okay?"

Grace's heart pounded. Was it because of the memory, because the knock had startled her, or because in another world it would be so tempting to say, "Come in"? "Fine. Water just got too hot."

"Be careful." God, that accent. She'd better hurry and find Jake because he was not going to like her hanging out with Jean Sebastian. She turned the water back on and proceeded to rinse off.

If she had really said all those things to Carrie Ann last night, then Grace could see Carrie Ann leaving her on the bathroom floor.

Why? Why wouldn't you tell something like that?

A realization, as cold as the water blasting her, hit Grace. Carrie Ann might have been telling the truth about Lionel.

It had honestly never occurred to her. And Grace had done nothing. Said nothing. And Carrie Ann had hated her ever since.

Oh, God. Grace turned the water off, but leaned her head against the shower wall. Lionel Gale. Carrie Ann. Stan. It was all so painful. Time hadn't done anything but make the memories worse. And they were coming back to haunt her. She had to squelch her emotions. She had to think.

She had been drugged first. Where had Jake been when they were fighting in the bathroom? What had happened next? And if she was remembering things, was Jean Sebastian? She glanced at the bathroom door. She wondered what he was doing out there. She trusted him, and yet he was a complete stranger. She didn't have much of a choice. And if he did start remembering things, she prayed whatever those memories were, they would help lead her back to Jake.

Jean Sebastian was standing over Jake's laptop when she came out of the shower. Wrapped only in a towel, she hurried to the bedroom to change. She slipped on a yellow sundress and slid into her comfy flip-flops. She brushed her hair out and stuck a band around it. She almost called out to "Jake" in the other room. She sat down on the bed, suddenly aware of how fatigued she was. Jake was missing. Where the hell were Carrie Ann, Rafael, and Jake? She wanted him more than she'd ever wanted anyone in her life. Why had she lied to her parents? What was she supposed to do now? She just wanted Jake, and she wanted to be on a plane back to Nashville. Tears came easily, and hard. Soon she felt a presence in the doorway.

"I'm sorry," Jean Sebastian said. "Don't worry. We'll find them."

"You don't know that."

He walked closer. "We know someone is deliberately doing this, right? They drugged you; they drugged me. So this is not an accident. Whoever this is will have to start communicating with us."

"What if they hurt him?"

"Before we even know what they want?" Jean Sebastian said. "This is not very likely."

"When you were in the Congo, did you ever face anything like this?"

"Yes. Twice armed men with masks and guns took us hostage in the center. The first time for two days; the second time for twelve days."

"My God. Was anyone hurt?"

"I don't want to talk about it."

"I'm sorry. I'm sorry. I've just—never dealt with anything like this before."

"No, I'm sorry. I wasn't trying to be rude. It's just—not something I like to talk about."

Grace looked up. "Believe me, I know what you mean."

"You do?"

"Carrie Ann. Carrie Ann is someone I never liked to talk about."

Jean Sebastian took another few steps. "You might have to. If you think she's the reason this is happening."

Grace sprung from the bed. "I know she's the reason this is

happening. She lured Jake and me here under false pretenses. She left little clues—a matchbook, writing in another book, tickets under the door—"

"Why? What did she want?"

"She said she wanted to see me. She said her husband was after her. But I remembered something from last night when I was drugged. It came to me in the shower. Are you starting to have any flashbacks?"

Jean Sebastian shook his head. "What did you remember?"

"I had a little fight with Carrie Ann in the bathroom. About our past."

"Okay. You're going to have to tell me everything. But for now—do you think Carrie Ann is doing this, or is her husband doing this?"

"I don't know. When I Googled Carrie Ann, I couldn't find a single thing. And all her ID—which I have, by the way—has her last name. Gilbert. Not Gale."

"So she could be lying about being married? She could be doing this all on her own?"

"I don't know. Manipulating, playing games—sure. But drugging and kidnapping? It seems a little out of her scope."

"Even if she strangled your cat?"

And drove Lionel Gale to his barn with a rope in his hand—"I don't know. I don't know."

"It's okay."

"It's not. None of this is okay. And if Jake is hurt, it's my fault. It's all my fault."

"Gather everything you need. We're not coming back here until we find them."

"Why? This is exactly where Jake will come the minute he's able."

"We'll leave him a note with your new mobile number. I think we need to buy two more phones. One for me and another one for you. The phone you already have will just be the number for Jake. Only give the other phone number to Carrie Ann or anyone else you get in touch with. That way—if she is behind this—you know the first phone number won't be compromised."

"Okay. That's good. That's smart."

"Besides Jake, have you made or received any other calls on the phone we just bought?"

"No."

"Not to your parents, not to anyone?"

"Just Jake."

"Okay. Pack whatever you need and leave him a note with the number."

"After we buy the phones, where are we going?"

"I have to stop by my place. Then we'll go to the police. I don't think they're going to be much help. But I can see it will make you feel better. After that we'll hit social media, then at seven o'clock tonight we'll be back at the club."

"Oh, God."

"We have to talk to bartenders, bouncers—anyone who might have seen anything."

Grace nodded, threw a few things in her bag, and left Jake the same note she'd left on his e-mail and voice mail. Once outside, Grace couldn't help but check her map for the police station. "It's on La Rambla," she said.

"You want to go there before going to my place, don't you?" Jean Sebastian said.

"Yes. I think we need to report this right away."

"Okay. I will not worry about my smell."

"I didn't even think to offer you my shower," Grace said. *Because I was too worried about sharing one with you.*

"That's okay. I need fresh clothes."

"If it helps, I think you look fine. I'm the one going in with wet hair."

"You look beautiful."

The compliment hung in the air. Grace waited a few beats too long to thank him. "Lead the way." She said it with extra volume as if that would negate her awkwardness. On the steps of the police station, a discarded poster caught Grace's eye.

VOLEM UN BARRI DIGNE!!!

"What does that mean?" Grace said.

"We want a decent neighborhood," Jean Sebastian translated. "You see this sign in a lot of Barcelona neighborhoods. Too many pickpockets and prostitutes."

"And kidnappers," Grace said.

"Before we go in"—Jean Sebastian touched her elbow—"I don't want you to be disappointed. It will be a lot of paperwork. Questions. They will want photos too—"

"I didn't even think of that. I'll have to log on to my Facebook page. Will they let me do that here?"

"I doubt it. In addition they will probably advise you to contact the American embassy. The embassy won't be able to do much either. And they will ask if you have contacted his family."

"I am his family."

"Yes. But his mother, father. The same with Carrie Ann."

"I'm her family too." According to Carrie Ann, at least. "I don't have any pictures on me. Jake took videos of us, and he said he uploaded some. If I can get into his e-mail, maybe I could show the police the videos."

"They aren't set up to let everyone start downloading things from the computer. I know we're going to have to come back with a photo we can put in their hands. This is what you will need for any media coverage too."

Media coverage. The news. A "Missing" poster. She wanted to crumple on the steps and cry. But she couldn't. She had to have tunnel vision and find Jake. "Damn it. I'm not sure I even know how to print pictures from Facebook. Do you?"

"We can figure it out."

"Would an Internet café let me do that?"

"I have a printer at my hotel."

"I guess we should have stuck to your plan," Grace said. "Now it's your turn to lead the way."

"Let's stop and get a few more phones first," Jean Sebastian said.

* * *

Grace was afraid to use up her cash on additional phones. She would also have to cancel her credit cards the minute they got to Jean Sebastian's hotel. Or hostel, or wherever he was sleeping. "You have Carrie Ann's credit card, right?" Jean Sebastian said. Grace nodded. "Use it."

"I don't know."

"At the least maybe it will get her attention."

Grace hadn't thought of that. "Smart. Okay. I'll use her credit card to buy the phones and if you think spending more might get her attention, draw her out of hiding, then I'll buy out the whole kiosk."

"Let's not go overboard," Jean Sebastian said. He patted her on the back. Grace nodded.

In addition to phones the kiosk sold the usual tourist fare. T-shirts, and postcards, and cigarettes, and maps, and hats, and sunglasses. Grace bought the two phones, T-shirts for her parents, then one for Jake's mom, then figured the heck with it and bought one for herself and one for Jake. WISH YOU WERE HERE. It was never so true as it was now. She also picked up a pair of sunglasses, a few candy bars, and another camera. She hoped wherever Jake was, he still had his second video camera. Maybe she would take Carrie Ann's original advice and buy him an expensive one with Carrie Ann's credit card. The bill here came to one hundred and forty euro. She wasn't prepared to sign Carrie Ann's name, so when the slip was pushed her way, she hesitated. She tried to remember what Carrie Ann's signature looked like. Did it really even matter? She made the signature neat and loopy, like the writing on the invitation to Casa Batlló that Carrie Ann had slipped under the door. That felt like ages ago. Grace was suddenly so tired. She stumbled, and Jean Sebastian had to grab her elbow to keep her from hitting the pavement.

"When we get to my hotel, you're taking a nap," he said.

"I can't. There's too much to do."

"We were drugged last night. Our bodies are still feeling the effects. You won't be any good to Jake if you faint. You are taking at least an hour's nap."

Did he have a tiny room? She wasn't sure she'd even be able to fall asleep. She'd probably feel too guilty. First showering with Jean Sebastian in the other room, then sleeping nearby? Then again, she might not have much of a choice. He was right; they needed their strength.

"An hour," she said. "Maybe I can even get my own room."

"You won't need to do that," Jean Sebastian said.

"I think you're right about the credit card though," Grace said. "The more I use it, the more someone—hopefully Carrie Ann—will come out of hiding."

"As long as we don't waste it," Jean Sebastian said. "You can decide when you see my place. We could walk, but given our hurry I think we should hop in a cab. I can get it."

Jean Sebastian flagged down a cab before Grace could agree or disagree. She did want to get the picture of Jake and get to the police office. She tried Jake's phone again as they raced down the street. Jean Sebastian must have told the cab driver to step on it in Spanish or perhaps they all drove like they had a death wish. Grace was expecting Jake's phone to be shut off, but this time voice mail was working. Did that mean Jake or someone else had done something with the phone? It was encouraging.

"Jake. It's Grace. My God, I hope you get this. If this is someone else, please call and tell me how you got this phone. Or tell me what I need to do to see Jake again. Please." Her voice cracked; she didn't know what was the appropriate thing to do in this situation. Beg? Threaten? "Whoever is listening to this, call or text this number right away. I'm going to the police in exactly one hour." There. A little bit of begging, a little bit of threatening. Grace left the number slowly and clearly. "I love you, Jake." When she hung up she was aware of Jean Sebastian staring at her. They were driving along the walkway to the beach; the ocean shimmered in the background. Grace had to bite the side of her cheek really, really hard.

"How long have you been together?" Jean Sebastian asked quietly.

"Three years."

"Was it love at first sight or did it take time to fall in love with him?"

Grace wasn't expecting the question. But the memory brought her instant comfort and fueled her resolve that they were going to find Jake as soon as possible. "I found a stray kitten," she said. "Jake was my vet. The kitten had been thrown out of a moving car. We had to put him down."

"That must have been very upsetting."

"It was. But get this—Jake was the one who cried. I hadn't been paying attention to him up until then, but when he saw what shape that kitten was in—his eyes filled with tears. That's the moment I fell in love."

"A sensitive man," Jean Sebastian said.

"Yes," Grace said. God, Jake would hate her for telling that story to Jean Sebastian of all people. But Jean Sebastian didn't look like he was judging Jake. He was trying to keep Grace calm. She and Jake had a reoccurring joke about their "how we met" story.

"When you tell that story, can you leave out the part about my bawling like a little girl over a kitten?" Jake would say.

She laughed quietly to herself, then was immediately overtaken by a sob. She knew Jean Sebastian heard her, but luckily he let her have her space. She looked out the window as they approached a tall building with interspersed glass and steel squares rising from the beach. It looked like a resort. They were in the little neighborhood of Barceloneta, right near Port Olímpic. The driver pulled in front of the building. Grace was about to ask him why they had stopped when Jean Sebastian opened the door. Jean Sebastian spoke to the driver in Spanish, and he grinned and nodded.

"What's going on?" Jean Sebastian was holding the door open for Grace. She got out, and the driver scrambled around for her bag. "Why are we stopping?" Grace asked.

"We are here."

They were at the Hotel Arts Barcelona/Ritz Carlton. Right on the beach. So much for living in a hostel. So, Grace thought, as Jean Sebastian took the bag from the driver and they headed for the entrance. He's Belgian. He's hot. He speaks God knows how many languages. He used to work for a prestigious, charitable organization in a dangerous territory, and he's now playing my knight in shining armor. Oh, no. Jake would not like this one bit. But she couldn't help it. She liked it way more than she should have.

"Travel writer?" Grace said, raising an eyebrow.

"My old job," Jean Sebastian said. "Being the director of a rescue agency gets you a few perks. A few still linger." Grace nodded as they stepped into the lobby dripping with marble, and glittering chandeliers, expensive furnishings, and an ocean view. Port Olímpic was just outside their door.

"Don't tell me you're in a penthouse suite," she joked.

"How did you know?" he said without a trace of sarcasm.

CHAPTER 25

Jake woke to the sound of a drip. He was in a small room, but the drip echoed as if he were in a giant tunnel. He was sitting on a floor with his back against a pipe, and his hands were cuffed behind him. Had he been arrested and thrown into some strange Spanish jail? It smelled moldy. He tugged on the handcuffs, and they cut into his wrists.

"Hey," he yelled into the dark. "Grace?" As his eyes adjusted he could make out a single bed in the room and a dresser. Was he in a house? An apartment building? There seemed to be a window behind him, but heavy shades prevented him from being able to tell what time of day it was. There was a figure on the bed, underneath the covers. "Grace?" This time he yelled as loud as he could. The figure stirred, then sat up. It wasn't her. Too chesty, hair too light, even in the dark. "Carrie Ann?"

"Where am I?" she said, rubbing her eyes.

"Is there a light next to the bed? Can you turn it on?" Jake said. Interesting. She wasn't handcuffed, but he was. She turned and reached out to something. He heard a click, and a dim light filled the room. When Carrie Ann turned to him, he got a fright. Mascara streaked from both eyes and down her cheeks, and her lip was swollen and slightly bloody. He tried not to react.

"Are you okay?" he asked.

"Where are we? Why are you sitting on the floor?"

Jake jerked on the handcuffs by way of an answer. Carrie Ann scrambled to the end of the bed and stared down at him. "Oh my God," she said. "Stan."

"What about Stan?"

"I saw him last night. At the club. Just before I took Grace to the bathroom." She looked around. "Where is she?"

"I just woke up," Jake said. "But obviously she's not in here."

"Oh my God," Carrie Ann said. "I'm going to kill him."

"You took Grace to the bathroom and what happened?" Jake said.

"She was out of it. She was sliding down the wall—I couldn't keep her up—"

"Somebody drugged all of us."

"I'm sorry, Jake. I'm really, really sorry."

"So you're saying you knew nothing about this?"

"Nothing. No."

Jake got the feeling she was holding something back, but pressuring her could backfire, so he let it go for now. "What happened to Grace?"

"I don't know, I don't know."

"What's the last thing you remember?"

"Grace and I were fighting—"

"About what?"

"Let's leave that for later, shall we?" Jake stared at her, then nodded. "Then she kept sliding down the wall, and . . ."

"And?"

"And I heard the door open because it made this loud groaning sound, and then I felt something smash into the back of my head." Carrie Ann reached around and felt her head. "I have a lump."

"You also have a busted lip."

Carrie Ann put her hand up to her lip. "I think I hit it on the sink as I fell."

"And then what?"

"That's all I remember."

"You think your husband did all of this?"

"I know he did. I know he did."

"By himself?" Carrie Ann stared at Jake, unblinking. "Who else?" Carrie Ann looked toward the door.

"Do you recognize where we are?" Jake said.

"No."

"Why do you keep looking at the door?"

"Because somebody has to be on the other side of it. Unless you think we did this to ourselves." There was a definite edge to her voice.

"You're not handcuffed," he said.

"My husband is a jealous psycho. He probably didn't want you touching me."

Great. A jealous psycho. Where in the hell was Grace? She'd tried to warn him about this Carrie Ann girl, and he hadn't listened. Was Grace with Jean Sebastian and Rafael? He didn't like Jean Sebastian either, but he'd feel better if she wasn't alone. "When you say . . . psycho . . . What are we talking here?" Once again, Carrie Ann just looked at him with that maddening stare. "I want to know if he would hurt Grace."

Carrie Ann lay back down. "My head is killing me."

She wasn't kidding. His head was throbbing something awful. "Answer me. Would he hurt Grace?"

"I don't think so."

"You don't think so?"

"He's more of a manipulator."

"Your busted lip says otherwise."

"I told you—I must have hit it on the sink—"

"After someone smashed something into the back of your head."

"If you know everything, then why are you grilling me?"

"Why is he doing this?"

"Because I'm trying to divorce him." Her voice swelled with emotion. Jake got the feeling there was more to the story, but she suddenly stopped talking. Once again, he heard a drip. So he was chained to a pipe. Carrie Ann had a busted lip, but was free and on the bed. Why was she just lying there?

"Do you have your phone?"

"No."

"Did you even check?"

"I'm wearing a dress. It's not down my bra. Where else do you want me to check?"

"Oh, I don't know. Why don't you get up and see if your purse is here? Open the bedside drawer. See if you can open this window behind me. See if you can open the door."

Carrie Ann slowly sat up again. "I think I'm going to be sick."

"Focus, Carrie Ann. Please. Before someone comes."

Carrie Ann opened the bedside drawer. "Not even a Spanish Bible," she said. She slowly got off the bed, then got on all fours and looked underneath it. "Dirty, but I don't see anything." She approached Jake, looked down at him. "Does it hurt?"

"Yes," he said.

"Sorry." She slowly took a corner of the curtain and peeked out. Then she slid the curtain to the side. The window was entirely grayed out. Jake couldn't tell what time of day it was. She turned and stared at the door. "What if they hear me?" she whispered.

"They know we're in here," he said. "So I don't think that's going to matter."

Carrie Ann still tiptoed over to the door. She put her ear against it. Then, she tried the knob. "We're locked in," she said.

"Great." Now he really had to pee. "Pound on it," he said.

"Seriously?"

"I have to go to the restroom."

"Oh, God," Carrie Ann said. "So do I." She turned to the door and began to pound on it with her fists. "Rafael," she yelled. "Rafael. We have to use the bathroom!"

"Carrie Ann," Jake said. He didn't even try to hide his anger. She turned and took in his demeanor.

"What?" she croaked.

"How do you know it's Rafael on the other side of that door?"

"Shit," Carrie Ann said.

"Carrie Ann?"

"All right. There are a few things I can tell you. Just, please, hear me out and try not to overreact."

"I can't promise I won't overreact," Jake said. He jerked on the handcuffs. "But it looks like this is your lucky day."

CHAPTER 26

Jean Sebastian's room, or rooms, as he had a main living room and a ginormous bedroom, also had a large balcony with an ocean-front view. The bathroom had a sunken whirlpool tub and a rainforest shower. He could have mentioned this before she showered in her rusty box, she thought. Not that she should be enjoying anything right now, especially little luxuries like a waterfall shower-setting.

While Grace wandered around with her mouth open, Jean Sebastian disappeared into his room and then came back with nothing but a towel wrapped around his waist. He was so tan, and was definitely a man acquainted with a gym. She tried not to stare at the muscles in his stomach. She thought of Jake's sweet, normally pale, not-quite six-pack stomach, and she wanted to cry. Was Jean Sebastian trying to flaunt himself in front of her?

"There's a lovely roof deck and gardens if you'd like to wander around there while I shower. There's an elevator at the end of the hall that will take you up."

"You mentioned you had a printer?"

"Right. Of course. But we'll have to figure out how to print pictures off Facebook. I think we'll need to set up an outside account with a photo-sharing album. You'll need all my passwords. You might as well enjoy the roof deck for a few minutes." Grace nodded. At least she wouldn't be thinking about him in the shower. Well, now she might, but she wouldn't be just a few feet away. She could clear her head.

The terrace had a sculpture garden, flower garden, seating area with fire pits, and of course an expansive, in-ground pool. Grace sat down on one of the outdoor sofa benches. Jake should be here with her. Her cell phone rang. Her heart leapt out of her chest. It stopped after one ring. It wasn't until she looked at the phone that she realized it was a text message.

Jake saw your Facebook page.

Heart leaping, Grace texted back immediately. What about her Facebook page? She hadn't been on Facebook since she had arrived in Spain. Not that it mattered. Whoever had Jake was making contact.

Who is this? Is Jake okay?

It felt like years that she sat with the phone cradled in the palm of her hand, staring at it. Beep again. Say something, anything. If Grace and Jean Sebastian had gone to the police already, maybe they could have set up a trace.

Not after he saw your Facebook page.

Please. Carrie Ann? Rafael? Stan? I need to talk to Jake.

Check your page. Then we'll talk.

Grace's legs were rubber as she ran back to the room. The shower was still going when she let herself in. He was taking his sweet old time, wasn't he? Shoot. He never did tell her where she could find his laptop. She raced around the apartment, hoping it would jump out at her. *If it was a snake, it would've bit you. . . .* Her mother loved that expression. Grace had always been the type of kid who misplaced things. Right now she'd be fine with the laptop's jumping out and biting her. Should she knock on the bathroom door, tell Jean Sebastian to hurry?

She put her ear to the door. Suddenly, it opened. Jean Sebastian stood there, naked and wet, and she fell into his chest. Oh, God. Why was the shower still running? She backed up as soon as she could, but it was still long enough to feel his hard body against her.

"I'm so sorry," she said.

"I thought I heard something," Jean Sebastian said.

"I was going to knock. I just got a text." Jean Sebastian nodded, then turned and shut off the shower. He didn't seem to mind being naked in front of her, and that made Grace blush even more. She stepped back into the living room and paced until he came out, towel once again loosely wrapped around his waist.

"Show me." She handed him the phone. He scrolled through the messages, then headed for his bedroom. "Follow," he said. She entered his bedroom, which had three floor-to-ceiling windows with views of both downtown Barcelona and the ocean. Everything else was white. His laptop was in the middle of his bed, and he jumped on it, and lay on his stomach as he pecked at the keys and brought up a search engine. "Join me," he said casually. Well, there just wasn't time to argue about how this might look. Grace carefully sat next to him on the bed. He turned and looked up at her, then gave a little smile as if he knew exactly how uncomfortable she was with this situation.

"Here," he said. He swiveled the laptop in her direction, and she quickly brought up her Facebook page. The first thing that struck her was her message bar. She had over fifty comments. She barely got any comments, even when she posted info about shows. She scrolled down and was confronted by a photo. It had been taken in the club. She was on the dance floor. With Jean Sebastian. The two were plastered together. There were three photos. Grace clicked on each to bring it to full size. In the first picture they were dancing, bodies pressed together. In the second picture Jean Sebastian had her by the hand, and she was twirling back, laughing. But it was the third picture that stopped her heart. She and Jean Sebastian were lip-locked.

Jean Sebastian immediately sat up. "Oh, God," he said.

"Is this Photoshopped?" Grace said. But even as the words left her lips, she remembered the kiss. Brazenly making out with Jake on the dance floor. Only it hadn't been Jake. Oh, God. She had even noticed he had been wearing a different shirt. The drugs had taken a strong hold by then. She'd loved the kiss. Shame flooded her. Where had Jake been when she was kissing Jean Sebastian? Had he seen and run out of the club? Was there a chance Jake was out there on his own and furious with her? In some ways that would be better than the alternative. "Do you remember this?" Her voice sounded desperate and accusing.

"Not a bit of it," Jean Sebastian said. His eyes stayed steady on hers. She didn't know if she believed him. "Believe me," he said as if he could read her mind. "I would *want* to remember that." He held her gaze until she broke it off.

There were a ton of Facebook comments underneath the photos, ranging from the "Way to go" variety to "How could you?" One person called her a whore. So much for her "friends."

Grace immediately removed the photos and posted a comment.

> My Facebook page was hacked. I did not post these pictures.

She hesitated. Did she tell them she had been drugged? Would people believe her? *I was drugged.* That sounded so lame! But saying she had thought she was kissing Jake would sound even worse. Should she tell them that Jake was missing?

"Don't say too much," Jean Sebastian said as he watched her wrestle with what to say. "We want whoever is doing this to communicate with us."

Grace scrolled down, but there were no other pictures or postings. "Jake saw this," Grace said.

"Or so they say."

"What if they hurt him? What if . . . ?" She couldn't even bring herself to say it out loud, but the fear echoed through her mind at top volume. *What if he isn't even alive?*

I was also robbed. I'm about to go to the police station to fill out a report. . . .

"That might get their attention all right," Jean Sebastian said.

"I should try again to see if Carrie Ann has a page," Grace said. With all this game-playing maybe Carrie Ann had set one up to send her clues. She typed in *Carrie Ann Gilbert.*

The first search result misunderstood what she was looking for. "People named Carrie Ann who live in Gilbert, Arizona," Grace read off the screen. "I don't think so." She tried it again: *Sorry, we couldn't find this search result.*

"Maybe just Carrie Gilbert?"

"I doubt it. And I don't have time to go through all the variations."

"Does Jake have a page?"

"God, I'm not even thinking." Grace brought up his page. No postings, but the picture of her kissing Jean Sebastian was on there, again with a million messages from "Dude, what gives?" to "Did you dump the bitch?"

She had no authority to delete the photo from his page. I did not do this, she commented. This is a hack and a scam!

Suddenly, an instant message popped up. "Jake," Grace exclaimed.

"Or just his account," Jean Sebastian cautioned.

Although the instant message screen with Jake's name popped up, no message came through. Grace typed:

Jake? Jake? Jake?

When she saw *Jake is typing* appear in the little screen, she cried out.

No police . . . Denuncia equals death

"Oh my God," Grace said. "What is *denuncia?*"
"It's Spanish for 'police report,' " Jean Sebastian said.
"What do I say?"
"Just ask what they want. But that's it."

> We want Jake. What do you want?

Who is we?

"Oh God," Grace said. "I'm already fucking this up."
"They're messing with you. They have to know we'd stick together."
"Okay. So I just tell them?"
"Just tell them."

> Jean Sebastian is here. What are your instructions?

Jake is offline. They were gone. "Damn it," Grace said. She glanced at Jean Sebastian. Why had she listened to him? Grace hurried and typed in her phone number again on Facebook. Then, on second thought, she added:

> We were both drugged. I was scared. He's just helping me until I find Jake. If you do not respond with a request I will immediately go to the police station. No response equals denuncia. And if you hurt Jake, I will hunt you down and kill you.

"Wow," Jean Sebastian said.
"I'm pissed," Grace said, tears rising into her eyes. "I'm really pissed." What she really wanted to do was throw his laptop through the giant-sized windows. "This can't be Carrie Ann. It can't be."
"Are you sure?" Jean Sebastian said.
"No. I'm not sure of anything." *Happy, Marsh Everett? I love*

Jake and I want him back, and I would be willing to physically hurt anyone who hurts him. I guess I've learned that about myself, Marsh. Turns out I'm an eye-for-an-eye kind of a girl. What do you think about that? She turned to Jean Sebastian. "I want to take my Facebook page down."

"You can't. Anything they do is a piece of the puzzle. Every little communication or lack thereof could mean something."

"Now what?" Grace still wanted to go to the police. *Denuncia* means death. Her phone beeped.

Park Güell
6 PM
No sidekick

Where exactly? Who is this? I will be there

Alone

Alone

"I don't like this," Jean Sebastian said.

"It's better than no contact," Grace said. "At least I'll find out what I'm dealing with."

"What we're dealing with." Jean Sebastian looked at her. A surge of attraction ran through her. It was natural. He was trying to protect her, and that was a definite aphrodisiac. She looked away. "It's a huge park. Ask them where."

Please. Where exactly shall we meet?

Enter and sit on the serpentine bench. Will text again.

"Could the police trace where this is coming from?" Grace said.

"It's probably a throwaway. Like ours."

"How would they know? If we go to the police, how would the kidnappers know?"

"Well—the police might contact the media, and then the kidnappers would hear it on the news or see a poster."

"So no police."

"I didn't say that. But you're definitely not going to the park alone."

"Jake couldn't wait to go to that park," Grace said.

"Maybe that's why they picked it."

"Do you think he's okay?"

"I don't know, Grace. I want to reassure you. But I don't know who's doing this, so I can't give you an honest opinion."

"What would you do?"

"I would go to the park. But not alone."

"But you heard them."

"And what? Will they have spies all over the park? I will get there an hour before you. I'll throw on a hat and glasses. You won't even know it's me. Do not get in a car or into an enclosed space with anyone, no matter what. Otherwise, we'll see what they have in mind, and after, we'll decide whether or not to go to the police."

"I agree," Grace said. *With some of it.* As for the rest of it, Grace had a few ideas of her own.

CHAPTER 27

Stepping into Park Güell was almost like stepping into Dr. Seuss land. The two buildings flanking the entrance of Park Güell were an example of Gaudí's intentions to marry his whimsical architectural elements with nature. They were solid stone structures with roofs that looked like jester's hats. Grace loved the white-laced edging that dripped over the tops like icing on a cake. The one to the right sprouted a blue-and-white-striped spiral. Pastel mosaic tiles and crosses at the top of each building completed the picture. This was where she would re-unite with Jake, she prayed. In this fantastical park, this was where her nightmare would end. From now on she would stand up for herself, she would sing whatever the hell she wanted, and she would shed the shame of her past with Carrie Ann. *You were right, Mom,* Grace thought. *You were right all along about Carrie Ann.* She was going to have to call her parents again soon, but she was putting it off because the next time she was going to have to tell them the truth. Hopefully, Jake would be at her side, giving the tale the necessary happy ending.

She was two hours early, and alone. She was also carrying her guitar. As much as she appreciated Jean Sebastian's suggestion that he arrive an hour early and plant himself somewhere nearby, she couldn't take the chance of its coming back to bite her. On top of that, she couldn't stop thinking about the Facebook pictures. It wasn't just an innocent kiss—they'd been full-on making out. But Jake was the one she had thought she'd been kissing. The point was—she remembered kissing someone. Jean Sebastian said he remembered none of it. Could she really trust him? And what did it mean if he did remember kissing her?

There was another reason she didn't want him tagging along. If Jake came to the park, she didn't want him to see her with Jean Sebastian and get the wrong idea. Not if he really had seen the pictures. Besides, the text had said to come alone. So she had snuck out of the Hotel Arts Barcelona while Jean Sebastian was getting dressed. Then, she had gone back to her apartment for her guitar. Stefano wasn't at the desk, nobody answered at Carrie Ann's, and her place was exactly the way she had left it. Jake hadn't been back. But at least she was able to grab her Taylor Hummingbird.

Musicians playing drew a lot of attention. If she was frightened at any point, she could set up somewhere and play, hopefully draw a crowd. She also picked up a small bottle of hairspray that she could use like mace in a pinch, and a pocketknife, though the thought of using it truthfully scared her to death. But having the small items in her pocket made her feel slightly more empowered.

Grace had been told to meet at one of the highlights of the park, the serpentine bench winding the length of the large terrace. It boasted colorful tiles along the top of the serpent's spine. The winding bench tilted upward so that it would dry quickly after it rained. Gaudí had thought of everything down to the tiniest detail. Grace needed to do the same if she wanted to get Jake back. There was no fear of a storm today, even though it was moving toward late afternoon; the sun was still high and bright in the sky. Grace stood at a prime viewing spot on the terrace overlooking lush treetops and the city. In the distance she could make out the familiar spirals of the Sagrada Família and the peaks of the Montjuïc mountain range. Under normal circumstances the view would have infused her with a sense of calm. But this was anything but normal, and everything, even the gorgeous views, set her nerves on fire.

Her phone rang. It was Jean Sebastian. She thought of ignoring him, but realized that could backfire. He seemed like the worrying type. *Say what you mean. He seems like he would worry about you, Grace. He isn't doing this for Jake; he's doing it for you.*

"Please don't come," she said quickly and quietly. "I have to do this alone."

"You are there now?"

"Not yet," Grace said. She didn't think he needed to know every move she made. Even though she felt so comfortable around him, she had to constantly remind herself he was a total stranger. And her guilt had doubled ever since she had realized it had been him she'd kissed and not Jake. The sexual tension had definitely increased since the discovery. She'd find him looking at her as if he remembered that kiss as much as she did. *I'm sorry, Jake, I'm so, so sorry.*

"I thought we had a good plan. You leave while I'm dressing? Did I do something to offend you?"

"No. I'm sorry. I just—after that picture—I don't want Jake to get the wrong idea."

"Ah. You actually think they will bring him?"

"We don't know that there even is a 'they.' Maybe it's just Carrie Ann carrying a joke a little too far. Either way I'm going to find out. Alone."

"It is a public park, no?"

"Jean Sebastian. Thank you for watching over me so far. But you shouldn't be involved in this anymore. Please. Just enjoy the rest of your travels."

"I don't think you—"

"Good-bye." Grace hung up. She turned the phone off. At least he'd had one good idea—getting two phones. The contact number she'd put on Jake's voice mail and Facebook page was for her second phone. Jean Sebastian didn't have that number. She wouldn't have to worry about him interrupting again. There was a chance he would show up at the park, however. But she had a plan for that too.

I am alone but Jean Sebastian knows where we are meeting. I don't know how to stop him from showing up at the bench. Please text another place to meet.

Was she the biggest idiot on the planet? If so, it was all because of Jake. If the roles had been reversed, he would have done anything to find her. She was going to play by the kidnappers' rules for now. At least until she had some clue what she was up against. She didn't even know if they would read and respond to the text, but at least she had to try. It couldn't have been Jake communicating or he would have answered the phone. So she had to assume someone had him. Unless Carrie Ann had tied him up while he was drugged, Grace didn't know how Carrie Ann could pull it off alone. So Grace decided to go with the assumption that Carrie Ann had married Stan Gale, that he was psychotic and blamed Grace for the past, and that he had taken Jake hostage. The goal for today was to find out what he wanted her to do, and then she would probably do it. But first she was going to demand proof that Jake and Carrie Ann were all right.

Which brought her back to Rafael. He had to be in cahoots with Stan. It was his club. And he was a tall and strong guy—heck, just wearing that eagle costume all day and walking around on stilts took a certain amount of stamina. He was weird enough to be involved too. He'd better not hurt Jake. Grace sat on the bench and propped her guitar on the ground. She suddenly felt foolish for bringing it. She longed for two days ago when the stupid review from Marsh Everett was her biggest worry. Life was so simple, and because of it, tragic. Simple because the only things that ever really mattered were the people you loved and the things you loved to do. Tragic, because those things were often overlooked, and yet at the core they were so fragile. Fragile, delicate, beautiful. So easily broken. Mistreated. Ripped away. *Just give me back Jake. I will never want for anything else ever again.* Her phone beeped.

Footpath under the viaduct

She had no idea where that was. *Whatever you do, don't get in a car with anyone or meet in an enclosed space.* Jean Sebastian was right about that. Did the viaduct count as an enclosed space? Well, there was nothing she could do about it now; she was the one who had suggested a second location.

I will be there

She'd start looking for it right now. If it seemed too dangerous, she would figure out an alternative. At least they were still communicating. Speaking of which, it was time to send her first demand.

I need proof that Jake is okay

If I do that, there are rules

?????

No crying out. No screaming. No reaching for anything.

"No reaching for anything" she could understand. But—No crying out? No screaming? What was he planning?

Fine. Who is this?

No questions. 6:00 sharp.

Grace began to walk the park, taking note of any landmark she could easily find, just in case she needed to exit quickly. She loved how Gaudí had built bird nests into the terrace wall. She noted a section where there was an overhang with mosaic tiled ceilings—a bright yellow sun against a blue background. That would be easy to spot. Another audience-pleaser was a large, mosaic-tiled salamander lying in the middle divide of a set of stone steps. He was called *el drac*, which meant dragon—even though he was a salamander. The park had several levels and three viaducts, all built with stones from the park. The lower level, where Grace was to meet whoever was doing the texting, was supported by sloping or inclined columns, angled in to handle the weight from above. Entering the footpath below felt like being in an ancient underground tunnel. It wasn't entirely enclosed, but there were also fewer people down here. She could see how screaming might get someone's attention; voices probably echoed down here. Grace took out her guitar. Wouldn't hurt to draw a little crowd.

The instant she held her Hummingbird against her body, she felt calmer, more confident. She'd missed it. She started with some simple instrumental tunes, just to check out the acoustics. As she suspected, there was a slight echo through the tunnels, but she kind of liked the effect. Sure enough, after five or so minutes, people nearby stopped to listen, and soon she had drawn a little crowd. A few even walked up with money, searching the ground near her for a hat or a tip jar. Under normal circumstances this is when she'd start singing. And a tiny part of her was dying to do it. A single ember, burning a hole in her heart. But now was not the time to lament the death of her dream. People weren't the only things in this life that were fragile. The only thing that mattered now was Jake. It was five-thirty. She didn't need to risk the crowd's keeping Stan away, so she stopped playing and moved on. Fifteen minutes later, she returned, guitar tucked up tight in its case.

And then, it was time. Exactly six p.m. according to her phone. Her heart hammered in her chest. Grace didn't know where along the pathway she would meet up with whoever it was, which was why she had taken to walking a section back and forth, hoping to see or be seen. If Jean Sebastian was in the park, she had yet to spot him either. Perhaps he was waiting on the serpentine bench, or maybe he'd realized he'd rather go out for sangria and tapas and tango dancers than follow her crazy predicament all over Spain. Either way she wished him well. There was a teeny tiny part of her that wanted him to be waiting on the bench above. Despite her guilt and the regrettable kiss, he had been a great comfort to her. She hated being alone and second-guessing every move she made. She turned to pace in the other direction and came to a dead halt. Carrie Ann and Jake were standing in front of her, just a few feet away. Despite her promise, she cried out. Immediately, Jake shook his head, "no." Grace clamped her mouth shut and waited. "Jake," she said after a few seconds. It came out as a strangled whisper. Carrie Ann and Jake hadn't moved, were just standing as still as statues, both wearing very serious expressions.

Grace walked closer, and then closer, until she couldn't help it, she was running toward Jake, planning on throwing herself in his arms. His arm jerked up, and he held his hand out in a "stop" position. And it wasn't just his arm that went up; Carrie Ann's did too. They were handcuffed together.

Grace came to a stop, tottering back on her heels and almost losing her balance. Tears flooded her eyes as she stopped and stared. Jake slowly nodded, and their arms went back to their sides. As far as Grace could see, they were alone in the tunnel.

"Let him go," Grace cried out. "Let him go."

"Gee, thanks," Carrie Ann said. Grace made eye contact with Carrie Ann, but she couldn't bring herself to apologize. She wasn't convinced that Carrie Ann was a victim. It was very likely that she was actually spearheading the whole thing.

"Is this a game, Carrie Ann?" Carrie Ann didn't answer, move, or even blink. "I'm going to find out. I'm going to find out everything," Grace said.

"He's watching," Jake said. His voice was low and measured. She searched his face for any sign of harm. And then looked at Carrie Ann. Besides looking tired and smudged, she had a swollen lip. Otherwise, they appeared to be okay. Grace had to ask anyway.

Jake nodded. "How about you? Are you okay?" he asked. His voice caught.

"I don't remember that kiss, Jake," Grace said. "I was drugged."

"I know. So were we." His voice was strangled. The way he said it made Grace wonder if there was a picture somewhere of him kissing Carrie Ann. But none of that mattered now. Grace wanted to touch him so badly. She took a step forward.

"No," Carrie Ann said. "He's watching."

"Stan and Rafael?" Grace said. "Are they doing this to you?" Grace's phone dinged, and she jumped. She glanced at the screen.

No questions. I hear everything.

"The threats are real, Grace," Jake said. "So please. Just do everything he says, okay?"

"What does he want, Jake? I can't take this."

"Here," Carrie Ann said. She extended her hand. In it was a piece of paper. "The first clue," she said. Grace took the paper and opened it. A series of dashes made up the middle of the page with a message underneath.

———————

(Go to Picasso Museum)

Grace looked up and around the tunnel, wondering where Stan was hiding. "Please," Grace said. "No games. Just let them go. If you want money, I'll get money." She lifted her guitar. "This is a Taylor Hummingbird. It's worth a lot. Take it."

"He doesn't want money," Carrie Ann said.

Grace opened her arms. "You want me? Here I am. Take me and let them go."

"Grace," Carrie Ann said. "For once in your life shut up and listen to me."

"Just come on out, Stan. Let's talk."

"Person," Carrie Ann said.

"What?" Grace said.

"Skirt," Carrie Ann said.

"What?"

"Go," Carrie Ann said.

"But—" Grace's phone dinged again.

Now or I punish them. Text when you know the word.

Grace stared into Jake's eyes. He stared back. *I love you,* she mouthed. He nodded.

"He's okay with you being with Jean Sebastian," Carrie Ann said. Jake made a noise; Carrie Ann jerked on the handcuff.

"Jake?" Grace said. It took a minute for Jake to look at Grace. When he did she got the feeling there was so much he wanted to say. She wished he could tell her something without anyone's knowing. They could probably manage to talk in code, but whoever was behind this wasn't letting them talk. What exactly was he threatening them with? What was stopping them from running right now? Grace didn't have the answers, but she wasn't stupid. They were terrified. Something was keeping them from turning and coming with her. Was he hiding somewhere with a gun on them? Were there explosives under their clothing? Whatever it was, it was enough to keep them in line, and Grace wasn't going to jeopardize them. "You're saying it's okay if Jean Sebastian helps me?"

"Yes," Carrie Ann said.

"There's nothing to worry about, Jake," Grace said. "I love you." Jake nodded, then looked away. It took everything Grace had not to run to him and hug him and kiss him. When this was over, she was going to be the best girlfriend ever. Or wife. Maybe she would propose to him. She couldn't imagine the rest of her life without Jake Hart.

"Hurry," Carrie Ann said. "There's a time limit."

"What time limit?"

"Eight hours for the first clue," Jake said.

"Or what?" Grace said.

"Please, Grace," Jake said. "Please." The tone of his voice got her attention. Jake sounded so vulnerable. Was Stan threatening to hurt him? She wanted to scream; she wanted to rush to Jake, throw herself in his arms, and never let go. She was going to get Stan for this. She would go along for now, but she was going to get him for this. Carrie Ann too if she was in on it.

"Is that it? Person? Five letters? The Picasso Museum?"

"The true victim," Carrie Ann said. This time it was her voice that caught. *The true victim?*

Jake looked at Grace again. He had the same look on his face as when he had found out about Carrie Ann. Grace knew that look. Whatever this was, it was her fault this was happening. She wished to God she knew why.

"Go," Carrie Ann said.

"Wait," Grace said. "I have to ask a question. Whoever you are. I have to." She looked to the stones in the ceiling above as if he were part of them. Her phone dinged.

What?

"Jake's mom has been calling my parents. She wants him to call her. If he doesn't, she's going to worry. Then my parents are going to worry. Then they're all going to keep calling me. I'm already stressed, and I'm not a very good liar." Grace couldn't help but glance at Carrie Ann on this. But she didn't react, didn't even blink.

I'll deal with it.

Grace wondered if this meant Stan was going to let Jake call his mom. She hoped so. She hoped wherever they were going back to wasn't horrible. She hoped they were eating, and sleeping, and being treated fairly.

"One more thing." Grace's phone didn't ding again, but she knew Stan was listening. "I see Carrie Ann's lip is busted. If you lay a hand on her again, this deal is off and I go straight to the police."

Grace glanced at Carrie Ann. She was surprised to see tears spilling out of Carrie Ann's eyes. Then, Jake took Carrie Ann's hand and held it. A wall of mixed emotions hit Grace. Of course Jake was going to comfort his fellow hostage. But it also felt like a knife to the chest. She wanted to crumple to the ground.

"Go," Carrie Ann said again.

CHAPTER 28

Every time they went outside, Jake waited for an opportunity to bolt. But Rafael was always their shadow, flexing those ridiculous knives, and situating himself so that he could easily overtake Jake if he tried to run. Rafael also had the home-field advantage; Jake was new to the neighborhood of Nou Barris, located in the northeast of Barcelona.

Although they were only a short metro ride to La Rambla, Jake might as well have been in a different country, given the odds of Grace's stumbling upon him here. It wasn't a tourist destination, and the two hadn't discussed coming here at all. Besides, Carrie Ann's psycho husband was never going to let Grace come here. And even if he did, even if as part of his sick game he tipped her off that they were here, there was no way she would be able to find their exact location. Known as a working-class neighborhood, Nou Barris was also home to several parks. Carrie Ann and Jake were given a half an hour to sit in one of them. Under the ever-watchful eye of Rafael of course. They were also told they were going to be allowed to have one meal out. Today it was to be at a café around the corner from the flat where the psycho was keeping them. After entering the café, Jake and Carrie Ann were told to sit against the far wall, while Rafael chose a table close to the door. This worked in Jake's favor, for Jake decided to keep his eye on *him.*

"Stop staring at him," Carrie Ann said. "He's not going to budge."

Jake turned back to Carrie Ann. She was ripping apart a piece of bread. Her fingers made him think of talons.

"How did Stan meet our Spanish friend in the first place?"

Carrie Ann shrugged, swept the piece of bread through the little plate of olive oil in front of her, and popped it into her mouth. Jake waited while she chewed. "He lived in Barcelona for a year," she said. "Right out of high school. Raf was his roomie."

"But you're the one who contacted Rafael this time? So we'd all have a free place to stay?"

"Stan wanted to see Grace. So did I. But I had no idea this was part of the plan, okay? I'm just as shocked as you are."

"Forgive me if I don't believe everything you say."

"Do you really think I care?"

"No," Jake said. He leaned forward. Rafael started to get up. Jake put his hands up and leaned back. Rafael sat down again, with a shake of his finger. "I don't think you care about anyone but yourself."

Carrie Ann slammed her hands down on the little table. The silverware clattered.

"Shhh," Rafael said, although the only other patron was an old man by the front door who definitely looked too old to hear much of anything. The waiters were all in the kitchen, only coming out when pressed, and giving them looks that conveyed they'd rather not be bothered. Jake wondered how fast they'd be if he and Carrie Ann decided to do a dine-and-dash.

Jake kept his voice as low as possible. "Is there any kind of leverage you might have over Rafael?"

"He wants to sleep with me," Carrie Ann said. "Would you like that? Should I whore myself out for Grace?"

"I don't care about your 'tough girl' act, Carrie Ann. If

you're truly a hostage—like me—I would think you'd want to do almost anything to get away from him and find Grace."

"I'm not sleeping with him. How dare you."

"What's your plan? Let Stan control everything? Hurt us. Hurt Grace? Tell me something—those tears in the park. Were they real?"

Carrie Ann looked away. She took a pack of cigarettes out of her purse. "Grace is smart, you know. She'll figure it out." Carrie Ann stuck the unlit cigarette in her mouth. She'd been smoking nonstop in their tiny little room. If she lit up here, Jake was going to rip up every single cigarette in her pack. That night, Jake was handcuffed to the pipe, stuck on the floor, while Carrie Ann was uncuffed on the bed. He hadn't figured out which team she was playing for. He wouldn't be surprised if it was a little bit of both. Whatever suited her in the moment. He felt a surge of anger that this girl had descended on Grace's life. Carrie Ann was cunning and mean at times, vulnerable and sweet at others. She was hard to look away from, but even harder to be with. He'd only been in her presence a few days, and he was already thoroughly confused. He could only imagine Grace's trying to deal with her as a child. Of course Carrie Ann would have been a child too, but this was almost impossible to imagine. And from what Grace had said, Carrie Ann had been forced to grow up awfully fast.

The puzzle. The stupid game. Another bit of information Carrie Ann was keeping from him. He was damn sure she knew the answer, and she wouldn't tell him. "It's between them," she said whenever he asked. Jake lifted the little container of sugar on the table. He shook the single rose in a little vase. He rattled their plates and shook out their napkins. Carrie Ann glanced at Rafael, then lowered her voice. "What are you doing?"

"Proving there's no bug. Rafael is way over there. He can't hear us."

"So?"

"So you're going to tell me what that 'clue' was all about. You're going to tell me everything you know that pertains to my wife—"

"Your wife?"

Jake stopped. It had just slipped out. The engagement ring was back in their flat in La Rambla. Had Grace found it? He should have proposed when he had the chance. It was torture being stranded from her. Her thirtieth birthday was in a few days. It was supposed to be their last full day in Barcelona. "Girlfriend, whatever," Jake said. "Start talking." He watched Carrie Ann's face contort. She was either a consummate actress, or she was truly afraid. What was stopping her from running? Besides Rafael? Jake couldn't figure it out. He wasn't running because the psycho had said he'd hurt Grace. And, of course, Rafael. Those stupid knives. He wore them constantly, missing no opportunity to clench his fists so they could see and hear the knives shoot out. But would Rafael actually try and hurt Carrie Ann? Jake didn't think so. Which meant she was either a part of this sick plan, or she was just as worried about Grace as he was.

"Look. I know you're upset," Carrie Ann said, leaning in. "But you got to see her. She's okay. You saw for yourself."

"For now. And—are you really that clueless?"

"I guess I am, Romeo. What?"

"I had to stand a few feet away from the girl I love. I couldn't touch her. I couldn't warn her. I couldn't protect her. It killed me. Don't you get that?"

"She's worried about you too."

"I want to meet him. I want to talk to him. Tell Rafael to tell Stan to face me. Man to man." Carrie Ann looked at Jake. He couldn't help but think she was beautiful. But it wasn't the kind of beauty that inspired joy. It was the kind of beauty that ripped out hearts and lied to your face.

"Do you want to challenge him to a duel?"

"Whatever it takes."

"He's already doing what it takes. Just let him play his little word game with Grace, and before you know it this will all be over."

"You really think someone who is psycho enough to play this

sick game in the first place is just going to let us all go when she gets the answers right?"

"I'm counting on it."

This time it was Jake who slammed his fist on the table. "Not good enough for me," he said. "I'm out of here." He stood. Rafael stood. Jake threw open his arms. "What are you going to do? Kill me in the middle of the restaurant?"

"No," Rafael said. "I will chase you. I will kill you near one of the aqueducts."

"What do you want? Money? Grace and I can get you money."

"Sit down," Carrie Ann said.

Jake leaned down. "If I run, Rafael chases me. Maybe he catches up with me; maybe he doesn't. But you'll be free. Then you can run."

"And then he kills Grace."

Jake sat, stared at her as hard as he could, as if that would help dig the truth out of her. "And you really care about that?"

Carrie Ann opened her purse. She took out her wallet. She opened it, then handed it to Jake. At first, he didn't want to take it. "Look through it," Carrie Ann said.

Jake took the wallet. The driver's license caught his eye.

"Pull it out," Carrie Ann said.

"It's Grace's license," Jake said.

"Her credit cards are there too." Carrie Ann pulled a passport out of her purse.

"You stole her ID?"

"Guess what ID she has?"

"Carrie Ann."

"Bingo. She even used it to get into the club. She also has my engagement ring."

"You dropped that into a beer. She was saving it for you."

"The police won't know that. They'll think she used my credit card to pay for the flat you were staying in."

"Why would they think she used your credit card to pay for the flat? We thought we won the trip. That it was paid for."

"Yes, but it was actually paid for on my credit card."

"Grace didn't know that!"

"Jake. Don't you see? It doesn't matter. What matters is how the police will view it. Especially when they find out that she used my credit card later for a few items while shopping."

"Just what are you getting at?"

"Identity theft."

"You're stealing her identity?"

"No. She's stealing mine."

"Come again?"

"Remember when we were separated?"

At one point Rafael had come into the room and "taken" Carrie Ann. She had been gone for several hours. When she had returned, she wouldn't talk. "Yes."

"He took me to the police station."

"What?"

"I had to fill out a report. Accusing Grace of stealing my identity."

"Come again?"

"She has my ID, my credit cards—she even used one yesterday morning at a kiosk in La Rambla. The bouncer will remember her using my ID. She has my diamond ring—"

"It's all innocent!"

"You have no idea how ironic it is."

"What does that mean?"

"I'll get to that. The point is, he's orchestrated all of this. Don't you see? He's ten steps ahead of all of us."

"So now if Grace tries to go to the police—"

"They'll detain her. Which is why he keeps warning her. No police. For her own good I hope she listens."

"Why? Why is he doing this?"

Carrie Ann opened her purse. She removed a picture and showed it to Jake. The picture looked old. It had been taken underneath a tree house. Two little girls, one blond, one brunette. Maybe ten years old. Their faces were dirty. Their arms were looped around each other. Big grins on their faces.

244 • *Mary Carter*

In the background stood an overweight boy with hair that desperately needed a cut. He looked out of place. He was staring at the girls, not smiling.

"You and Grace," Jake said. "Is that Stan?"

"The one and only."

Jake brought the picture closer and studied it, trying to figure out what Stan would look like now. It was useless. "So, what? This picture is proof that you care about Grace?"

"Point to Grace," Carrie Ann said. Jake took the picture and pointed to the brunette. Carrie Ann looked just as Grace had described. Blond, scruffy, tough. But vulnerable too. There it was again, the ambivalence he felt toward Carrie Ann. If he was honest, there had been moments of sexual attraction too. He couldn't help it. She was a beautiful woman. And Grace was probably attracted to Jean Sebastian as well. That killed Jake. Because he trusted himself. He didn't trust that asshole no matter what anybody else said.

"Point to me," Carrie Ann said. Jake hated these games, but he went ahead and pointed to Carrie Ann. "I'm sure Grace has told you the story of Carrie Ann since you've been here?" Jake shrugged. That was between him and Grace. "Orphan girl? Nothing to her name but a little vinyl suitcase? A chip on her shoulder bigger than she could carry? More foster homes than she could count? No better than one of the strays you treat in your practice, Jake. Carrie Ann had nothing. No love. No family. No hope. Until Grace. Grace was the only good thing in her life. Ever. To this day. You can think whatever you want of me. But these two—" Carrie Ann held up the picture. It shook in her hands. "They're family. And I'm not going to abandon her. I did that once. Not this time, do you hear me? Not this time."

"I hope you're telling the truth. Because we have to do something. We can't just sit around and let Stan take control like some kind of Wizard of Oz. You have to tell me everything you know."

"Well, for starters—Carrie Ann? I know her."

"What's that supposed to mean? Why are you talking about yourself in the third person?"

"You have no clue who that girl really is. No clue."

"You are a game player, aren't you? I don't care about what-ever little secret from the past you're holding over her head—"

Carrie Ann opened her purse. She handed him Grace's ID. Jake picked up Grace's driver's license, ran his finger along the picture. "Why are you showing me this again?"

Carrie Ann picked up the photograph of the three children. She pointed to the brunette. "That's me," she said.

"No," Jake said. "That's Grace."

"It is Grace, and it's also me."

"Excuse me?"

"Just like this driver's license." She held up Grace's driver's license. "This time it's her picture," Carrie Ann said. "But it's my identity."

"Stop it. Just what the fuck are you saying?"

"I'm saying my name isn't Carrie Ann. It's Grace. I'm Grace Ann Sawyer."

CHAPTER 29

Grace held the piece of paper with the little dashes clutched in her hand. On it she had written the clues.

Skirt. Person. The true victim.

"Do you have any idea what we're looking for?" Jean Sebastian said. "A painting of a woman in a skirt?" They stood in the Palau Aguilar, the first of a series of courtyards connecting the townhouses that made up the Museu Picasso. After the incident in the viaducts, Grace found Jean Sebastian waiting for her on the Serpentine Bench. She had promised Jean Sebastian that she wouldn't try and go it alone anymore. It wasn't safe. Seeing the fear on Jake's and Carrie Ann's faces convinced her of that.

"I have no idea," Grace said. "But look at this place. I read that it dates back to the thirteenth to fifteenth centuries."

"The architecture is stunning."

"It's a mutt," Grace said.

"What does this mean, 'mutt?' " Jean Sebastian said.

"It's a mix of medieval, Renaissance, and baroque styles."

"You've always had your nose in a book," Jean Sebastian said, pointing at her as if he had her pegged.

"How did you know that?"

"I just have this theory about people." He didn't tell her what it was. Instead, he took in their surroundings. Grace watched him as he looked around and found herself wondering what he had been like as a boy. Had he ridden his bike up and down cobblestone streets? She imagined he had been active, and friendly, and charming. Just like now. She'd better stop thinking about him like that. Silently they headed up the grand staircase that led to the first-floor balcony. The windows adorning the beautiful stone palace were also from various time periods, but Grace had already said enough. She could have spent an entire day in the first courtyard alone. She felt a spasm of anger. She should be enjoying the architecture. With Jake. This was supposed to be a holiday, and instead she was on some kind of demented scavenger hunt. It took everything she had to keep her emotions under control. Throwing a fit would not help her find Jake any faster.

Jean Sebastian touched her elbow as they entered the museum. "What's your theory?" Grace finally asked. She was dying to know.

"That we are born with our personalities," Jean Sebastian said. "If you read a lot now, you read a lot as a kid. A mean old lady was a mean little girl. We cannot hide who we are. Oh, we can change the outside, maybe, like this museum has done, but inside, we are who we are. I find that comforting."

We are who we are.

The true victim. So what did that mean? Who was to say which one of them had endured the most torture? *Torture.* Did the clue refer to some masochistic piece of art? That sounded more like Salvador Dalí than Picasso. "I honestly have no idea what we're looking for," Grace said after they paid for their tickets.

"Did Stan Gale used to play word games with you?"

"No. Then he would have actually had to speak to me. And I would have had to look at him."

"You mean he was shy?"

"Not exactly. He was just—awkward. He'd stare and stare at me without any kind of awareness that he was being rude."

"Sounds like he had a crush on you."

"That's what Carrie Ann said. But at the time I didn't know that. I just thought he was creepy."

"So you wouldn't look at him?"

"I know it sounds awful."

"I'm not judging. I'm just curious."

"Stan didn't win the looks lottery. He was overweight. He had acne. He had these greasy, floppy bangs that hid his eyes—which frankly were his best feature. I felt bad for him. But he just had this intensity that gave me the creeps. I'm not proud of it now, but I could barely make eye contact with him."

"It seems as if he's definitely trying to communicate now. I'd say it would be well worth your while to try and figure out exactly what he has to say." Grace shook her head, not because she disagreed with Jean Sebastian, but because she had no idea how to figure out what Stan was trying to say. She still wasn't even a hundred percent convinced it was really him. She had yet to look up a phone number for Lydia Gale, because she was still the last person Grace wanted to disturb. Or face. Who knew what hearing from Grace might do to her. Grace's family had been the one that foisted Carrie Ann off on the Gales. It had been Grace's tears that had moved Lydia to invite Carrie Ann into her home. Grace would only contact Lydia if she had no other choice. If this was all just a big lie, if Stan had nothing to do with this, Grace wasn't going to be the one to stir up a hornet's nest.

So for now Grace and Jean Sebastian hurried through the museum, feeling totally lost. There were so many stunning works. Picasso had such a range. There were so many variations, starting with his work at nineteen, which was very realistic, all the way through his Blue Period, and Rose Period, and Cubist works. Grace wished she could just enjoy the experience, pretend she was a tourist strolling through the masterpieces with her boyfriend before dinner. Jake should have been at her side. What were they doing to him? Was he all right? This was insane. Why was she wandering through this museum without a clue as to what she should be looking for besides "female" and "skirt." Picasso had too many paintings of females, and mistresses, and yes, most of them were wearing skirts. In the few seconds she wasn't panicking, Grace had to marvel at how unbelievably beautiful some of his simplest sketches were—just curving lines, a brief sketch of an owl, a goat, or the famous bouquet of flowers. How was it possible to sketch a line so beautiful that everyone stopped to stare?

Grace stopped and turned to Jean Sebastian. "I love his works," she said. "But I don't understand this game. Or the puzzle. We could be in here for days and still not have a clue."

"Why don't we buy the catalogue with all his works. We can go sit somewhere, have a drink, and go through it."

"But why are we even playing this game? I think I made a mistake. I should have gone to the police."

"Whatever you say. If you want to go, we will go."

He was being so reasonable. She was starting to feel like she wanted to just lose it, have a complete mental breakdown. Call her dad and tell him what was going on. Go to the police. But she'd heard it directly from Jake's mouth. *Just do what he says.* "I agree. We'll buy a catalogue. But if we go through it and don't understand the clue—it's straight to the police station."

Grace usually loved taking her time in museum gift shops. This time, she went straight to the counter and asked for their most recent catalogue. It was beautiful and thick. Even this would take time. She went to pay cash for the catalogue, then stopped. The saleslady watched Grace as she clutched her euros. She should save her cash. She didn't have her ATM card and wouldn't be able to get more. She'd also forgotten to cancel her credit cards and call her bank. There was just too much going on. She took out Carrie Ann's credit card and handed it to the saleslady with a smile. "Better save my cash."

The lady smiled back, although Grace could tell she was only being polite. She swiped the credit card and slid it back to Grace. Then, the saleslady looked at her computer screen and frowned.

"May I see your card again?"

"Of course." Grace slid the credit card back and the woman

snatched it up. Keeping it aloft in her left hand, the woman opened a drawer with her right. Grace was a little slow. In the second it took her to think—*why is the saleslady holding up a pair of scissors?*—the lady had already snipped Carrie Ann's credit card in two. "Go," Jean Sebastian whispered in her ear. He took out his wallet and gently shoved Grace. Without looking back she quickly headed out to the courtyard. By the time she reached it, she was breathing hard. Why had she run? Obviously the card had been canceled, but she didn't need to behave like a criminal. Of course she was using someone else's credit card. Stan, or Carrie Ann, or whoever had kidnapped Jake wanted her to run out of money. Jean Sebastian was going at a fast clip when he tucked his arm around Grace's shoulder, and together they hurried out to the street.

"This way," he said, plunging them into the most crowded spot.

"Don't tell me she's chasing us," Grace said. "I hardly think a canceled credit card—"

Jean Sebastian stopped, and Grace bumped into him. His cologne was incredible. She felt a shot of desire. How could she? With Jake in trouble. She jerked away from him. "You replaced your wallet," she said to Jean Sebastian.

Jean Sebastian patted his pocket. "Yes. I bought a new one. And I always keep extra credit cards back in my room."

"Smart. Jake tried to tell me not to keep all my belongings in one place."

"You can never be too careful." He handed her the catalogue.

"Thank you," she said. "I'll pay you back."

"It's the least thing on my mind."

"It's getting too complicated," Grace said. "I think we have to go to the police station. Now."

"Stan or Carrie Ann must have reported the credit card stolen," Jean Sebastian said. "I don't think you should go to the police."

"They won't know I had her credit card," Grace said. "I don't have it anymore." Grace headed toward the metro. "Besides, maybe it was just at its max. We don't know it was reported stolen."

"It's a good guess," Jean Sebastian said. "Especially if someone is playing games. Think about it. Don't you think they've anticipated your going to the police?"

"I think they're trying to scare me off going to the police, which means they don't want me to go to the police, which means I should go to the police."

"I don't like it. I think they're three steps ahead of us."

"You don't have to come with me."

"But I'm a witness."

Grace stopped, and Jean Sebastian bumped into her. He put his hand on her hip to steady himself. Peered down at her with those intense light brown eyes. She backed away. Another three seconds and she would have kissed him. *I'm sorry, Jake. It's just chemical. And it's so unbelievably strong. But I love you. I love you.* Grace looked away from Jean Sebastian as she spoke. "You'll tell them you were drugged too?"

"Of course. Although there's no telling if they'll believe us. It's not like we have proof."

"You said you passed out after one drink. That's not proof?"

"The drugs are no longer in our system. We don't have the glasses we drank from—and we didn't see anyone put anything in our drinks. Even if they thought we were telling the truth, police need evidence."

"It doesn't matter. We have to get it on the record anyway." As they neared the police station on La Rambla, Grace could see a line winding halfway down the block. "Oh my God," she said.

"There is a lot of theft in Barcelona," Jean Sebastian said.

"And we forgot a picture of Jake. Again."

"*Ayayay.*"

"It doesn't matter. I'm reporting it anyway. I'll bring a picture later." Grace watched the people in line, wondering what had happened to them. Most likely here to report stolen wallets and passports. What she wouldn't give to have just that problem. Although her passport was gone too, and she was going to need a police report to be able to fly home. Home. She ached for it. But she wasn't leaving without Jake. No matter what.

As Grace stood in line, thinking, worrying, she came to a conclusion. Carrie Ann wasn't married to Stan. Carrie Ann had upped her game. Rafael was helping her, and that was it. Carrie Ann was the one who liked to drop clues like a demented tale of Hansel and Gretel. There was no other explanation as to why Carrie Ann and Jake were handcuffed together and why Jake seemed so afraid. The long silences, the way he had looked at her. He'd been trying to tell her something. Was it—*Open your eyes, she's doing it again! . . . ?*

Unless Jake had bought Carrie Ann's victim routine. Grace hated the thought of Jake's falling prey to Carrie Ann. Just look at the way he had held her hand. Comforting her crocodile tears. What other lies was she feeding him? Normally, Jake was very astute. Analytical. But he was probably exhausted. Drugged. Handcuffed. He might not be thinking clearly. Especially if Carrie Ann was spinning a tale. About Grace. About their past. Everything according to Carrie Ann. It was a terrifying thought.

They had barely moved in line. Was she even in the right line? It seemed to her that drugged, identity stolen, and boyfriend kidnapped should trump lost wallet, but there didn't seem to be any weeding out. Jean Sebastian must have sensed she didn't want to talk, for he stayed silently by her side with his arms crossed. Once again, she realized how lucky she was that she had him. Even if Jake wouldn't be happy.

"I need to find a restroom," Jean Sebastian said when they were finally moving up.

"I'll be here," Grace said.

"If I don't see you, I'll meet you by the chairs." He pointed to a waiting area where those who had made it through the first portion of the line were filling out paperwork.

"Great," Grace said. When she got up to the desk, the police-woman spoke to her in Spanish. "Do you speak English?" Grace asked.

"Yes. What can we do for you?"

"I don't know where to start. Okay. Last night I was drugged." Was it really just last night?

"What drugs did you take?"

"I didn't take drugs. I was drugged. Somebody put something in my drink."

"Did you wake up somewhere you didn't recognize? Were you a victim of sexual assault?"

"No. I mean I kissed a guy without remembering it, but— no—I woke up in the bathroom of a club—"

The woman handed her a clipboard. "Fill this out. We will need the name of the club—"

"Wait. I'm not done. My ID is gone—my money, my passport—"

"Okay, okay. Yes, we will still need you to fill this out—" She was already looking to the next person in line.

"Wait—I was with a group of people—and they're missing."

"A policeman will speak with you after you fill out the paperwork."

"Okay, but I should have said this first—my American boyfriend has been kidnapped." She felt a little guilty, stressing *American*, as if somehow that would make him more important than anyone else who went missing in Barcelona. The clerk gave her a look that finally sent Grace to the wall of chairs with her paperwork.

She was halfway through filling it out—name, address, how long have you been in Spain, what is the address where you are staying, what is the date of your return flight, what is the airline, what is the date the incident occurred, etcetera, etcetera—when she realized that Jean Sebastian was taking an awful long time in the bathroom. Maybe he was sick, or maybe he had just decided this wasn't his idea of a holiday and he had taken off. The thought left her feeling panicked. Even though she had tried to let him off the hook, he was on it now, and she didn't think she could handle this alone. From her seat in the waiting room she couldn't even see where the restrooms were. Short of finding them and going into the men's room, there wasn't much she could do.

Wait. She did have his phone number, and now that she had two phones, there was no reason why she shouldn't call him. Although it really wouldn't be very polite of her to call him given that he was a grown man who was in a restroom and he knew exactly where to meet her when he was finished doing whatever it was he was doing.

At least she was here, doing what she should have done the minute they returned from the nightclub. And so she waited. And waited. And waited. And listened to people speak Spanish, or Catalan, all around her. There were a few other tourists as well, but no Americans that she could tell. She tried to imagine what it would be like for a Spanish tourist in an American police station. Not fun, wherever you go; not in the guidebooks for a reason.

She was about to give up on Jean Sebastian, when he returned. He sat next to her. She could smell stale smoke. Mystery of why he'd taken so long solved. She almost wanted a cigarette herself. Anything to dull the nightmare.

"I don't know if I should give the name of the club," Grace said. "If they ask."

"Because if Rafael is somehow involved—"

"They'll know I went to the police."

"But you're here. This is the decision you made—to go to the police. Now would be the time to tell them everything."

"I'll take that into consideration."

"Otherwise, we shouldn't be here."

"I hear you." But she disagreed. She didn't have to play all of her cards. If a bunch of police officers showed up at the club, Carrie Ann would know. And she could use it against Grace. Jean Sebastian meant well, but it wasn't his lover at stake here. If, at a later date, Grace thought it could help, she would call the police and tell them she remembered the name of the club. "Listen," she said to Jean Sebastian. "I'll meet you somewhere. Back at the hotel even. There's no use both of us hanging out here."

"But we agreed I am a witness—I was drugged too." If Jean Sebastian stayed then he might blurt out the name of the club.

"I think you'd have to fill out a report of your own if you plan on telling them you were drugged too."

"I see," Jean Sebastian said.

"Otherwise, what's the point of mentioning the crime, right?"

"You are probably right. So you want to be all alone, is that it?" He looked at her, as if trying to analyze her on the spot. "You are a rock; you are an island," he said. "Is that the song?"

"I appreciate your help. It's just that—"

Jean Sebastian stood. "I understand. I will see you back at the hotel." And with that, he was gone. It was strange, and she felt guilty. Because, for some reason, it felt as if they'd just had their first lovers' quarrel. *I miss you, Jake. I just want you back. I don't think I can help it if there's something so attractive about Jean Sebastian. I just feel comfortable with him. Maybe because subconsciously I know that without him I'll really start to panic.*

Or maybe she was just a terrible person. Finally, an officer came out and called her name. Grace followed him to a busy room filled with desks, filled with people just like her. He indicated where she should sit. Across from her was a short, female police officer who looked as if she was ready to go home. Grace would be too. It was noisy in the station. Chairs squeaked, keyboards clacked, phones rang, and various conversations skittered throughout the space. Next to the officer sat a rotund middle-aged woman who introduced herself as the interpreter. The officer looked over Grace's paperwork. Even though the interpreter was present, the officer spoke in English when she could.

"You have had your wallet stolen?" she began.

"Yes. All my ID. Credit cards, cash, and my passport," Grace said. The officer shook her head. Grace didn't know if it was an empathy shake, or a how-could-you-be-so-stupid.

"Where was this stolen?"

"I'm not sure. I mean at a dance club, I think, but my friend—well, enemy is more like it . . . or frenemy—took my ID before that—"

The officer waited while the interpreter clarified. Grace won-

256 • *Mary Carter*

dered if she understood "frenemy," but kept quiet. The officer held up her hand as if Grace were going too fast, even though she was already finished speaking.

"Wait, wait, wait. *Un momento.* Your friend stole your ID?"

"Yes. Her name is Carrie Ann Gilbert." Oh, God. She hadn't really meant to blurt that out. The officer turned a piece of paper toward her.

"Write down the name," the interpreter said.

Grace hesitated. "The real reason I'm here is because my boyfriend is missing."

"Your boyfriend is missing."

"Yes."

The officer looked over her statement on the report. "You were out dancing, and drinking, and doing drugs—"

"No. No. I wasn't doing drugs. I was drugged. They put something in my drink."

"They. Who are they?"

"I don't know. Carrie Ann maybe—"

"Your friend who stole your ID."

"Yes."

"She also drug you."

"I think so. She was the last person I remember seeing. I woke up on the floor of the bathroom."

"Where? Where did you wake up?"

"Um—it was a dance club—here in Barcelona."

"What is the name of the club?"

"I don't remember."

"Where was it?"

Grace hesitated. If she said it was on the ocean that would certainly help them nail it down. "I don't remember," she said.

"We can write a police report documenting your missing identification. You can bring this police report to the airport. Okay?"

"Great. But I'm really here about Jake."

"Jake?"

"I told you! My boyfriend. He's—missing." Grace hadn't meant to yell at the officer, but her frustration was boiling over.

"Missing?"

Hadn't Grace said this already? "Yes. Missing. Kidnapped. Held hostage!" The police officer looked at the interpreter. The interpreter spoke in low, fast tones. Shoot. They thought she was nuts.

"Jake," the police officer said, once again looking over Grace's notes. "Carrie Ann," the officer said. Then she looked at Grace. "Carrie Ann Gilbert," she repeated. "American." She turned and shouted in Spanish to an officer a few desks behind her. The only parts of the sentence Grace understood were "Grace Saw-yer" and "Carrie Ann Gilbert." The male officer stood, then rummaged around his desk. He brought over a folder, handed it to the female police officer, and then stood, staring at Grace without a word. The female police officer slowly opened the folder.

"Your friend. Carrie Ann. She was here."

"She was here?" Grace said.

"Yes, she too had her wallet stolen."

"Wait. When was she here?"

"Do you want to know who she say stole her ID?" She looked up at Grace with infinite patience.

"Her husband? Stan Gale?"

"No, no, she did not say husband." The officer picked up something from the folder and turned it around so Grace could see what it was. It was a photograph—of her. Sitting in La Rambla. No doubt the one taken by Rafael. And she had thought she was being paranoid then. Whatever game this was, it had begun the minute Grace had arrived. And here she was, playing her part, going to the police, just like Carrie Ann had known she would. Grace stared at the picture, her mouth open, unable to speak. Should she tell the male police officer that a demented street performer, dressed like a serial-killing eagle, had taken the photo? It probably wouldn't help her credibility. The officer held up another photo. "Is this your missing boyfriend?" It was a picture of Carrie Ann and Jake sitting at a café. Carrie Ann had her arms around Jake, and her head was resting on his shoulder. Grace didn't answer. It was hard to answer when you were trying to remember how to breathe. The officer turned another page of the report and read: "Grace Sawyer is staying at my apartment without paying, and has stolen my driver's license, my diamond engagement ring, and my credit card. She is acting out because she discovered that her boyfriend and I are in love."

Grace shot out of her chair. "It's not true. He's being held against his will."

The officer shook her head at Grace as if she was disgusted with her. She looked at the photo of Carrie Ann and Jake with her eyebrows raised. She showed it to the interpreter and spoke in Spanish, then laughed.

"Interpret that," Grace said. "That's your job."

"She said he does not look like he is being held against his will."

"I know what it looks like. She planned this. Every single detail."

"Do you have her ID, or her engagement ring, or her credit card?" the officer said as her eyes landed on Grace's purse.

"She put her credit card in my purse, and she threw her ring into a pint of beer—"

"So you do have her credit card? You do have her ring. And her ID? Are you still staying in her flat?"

This wasn't good. Grace looked at her purse, wondering how she could just pick it up and run out without drawing attention to herself. "You know what?" Grace said. "It's true what they say. It is hard to travel in Europe with a friend, right? I guess we're a little mad at each other. She took my ID, she stole my boyfriend—it's just a girl thing. We'll work it out. I'm sorry to trouble you." Grace stood.

"Please, sit down. This report says you are attempting to commit identity fraud. Are you acknowledging you are in possession of the ID and credit card and ring of Carrie Ann Gilbert?"

"No, no. Carrie Ann has them back now. And I wasn't attempting identity fraud. She wanted me to hold on to her ID and credit card because they wouldn't fit in her purse. We were drinking. Dancing. You know?"

"This is not what my report says."

"Well, bring her into the station then, and the three of us can have a little chat." Grace wanted to grab the folder, and her own report, but they were on the other side of the desk. This officer wasn't going to care about Jake. Not now. Grace clutched her stomach and moaned.

"I'm going to be sick," she said. *"¿El baño?"* The interpreter and the officer pointed at the same time. *"Un momento,"* Grace said. Then she was down the hall and out the door. Once she hit La Rambla, she started jogging, then broke into a full-out run. Would they have arrested her? Grace wondered. She had no idea, but she couldn't afford to stick around and find out. The catalogue from Museu Picasso was weighing down her bag. She dug out her phone and texted "Jake."

You are not going to get away with this. I know this is all you, Carrie Ann. I'm coming for you.

Grace was almost to the beach when her phone dinged. She opened up her text to find nothing but a circle in the middle of the screen. One of those text image software programs no doubt, but what did it mean? Who draws and sends a circle? Grace sent back her confusion with a series of question marks.

???????????

Next she received a circle with a stem sticking out of it. Like a petal-less flower. Or a human head—

Oh, God. The clues. The blank slashes standing in for letters. The circle and now the stem. The head and the body. Hangman. They were playing a game of hangman.

CHAPTER 30

"This is impossible!" Grace said. Disgusted, she shoved the catalogue away from her. They were seated at an outdoor café high atop Montjuïc on fortress grounds that also held an ancient castle. It was past dark and they probably weren't supposed to be here, but somehow Jean Sebastian had convinced one of the workers to let them in. He'd even wrangled them each a cup of coffee. It must be nice to have money to bribe people, Grace thought. She was lucky he was on her side.

Now open to the public as a museum, back in the day the grounds had been protected by a moat and 120 cannons. Grace could imagine a sign hanging on the stone wall. BEWARE OF 120 CANNONS. She wondered if there was a fun song in there somewhere—*Forget the pool, build me a moat. . . . Get rid of the lawnmower, I want a goat. . . .*

Jake wasn't here to tease her about composing in her head, and the pain of it hit her so hard she almost cried out. The other thing crying out to her was the picture in her pocket of Carrie Ann and Jake in the café. She'd swiped it off the police officer's desk just before her run to the bathroom. It was true. He didn't look as if he was being held against his will. His hands were visible atop the table. Why didn't he just run?

She hadn't said a word about it to Jean Sebastian, nor did she mention that the word game was a version of hangman. She just couldn't bring herself to tell him everything. She wouldn't be able to take it if he pointed out the obvious in the photo— that Jake and Carrie Ann looked awfully cozy. And when Grace had seen them in Park Güell, Jake had taken Carrie Ann's hand right in front of her. One thing was for sure: He didn't see Carrie Ann for the manipulator that she was.

"Don't bother," Grace said. "I think we've been led on a wild-goose chase." Jean Sebastian was intently studying the Picasso catalogue. Grace's coffee was growing cold. She needed it though; she felt fatigued to her bones. She wanted to share every little thing she was thinking or feeling with Jake. She wanted to text him every thought, every sight, every song lyric. Where was he and what was he doing right now? She knew she should have been paying more attention to the catalogue like Jean Sebastian, but she was too numb. Instead, she mused about the history of the fortress, guiltily taking comfort in the fact that life had been harsh and cruel back in the day. In a strange way, it gave her comfort. She was suffering. Jake was suffering. The people who lived in this castle back in the day had suffered, and in life you had no choice but to build fortresses, and moats, and set up your cannons.

How did she go about building a fortress? What were her cannons against Carrie Ann?

She's angry with me. I forgive you, she had said about Lionel Gale. I forgive you. She thinks I betrayed her. Did I?

Was there the teeniest, tiniest chance that Carrie Ann had told the truth way back when about Lionel Gale? The returning thought literally made Grace sit as straight as a rod. There was a warm breeze, but all she could feel was a cold chill working its way inside her blood. Back then, Grace had never, not once, considered the fact that Carrie Ann might have been telling the truth about Lionel Gale.

I have something to tell you, Grace. But you have to swear—blood swear—you won't tell anyone ever—

Don't think about that.

Five letters. Skirt. Person. "It has to be a woman," Grace said. "Right? Skirt and person."

"Unless it's a kilt," Jean Sebastian said.

"I don't think Picasso was painting Scottish bagpipers," Grace said.

"True," he agreed. "He does like Harlequins though." Jean Sebastian turned the catalogue around to show her a self-portrait of Picasso dressed as a Harlequin.

"Too many letters," Grace said. "Jester doesn't fit either."

"The true victim," Jean Sebastian said. "That's a clue too."

Lionel? Way too many letters. But he was a victim. He had been Carrie Ann's victim. And there had always been a part of Grace that feared she was to blame too. Maybe if she'd gone to her parents the instant Carrie Ann had told her story—

"Here's another one of Picasso as a Harlequin. *At the Lapin Agile*. A French club. This painting actually hangs at the Met in New York City. It is a portrayal of Picasso with a famous artist's model of the time—it says she was the unrequited love of his friend, Carlos. Carlos killed himself because she didn't love him back."

"What?" Grace grabbed the catalogue out of Jean Sebastian's hands. Picasso, dressed in a Harlequin outfit, was sitting at a bar next to the actress. It was amazing how red he had been able to paint her lips. The woman who drove his friend to his death. Suicide. Was that the clue she was meant to find? All because of the woman and a reference to suicide?

"What? What are you thinking about?"

"What's the name of the model?"

Jean Sebastian leaned into the catalogue. "Germaine Pichot."

"Doesn't fit."

"But it sounds like you're on to something. I feel left out."

Grace looked at Jean Sebastian. "I think this is about our past."

"You and Carrie Ann?"

Grace nodded. "And Stan."

"How so?"

"There's a . . . shared tragedy—a big mess actually, from when we were kids. And even though it was the briefest conversation, Carrie Ann said something that really disturbed me."

"What?"

"She said she forgave me. As if she wasn't the one to blame."

"Blame for what?"

Grace looked out at the distance. Ironic—she was in a fortress, but felt wide open and vulnerable. "I don't like to talk about it. I've never even told Jake the whole story."

"But you think it has something to do with this puzzle?"

"I thought—the true victim—but the person I'm thinking of—the name doesn't fit."

"Your name fits," Jean Sebastian said.

Startled, Grace turned to Jean Sebastian. "Me?"

"Did they—do something to you as a kid?"

"They?"

"Carrie Ann and—Stan?" Grace didn't answer. Jean Sebastian watched her with a quiet intensity. "I'm here to help," he said. "But I can't do much if I'm in the dark."

"I know. I know. I just hate thinking about that part of my life."

"Whatever it was—you were a kid, right?"

"Fifteen years old. Old enough to know better. Old enough to do better."

"Look. I'm not trying to pry. Or judge you. I've done a lot of things I'm not proud of. I've seen a lot of things. There's nothing you could tell me anymore that would shock me. I just want to help you get your boyfriend back."

"Why? Why are you helping me?"

"Must I have a reason?" He held her gaze long enough for her to deduce exactly what that reason was.

"I have a boyfriend. I love Jake." A look flashed across Jean Sebastian's face and then it was gone. He looked away. "What?" Grace said. "Tell me."

"Sometimes it is easier to believe what we want to believe. Sometimes the truth can do more damage than a lie. At least when one is in the middle of a crisis."

"Oh, God," Grace said. "What is it?"

"When you kicked me out of the police station, I went back to the hotel. I checked Jake's Facebook page. He had posted a video."

"What was it? Is he okay?"

Jean Sebastian lifted his shirt to reveal a small traveling pack.

"Is that a fanny pack?" Grace said.

"What is that?"

"That's just what we call it."

"It is a leather traveling bag that straps to your waist," Jean Sebastian said.

"Right, right," Grace said. No use antagonizing him by pointing out that he was indeed wearing a fanny pack. A deep longing hit her as she remembered joking about fanny packs on the beach with Jake. How they were hurrying back to the hotel room to make love. How she had bumped into Carrie Ann and didn't even recognize her. What was wrong with her? How could she literally bump into the girl who was once her sister and not even recognize her?

Jean Sebastian brought out a mini iPad, set it on the table and pressed PLAY. There were Jake and Carrie Ann in the same café where the picture was taken. "Who are you, Grace?" Jake said. "Just who the hell are you?" Carrie Ann put her arm around Jake, then rested her head on his shoulder. Grace put her hands over her face, then slammed them down on the table and clenched them into fists. Breathe, breathe, breathe.

"She's feeding him lies. Or she made him say it."

"She?"

"This is Carrie Ann. All Carrie Ann."

"No Stan?"

"No Stan. I'll bet he's back in Tennessee living with his mother. And I'll bet you anything he's not married to Carrie Ann."

"Why did she lie? What would she gain?"

"She's torturing me. Can't you see that? She's trying to make Jake doubt me." Grace buried her face in her hands again, trying to keep back the tears. "I'm so alone."

Jean Sebastian reached over and gently pried her hands from her face. "You're not alone. I'm here. I'm right here."

"Thank you," Grace said. "I don't deserve you."

"You deserve everything."

"I don't know what to do, Jean Sebastian. Tell me what to do."

"I think we've got to figure out this puzzle. And it has something to do with your past."

"But what?"

"Let's just go through this. When did the trouble begin?"

"That should be easy," Grace said. "Because the trouble always began with Carrie Ann."

CHAPTER 31

Two little girls, sitting in a tree house. They poured out their secrets in low, hot whispers, sitting cross-legged on the rugged planks. Carrie Ann was always nicer if Grace brought a pile of candy from the cupboard. Candy necklaces and bracelets were Carrie Ann's favorites. Grace's favorite was Tootsie Pops, but she pretended to also love the candy necklaces. Otherwise, she was afraid Carrie Ann would take a sharper liking to the Tootsie Pops. It had taken Carrie Ann a good three weeks to warm up to Grace, and then it was only with the help of the tree house and the sugar stash.

The first time Carrie Ann climbed up, she simply stood at the top of the ladder, surveying the digs. It was a nice platform, at least ten by ten, supported by an old, sturdy oak. Grace's father had built it for her eighth birthday. Together they had painted it red.

"I would have preferred blue," Carrie Ann said as she gave it the once-over. And then she was gone.

"Me too," Grace called after her. "They were out. Totally out. I was so mad. Ask my dad." She kept her fingers tightly crossed behind her back. But Carrie Ann didn't appear to be listening; she was already playing with one of the boys. Grace squeezed the two by four she was clutching so hard that she drove a splinter through her palm. She couldn't lose Carrie Ann to those stinky boys! Not after all these years of wanting a girl. That night, when her father was ensconced in his study, Grace knocked on the door.

"Come in." Grace approached his desk, trailed her finger along the edge.

"You didn't come in to dust, so what is it?"

"Do we have any blue paint?"

"Like watercolors?"

"No. For my tree house."

"Why do you want to paint your tree house blue, Graceful? Are you feeling sad?"

"No. I just realized I like the color blue better."

"I see."

"Can I?"

"The tree house is fire-engine red. If you paint it blue, it's going to turn out purple."

Grace wondered what Carrie Ann thought of purple. "How do we get it blue?"

"We'd have to prime it, and that's pretty involved, honey. Why don't you just bring some other things that are blue up to the tree house? Throw some white in there too. You'll be patriotic."

The next time Carrie Ann climbed up the ladder, Grace was ready for her. She had brought everything blue she ever owned up to it. A snow globe with a blue back. Her blue dress. And a bowl full of blue gumballs. It had taken a long time to pick out all the other colors. Brady sat on Grace's lap, purring. Carrie Ann stared at him. It was as if she didn't even notice the blue.

"He won't hurt you," Grace said. Instead of answering, Carrie Ann spit on the ground like a boy.

"She's a bit rough," Grace heard her mother say to her father later on that evening.

"Never in a foster home more than a year," her father replied. "I wouldn't expect less."

"You think she'll come around?"

"How could she not?"

"Hmm," her mother said.

"I think Gracie likes her."

"She just wants another girl. We're going to have to keep our eye on her."

On who? Grace wondered. *Carrie Ann or me?*

From then on, Grace also kept an eye on Carrie Ann, just in case she saw something before her mother did. If it was something she thought her mother wouldn't like, she would gently bring it up to Carrie Ann, usually after an extra treat, like a ring pop. The first time it happened, Grace's voice quivered with anticipation and fear. Carrie Ann was admiring her ring pop, and they were lying on their stomachs in the tree house listening to the radio and painting their nails.

"You know when my mom asks you to wash your hands for dinner?" Grace said.

Carrie Ann looked up at her, nail polish brush poised in the air. "What?"

"Yeah. You know how she always asks us that?"

"Uh-huh."

"I think you should do it. You know. Like the first time she asks. You can come with me. I'll help you."

"You think I need help washing my hands?"

"No. I just thought—"

"Well, don't." She poked the nail polish brush in Grace's direction, spattering hot pink on the floor planks. "Don't think."

Grace fell silent, but inside the wheels were still turning. She looked at her pile of candy, then tossed a bracelet Carrie Ann's way. Carrie Ann stopped polishing once more and stared at the candy bracelet. Then, she looked at Grace for a long time. Finally, she nodded, put the bracelet on, and then said, "Okay."

Grace felt a rush of relief. Then she felt triumphant. Carrie Ann had listened to her. And it didn't cost her too much. That evening, when Grace's mom yelled out, "Wash your hands for dinner," Carrie Ann was the first to the bathroom. And although she dried her hands on her pants instead of the towel, Grace still counted it as a victory.

And for about a year it was just the two of them. Against other foster kids, against mean girls at school, and increasingly against her parents. Grace came to love Carrie Ann with the fierceness of a mother bear. And things might have stayed that way forever. If it hadn't been for the day that Grace was late coming home from school because she had to resew a pillow in home ec. It was an elephant. The teacher scolded her for sewing the trunk shut. Grace hated that teacher to this day. She was forty-five minutes late. She climbed up to the tree house. There, sitting next to Carrie Ann, was a boy. And not just any boy—Stan Gale, the most hated kid in their school. Not that he was a bully; just the opposite. Stan was just so—awkward. Overweight and tall, with braces and greasy hair always hanging in his eyes and, worst of all, big red pimples all over his face. Grace could barely look at him, even from a distance, and here he was sitting in their tree house. He lived nearby, just on the other side of the woods. She'd found him sneaking around her yard a couple of times, but she'd never actually talked to him. She couldn't. He gave her the creeps. She almost fell backward. That could have been the end of her, splatted on the ground underneath the oak tree.

"There she is," Carrie Ann said. "Carrie Ann, this is Stan."

"She knows me," Stan said.

"Not really," Grace mumbled. What was he doing here? Grace started to climb down.

"Where are you going?" Carrie Ann said. "Get up here."

"I have to check on Brady," Grace said. She didn't know what Carrie Ann was thinking, but Grace did not want to sit in her tree house with Stan Gale. She'd heard his name paired with "cooties" so many times, she'd rather just play it safe. Besides, if he was up here, then Carrie Ann wanted something from him. And usually, when Carrie Ann wanted something from somebody, it was never good.

"You know who Stan's mother is?" Carrie Ann said.

"No," Grace said.

"She's the art teacher," Carrie Ann said. "The one you like."

"Lydia?" Grace said. Carrie Ann just smirked; Stan turned as red as the planks in the tree house. Grace waited for someone to laugh. They had to be joking. Lydia was Stan's mother?

Lydia Gale was the prettiest woman Grace had ever seen. She had long curly blond hair, and even longer skirts. Always with something on them. Flowers, or patterns, or even paintings. Later, Grace learned that despite having a husband who could afford to buy her clothes, Lydia made the skirts herself. It made Grace love her even more.

Grace was the kid in the farthest corner of the room, the kind who held her breath when any teacher asked a question, praying she wouldn't be picked to answer. Being called on by the teacher in front of the whole class was like standing in front of a firing squad. But in art class, Lydia, as she whispered the kids could call her, never asked any questions. Another reason Grace loved her. On free days, if you wanted to draw, you could draw. Or work with clay. Or paint. Even finger paint. Even cut out pictures from magazines and stick them on paper. Lydia didn't care. As long as you were creating. Lydia, quite frankly, was Grace's favorite person in the whole world outside of Carrie Ann and her mother.

Carrie Ann patted the planks next to her. "So he can't be all that bad, right?"

Grace still wanted to know what Carrie Ann was up to. But Carrie Ann was right about one thing. If Lydia was Stan's mother, then he couldn't be that bad at all.

"Lydia," Grace called out in the present. She reached for her phone.

"Lydia?" Jean Sebastian said.

"I think she's the answer to the puzzle—her name fits." Grace didn't have a pen, but she pretended to write the letters in the spaces. "Lydia."

"Why would she be the answer?" Jean Sebastian said.

"She made her own skirts."

"The true victim—does that fit?"

It was her husband who was accused of being a degenerate, a pervert, a Peeping Tom. Her husband hanging from the rafters of their barn. She lost everything after that. "It fits," Grace said.

"You can't stop the story there."

Grace took out her phone. She texted Jake.

Lydia.

"Seriously. Can you keep going with the story?"

Grace's phone dinged. "Brava," she read aloud.

"You got it right?"

"I got it right." She was right; they had been on a wild-goose chase. She hadn't needed to go to the Picasso museum to figure out the clue was Lydia. Grace was being toyed with.

"So what does Lydia have to do with any of this?"

"She went downhill after Lionel's death."

"Lionel?"

"Stan's father. Lydia's husband."

"Okay. I'm sorry. I'm lost."

"Please. Please don't make me relive all this tonight."

"Okay, okay. It's okay. Don't cry."

"It was such a mess. The whole thing turned into such a mess. And I think Stan partly blames me for making the mess." Grace looked at Jean Sebastian. "He's not wrong. I am partly to blame." Jean Sebastian still looked confused. "Please. I can't get into all of it tonight."

"I said it's okay. I meant it. You don't have to talk about it."

"So I guess he blames me for ruining Lydia's life too." And Grace didn't exactly disagree. She was the one who had cried to Lydia about Carrie Ann's not having a place to go.

"Brava? That's all he said?"

"That's all."

"Is that also a clue?"

"Beats me."

What now? Grace texted. Her phone remained silent.

"Let's go back to the hotel and get some sleep," Jean Sebastian said. Grace wanted to argue, but just then realized how tired she was. It was better to conserve their energy while they could. God only knew what little puzzle they were going to have to deal with next. Nightmare. This day had felt like a never-ending nightmare.

CHAPTER 32

Sleep did not come easily to Grace with what was left of the night, and she was up before the sun. She watched the video of Jake and Carrie Ann over and over. Grace cried. She pounded her fists on Jean Sebastian's bed. Several times when he cried out—"Just who the hell are you?" Grace yelled back, "It's me; you know me."

Finally, when she couldn't take another second of feeling this bad and this alone, she called her mother. There was no answer. Someone was always in her mother's room. Where was her father? Or a nurse? She'd certainly let it ring long enough. She called the front desk of the hospice. A girl answered and admonished her. No wonder no one was answering; it was after eleven p.m. in the States. She almost woke the entire floor. Grace apologized profusely and hung up. Then she cried some more. She called Jake's number. Got voice mail. Jean Sebastian walked in when she had just started crying again. Without hesitation he crawled onto the bed next to her and held her.

"I can't take any more," she said. "I'm going to tell my father."

"I'm sure he'll be on the next plane out here," Jean Sebastian said.

Oh, God. Of course he would. She couldn't have that. She couldn't leave her mother all alone.

"I have some sedatives," Jean Sebastian said. "They are very light, but you would definitely sleep."

"I can't, I can't," Grace said. "What do you think is coming next?"

"That's just it. We don't know. And you're not going to be able to do anything if you don't get some sleep."

"What about you?"

"I'll take one too."

Grace was completely exhausted. "Give it to me," she said.

She awoke, a few hours later, to the sound of her phone dinging. Jean Sebastian was lightly snoring beside her. They'd slept on the same bed, but on top of the covers and both fully clothed. He'd been a perfect gentleman even though she knew he had feelings for her. She owed him so much. She opened her text.

It was a picture of a couple standing by the sea. It looked like a small inlet, scattered with rowboats. Behind them was a multi-leveled white-stone farmhouse. Grace enlarged the picture and gasped. It was Jake. With Carrie Ann. Except she had brunette hair, just like Grace, and she had even styled it in waves like Grace, and to top it off she was wearing faded jeans with a cowboy belt, and a tight, colorful blouse. Grace's signature outfit for shows. With Carrie Ann wearing sunglasses and flat sandals, not to mention the distance at which the picture was taken, nobody would have guessed it wasn't Grace. In the photo Jake and Carrie Ann were arm in arm. Most disturbing of all was Jake's lip. Even from a distance Grace could tell it was grotesquely swollen. Somebody had punched him in the mouth. The caption read: *Jake and I at the Salvador Dalí House in Port Lligat. Wish you were here!*

Grace waited twenty minutes, then gently shook Jean Sebastian awake. As soon as he sat up she showed him the picture and the text. "Port Lligat," Jean Sebastian said. "That's a couple of hours' drive from here."

"I know," Grace said. "A small fishing village in Cadaqués, Spain."

"And I thought I was the travel blogger," Jean Sebastian said. "How in the world did you know that?"

"Lydia. She used to teach us about the lives of the artists she was introducing."

"She introduced Salvador Dalí to kids?"

"Oh, yes. She showed us slides of the house and even the village. She was so in love with it. She said Dalí and his wife split their time between New York, Paris, and Cadaqués. But it was in Cadaqués that he did his best work. For some reason that stuck with me. I had never been out of Tennessee. I remember rolling the name Cadaqués around in my mouth. I know that sounds stupid."

"It doesn't. I like the image of you rolling words around in your mouth."

Grace stared at Jean Sebastian for a moment. It was the first blatantly sexual thing he had ever said to her. Was he going to break his streak of not crossing any lines?

A small smile played across his lips. "Sorry," he said. "Sometimes I'm bad." He held his arms out in a shrug.

Grace reached out to touch the picture. "Look at her," she said. "And look at him. He's hurt."

"What?" Jean Sebastian leaned in. "His lip?"

"Yes," Grace said. Tears welled up in her eyes. "I'm going to kill her."

"Carrie Ann seems tough, but I doubt she could do that."

"She had Rafael do it. I'm sure of it. Jake probably tried to get away."

"So what does this place have to do with you?"

"I guess Stan wanted to pick a place I'd remember from my connection to his mother," Grace said.

Jean Sebastian's phone rang, startling them both. He answered it, and they locked eyes for a few seconds before she heard him tell the caller to hold on. Grace took the cue and slipped out of bed. She nodded at Jean Sebastian and headed out to the living room. He tucked the phone under his armpit, followed her to the doorway, and looked at her. "Grace?" he whispered.

"Yes?"

"I want to say something really inappropriate."

Grace hesitated. She should tell him she didn't want to hear it. Whatever it was. Then again, he'd stuck with her so far—maybe he'd earned it. "Go ahead."

"I wish to hell I remembered that kiss." He left her standing dumfounded and slipped into his bedroom. She could hear him speaking in soft tones as if he was talking to a girl. Why did he have to tell her that? And why did she feel a shot of desire when he did? *I'm sorry, Jake. It doesn't mean anything. I love you.* She wondered whom Jean Sebastian was talking to. She'd been so wrapped up in her own drama that she hadn't even thought about the fact that Jean Sebastian had friends, and family, and a life outside Barcelona and her.

Grace wandered out onto the balcony and leaned against the railing, gazing out onto the ocean. It had always calmed her in the past to lose herself in the waves; it always made her problems seem so small. But not this time. She just couldn't shake the dread, and guilt, and desire. Desire for Jake, desire to be selfish enough to kiss Jean Sebastian again, desire to erase every trace of Carrie Ann and Stan from her life. She had too many wishes. Wished her mom were healthy, wished she were back home with Jake and Stella.

Before you dredged up any deep, dark secrets. Is that what her past was? An abandoned well of deep, dark secrets? She'd spent most of her life trying to cover it up. Now she wished more than anything that Stan and Carrie Ann were here so they could get it all out into the open. Because one thing was becoming very clear. This situation wasn't going to just go away. If Grace wanted out of this, she'd have to go through it. Grace took a deep breath and dove headfirst into the past.

* * *

Stan started to bring them "goodies" from his home. That was Carrie Ann's word for it. It started with a can of Budweiser. After all, they were teenagers now, and the kid stuff was behind them. Carrie Ann had him open it inside his backpack. Grace would never forget the snap and fizz of it opening, slightly muffled inside his pack. Carrie Ann lifted it out and brazenly poured it into cups that originally had had homemade lemonade in them. Grace watched the lemonade trickle through the boards and drip below. Her mother was so proud of her lemonade, and actually spent quite a bit of time making it. Betrayal and guilt crawled up her spine. "Maybe we should drink our lemonade first," she said.

"It's too late," Carrie Ann said. She handed Grace the beer. "Have you ever had beer before?"

"Yes," Grace lied. She choked on the first sip. Carrie Ann laughed. Stan just stared. Grace wiped her mouth and looked away as she tried not to cough again. Stan was awfully quiet, although that's what Carrie Ann said she liked best about him. Grace thought the beer tasted like dirty socks. Was she really going to drink the whole thing just to please the Queen?

She'd taken to silently calling Carrie Ann "the Queen."

"Chug it," Carrie Ann said. Both Stan and Carrie Ann tipped their glasses back and drank their entire cups of beer in one go. Grace heard the screen door slam.

"Thirsty kids," Jody said, smiling and holding aloft her pitcher of lemonade.

"Oh yes," Carrie Ann said. "It's so good." Jody smiled as she started to climb the ladder.

"I'll come down to you, Mrs. Sawyer," Stan said. "So you don't spill a drop."

"Thank you, Stan," Jody said. She liked Stan; Grace could tell. Grace saw Carrie Ann's eagle eyes on her. She wanted her to drink the rest of the beer before her mother caught on. Grace took a deep breath and drank. When she was finished, the last bitter swallow went down the wrong pipe. Grace coughed and coughed. *It's what I deserve,* she thought as her mother's concerned face tilted up to the tree house. *It's what I deserve.*

"Next time," Carrie Ann said later as Stan was preparing to go home, "bring us a cigarette." Stan's father, Lionel, an insurance salesman, smoked a pack of Camels a day. Two, Stan said, when he had a bad day.

"We can't smoke up here," Grace said. She was whispering even though her mother had already gone into the house and turned on her radio. Grace could hear her mother singing along to The Mamas and the Papas through the screen door.

"There are a lot of things we can't do here," Carrie Ann said. "Which is why we're going to have to find another hangout."

"We can hang in my barn," Stan said.

"Will your mother be there?" Grace said. She loved the thought of seeing Lydia outside of class.

"It will be just us," Stan said. "Mom paints in the basement. The barn is a million miles from the house."

"Perfect," Carrie Ann said.

Bummer, Grace thought.

"Tomorrow after school?" Stan said.

"We'll meet you there at like four," Carrie Ann said. "We have a few chores to do here first." She looked at Grace for support. Carrie Ann did indeed have a list of chores, but Grace was always the one doing them for her. Despite befriending Stan, and letting him stay in the tree house, Grace did care what the other kids at school thought. She never associated with Stan at school, and she certainly didn't want any of them to know she was going to his house.

"Cool," Stan said. He zipped up his backpack and scrambled down the ladder. He looked back up with a last smile. It was aimed at Grace. She looked away.

"Somebody has a crush," Carrie Ann said when he was gone.

"Eww," Grace said. "Besides, he probably likes you."

"I wasn't talking about him," Carrie Ann said. Grace opened her mouth to protest, to insist she did not have a crush on Stan, but then thought better of it. Carrie Ann was winding her up again. If she protested too much, Carrie Ann would whoop like a pirate who had just discovered gold and shout, "See?! See! I was right!"

There are a lot of things we can't do here. Carrie Ann's words came back to Grace that evening as she was trying to sleep. What things? Grace realized, deep down, she didn't even want to know. If it was just the two of them, she could sometimes set Carrie Ann straight. But Grace had to admit, as much as she liked to filter him out, Stan was always there. They were a three-some. And Stan was always eager to go along with whatever Carrie Ann dreamed up. Grace didn't know what else Carrie Ann had in mind besides beer, but Grace knew, as usual, she wasn't going to like it.

Grace was startled out of the past by a hand on her shoulder. She turned and looked at Jean Sebastian.

"Beautiful," he said, gazing into her eyes. She must have looked confused, for a slight smile played across his lips. "The sky," he said. Grace turned back. The sun was high, the ocean glowed.

"It's stunning," Grace said. She still wanted to know who he had been on the phone with, but she didn't pry, and he didn't volunteer any answers. "I have to go to Port Lligat," Grace said.

"I figured you'd say that," Jean Sebastian said. "I don't like it. Luring us off to a small village."

"Not us," Grace said. "Me." Jake was there. He needed her. She had to end this nightmare one way or another. But Jean Sebastian had his own life. Maybe even a girlfriend. This wasn't his problem. *Face it, Grace. You're close to crossing lines. You don't want the temptation.* Was Jake feeling this way toward Carrie Ann? It made Grace almost physically ill, and jealous. No, continuing to have Jean Sebastian tag along was not right.

"Don't start this, Grace. I told you. I'm not leaving you until you're back with Jake. And I want to make sure Carrie Ann is safe too."

Grace was suddenly aware of how close Jean Sebastian was to

her. She moved past him and back into the hotel suite. "I'm not going until he lets me talk to Jake. I have to hear his voice. Make sure he's okay."

"Whatever you do, I'm going with you."

"You shouldn't be involved with this. Or with me."

"I'm a travel blogger, remember? I love Cadaqués. It's right on Costa Brava on the Mediterranean. Only a few hours from Barcelona. We could rent a car."

"I can rent a car."

"With what? You don't even have your license, or your passport, or a credit card." He had her there. "And if you did get there on your own—somehow—would you know exactly where to go?"

Oh, God, he was right. She needed him. Without thinking it through, Grace threw her arms around Jean Sebastian and hugged him. Slowly his arms wrapped around her waist, and he hugged her back. When she started to pull away, he dropped his arms and stepped back. He had been telling the truth. He wasn't going to take advantage of her. And Grace knew she needed all the help she could get.

"Thank you," she said.

"I'll start packing," he said. He went into his room. Grace texted Jake's phone.

I won't come until you let me speak to Jake.

By the time Jean Sebastian was finished packing a small bag, Grace still hadn't heard back from anyone. "I mean it," she said. "I'm not going until they contact me directly and let me talk to Jake."

"Let's go up on the roof deck and get a bite?"

"I don't think I can eat."

"A glass of wine then?"

Grace nodded, although she immediately felt guilty. The roof deck was like a sanctuary. The ocean was their backyard. Jean Sebastian and Grace sat on one of the sofas, and Jean Sebastian ordered a bottle of wine and some appetizers. As they ate and drank, Grace wondered where Jake was and what he was doing. He certainly wasn't drinking wine on a roof deck. If she was allowed to talk to him, maybe he would give her some sort of clue as to where they were keeping him. Maybe he was in Port Lligat. That could be a good thing. Wouldn't it actually be easier to find him in a small fishing village than in all of Barcelona? She could go to the police, or, hell, hire Spanish thugs. They could raid the place. Break down the door and get Jake back. Her cell rang. She almost dropped it, she was so jittery. She didn't even look at the screen.

"Jake?" There was a moment of silence and a hum, as if the caller were in a tunnel. "Jake?"

"No," said a familiar female voice. "This is his mother."

CHAPTER 33

"Barbara," Grace said. "How did you get this number?"

"That's how you greet me?"

"I'm sorry, it's just—I just bought this phone."

"Your father gave me the number, Grace."

"Oh, that's right." Even though Jean Sebastian had warned Grace about giving out the new cell phone numbers, Grace had managed to sneak a call in to her father. She wanted him to have the number in case he needed to call about her mother. Barbara Hart must have called her father when Jake didn't return her calls. She'd told Stan at Park Güell to have Jake call his mother back. She'd warned them.

"Where is Jake?" Barbara asked. "Why isn't he calling me back?"

"Oh, so sorry about that. He ran into some old college friends." Across from her, Jean Sebastian raised his eyebrow. Grace shrugged.

"Old college friends? In Barcelona?"

"Yes. Small world, huh?"

"What old college friends?"

"I don't know. Mike and Jimmy?" She desperately tried to remember any guy friends Jake had ever mentioned.

"Tell me the truth," Barbara said. "Are you two having problems?"

"Europe is stressful," Grace murmured. She hated lying, and hated Jake's mother's thinking that they were fighting. But it was better than leaving her thinking something awful had happened to her son. Which, of course, it had. But if Grace had told her, that woman would have been on the next plane to Barcelona. Grace's parents would be notified. The police would be involved. Grace had to at least talk to Jake one more time and try and find out what he thought she should do. Grace got off the phone as quickly as possible, with a hundred more promises that Jake would call Barbara soon.

Please, Jake, call me. Call me, Grace thought. The kidnappers would be monitoring the call, but she and Jake knew each other well enough that she was praying he could give her some kind of hint. Then it would be off to the Salvador Dalí House for the next "clue." Jean Sebastian had already hired a driver. He had said they were both tired and stressed, and this would give them a few hours to relax. She didn't know how to thank him or repay him. Grace was almost finished with the glass of wine, and pondering sending another text, when her phone rang. This time she looked at the screen.

"It's Jake's phone," she told Jean Sebastian. He nodded. Grace moved away from their little table to the edge of the roof deck. "Jake?" she answered, well aware of the quiver in her voice.

"Grace," he said.

A sob escaped from her. "Oh, God. Jake. Jake."

"Are you okay?" he said.

"Me? I'm okay. What about you? I saw your lip."

"You did?" Jake said. "How?"

"They texted me a picture," Grace said.

"This is so messed up, Grace."

"I know. She dyed her hair? She's dressing like me now?"

"Grace, I can't speak off the cuff. I have a list of approved things I can say."

"Okay. Okay. Tell me you're all right. Tell me they're not going to hurt you again."

"I'm okay, Grace. It's going to be okay. We just have to do what they say."

"We're leaving for Cadaqués tonight." There was silence. Grace knew Jake wanted to say something, but he couldn't. "Is that really where you are?" Again, that awful silence. "Cough if you're in Cadaqués."

"They're listening, sweetie. They just heard you say that."

"I hate this."

"I do too. But I love you."

"I love you more. I'm going to find you, Jake."

"I have to go, Grace."

Panic seized her along with an uncontrollable anger. "Wait. Is she going to hurt you again?"

"Who?"

"Carrie Ann. Who else?"

"She's not doing this, sweetie."

Grace hesitated. She didn't want to admit it, but she was stung. He sounded like he was defending her. Was he falling under her spell? Stockholm syndrome. If anybody could pull it off, Carrie Ann could. And he hadn't even acknowledged the weird photograph where Carrie Ann was dressed up as Grace. Because "they"—whoever "they" really were—were listening. Grace wasn't going to get him busted up again. But she was going to pry just a little. "Have you seen Stan?"

"Yes," Jake said. His voice was very measured.

"Can you tell me anything?"

"No."

"Because you don't know anything?"

"No."

No, he didn't know anything, or no, that wasn't why he couldn't tell her? She wasn't too good at this type of questioning. "Because they're listening?"

"Of course."

"Is Rafael helping him?"

There was a pause, as if Jake had to check whether or not it was okay for him to answer. "Yes."

"I knew it." She made a mental note to try and figure out Rafael's connection to all of this. Grace lowered her voice, even though it was probably pointless. "You can't escape them? Run away?"

"Grace."

"Tell me what to do. Should I go to the police?"

"No. Don't cry. You know I hate it when you cry."

"I can't believe this is happening."

"Listen to me. Just do what he says."

"He wants me to go to the Salvador Dalí House for the next clue. Jean Sebastian says it's only a few hours' drive."

Jake's voice caught, as if he too were crying. "I know," he said.

"So you think I should go?"

"I just want you to be safe," he said.

"Jean Sebastian has been amazing," Grace said. Shoot, she shouldn't have said that. It just slipped out, and she didn't want Jake worrying about her being on her own. But he didn't like her being with Jean Sebastian any more than she liked him being with Carrie Ann.

"Be careful," Jake said. "I have to go."

"Wait. Don't react. Just listen. Your mother called me."

"You?"

"Yes. My father gave her my cell number."

"Okay," Jake said.

"She thinks we're fighting. I told her you met up with friends from college."

"Okay," Jake said.

"If she doesn't talk to you soon, she'll be on the next flight out here."

"I'll tell him."

"Don't trust Carrie Ann, Jake. She could be lying. She could be in on this with him."

"You're the one I'm worried about, Grace."

"How do we know he'll keep his word? If I figure out this stupid puzzle?"

"We pray."

"This is because of my past, Jake."

"I know, Grace."

"What do you know? Did Carrie Ann say something?"

"None of it matters now. Do you hear? I don't care about any of it. I don't care who you are. I just want you back."

Who she was? Grace had been so relieved to hear his voice that she'd forgotten all about the video he made. What was Carrie Ann saying to him? Grace was going to kill her. How could Jake believe a word of it? Maybe he was just playing along, following his approved "script." "I can tell you're holding things back," Grace said. "I know you can't talk freely. This is making me crazy."

"I love you," Jake said. "Do you hear me? No matter what."

Grace's composure crumpled. "What does that mean? Oh, God. Carrie Ann has been filling you with lies, hasn't she?"

"She said you were really Carrie Ann. That you've only been pretending to be Grace for the past fifteen years. She told me that she is Grace Ann Sawyer."

"She what?" What in the world? "And she thinks you'd believe that for a second? Jake? Jake?"

There was a silence. When he spoke again, he sounded extremely strained. "How come I've never been to your father's house?"

"What?"

"We always see him at the home. I've never been to his house."

"When my mom was healthy my parents preferred to get out of the house. A lifetime of foster children will do that to you. And lately, it's because he spends all his time at Mom's facility." Grace started to get ramped up, then paused. Wait. Why was this important right now? Was he trying to tell her something?

"I'm a little confused. I feel like I don't know anything anymore."

He was trying to tell her something. She could tell from his voice, his manner. She just didn't know what. She spoke carefully and slowly back, as if that would help. "You know me, Jake."

"Do I? Are you Grace Sawyer? Or are you Carrie Ann Gilbert?"

"We know each other, Jake. Like the back of our hands."

"I thought so," Jake said. "But sometimes you just never really know who you're with."

"That's true," Grace said. She thought of the picture of Carrie Ann and Jake in front of the Salvador Dalí House. Carrie Ann dressing up exactly like Grace. "Sometimes people are pretending to be something they're not."

"Exactly," Jake said.

"Like Carrie Ann. Pretending to be me on Facebook. Filling you up with lies. Stealing my ID. Luring us to Barcelona."

"That's cold, Grace," Jake said. "You're so cold."

She knew Carrie Ann was probably listening. She hoped Carrie Ann was listening. "You know me, Jake. No matter what she says—don't ever forget that."

"I have to go, Gracie." And with that, he hung up. She slowly walked back to Jean Sebastian. *That's cold, Grace. You're so cold.* He'd never spoken to her like that before. Never accused her of being anything other than too nice. He was definitely acting. But she didn't get it. Whatever he was trying to say, she had failed to get it.

"Is he okay?"

"No. I mean, physically—I think so. Yes. But he says Carrie Ann has nothing to do with this. He also told me something pretty crazy that Carrie Ann's been saying."

"What?"

"I don't even know how to say this."

"Tell me."

"She told Jake that I'm Carrie Ann."

"I don't understand."

"She told him that I was Carrie Ann and she was Grace. That I've just been pretending to be her for the past fifteen years."

"Pardon the American expression but—that is fucked up."

"Oh, believe me, I know."

"Wait. He doesn't believe her, does he?"

"I don't think so. But they weren't letting him speak freely."

"Stan was there?"

"I think so. He said he'd seen him."

"At least that's one mystery solved."

"And Rafael is working for Stan."

"We suspected that. Anything else?"

"No. That's the gist of it."

"You said Carrie Ann was crazy. I know it was an American expression. But is there any chance she actually is crazy?"

"What do you mean?"

"Telling Jake she's you. Dressing as you. Switching ID. Posting pictures dressed as you on Facebook. Is there any chance she actually thinks she's you?"

"No. Not a chance."

"Are you sure?"

"I was alone with her several times before all this happened. She always knew who she was."

"All right. Whatever it turns out to be—they won't get away with this," Jean Sebastian said. "Not if I can help it."

"I can't thank you enough," Grace said. "How does your driver feel about going now?"

"He's waiting downstairs," Jean Sebastian said. "Let's go." On their way out, Grace passed her Taylor Hummingbird. For a few seconds, her fingers ached to touch it. For the first time in months, she actually missed it, wanted to play, wanted to sing. Maybe she *was* the type who could sing her pain. Who knew? Her gut told her to bring it. It wasn't logical, but then again, neither was her life at the moment. She picked up the guitar on the way out the door.

"We've got a long ride ahead of us," Jean Sebastian said. "You can tell me more about the past."

It was the last thing Grace wanted to do. But he was right. The answer lay somewhere back there, and if she couldn't figure it all out, maybe Jean Sebastian could.

CHAPTER 34

Carrie Ann sat on the bed in the tiny, musty room, absolutely fuming. She was going to kill Stan. He had completely usurped her power and changed the entire plan. She was the one who was supposed to get kidnapped. To see if Grace would try and find her. She was the one who was supposed to leave the clues. And she certainly wasn't supposed to be spending her "missing" time in this hovel of a room. She was supposed to be at the Ritz Carlton on the beach. She could just kill Stan. She hadn't had a single second to talk to him or Rafael alone. Although she had to admit, he'd successfully raised the stakes of their little game, but at her expense. At least it was almost over. The festival and Grace and Carrie Ann's mutual birthday were only two days away. So why the hell was Stan luring Grace all the way out to Cadaqués? Several times Carrie Ann had almost blown it, by going off on Rafael. He was enjoying his little power trip way too much. But she could endure two days. She just prayed that if Jake and Grace decided to press any charges that they would believe she hadn't been in on the drugging and kidnapping. Jake might believe her, but not Grace. They wouldn't be in the spot they were in right now if Grace had ever believed her. And if she would just open those damn letters, she would know that this was all a game. But Grace hadn't opened the letters. Because Carrie Ann and Jake were still here. And Stan had ruined everything. It was Jake that Grace was searching for, not Carrie Ann. That wouldn't prove Grace's loyalty to Carrie Ann. This had all been a huge mistake. And it was all because of Stan.

Because he was still obsessed with Grace. Carrie Ann should have seen it. She never should have enlisted his help. And once again, she was going to be guilty by association. Maybe she was going to have to end this thing sooner rather than later. Plan or no plan, at this point, she just wanted to stick it back to Stan. She was going to kill him. She was absolutely going to kill him.

Jake had never seen Rafael with a gun. They used some kind of sedative, and the handcuffs, and besides Rafael flashing his knives, the real weapon that kept Jake from escaping was the constant threat of what they would do to Grace if he tried to interfere. He could barely look at or talk to Carrie Ann after what she had pulled in the café. What she had made him do. He couldn't get it out of his mind, kept replaying it over and over.

I'm Grace Ann Sawyer.

Jake had not fallen for it. "Lady, you are out of your fucking mind." He had gotten up and headed for the door. Within seconds Rafael's hands were planted on Jake's shoulders. Jake had tried to jerk away, but Rafael had dug into his arm and turned Jake around to face him. Then before Jake could defend himself, Rafael's fist had connected with Jake's mouth. Jake had felt the blow, his teeth cut into his upper lip, and a few seconds later he tasted blood.

"Stop," Carrie Ann had said. She had hurled herself at Rafael. He had given Jake a final shove into the wall, then backed away. Jake had sat on the floor, mouth bleeding. The staff had remained in the back as if they were all deaf. Carrie Ann had knelt down beside Jake. "Do you see now?" she had said.

"See what?" Jake had said.

"Grace isn't who she says she is. You don't know her at all."

"I know her. And I'm starting to know you." He had pointed at Carrie Ann. His finger had shaken. She had pulled Jake up, leaned in to wipe the blood off of his mouth with a napkin, and whispered.

"Go along with it, Jake. They're going to let you talk to Grace soon. When they do, pretend like you're starting to doubt her."

"Why would I do that?"

"Because I'm trying to help her. I'm trying to feed her clues."

"This is unreal. This is unreal."

"Say it right now so Rafael can hear you."

"Say what?"

"Something that shows you're starting to doubt her."

Jake had squeezed his eyes shut. Did he trust her? God, she was good. She sounded so sincere. "Who are you, Grace?" Jake had said loudly. "Just who the hell are you?" Carrie Ann had nodded, and then put her arm around Jake before bringing her head to rest on Jake's shoulder. Jake had heard something whir. He had looked up to see Rafael holding a camera with a little red light glowing in the corner. Rafael had caught it all on video.

And now Jake was freaking Grace out, making her think he doubted her. He had played right into their hands! But what choice did he have? He had tried to warn her on the phone, the only way he could. Would it sink in later? And even if it did—then what? What was the true endgame here?

Carrie Ann had been the one to coach him. "Grace and I used to play Hot and Cold all the time. If she doesn't pick up on what you're saying to her, tell her she's cold, very cold. If she does, tell her she's hot."

But Grace didn't get it. All he did was upset her, and he wished he could take it back. She wouldn't fall into the arms of a handsome stranger at a time like this—would she?

No. Don't think like that. This was their game. Messing with Grace's and Jake's heads, making them paranoid, creating doubt. Jake loved Grace, and Grace loved Jake, and they were going to get through this somehow. But he was starting to think they weren't going to get out of it without a fight.

How could they trust that the psycho was really just going to let them go? Grace thought Jake and Carrie Ann were in Cadaqués, and now she was off to find them, yet here they were in Barcelona, still stuck in a shoebox of a room.

There was only one window, toward the top of the wall, and it wasn't large enough for him to fit through. The door was kept constantly locked. Any time they were allowed out to walk the perimeter of the neighborhood or get something to eat, Rafael was their constant companion. Carrie Ann was supposedly in a room down the hall. It made it impossible for Jake to figure out whether she was a victim or a mastermind. Sometimes, she was "allowed" into Jake's room. She would sit and tell him stories about Grace—who she was still calling Carrie Ann—either in an effort to ease her own loneliness, or as just another sick mind game. Bit by bit Jake was learning about Grace's past, everything that had brought them to this point. Once in a great while, Jake had to step back and admit that Carrie Ann had told a partial truth. He hadn't really known Grace, not in the way he had thought he had. She had kept her past locked away. She had never told him about Carrie Ann.

He had decided. He would never hold it against her. Whatever past drama that was being played out, he knew it wasn't her fault. She was a good soul. She had a huge heart. And the years of secrets had hurt her most of all. It made him furious that Stan was still trying to make her pay—for whatever reason. Carrie Ann had hinted about Stan's having a crush on Grace. That worried Jake most of all. And—Jean Sebastian. *He's been amazing,* Grace had said. Jake wanted to wrap his hands around Mr. Amazing's throat and squeeze. Mr. Belgian. Mr. Congo.

He had to get out of this room. He was sick with worry over Grace. He was disgusted by the dirty linoleum floor. The plain walls. The musty, maroon bedspread. The cloying heat, hardly dissipated by one loud, whirring fan. He was pacing the room when the door opened and Carrie Ann was shoved in. Rafael entered behind her, shut the door, and threw something at

Jake. His initial reaction was to duck, until he realized it was his cell phone. He caught it, then just looked at Rafael. Carrie Ann scrambled onto the bed and huddled near the headboard. She was sniffling. It was the first time he'd seen her cry.

"Stan says you need to call your *mami*," Rafael said. "And no funny business." Shit. Jake looked at the phone. Should he call Grace instead? But what would he say? The calls were still being monitored somehow. "Now."

Jake called his mother. She picked up on the first ring, which meant she was truly pissed.

"Jake?"

"Hey, Mom."

"Oh my God. I thought you were dead. I've been calling Jim Sawyer nonstop until he finally gave me Grace's number. I was just about to call the police."

Should she? Should Jake let her call the police? And say what? My son has been kidnapped, but I don't know where he is, and his girlfriend is also somewhere? No. There was nothing they could do. "Mom, I'm sorry. We're on vacation—I just thought it would be fine if I talked to you when I got back. Between the time difference and the expense—"

"But you know how I worry."

"I know. I'm sorry. I am. I'm fine, Mom."

"Every time I called Grace was there without you. Why is that?"

"Nothing sinister, Mom. You know me—I like to wander around checking everything out. Grace wasn't feeling well for a few days so she stayed in—"

"She didn't say anything about not feeling well."

"You know Grace, Mom. She's a very private person." From the bed, Carrie Ann snorted. Jake glanced at her, then turned away.

"And what's this business about you meeting friends from college? Who did you meet from college?"

"Grace misunderstood. I just met some guys who went to the same college as I did—you know how it is—we got to shooting the bull."

"As long as you're not running with the bulls."

"Funny."

"You're not, are you?"

"No. I'm not. And I'm actually kind of ready to come home."

"You'll be home in three days, right?"

Three days? Could that be right? That meant that Grace's birthday was the day after tomorrow. He couldn't let her turn thirty without him. He had to do something. "Right, Mom. Listen—I'm out of minutes—"

"You don't sound like yourself. Tell me the truth. Did you and Grace break up?"

"No. I love you, Mom. Sorry, there's a beep—we're going to be cut off." Jake hung up the phone.

"Toss it here," Rafael said. Jake tossed the phone. Then he took a few steps toward Rafael. Rafael crossed his arms against his chest. He was tall, but skinny. He also smoked a lot of dope. Jake could take him, couldn't he? And wouldn't that be the moment of truth? Carrie Ann would either help tackle Rafael or Jake would find out once and for all whose side she was really on.

"Back up," Rafael said. He put his hand in his pocket, then brought out a long, gleaming knife. Shit.

"Grace's birthday is the day after tomorrow," Jake said.

"So is mine," Carrie Ann said. "We'll be thirty."

Jake stared at Carrie Ann. "I don't believe a word out of your mouth," he said. "And if you two think I'm going to let this psycho lure my girlfriend out of Barcelona and to this Salvador Dalí House, well, you all have another think coming."

"Bringing fists to a knife fight?" Rafael said. He sounded as if he enjoyed the prospect.

"Are you ready to kill me?" Jake said. "Because that's the only way I'm staying here another minute."

"Are you sure that's how you want to play it?" Rafael said.

"No," Carrie Ann said. "Look. He might not kill you, but he'll hurt Grace. Is that what you want?"

"I'm sick of these mind games." He pointed to Carrie Ann. "You start telling me the truth right now, or so help me—"

Rafael approached with the knife held aloft. "You touch her, I kill you with pleasure," he said.

"Let's all calm down," Carrie Ann said. She shot Jake a look. He shook his head, then retreated to a corner of the room. He was going to cry in front of these assholes, and he didn't want to. He'd let Grace down. He never should have left her alone with Carrie Ann. He shouldn't have accepted that drink. He should have believed Grace when she said that Carrie Ann was evil. Jake turned and lifted a small table by the bed. He held it over his head.

"Jake," Carrie Ann said.

"Let him," Rafael said. "He's a man. Men need to smash." Jake slammed the table into the wall. One leg broke off. A splinter lodged itself in his palm. Rafael let out a torrent of Spanish that had the sound of attaboy. *"Bueno, bueno,"* Rafael said. "Feel better?"

"Next time it's coming down on your head," Jake said. He picked up the table again. Rafael frowned as if not sure whether to believe him.

"Can you just give us some space?" Carrie Ann asked Rafael.

He glared at Jake, waved the knife around. "I'll be just out-side this door," he said.

When the door shut, Jake whirled around to Carrie Ann. "Why would he listen to you? If you're just an innocent victim like me?"

"Maybe he's sick of listening to you whine."

"Excuse me?"

"If you want to bust out of this place, announcing that fact in front of the guy we have to escape from is not exactly the smartest plan."

"You have a better suggestion?"

"I've done all I can do."

"Oh, yes. You're a regular Mother Teresa."

"I told you that crazy story in front of Rafael so that it would get back to Stan. He thinks I'm doing my part to make Grace feel as if she's going crazy. That's why Rafael let you repeat it to

Grace. With a little bit of luck she'll figure out what you were really trying to say. It was the best I could do."

"It wasn't good enough. She didn't get it."

"Just give it time to sink in."

"What if it doesn't? What if it's too late?" Carrie Ann didn't answer. She didn't have to. Jake didn't know how, but he was going to have to bust out. What was it they said about kidnappers? *Never let them take you to a second location.*

Don't go, Grace. Don't leave Barcelona. Jake repeated the plea over and over in his head, knowing all the while it was too late. She was already gone. Ignoring Carrie Ann, he picked up the table and alternated between yelling and smashing whatever pieces were left of it against the wall until Rafael came in with the handcuffs.

"You'll have to cut me," Jake said when he saw what Rafael had planned.

"No problema," Rafael said.

CHAPTER 35

Grace had hated Stan's barn from the minute she walked into it. It was looming and dark; a heavy, sad feeling had worked its way into the joints and settled. And that was before. It smelled of oil and manure. The Gales only had a couple of cows, which were currently grazing in the field, but boy did the large, messy barn stink. Stacks of hay, the carcass of a rusty old car, a John Deere tractor, moldy feed buckets, and empty horse stalls filled the bulk of the space. Carrie Ann, Grace, and Stan headed for a ladder leading up to the hayloft, tucked away beneath the old, thick rafters.

Stan was more animated than usual, which for him meant a bounce in his step and slightly more chatter. Grace brought up the rear, dragging her feet, not at all happy with their new meeting place.

"Did you get it?" Carrie Ann asked Stan.

"I got it," he replied.

What now? Grace wondered as they climbed up the ladder. Grace was the last to reach the loft. When Stan held out his hand at the top, she was forced to take it. There was a gap of about a foot between the last rung and the floorboard of the hayloft. She wanted to go home. Stan's hand was cold and clammy. As soon as she was sitting on hay, she wiped her hand on her pants over and over, as if trying to rub off his touch. As soon as they were all seated, Stan dug around in his backpack. He pulled out a tall bottle. The liquid was gold.

"Scotch," Carrie Ann said. "Nice." Next he pulled out a single Camel cigarette.

"We'll have to share," he said. "It's all I could get."

Grace didn't want to drink scotch and share a cigarette. She wanted to go home. She could do that, right? She could say she was going home, walk down the ladder. She was more afraid of going down than up, terrified of that gap. Maybe Lydia would come up from the basement of her house, where she had her painting studio, and see what her son was up to. Grace's mother was probably home ironing a shirt for her dad or scolding one of the boys.

Carrie Ann lit the cigarette. The tip glowed orange, and a sharp smell hit the air along with a cloud of smoke. That was worse than the manure. Surely Lydia would smell that? Carrie Ann didn't even cough. She inhaled, blew smoke, then inhaled again.

"You're good at that," Stan said. He sounded impressed. Grace was kind of impressed too, although she knew it wasn't something she should be impressed about. She could see Carrie Ann leaning against an old building, smoking with a group of ragtag little boys. Carrie Ann was tougher than Grace would ever be.

"I should be. We smoked at the orphanage all the time."

"Really?" Stan said. He sounded in awe. Grace had heard it before. Carrie Ann's stories were always horrifying but gripping.

"I was seven when I smoked for the first time," Carrie Ann said proudly.

"Wow," Stan said.

Carrie Ann passed the cigarette to Stan as he handed her the bottle of whiskey. It was now or never.

"I don't want to smoke," Grace said. "And I don't want to drink."

"Then go home," Carrie Ann said. It was the last thing Grace had expected to hear. "Be careful climbing down," Carrie Ann added with a smile. She knew. She always knew what to say, what button to push, what scared Grace most of all. How did she always know?

"Is there another way down?" Grace said, looking around. Carrie Ann laughed.

"You could jump," she said. "Try and land on a bale of hay." Grace considered it for a moment. Hay was pretty soft. But most of it was up here, not down there. Maybe Stan would let her throw some bales down. "I'm kidding," Carrie Ann said. "Just climb down the ladder already."

Now Grace had to pee. She was terrified of the ladder, but even more terrified of peeing her pants in front of Stan and Carrie Ann. She crawled over to the ladder and looked down.

"Go down backwards," Stan said. "It's the best way."

Grace shut her eyes and started the descent. Each rail felt like death was near. She was halfway down and almost breathing normally when she felt the ladder sway. She screamed and opened her eyes. The ladder was falling backward. Carrie Ann's and Stan's faces hovered over the edge. Grace locked eyes with Carrie Ann. *She's trying to kill me,* Grace thought. She quickly let go of the ladder and tried to curl into a ball. She landed hard on her left arm and screamed in pain as the ladder barely missed knocking her on the head. She knew, before she even tried to move, that she had broken her arm. Carrie Ann was the first to sign her cast. *Smoking Kills,* she wrote. Then she added a smiley face.

I'm sorry, Stan wrote.

Grace couldn't wait to get the cast off, not because it was itching her, not because it was bulky and sweaty, not because she was tired of not being able to use her arm. All those things were true. But the biggest reason she wanted to get that cast off was so she didn't have to stare at Stan's signature on her arm. It made her feel sick. Because, under his name, so tiny she almost missed it, he had drawn a heart.

CHAPTER 36

Captured between the Mediterranean Sea and the extension of the Pyrenees Mountains, Cadaqués, Figueres, and Roses, Spain, glimmered like little gems sprinkled along Costa Brava. The town car that Grace and Jean Sebastian were riding in wound up and up and up. Bright skies stretched above them, and the wild blue sea churned below. Grace couldn't believe she was able to appreciate the beauty given the circumstances, yet one would have to be dead not to.

The peninsula encasing Cadaqués was the Cap de Creus, and the surroundings were composed of geological wonders. The rocks dotting the rugged coastline were formed along with the Pyrenees Mountains. Costa Brava, which meant wild coast, was named for the temperamental winds that would whip through at terrifying speeds, stirring the sea into a boiling frenzy.

Is that what had happened to Carrie Ann and Stan? Had the years stirred them into a boiling frenzy?

Salvador Dalí grew up in Figueres, where now the Dalí Theatre-Museum stood, showcasing a broad range of his work, but Grace and Jean Sebastian were headed instead to his house, the Casa-

Museo Salvador Dalí, in Port Lligat as the clue had instructed. It would be too late to go this evening, but Jean Sebastian had managed to book them adjoining rooms at Hotel Port Lligat. It was a longer drive than if they stayed in Roses, or Cadaqués, but it would pay off the following day; their hotel was only a few meters from the Salvador Dalí House.

The entrance to the Island of Port Lligat was separated from the mainland by a narrow thirty-meter-wide canal. Dalí was known to have incorporated the island into several of his paintings: *The Madonna of Port Lligat, Crucifixion,* and *The Sacrament of the Last Supper.* Grace was infused with a sense of peace as they pulled up to the hotel. Check-in was a breeze, and soon Grace and Jean Sebastian were standing on the shared veranda of their adjoining rooms.

The small family hotel offered stunning views. The building itself seemed to grow right out of the sea, just like the Dalí House, which Grace could see from her vantage point. Dalí's villa was a white-stone building topped with terracotta roofs. It rose from the bay at irregular levels, encompassing over three stories, although it still wasn't very tall. Simple, fisherman beauty, a marriage of land and sea.

"You've been here before?" Grace said as they stared out to sea.

"This is my third time," Jean Sebastian said. "I think it's one of the most beautiful places in the world."

"I can see why."

"In fact . . . No. It's silly."

"Tell me."

"If I had a choice—this is where I'd spend my last day on earth." Jean Sebastian pointed to the small cove in front of the Dalí house. "I'd like to be lying in a rowboat, right there. Just bobbing along until I take my last breath."

"Who wouldn't want that?" Grace said.

Jean Sebastian laughed. "I guess I'm not as unique as I like to think I am."

"I'd say you're pretty unique." He stared at her until she found herself trying to remember how long average human eye contact lasted and if they had gone over the average time limit.

They'd definitely gone over it. And this was the most romantic setting on earth. Grace could only imagine it at sunrise and sunset. The air was warm, and she could hear the water lapping on the rowboats scattered along the bay below. Where were Jake and Carrie Ann? Were they still here? Was he close enough to touch? "Tell me something about yourself," Grace said.

"Like what?" Jean Sebastian said.

"I don't know. I just realized I don't know the first thing about you. I haven't even read your travel blog."

"I am a simple guy," Jean Sebastian said. "But I'll show you my blog sometime."

"Do you have any brothers or sisters?"

"No. It's just me."

"Do your parents still live in Belgium?"

"Only my mother is alive."

"I'm sorry."

Jean Sebastian shrugged. "It is life."

"I wish it weren't. Don't you?"

Jean Sebastian moved closer. Grace's hands were resting on the veranda wall. Jean Sebastian put his hand on top of hers. "I hope your mother will be all right," he said. For a second, Grace was startled, but then she remembered he had been in the room during her last video chat.

"That's not going to happen," Grace said. "But thank you."

"How long does she have?"

"A few weeks ago the doctors said one to six months." Tears filled Grace's eyes, and Jean Sebastian stepped closer and put his arms around her.

"You're going through too much," he said. "Too much for one person."

His cologne smelled so good. It was probably expensive, designed to be irresistible. His body felt nice next to hers. This just wasn't fair. She had to admit, if she could carve a little time out of her life and step out of it, just for a moment, she would be tempted to kiss him. God. She already had kissed him. On the dance floor when she had thought he was Jake. It had felt exciting and new because it was exciting and new. Grace gently pulled out of Jean Sebastian's arms. "I just want to get Jake and go home," Grace said. "I just want to go home."

"And I won't tell you what I want." Grace waited, holding her breath.

"What?" she asked, even though she knew she shouldn't.

"You." His face was so handsome by the moonlight. The air was thick and warm. Their faces were only inches apart. *He's going to try and kiss me,* Grace thought.

"I can't," she said. She stepped back.

"I'm sorry," Jean Sebastian said.

"Don't apologize. Look. I'm attracted to you too."

"You are?" He stepped forward. "Do you really mean it?" He seemed so intense. Had she made a mistake in mentioning it?

"Of course I mean it. Come on—you must have a million girls after you."

"Last count it was under nine hundred thousand," Jean Sebastian said.

"Funny."

"I don't get close to many people," Jean Sebastian said.

"Why not?"

"I guess it was just the way I was brought up. Protecting myself."

"From what?"

"From everything."

Grace knew there was more to the story, but she didn't want to feel any closer to Jean Sebastian. She had come this far; she just wanted to focus on Jake. "You're a catch. There, I said it. You're handsome, and you have had a very exciting life, and you're funny—"

"Okay, okay. Please. Keep talking."

Grace laughed and slugged him on the shoulder. He grabbed her hand and held it for a moment. Her breath caught. *Please, don't. Not tonight.* She felt too weak, too vulnerable.

"Get some sleep," Jean Sebastian said. He turned her hand over, kissed the top of it, and let go. Grace nodded and turned to go back to her room. Then, she turned again, and kissed Jean Sebastian on the cheek.

"I'm sorry," she said. "Maybe another time. Another place."

"Then I wish this were another time," he said. "Another place." It took Grace an eternity to fall asleep.

They were at the Dalí villa the minute it opened. Jean Sebastian gave Grace a rundown on the history. Salvador Dalí moved into his fishing cabin in 1930 with his wife and muse, Gala. He worked on and added to the house over the next forty years. The result was a maze-like structure within the Spanish-style home, consisting of his workshop on the upper level with a view of the bay, the bedroom he shared with Gala, a kitchen, an expansive library room, and the "whispering" room where it was said you could hear someone whispering to you from way across the room. The outside consisted of an elaborate outdoor pool, sculptures, and gardens.

Grace stepped into the entryway and was confronted by a giant grizzly bear standing upright. It had paws out, mouth open, teeth showing. His fur was the color of toffee, and he was decked in silver and turquoise jewelry, complete with a rifle slung over his shoulder. A few other stuffed animals sat on shelves above him; Grace couldn't tell if they were possums or something else—she'd never thought of taxidermy as art until this moment. *Who in the world was this man?* Grace couldn't help but wonder as she toured the house. It was hard to tell if he was a genius or a madman, and she concluded he was definitely both.

At the top of the house, facing the water, was an attic room with a circular window. An easel faced the window. Upon it sat a half-finished canvas. A paintbrush lay across the ledge of the easel, and a rag was balled-up at the base. It looked as if Dalí had just been here, stepping away momentarily for a cup of coffee, or a phone call, or a kiss from his wife. Grace wondered what he would think of all these strangers traipsing through his house. One thing was clear: He had spent his days doing what he loved, surrounded by the things he loved. It was really that simple, and yet so few people got to live their lives that way. It made her ache for Jake, and her stomach had been in knots since they had arrived.

Every time she turned a corner, she held her breath, praying Jake and Carrie Ann would just appear as they had done in the park.

Instead, every corner was filled with unique objects: dried flowers, stuffed wildlife, painting easels, artwork, jewelry. The windows in every room varied drastically in size and shape, and sometimes passages seemed to lead nowhere. Candelabras, vases, animal heads and animal bodies stuffed everywhere. Strange dolls, and ornate, tall birdhouses, and velvet built-in sofas. She hadn't been paying much attention to where Jean Sebastian was, but they ended up stepping into Dalí and Gala's bedroom at the same time. They had separate beds covered in red and gray bedspreads. The same material was draped on the wall behind the beds, held up at the ceiling by a golden eagle.

"Don't get the wrong idea," Jean Sebastian whispered in her ear as she took in the pair of beds. "They were very sexual. Especially Gala. And Salvador liked to watch her make love to other men."

Grace felt little pinpricks on the tops of her arms, and she shivered. Jean Sebastian took a step back. Grace felt slightly nauseous. Why? Because he had whispered in her ear? Because it was too intimate? She couldn't put her finger on why she was reacting this way. It was probably because a man she was attracted to was whispering in her ear about Dalí and Gala's experimental sex life. Grace didn't want Jean Sebastian to know he was sparking this reaction inside her. "Really?" She hoped she sounded nonchalant.

"She had quite the appetite. Even in her seventies she was bedding much younger men."

"My God," Grace said.

"You're shocked?" he said.

"A little bit—but mostly because—is it me or was she really homely?"

Jean Sebastian burst out laughing. Grace felt guilty saying it, but from every painting and photo she had seen of the woman, the best compliment she could give was that maybe, in certain lights, Gala was handsome.

"She must have had other enticing qualities," Jean Sebastian said with a wink as they exited the room.

The most unusual object to catch Grace's eye was hung on the wall in a small alcove above a built-in table. It was the head of a rhinoceros with the wings of an eagle. Around his neck hung a bell.

"Wild, isn't it?" Jean Sebastian said.

Salvador's artwork hung on the walls, and pictures of himself with his curled-up mustache, and again, pictures of Gala. Jean Sebastian was right. Gala must have had something going for her, for it was obvious that Dalí had been absolutely mad about her.

There was that word again—*mad.* Everything about the house screamed madness, and yet somehow it totally worked.

"Wouldn't you love to live here?" Jean Sebastian said.

"The views are pretty," Grace said. "But I don't know how I'd feel about all these dead animals staring at me all day long."

Jean Sebastian laughed again, and Grace joined in. It wasn't right, was it—these little moments of mirth? When Jake was God knows where?

"Let's go outside," Jean Sebastian said.

Out back was an in-ground pool consisting of two round sections separated by a narrow passage, like a hallway made of water. The swimming pool dead-ended into a little seating cove, complete with a hot-pink sofa in the shape of giant lips. Next to it, enormous tires were propped up, with Firelli signs adorning the tires like Miss America sashes. More windows, and sculptures, and animals. There were stone swans, and the remains of a huge python twisting above the archway. The plants—a mix of cacti, flowering shrubs, and overhanging trees—blended into the architecture. A white stone wall surrounded the property, and in various positions giant white egg sculptures sat on top, as well as a pair of giant heads cuddled together.

"Totally trippy," Grace whispered to Jean Sebastian. Her phone dinged.

"I like to be a clown, a buffoon, I like to spread complete confusion."—Salvador Dalí

"What in the world?" Grace said. She showed it to Jean Sebastian.

"More games," Jean Sebastian said. It had Carrie Ann written all over it. Grace's phone dinged again.

Whispering room. Alone.

"Oh my God," Grace said. "Do you think they're here?" She looked around as if Carrie Ann or Stan might be crouching in the bushes.

Jean Sebastian sighed and looked around too. There were others on the tour, but the number was limited due to the size of the house. "I doubt anyone would try to hurt you here," he said. "But I don't like it."

"I just want to get it over with," Grace said. "Stay here." She left Jean Sebastian by the pool and hurried back into the whispering room. *Please be here, Jake. Please be here, Jake.* She sat on the curved built-in sofa, turned her phone to silent, and waited.

Close your eyes. I'll whisper to you. Wait 30 seconds before you open your eyes again, or I will hurt them.

CHAPTER 37

Was Stan here? Was Stan actually here? Her stomach twisted in anticipation. A strange part of her wanted to see him. It was being in this perverse house. It was making the abnormal seem normal. Grace looked around. The room was empty. She closed her eyes and began to count. It was excruciating not to open her eyes and see if Stan was here. When she reached fifty-nine, she heard a whisper, clear as day.

"We can bring her down." *Oh my God. Don't open your eyes; don't open your eyes; don't open your eyes.* Could she open one eye? Would he notice? *We can bring her down.* What did that mean? She couldn't believe how clear the whisper sounded. It was a male voice with an American accent, and it sounded familiar. She knew that voice. It made her stomach turn. It was Stan. *We can bring her down.* He was talking about Carrie Ann. Or he wanted her to think he was talking about Carrie Ann. Was he sitting directly across from her? It was excruciating not to open her eyes, but she didn't want to lose any chance she had of getting Jake back, so Grace silently began to count. When she reached thirty, her phone buzzed yet again. Her eyes flew open. She was alone. She shot off the bench and resisted the urge to run through the house, trying to catch him. She forced herself to at least read the message first.

Salvador Dalí married an ugly woman and worshipped her. I married a beautiful woman and despise her. You are the one for me, Grace. Be mine and I will set them free.

He was crazy. Not part genius like Dalí, just pure crazy. Grace stood and called out. "Jake? Carrie Ann?" There was no answer. She ran to the pool to find Jean Sebastian pacing. "Thank God," he said. "I was just coming in there."

"Let's get out of here," Grace said.

"What happened?"

"Nothing," Grace said.

"What do you mean?"

"I mean I sat there. I waited. And nothing. I'm getting the creeps. I just need to get out of here."

"Okay," Jean Sebastian said. "Let's go." Once they exited the house and grounds, Jean Sebastian suggested they sit down, get something for lunch, discuss their options.

"I'm sorry," Grace said. "I'm going to take a walk. I need to be alone." Jean Sebastian gently grabbed her arm and swung her around to him. Grace could feel her heart beating at their proximity, and she feared he could too.

"Is there something you're not telling me?"

"Like what?"

"Did you get another message? Did he threaten you?"

"No, I swear. It's just me. Whenever I'm upset, I need to be alone and walk it out. Compose in my head. You can ask Jake."

"I've been thinking about Jake," Jean Sebastian said.

"What?"

"How long have you known him?"

"Three years. Why?"

"How did you meet?"

"What's this all about?"

"Look—don't get too upset—but didn't Jake say, 'You never know who you're with?' "

"Yes."

"What if—just bear with me—what if he was talking about himself?"

"What?"

"What if—he's Stan?"

Grace burst out laughing. "Jake? Stan?"

"Isn't it possible?"

"No. God. No."

"Why not?"

"Besides the fact that Stan was fat and covered in pimples?"

"People lose weight. Their skin clears up."

That was true. And back then she could barely even look at Stan, so there was a good chance she wouldn't recognize him now. "Stan had the lightest blue eyes I've ever seen. Those wouldn't have changed. And before you say colored contacts— Jake doesn't wear contacts. I should know. I've been living with him for the past three years."

Jean Sebastian put his hands up. "Okay, okay. I just don't want to leave any stone unturned."

"I'm going for a walk."

"I'll go with you."

"I want to be alone."

"But Stan could be here somewhere. It's not safe."

"Nobody whispered to me in the house. That means they're not here."

"Are you sure? I get this feeling you're holding something back."

"You're right." Grace took a deep breath and threw her arms open. "I need to get some feminine items from the market at the top of the hill, and I'd rather do it alone."

"I'm a grown man. I can handle your buying feminine products."

"It's not dark out. There are people around. If anyone comes near me, I'll scream. I'm sure you'll be able to hear me all over town."

"I don't like it."

"I just need to clear my head. Do you want anything?"

"I want to go with you."

"You're starting to make me feel like a prisoner."

"I'm sorry. All right. Just be careful."

"I will. I'll see you later."

"I'll be at the hotel."

Grace nodded, then turned and walked up the hill from the house, making sure not to run in case he was watching, but dying to get away. When she was at the top of the hill, she looked down to the bay and pulled a stack of letters from her purse. The ones Carrie Ann had thrown back at her. All marked: RETURN TO SENDER. Grace had been going over and over every single thing she could remember Carrie Ann's saying to her since she had seen her on that roof deck.

She remembered Carrie Ann telling her that she should have made time to read the letters. She would do that now, read every single one of them just to see if there were any clues. Then, she had to find the nearest market, and then she had to find a computer with an Internet connection, and then she had to buy a phone card. She knew Carrie Ann better than anyone. So all Grace had to do was figure out the end game and beat her or Stan—or both of them—to it.

I married a beautiful woman and despise her.

You just never really know who you're with.

This time, there really is a wolf.

Grace paced underneath an old tree at the top of the hill and started opening the letters. The first few were pretty generic. Carrie Ann missed her. She wondered what Grace was up to. She wanted to see her. She "forgave" her. In later letters, the tone became more threatening. *Our thirtieth birthday. If you don't answer these letters, you'll see me then. We'll have our adventure. Maybe I'll enlist the help of an old friend.*

Old friend. Stan. Grace knew it. The two weren't married at all. It was Grace who Stan had a crush on.

You just never really know who you're with.

We can bring her down. That was what Stan had whispered to Grace in the whispering room. It was Carrie Ann he wanted to destroy. And apparently, he was under some kind of delusion that he loved Grace.

Grace flashed back to Park Güell. The look on Jake's face. He was absolutely terrified. At the time she had thought he was afraid of what Stan would do to him and Carrie Ann. Suddenly she knew, clear as day. Jake had been terrified for her.

The whisper had triggered a nagging suspicion, one too awful to face, but before she freaked out completely, she had to check it out. First, she had to find a computer. As she was putting the letters back in her purse, a flyer fluttered to the ground.

GREC FESTIVAL de BARCELONA

A spark of something akin to hope reverberated inside her. Grace had never called her agent to cancel her spot in the concert. There had been too much going on. Maybe she could use that to her advantage.

Although the scenery was spectacular, it was a hot day for a walk, and by the time Grace made it to a little market, she was damp with sweat and dehydrated. It was ridiculous of her to think there was an Internet café in this little village, but maybe one of the shopkeepers would let her use his computer. She could ask at the hotel, but for now she couldn't involve Jean Sebastian in any of her thoughts.

The small convenience store felt nice and cool. Grace bought a bottle of water and a calling card.

There was a middle-aged Spanish man at the register. His eyes had been on her since she entered the store. When he smiled at her, Grace pounced on the opening.

"Hola."

"Hola." He grinned. His teeth were yellow and crooked, but the smile was straight up.

"Por favor," she said. *"¿Habla inglés?"*

"Yes, English. Hello, American."

Wow. Grace would never get over how obvious it was to people. "Hello," she said. "Hello, Spanish man." She grinned. He grinned. "Have you seen any other Americans in here in the past week or so?"

He squinted. "Only I see French," he said. "And Spanish."

"I see." Just what she was beginning to suspect. Carrie Ann and Jake hadn't been here, had never been here. This old flirt seemed like he would remember Carrie Ann. It confirmed what Grace was starting to dread. "I was wondering—do you have a computer here with Internet connection?" He thumbed to a door behind him.

"My wife," he said. He mimicked her typing. "All day."

Grace laughed. "I'm so sorry to ask this—but do you think I could use it? I have to look up a phone number. It's very important."

"Sí, sí," he said. "I kick her." Grace prayed he meant "kick her off," but either way it looked like she was going to get to use the computer.

"Gracias," she said. "Gracias."

Grace's hands trembled as she held them over the keyboard. She didn't know his last name. She typed in Jean Sebastian, Congo, international rescue agency. Why hadn't she asked the exact name of the organization he had worked for?

Was it the International Rescue Committee? If so, she could find no mention of him on their Web site. Or anywhere else on the Internet. She also didn't know the name of his supposed blog. She'd been so wrapped up in herself, she'd completely ignored the person who had been right in front of her this entire time.

You never know who you're with.

She didn't find a travel blog, or a Facebook page, or anyone resembling the Belgian man who had been by her side.

She thanked the shopkeeper and hurried outside. Just as she was wondering what move she should make next, she saw him, coming up the hill in the distance. She hid behind the nearest tree, heart hammering. She was at the top of a steep, wooded hill. Just below was the hotel, but the only true path back to it was the way she had come. The way Jean Sebastian was coming. If she went straight down the hillside, she could reach the hotel room before he reached her. As long as she didn't kill herself on the journey. She ducked, then before she could talk herself out of it, she started scooting down the hill on her bottom. The terrain was littered with rocks and giant tree roots. Branches scraped the side of her face and clung to her hair. Leaves rustled and twigs snapped and everything sounded so loud, and even though she tried to slow down, she was picking up speed. If she went too fast she would slam into the back wall of the hotel. Speed plus stone wall would not a happy union make. Grace tucked her head into her body and gave in to a somersault. She turned at the last minute, and her side slammed into the wall. She lay for a moment, out of breath, adrenaline and fear pumping through her. She was all right. Nothing broken. Nothing bleeding. Slowly, she got on her hands and knees, then to her feet.

She forced herself to walk, rather than race, up to their rooms. Even though she knew he wasn't there, she opened the adjoining door and called out to him. "Jean Sebastian?"

She hurried into his bathroom and faced the medicine cabinet. She caught sight of herself in the mirror. Her hair was tousled with a few leaves stuck in the tangles. Dirt was streaked on her cheeks. For a moment, she just stared at the bedraggled girl in the mirror. Then, knowing full well what she would find, she took a deep breath and opened the medicine cabinet. And there it was. On the top shelf. A bottle of saline solution and a contact lens case. Of course he wore contact lenses. Colored ones, no doubt. He had to do something to cover up eyes so blue. Next to the saline solution was a prescription bottle. Shaking, she picked it up. Lithium. She closed her eyes before looking at the name.

The minute he had first whispered into her ear, not in the whispering room, but in the bedroom, when he had been all too happy to tell her about Dalí and Gala's sex life. Something about it had nauseated her. At the time she had blamed herself.

It was just guilt for being attracted to him. But then, when she had heard Stan whisper to her in the whispering room, something had clicked. Grace was a musician; she had an ear for pitch. The whispers matched. Disbelief and dread dropped into the pit of her stomach.

You just never really know who you're with.

That's cold, Grace, you're so cold.

This time, there really is a wolf.

Grace had been thoroughly played. People could lose weight. Their skin could clear up. They could cut and lighten their hair. Braces eventually came off. Contacts could color your eyes. An accent could be faked. Jean Sebastian's eyes were such an odd color, such a light, light brown. Because even with colored contacts it was hard to disguise eyes so blue. Grace couldn't deny it any longer. She opened her eyes and faced the name on the little orange bottle. And there it was in black and white. Hiding in plain sight. The prescription belonged to Stan Gale.

CHAPTER 38

The day after Grace got her cast removed, she climbed up to her tree house to find a note stuck on the wall.

You have to come see me. I have to tell you something.
Come tonight. CAG.

Tonight? In the dark? Grace had been grounded since she last snuck over to the Gales' barn. Part of her didn't want to go, wanted to pretend Carrie Ann had never existed, but the other part of her missed Carrie Ann as much as she'd missed using her arm. Grace's bedroom was on the first floor, and her parents rarely locked the doors (if only child services knew), so once the house was quiet and dark, Grace slipped out and made her way through the woods and over to the barn. The minute Grace saw Carrie Ann, huddled in the hayloft, she knew something terrible was going on. For once, Stan was nowhere to be seen. "Are you okay?" Grace said as she climbed up. Instead of hugging her, Carrie Ann scooted away.

"Get out of here," she said. Carrie Ann, at fifteen, had never lost her rough edges.

"But you told me to come."

"I did not."

"You left me a note."

"I *didn't*."

"It's not my fault," Grace pleaded. "I didn't know my mother was going to send you away."

"I hate it here," Carrie Ann said. "I hate Stan, and his stupid mother, and his evil father!"

Grace winced when she heard Carrie Ann call Lydia stupid, but she didn't challenge her. "He's pretty strict, huh?"

"He's a perv," Carrie Ann said.

"What do you mean?"

"You really want to know, Gracie? You want all the dirty details?" Grace could barely swallow. She nodded. "You know how I like to sleep in the nude?" Grace did know. Carrie Ann had done it ever since she came to live with the Sawyers. No matter how many pairs of pajamas Jody bought her, they, along with Carrie Ann's underwear, were always on the floor in the morning.

"He's been coming into my room at night with a flashlight."

"What?"

"When he thinks I'm asleep."

"Oh my God."

"He lifts the sheet and stands there staring at me. Running the flashlight up and down my body. Every night. And he's taking longer and longer."

A sick feeling crawled into Grace and lodged itself in her stomach. "No," she said. "No."

Carrie Ann, who had been clutching her knees, pulling them into her chest, suddenly shot out and grabbed Grace's shoulders. "Don't tell anyone. No one. Especially not your mother."

"But Carrie Ann—"

"Who knows where I'll end up, Gracie. At least this way I get to see you."

"We have to tell her—"

"Do you think if she knew—she would let me come back and live with you again?"

This time, when Carrie Ann looked into Grace's eyes, Grace saw it all. The pleading. The desperation. And the plotting. Carrie Ann was lying about Stan's father coming into her room at night with a flashlight. She was making it all up just so Grace would go running to her mother and tell. Because Carrie Ann thought Jody would take her back. What Carrie Ann didn't know was that Grace's mother wouldn't believe Carrie Ann in a million years. Grace could even tell she was lying. Carrie Ann was the girl who cried wolf, and anybody could see that the local insurance man, married to the art teacher, was anything but a wolf. He was just strict. He wasn't letting Carrie Ann rule the household. And she was lashing out.

"I have to go," Grace said. She suddenly wanted to get away from Carrie Ann, wanted to be anywhere but in the hayloft. When Grace stepped onto the ladder, Carrie Ann crawled over and grabbed ahold of it. Not again, Grace thought. This time maybe she'd break more than an arm. Why didn't she ever learn her lesson? Carrie Ann pushed the ladder back about two inches. Grace screamed. Carrie Ann brought the ladder back in. Grace was fine, but her heart was hammering so hard it was a full three minutes before she could move again.

"Tell her," Carrie Ann said. "Please."

"I will," Grace promised. "I will."

And then Grace went home and didn't tell a soul.

That was her dirty secret.

Not a whisper. Not a peep, not a soul. And maybe, just maybe, she should have.

But somebody told. Because it wasn't long before tongues started wagging in town. Whispers spread into full-blown rumors. Around water coolers. At the local diner. Grocery stores. Then at the pub. Faster and faster, rumors started to float around town. *Did you hear that Lionel Gale is a pervert? He comes into Carrie Ann's room at night.*

With a candle . . .

With a flashlight . . .
With a match . . .
With a knife . . .

The first time Grace caught wind of it was in the girls' bath-room at school. A group of girls swarmed Grace, asking her if it was true. Grace clamped her mouth shut and ran out of the bathroom.

The next week, Lydia Gale didn't show up for work. She was out for five days. When she did return, briefly, her eyes were bloodshot. She sat at her desk and cried. When somebody called her Lydia, she lashed out.

"My name is Mrs. Gale! You will call me Mrs. Gale!"

At the height of the rumors, Carrie Ann left Grace a ton of messages. Grace was too petrified to answer. Carrie Ann was going to think she was the one spreading the rumors. And she wasn't. She wasn't. Grace prayed it would die down. It didn't. Somebody said they'd seen a police cruiser at the Gales' home. No doubt questioning Lionel. Somebody else said he was fired from his job because they didn't want a pervert working there. Next, Stan dropped out of school. Grace was secretly relieved; ever since Carrie Ann had moved in with him, he'd stopped staring at Grace in that strange way, pretended to see right through her, even when they passed in the halls. And although she would have thought it would have brought her relief, being so blatantly ignored was even creepier than when he had been openly staring at her with those pleading blue eyes. Grace wasn't sure what had happened, why Stan was acting this way. She had thought he worshipped Carrie Ann. Now it was as if he blamed Grace for Carrie Ann's very existence. She could only imagine the tension in that home. And it was her fault, in a way. If she hadn't broken down in front of Lydia, the Gales probably would have never thought to take Carrie Ann in.

Then came the night that still shamed Grace to the core. It was before Lionel's death, at the peak of the nasty rumors. Jody Sawyer climbed up to the tree house where Grace had been holed up every day after school.

"Do you know anything about this situation with Lionel Gale?" her mother asked. "Did Carrie Ann say anything to you?"

Grace looked at her mother's face, contorted in worry. "No," Grace said. "She didn't say a word."

To this day her insides burned in shame. Why didn't she just tell her mother that she hadn't told because she knew Carrie Ann was lying? Her mother would have understood that. But just the fact that her mother had asked, in that voice ripe with concern, made Grace's blood feel like ice water running through her veins. Did it mean she should have told? Did it mean her mother thought that Carrie Ann might be telling the truth?

Then, one night, came another message from Carrie Ann. A note. Left in her tree house. It was the most frantic Grace had ever heard Carrie Ann.

Please. Help me. Come tonight. You're my sister. I need you. Meet me in the hayloft.

Below the note was a drop of blood. Grace ran to the Gales' house as fast as she could. She took the woods between their homes, tripped on several tree roots in her haste, then stumbled yet again at the entrance to their farm.

She passed the tree where Stan's tire swing usually hung. The tire was lying on the grass. The barn door was open. Just barely, just enough for Grace to slip through. A single light was shining in the middle of the barn. Grace took slow, quiet steps. As soon as she neared the hayloft, she saw something hovering in midair.

Shoes. Brown, leather, size-eleven shoes. Big, shiny brown shoes hovering right in front of her face. The smell of shoe polish was overpowering. At first, her brain couldn't compute what she was seeing. She thought it must be Carrie Ann, practicing magic. *She's made a man float,* Grace actually thought. Until Grace looked up, past the gleaming shoes. Lionel Gale dangled in front of her, hanging from the rafters by a thick, braided rope. Later she would realize it was the rope from Stan's tire swing. Lionel was the first dead person Grace had ever seen. The spotlight had been aimed directly at his face.

His face bulged, his skin was purple above the neck, and blood was dripping from his eyes. His blood vessels had burst. Grace didn't know a cadaver could look so gruesome. She whimpered. Then she moaned, and finally, she opened her mouth and screamed. And she screamed, and she screamed, and she screamed. She wished she hadn't.

She wished she had it to do over. She would calmly, bravely walk up to Lydia's house, and tell Lydia she was very sorry but she needed to call the police. Instead, Grace's screams brought Lydia flying from the house and into the barn. The horrific sight, coupled with Grace's hysteria, brought Lydia Gale to her knees. Grace would never again be able to imagine Lydia smiling, standing in the middle of the art room in her beautiful homemade skirts, smelling of vanilla or lavender, encouraging the children with what seemed to be an endless well of optimism. Instead, Grace would see Lydia on her knees, rocking back and forth, fists in her mouth to keep from screaming, head bent down and blond curls kissing the dirt.

Two things hit Grace as she replayed that awful memory.

One: Carrie Ann had told her she hadn't left the first note. So, what if she hadn't left the second note either? What if someone else had lured her out to the barn to find Lionel Gale?

And two: His shoes. They were so shiny. So polished. Gleaming. They looked like shoes that had never even touched the ground. Wouldn't there be some little scuff, at the least some disturbance to them from when Lionel had hanged himself? Or was Grace just imagining how shiny the shoes were—was it a detail she'd exaggerated in the trauma of the moment?

All these years it had haunted Grace that Lionel Gale, before he had slipped the rope around his neck and stepped into thin air, had stopped and taken the time to thoroughly shine his shoes. It meant something. Grace didn't know what. But she knew. All these years, like a secret message, like a name written in blood, those shoes had been trying to tell her something.

CHAPTER 39

Grace paced her room at the villa. She looked again at the text message Stan had sent her in the whispering room.

Be mine and I will set them free.

She took a deep breath and texted back.

Release Carrie Ann and Jake. Then I will be yours.

If Carrie Ann and Stan thought they were going to get away with this little prank, they had another think coming. She knew she should feel relieved. This was just a sick game. She wasn't in any real danger. Jake wasn't in any real danger. So then why didn't she feel relieved? Why was this heavy feeling of dread still lodged in her stomach? God, all those awful things she'd said about Stan right to his face. She tried to remember every single comment, and her stomach knotted more with each remembrance.

She was going to have to make sure she didn't let on that she knew. Thanks to Carrie Ann's securing a singing spot for her at the Grec Festival de Barcelona, Grace actually had a plan, a chance of turning this prank around. Every time she thought of the lengths they'd gone to, to pull this off, rage threatened to bring her down. Part of her wanted to confront Stan the minute he returned to the hotel. He and Carrie Ann had actually drugged and kidnapped Jake and Grace. They would not get away with this. They would not. She didn't know if her plan was going to work, but she was sure as hell going to try.

She'd arrange for them all to come together at the festival, and once she was reunited with Jake, they would actually disappear. For good this time. Carrie Ann and Stan wouldn't get the pleasure of saying "Gotcha," that was for sure. Grace would love it if Carrie Ann and Stan would get a little visit from the Spanish police, but at this point she just wanted to get as far away from them as possible. Maybe she'd hire an attorney when she was safely back in the States, and figure out her options. Grace pulled out the calling card she had bought at the market and made her phone call. Jim Sawyer answered on the first ring.

"Dad?" Grace said. "It's me."

"Grace, finally." Her father sounded agitated, which wasn't like him.

"Dad?"

"There have been some really strange things on your Facebook page, Grace. And then an official from the American embassy called me yesterday asking all sorts of strange questions about you."

"Oh, God."

"I've been telling everyone that my little girl is not a liar. I didn't know what to make of that picture of you kissing another fellow. And now I have Jake's mother calling me and telling me that she thinks you're lying to her about Jake—and that she talked to him, but he sounded funny. Grace—what are you mixed up in?"

"I'm sorry I didn't tell you, Dad. But it's true. Carrie Ann is here—and all my ID was stolen, and Jake was kidnapped."

"This sounds like your mother's soap opera. This can't be real."

"Dad. It is real. Or at least it was. Stan Gale is here too, Dad."

"Are you kidding?"

"No. I don't have much time to explain."

"You have to say something."

"Carrie Ann and Stan did this to mess with me. They're playing a game."

"The embassy said that the Spanish police suspect that you stole Carrie Ann's ID and her diamond ring. I told them my daughter is no thief. But I also didn't think my daughter made out in dance clubs with men who were not her boyfriend."

"Dad—please. Listen to me. It's all a setup."

"I want you on the next plane home."

"I have to find Jake, Dad. I've figured out how to meet up with him, and I need your help."

There was no hesitation. "Tell me exactly what you want me to do," he said. And so she did. "Wait," her father said before she hung up. "Happy birthday, Gracie."

A lump formed in Grace's throat. She'd forgotten all about it. Her birthday. She would turn thirty tomorrow. "Thanks, Dad. And give my love to Mom."

By the time Stan arrived back at the hotel, Grace was ready for him. She was out on the balcony, with her guitar.

"I'm so glad you're here." She took a moment to really look at him. Was there any part of him that looked like the old Stan? It was truly a remarkable transformation. He was in such good shape. His hair was lighter and out of his eyes. He did have some acne scarring, but nothing drastic. If those colored contacts had come out, and he had dropped the accent, she still probably wouldn't have known. But now that she knew it was Stan, the creepy feeling was back tenfold.

She felt like such a hypocrite. Just last night she had been thinking about kissing him. Maybe part of her aversion to him back when they were kids had been out of jealousy. She had been a young girl, and she had just wanted to be with Carrie Ann. Would telling him she was sorry change anything? Why was he still holding such a grudge after all these years? He must be thrilled, thinking he had completely snowed her. And he would be right. Not only had she not recognized him, but she had lusted after him as well. Carrie Ann had pulled off her greatest trick of all. She had probably been instrumental in giving Stan this makeover. She'd always wanted to make someone disappear, and she had. She had made Stan Gale disappear in plain sight. It was payback time. Grace stepped up to Stan and put her arms around him. This time, as they hugged, she didn't pull away. "I'm sorry," she said.

Stan backed up, held her at arm's length. "What for?"

"Getting mad at you about Jake. You were right."

"About what?"

"I think Jake is in on this with Carrie Ann and Stan."

"Seriously?"

"Yes. I think he's been having an affair with Carrie Ann. Which makes much more sense than Carrie Ann's being with a loser like Stan." Grace cringed a little to say this, but it was exactly what Stan deserved. She would have just run out of the hotel and gone back to Barcelona without him, but she got the feeling he was the one giving the go-ahead to Rafael, and she needed everyone to go along with the upcoming rendezvous.

"So what is your plan?" Stan said. Was it her imagination or was he already losing the accent?

"I need your help. Because they aren't going to like this." She forced herself to look up at Stan.

"Why not?" Stan said. His voice was a whisper.

"Because it involves my doing this again," Grace said. And with that, she put her arms around him, pulled his face close to hers, and kissed him. Stan was stunned at first, then slowly responded. Then abruptly, he pulled away.

"This is part of your plan?" he said.

"Yes," Grace said. "But I wanted to do that."

"Why? Don't get me wrong. I want to do that too. But you . . . Why now?"

"Don't make me say it; I feel too guilty."

Stan stepped forward. The intensity in his eyes was startling. "You have to say it."

"I have these feelings for you, all right? But I can't act on them. Not yet."

"Not yet?"

"I don't think Jake is in any real danger. I think I'm being played. And even though I don't think Jake is Stan, I do think Jake's involved in this."

"How so?"

"Look at how he's been acting! He took Carrie Ann's hand in front of me at Park Güell. Then there's that video—he's not handcuffed. He could have walked away. Instead, what does he do? Questions who the hell I am. Carrie Ann admitted that she's been in Nashville—she's seen me play in concerts. I think they've been having an affair that began long before this trip."

"My God."

"I know. I just don't know why Carrie Ann bothered to involve Stan at all. She must have used him just to get Rafael. I mean Stan didn't mastermind this—he's not smart, he's not strong, and he's certainly not the type a girl like Carrie Ann would ever have any romantic feelings for. I feel so dumb that I didn't realize it was a big, fat joke the minute she said she had actually married him."

Stan turned around for a minute and pretended to look out at the ocean. Maybe Grace had taken it a bit too far. Then she thought about how he'd been deceiving her this whole time. He was lucky she hadn't called the police or planned to stab him in his sleep.

"I thought you haven't seen Stan since you were a kid."

"I haven't. Thank God."

"Maybe he's changed. People change."

"Not Stan."

"Are you sure?"

"I'll bet he still lives with his mother. His own Bates Motel." Grace cringed as she said the words and saw Stan's eyes darken. To his credit, he quickly recovered.

"I'll take your word for it. I don't know any of them. I mean—I barely met Carrie Ann."

"I'm so lucky I've met you. You're almost too good to be true. You haven't been lying to me, have you?"

"What do you mean?" Stan's voice was tight.

"Someone as gorgeous as you? And that accent. God, it really gets to me. You aren't hiding a girlfriend or wife back home, are you?"

Stan broke out into a grin. "I'm a free man," he said.

"Good. I have a plan to get back at them. Are you in?"

"I guess it depends on what it is." Grace had been waiting for this. She handed him the flyer. "Grec Festival de Barcelona," Stan read. "I don't get it," he said.

"I'm supposed to play at this concert. Carrie Ann set it up as a surprise. Let's get them to meet us there."

"Then what?" Stan said.

"I play them the song I wrote about our childhood tragedy. In front of a huge crowd. In front of Carrie Ann, and Jake, and Stan."

"Why?"

"Because Carrie Ann might be doing this just because she's sick in the head—but I think Stan is doing this because he thinks I'm the one who spread ugly rumors about his father. He holds me responsible for his father's suicide."

Stan gave a low whistle. "Let's say you're right. So this song— this apology—you think that will be enough?"

"I think it's a start. I think Stan wants to see me. And I think I need to see him. I need him to hear what I have to say."

"Let's just forget about all of this and take off on our own."

"I need closure with Jake. And I need to look Carrie Ann in the eye and tell her that her prank didn't work. Then, I need Stan to hear the truth. From me. And that's it. I'm done. I walk away. With you." Stan put his arms around her waist and pulled her in. It took everything in her not to push him away. Instead, she played with a button on his shirt. "I think of all of them there might be hope for Stan. Maybe he'll see the light."

"The light? What exactly is the light?"

"You of all people should know. All of your experiences in

the Congo—the danger, the threats, the constant heaviness. You must know. Stan has probably spent the rest of his life since that Tuesday night when his father hanged himself in torment. Absolute torment." Grace stopped for a minute, took in their surroundings. The water was so peaceful. Small fishing boats bobbed along the shore, kissed by the afternoon sun. "The light is freedom, Jean Sebastian. The light is coming out of hiding and speaking the truth. The light is finally letting go."

CHAPTER 40

Carrie Ann and Jake sat at their usual table at the café near the apartment. Rafael sat on the opposite wall right near the door. His knee hadn't stopped bouncing since they had arrived. Jake got the distinct feeling that something was up.

"Did you notice the schedule is different today?" Jake said. The music festival was tomorrow. Grace's birthday was tomorrow. He should be with her, talking her into singing, and celebrating her birthday. Proposing even. But, no. They were still hostages. And instead of being allowed out for lunch, they were sitting in the café at breakfast time. Something was happening, he could feel it.

"No," Carrie Ann said.

"We're here a half an hour early."

"Whoopie."

"You're missing my point. See how Rafael keeps looking at the door?"

"Do you think they're coming?" Carrie Ann sat up straight, and some life actually came back into her eyes.

"I doubt that very much. But I definitely think Rafael is expecting someone."

"What are you thinking?"

"I'm thinking that if Grace hasn't figured out he's Stan by now, that she's not going to. We have to do something."

"He won't react well if we try and trick him."

"Do you think he would really hurt her?"

"A few days ago I would have said not on your life. But he's surprised me. This was supposed to be my plan. I was supposed to disappear. He not only defied it; he took it to a whole new level."

"If all he wants is some kind of grand apology, why doesn't he just tell her that? I know she'd do it."

"I don't know. He's not communicating with me." The door to the café opened, and the man Grace called the doorman-who-doesn't-open-any-doors walked in. Jake felt a pang, like a hit to the gut. He missed his Grace. Everything about her, including her cute little sayings. He was never going to let her go again. Carrie Ann had finally told him everything. Grace had been carrying the guilt of Lionel Gale's suicide all these years. It explained a lot. Jake's desire to protect her and heal her was stronger than ever. It wasn't her fault. And after spending just a little time around Carrie Ann, he could only imagine what years of being around her could do to a young girl. He had to see Grace. Hell, he was probably going to ask her to marry him the second he saw her. *Please be all right.* He wanted nothing more than to get his hands on Stan Gale. Rafael too for that matter. Up until Carrie Ann's recent confession, Jake had just thought that Jean Sebastian was helping Stan. He had had no idea Jean Sebastian *was* Stan. It made Jake's blood boil. During one of their phone calls, Grace had asked him if he'd seen Stan. Carrie Ann had emphatically nodded yes. And so he had fibbed. If he hadn't, maybe Grace would have figured it out sooner. There were so many things he wished he could take back. Instead, he had to focus on getting away from Rafael.

Across the room Stefano was handing Rafael a large envelope. Rafael slipped Stefano some money and booted him out as quickly as possible. Carrie Ann was seated so that she was facing Rafael.

"Can you see what he's looking at?" Jake said.

"No."

"He's distracted. I say we make a run for it. Through the back."

"Okay," Carrie Ann said. "Let's do it."

"On three." Jake scooted his chair back quietly. "One—"

"Rafael's getting up," Carrie Ann said.

"Shit." Did he literally have eyes in the back of his head? Rafael came to their table. He was holding a flyer. To Jake's surprise, Rafael thrust it in Jake's face.

"Have you heard of this?" Rafael said. Jake looked at the flyer.

GREC FESTIVAL DE BARCELONA

ROBERT LOVE LANDING

PRESENTS

MEET ME IN BARCELONA

A HUNDRED RED BALLET SLIPPERS PRODUCTION

AMERICANS IN BARCELONA

COSTUME CONTEST

PRIZE: $20,000 US DOLLARS

Are you an American living in Barcelona? Do you have a wild costume, like those of the street performers on La Rambla? If so, you could win $20,000 at our annual contest. Food, drink, music. To enter, you must have an American passport and ID. Will be checked thoroughly.

The concert was tomorrow. Jake had to use every ounce of willpower not to break out in a grin. *Way to go, Grace. Way to go.* She finally got it. She knew who Jean Sebastian really was. And she was trying to get them all in the same place. *Thank you, God. Thank you.*

"Your eagle costume would be perfect," Carrie Ann said.

"That's what I was thinking," Rafael said. "Do you think I could pass for American?"

"Not a chance," Jake said.

"I have your passport," Rafael said.

"For a $20,000 prize they aren't going to let anyone pull a fast one," Jake said. "You are Spanish through and through, my man."

"But we do have an American sitting right here," Carrie Ann said. Rafael didn't answer, but he did make a second out-of-the-ordinary move. He sat down at their table. Stared at the flyer. "He's just a little shorter than you, Rafael," Carrie Ann said. "But I could help tailor the costume."

Rafael looked up at Jake as if they were having a stare down. "I don't trust him with the knives," he said.

"That's too bad," Carrie Ann said. "The knives are the best part."

"They are, aren't they?" Rafael said. "They are divine." Rafael's phone rang. He gave a start. Jake and Carrie Ann made eye contact. Rafael held up his finger, then walked a few feet away to take the call.

"This is Grace," Jake said.

"I know that," Carrie Ann said. "A hundred red ballet slippers."

"Robert would have loved the landing." He laughed softly, then his face took on a more serious expression. "I think she wants me to wear the eagle costume," he said.

"Because you'll be easy to spot in a crowd."

"She's a genius."

"You'll also be easy for everyone else to spot—namely Rafael."

"There's a flaw in every diamond."

"If you're in the eagle costume and she can spot you easily, then you have to let me stay by your side. I don't want to be alone with Rafael."

"Do you think he's actually going to let me have the knives?"

"He's got twenty thousand reasons," Carrie Ann said.

"And a couple really good ones not to."

"I knew the knives were real. Psycho."

Rafael was off the phone. He strode back to them. He was actually rubbing his hands. "That was Stan. Grace is going to sing and play her guitar for a big crowd tomorrow. At this festival. This is a message from heaven. This is meant to be, no?"

"It definitely is," Carrie Ann said.

"Okay. So you will wear the costume. If you win—the money is mine."

"And you let me go," Jake said. "Or no deal."

"Where will you go?" Rafael said, throwing his arms open. "Will you go without Grace?"

Jake curled his fists and looked away. He needed to pretend to be nervous about this. Carrie Ann was right though. Rafael would be able to spot Jake in a second. Worse, Rafael was probably going to stick to him like glue. What happened when Rafael found out there was no costume contest? Nobody else dressed up like an idiot? Jake was going to have to take Rafael down for the count.

Would it jeopardize Grace's plan? She had sent the flyer to Rafael after all. Did she have some kind of plan of her own for neutralizing Rafael? Doubtful. Although Jake had no clue how she'd even pulled this off. Somebody had to have made the flyer and then delivered it to Stefano.

Rafael hopped up. "We'll do it," he said. He pointed at Jake. "You will not leave my side," he said.

Shit, Jake thought. The best-case scenario would be taking Rafael down somehow.

Jake shrugged. "You'll need to give me back my passport."

"I'll be your shadow," Rafael said. He grabbed the flyer and his phone and started to walk away again.

"Rafael," Carrie Ann said.

"*¿Qué?*"

"If you talk to Stan again, I wouldn't mention this costume contest." Rafael frowned. "I know Stan," she said. "He'll think it will distract you. He won't like it."

"I can handle it," Rafael said.

"I know that. But he won't see it that way."

"You're trying to set me up," Rafael said.

Carrie Ann put her hands up. "Tell him then," she said. "See for yourself."

Rafael glared and began to pace as he dialed his phone.

"What do you think he'll do?" Jake said.

Carrie Ann crossed her fingers. Jake nodded, then crossed his. "Who is Robert Love Landing?" Carrie Ann asked.

"Her grandfather was Robert," Jake said. "Something her mother says—'Robert would have loved the landing'—I don't know the whole story."

"Sounds like Grace," Carrie Ann said. "Never telling the whole story."

"Seriously?" Jake said. "She comes up with a plan to save our asses and you're still trying to cut her down?"

"Sorry," Carrie Ann said. "I couldn't resist."

"We've got another problem," Jake said.

"What?"

"Grace's parents." Jake swallowed hard. "Unless Grace has been allowed to speak with them, they're probably on a plane as we speak."

"To where?"

"Here."

"Here?"

"It was a surprise. For her thirtieth birthday."

"But I thought her mom was on her deathbed."

"The doctors have been working with them to figure out everything they could to let her take this last trip. Just for a few days. It was going to be a big surprise."

"Shit."

"As soon as I take down Rafael, I'm going to have to get to a phone."

"Wait. What do you mean—take down Rafael?"

"If I'm in that bird costume, he's going to be able to follow every move we make."

"So will Grace."

"Right—but how long until he figures out there's no costume contest, no $20,000?"

"I didn't think of that."

"So we're going to wait for an opportunity—both of us—and if one comes, we take it."

"What exactly does that mean?"

"Most likely hitting him on the back of the head with something heavy."

"Couldn't that kill him?"

"Our goal is just to render him unconscious. But anything we do in an attempt to escape is truly self-defense."

"I could try seduction one more time."

"No offense, but he's had us locked in our rooms for days and he has kept his distance. I think that ship has sailed."

"You have no idea what I'm capable of."

"Well, give it a try. But if that doesn't work, start thinking of everything that is in that apartment—anything you could grab when his back is turned."

"Me?"

"I'm assuming I'm going to be back in cuffs. So you either have to find the key to unlock me, or—assuming your little seduction plan fails—you're going to have to be the one to hit him over the head any second you get."

"But this is a prank, Jake. Not a real kidnapping."

"Tell that to Rafael. Any time I tried to leave I got a punch in the mouth."

"I could try and call Stan, make him realize that it's time to tell Rafael to let us go."

"Why would he do that?"

"Because he knows that we're all going to the festival. He doesn't need iron control anymore."

"Don't call him. We don't want to risk Rafael's telling him that I'm going to be wearing the eagle costume."

"Right."

"I don't want to kill Rafael or anything, but we're going to have to make sure Rafael doesn't follow us to that festival. I have an idea. But you're going to have to help me get ahold of Rafael's phone."

Carrie Ann stared at Jake for a long time, then slowly nodded.

CHAPTER 41

Jim Sawyer hung up the phone. He didn't know what to do. Jake couldn't talk long because he didn't want someone to notice his phone was missing, so he just said that they shouldn't come. He'd explain the rest later. Now Jim had to break it to his wife. There was a chance she wouldn't even remember they were supposed to take a trip. He wanted to get on a plane himself and rush out to save his little girl, but he wouldn't have a clue where to start. Instead, he had done as Grace had requested and made up that flyer, then sent it American Express to someone named Rafael in care of Stefano at the address where Grace had been staying.

When Jim walked into the hospice room, Jody was dressed, sitting on the bed with her travel bag by her side.

"Where's your bag?" she said.

"You remembered," he said.

"Of course I remembered. I've been good about taking my medication for this trip. I wouldn't miss this for the world."

Jim was filled with a sense of hopelessness and powerlessness that was debilitating. Not only was his little girl in trouble, but now he had to break that news to his wife. And it was no exaggeration to say that it could kill her.

"Sit down," Jim said. "I have something to tell you."

"I am sitting down," she said.

"We can't go to Barcelona," Jim said.

After over three decades of marriage, Jody must have picked up on the seriousness of the situation. "Start talking," Jody said.

Jim reluctantly filled her in. He told her everything. Jody sprang from the bed and grabbed her suitcase.

"Let's go," she said.

"But I just told you—"

"Our little girl is in trouble. It's even more reason to go."

"The stress won't be good for you."

"I'm not dead yet—and my daughter needs me. If you think I'm passing that opportunity up, then you might as well kill me yourself."

Three hours later, they were on a flight to Barcelona.

The car ride from Cadaqués to Barcelona was filled with a thick silence. Whereas he'd been chatty on the way to Port Lligat, "Jean Sebastian" was now spending most of his time staring out the window. Several times Grace had almost slipped and called him Stan. She prayed her father had been able to send the flyer and that it had made its way to Rafael. Hopefully Jake would be wearing the eagle costume. She could find him, and the two of them could decide what action to take against these three. Or maybe they would just slip away. They could talk to an attorney when they were safely back in the States.

Grace still wasn't sure about Carrie Ann. Part of this was totally something she would do. But Carrie Ann was more of a pomp and circumstance girl. Carrie Ann's grand schemes usually involved everything revolving around her. Was Stan really the mastermind behind this? If so, he had changed. Come out of his shell, so to speak.

"It looks like our plan is working," Grace said.

"How so?" Stan said.

"Well, ever since I texted Carrie Ann to meet us in Barcelona, she stopped playing hangman."

Stan turned, and his eyes bored into Grace's. "Hangman?" he said.

Had she just made a horrible mistake? She was trying so hard to say whatever she would have honestly said to Jean Sebastian. But she'd kept the fact that the clues were looking like a game of hangman to herself. Because she hadn't wanted Jean Sebastian to be drawn into all the psychodrama. How ironic.

"I forgot to tell you," Grace said. "The couple times I got the answer 'Lydia' wrong, Carrie Ann—or Stan—replied with a circle and then with a stem coming off the circle. It looked as if they were playing a game of hangman."

"That's bizarre," Stan said.

"You don't know the half of it," Grace said.

Stan gestured to the countryside. "We've got time."

Grace hesitated. Did she or did she not tell "Jean Sebastian" all the details about Stan's father? It was a tightrope. If she angered Stan, or touched on too many painful memories, wasn't there a very real chance he'd break character? And then maybe he'd call off meeting at the concert, and she'd never find Jake and Carrie Ann.

"You'll hear it in the song," Grace said.

"Why not both?"

"It's too personal," Grace said.

"But you're going to sing it in front of a festival full of total strangers?"

"It's different when I'm on stage. Playing for a crowd. Then the music takes over, as if it's performing, and I'm just the vessel."

"You're lucky," Stan said. He went back to looking out the window. "I've never had anything like that."

He was lying. Stan used to be terrific at doodling. It sounded silly, but jaws would drop at the things he would sketch in his schoolbooks. He could have been a great cartoonist, or a book illustrator, or a freelance artist. Why did some people ignore their talents and get sucked into the dark side? His obsession with Grace had really nothing to do with her. It was too bad she couldn't get him to realize that.

"It's almost over," Grace said. "I'm going to go to this thing, apologize publicly to Stan, make sure Jake is okay, and then . . ."

Stan slipped his hand into hers. "Then you and I can get the hell out of here. Maybe Italy?"

"Only if Carrie Ann brings my ID."

"Right. We'll have to make sure of it." They were nearing Stan's hotel. Grace wondered how Stan had come into so much money. She'd heard his father had had a hefty insurance policy. And maybe it was just in her head, but it seemed as if he was slowly dropping the "Jean Sebastian" act, and the real Stan was once again shining through. Unfortunately, the real Stan made her just as uncomfortable as ever.

And really—did he truly believe she was now in love with him and wanted to leave Jake? She wasn't an expert on the Stockholm syndrome, but surely it took people longer than a few days to fall for their captors. Because that's what Stan was, wasn't he? Her captor? She never would have stayed with him, traveled with him, or showered with him nearby, if she had known he was Stan. As soon as they got to the concert and she found Jake, the two of them would get away. As long as Jake was wearing that costume and had figured out how to deter Rafael, they would find each other.

Grace was relieved when they finally arrived at the hotel and they stepped into Stan's suite.

"Do you want to shower first?" Stan asked. At least he was pretending to be a gentleman and hadn't tried anything. Thank God for small miracles. But she felt odd, once again, knowing she'd be showering with him in the other room. She felt a deep shame at her earlier fantasies about and attraction to him when she had thought he was a Belgian man who headed up rescues in the Congo. What an idiot she'd been.

"Are you okay?" Stan said.

"Yes," Grace said. "Sorry, my mind is racing."

"Well, a nice shower should help it slow down. After all,

you're going to be on stage tomorrow. Have to look good for the fans."

"Right you are," Grace said. She hurried to the bathroom and shut the door. How dare they? Was this all a game, a manufactured drama, just to mess with her mind and get her on stage? Why would they care about her singing?

Because of what she'd said in one of her interviews after the Marsh Everett review.

"Do you have any painful songs?" a reporter had asked her as a follow-up to Marsh Everett's comment about singing her pain.

"I have one," Grace said. "It's about something tragic that occurred in my childhood."

"Why haven't you sung it? Shown the country world some pain like Mr. Everett suggested?"

"Because it's personal, and it involves other people, and it was just something I had to write to work through the truth."

Well, if they wanted to hear her take on the past, they were going to get it. Maybe shaming them in front of an international audience was exactly what was called for next. And then she and Jake would get the hell out of here.

There was a knock on the door, startling Grace out of her memory. "Yes?"

"I'll order room service," Stan said. "Should I choose for you?"

God, he was such a pompous ass. Now that she knew it was fake, she wanted to choke that phony accent out of him. Grace forced herself to sound cheery. "Too nervous to eat. But thanks." Grace slipped off her clothes and stepped into the shower. She needed a razor. She hadn't cared about it the past few days, but if she was going to sing, she wanted to look her best. Stan had a small leather bag on the sink. Maybe he had a razor in there. Grace stepped out and opened the bag. Lying on top was a small sketchbook, and underneath it were mounds and mounds of circular tins. At first she didn't know what the round tins were, but at the moment she didn't care. It was the top sketch that was rooting her to the spot in horror. It was of a cat. Her cat. It was Brady. His body lying on the steps of her house, his eyes open and glassy. The sketch clearly showed a scarf strangling his neck. Stan had even colored the scarf pink. Grace slapped her hand over her mouth. Above the sketch of Brady it said: DIE. Grace felt her insides turn to ice. On the next page he'd tacked a newspaper article. It was Lionel Gale's obituary, the one that had run in the newspaper after his death. In the photo, Stan had drawn a rope around Lionel's neck in red marker. He'd also sketched in the rafters of the barn from which Lionel had hung. Across his forehead Stan had written: DIE.

The next page was a picture of Carrie Ann. Dead. From a stabbing. Tears welled in Grace's eyes. Jake was next. It appeared Jake had been beaten to death with a baseball bat. The last page held an actual photo of Grace. The one Rafael had taken of her on La Rambla that second morning. She'd had good reason to be paranoid. Above her head someone had drawn a question mark.

Grace heaved and rushed to the toilet. Thankfully she hadn't eaten anything, but the reflex continued, so she grabbed a towel and held it over her mouth to mask the noise.

Carrie Ann had been out to play a prank. Stan had other plans for all of them. Grace looked around the bathroom for a weapon. Anything to arm herself with. That's when her eyes landed back on the leather case. And that's when it hit her. The round tins. She approached them slowly, and then, filled with dread, picked one up. Shoe polish. Stan's leather bag was filled with shoe polish.

CHAPTER 42

Grace and Stan sat on the roof deck. When Stan poured her a glass of wine, Grace tried not to down it all in one go, but she needed enough in her to stop herself from shaking. It had taken so much concentration to zip closed the leather bag, terrified the whole while that Stan was on the other side of the door, that he could hear it zip, that he would see drops of water near it, although she meticulously wiped the area with a towel and prayed she hadn't moved the bag or otherwise drawn any attention to it. Her heart was hammering so loudly when she emerged from the shower. She hadn't wanted to wash and condition her hair after that or shave, even though she did manage to find a razor tucked into her own bag. If she had found her razor in the first place, she never would have made the horrific discovery.

Killing animals. Drawing a noose around his father's neck and writing the word *die*. And shoe polish. Lionel hadn't shined his shoes before he hanged himself—which had never sat right with Grace; Stan had. Lionel hadn't killed himself. Stan had murdered him. Grace didn't know how it all had gone down, but she knew she was right. Stan was keeping the shoe polish as some sort of sick memento so he could relive the thrill. She was in the company of a true sociopath. And she would have to spend one more night with him. The festival was tomorrow night.

Did Carrie Ann know? No, Grace thought. Carrie Ann wasn't evil. She was immature and self-centered and manipulative. But not cold-blooded. She was just as much a victim of Stan as Grace and Jake.

Grace wondered what had happened. How had Stan killed Lionel and why?

Stan had gotten away with the perfect murder. So why was he coming after Grace like this?

Was this all because he had some secret obsession with Grace that she had never picked up on?

Or was he trying to find out if she suspected? Because of what she'd said to him at his father's funeral?

Lionel Gale's funeral was the last place on earth Grace Sawyer wanted to be, but guilt had drawn her there. She didn't know what to say to Stan, and quite frankly she didn't want to talk to him at all. He was skulking in the corner of the room, and he had worn jeans and a heavy-metal shirt. To his own father's funeral. Lydia seemed so out of it that Grace wasn't even sure Lydia noticed. Or maybe she just didn't care. Not many people were in attendance. By the time of the funeral Lionel Gale was one of the most talked about and detested men in town. But Grace had to show up. If she had managed to keep Carrie Ann with her, none of this would have happened. Or if she had told her mother the rumor that had begun on Carrie Ann's lips. So here Grace was. But she still didn't know what to stay to Stan. *I'm sorry for your loss.* It seemed so trite. *Your father was a good man.* She hadn't known Lionel, and she didn't want to lie. Instead, it just popped out. As she and Stan stood at the back of the funeral home. "Why do you think he polished his shoes?" Grace asked.

She'd never forget the look Stan gave her. "What?" he said.

"Never mind," Grace said. It was a stupid thing to blurt out. "I'm sorry." She turned to go. Stan grabbed her arm. It really hurt. She was forced to turn back to him.

"You noticed?" he asked.

"Yes. I just—I wondered why," she said.

"Did you tell the police?"

"No. But I'm sure they noticed."

"Are you kidding me? They're complete idiots. They noticed nothing."

"So was he like—a stickler for having polished shoes?"

"He had a shoe-polishing obsession," Stan said. "I hated that smell."

"I'm sorry," Grace said.

Stan stepped closer. "That's just it, Grace. I'm not."

"What?" She couldn't help it; she stepped back again. He was so intense. She wished she'd never come.

"I thought it was quite fitting. You're pretty smart, Grace. You noticed."

"Thanks," Grace said. Of course it was odd that she said "thanks," and it was even odder that Stan had said it like he was proud of her, and it was odder still that he thought it was quite fitting that his father had shone his shoes before he strangled himself to death.

I thought it was quite fitting.

"So what are you going to do about it?" Stan had asked.

"Do about what?"

"The things you noticed."

"I just—wanted to say I'm sorry. That's all." And then Grace did turn and practically run away. So creepy. What was that conversation about, anyway? At the time she had no idea.

Now that exchange took on a whole new meaning. *So what are you going to do about it? The things you noticed?* Had Stan thought they were sharing a secret back then? The secret that he had killed his father? Was he worried she was going to say something about it in her song? If that was the case, then he had no intention of letting her sing at the festival.

346 • *Mary Carter*

Carrie Ann was here to play games. Grace was sure about that. Carrie Ann wasn't a cat killer. Which meant Grace's mother had sent Carrie Ann away for the wrong reasons, and she had sent her directly to the boy who had actually done the cruel deed. Stan was the sociopath. Carrie Ann was just the drama queen. And if he picked up on everything Grace had just put together then she was going to be in real trouble.

Stan topped off her wine and then he held her gaze until she smiled and looked away. She was still shaking, so she was keeping her hands underneath the table as much as possible and doing everything to hint about how exhausted she was. "Cheers," Stan said, holding up his wine glass. Grace had no choice but to reach for hers and clink glasses. Stan's eyes bored into hers. "Why are your hands shaking?"

She thought she saw a flash of distrust in him, as if he was just waiting for her to slip. Did he know that she knew? He had to at least suspect. She tried not to think about the sketch he had done of her with the grotesque question mark hovering above her head. Or Carrie Ann stabbed and bleeding, Jake beaten to death.

Maybe he'd left the leather bag there on purpose. Maybe he wanted her to find it because he never intended to let her go. She had read that people often had a deep psychological need to confess. It was how a lot of evil people had been caught. They couldn't keep their mouths shut. Maybe all of this was Stan's idea of a game. Maybe the clues weren't meant to lead her anywhere but to the inevitable truth. Maybe the man hang-ing at the end of his game was going to be none other than her.

They were still playing the game. And there was no denying that her hands were vibrating like they had been electrified.

"I have a confession," Grace said.

"A confession," Stan repeated. "Does anyone else know?"

"Not a soul," Grace said.

"Tell me," Stan said.

"I'm an alcoholic." Grace drank the rest of the wine and then put it down. "I haven't been drinking much the past few days with you, so I'm going through withdrawal."

"I never would have known," Stan said. "That doesn't seem like you at all."

"I know, right? It's the music business. The pressure. The late nights. The fact that I work in a bar. I didn't even realize it myself until recently."

"Really?"

"Yeah. I mean—I haven't even admitted it to Jake. I know it sounds silly, but I was going to wait until after this trip to deal with it. What with coming to Spain, and my birthday, and my mom, and Marsh Everett—it just didn't seem like the right time to quit."

"And then here comes Carrie Ann to push you over the edge," Stan said.

"Right? Just makes me want to drink even more. But I'm looking forward to quitting. It's just not worth it. The hangovers, the cravings, the huge memory gaps—"

"Memory gaps?"

"Oh yeah. I mean I think I blocked out half my childhood. I mean half of that is probably because I don't want to remember it, but really—everything is just one big blur."

"Maybe you blocked out something traumatic."

"I think that probably applies more to you than to me."

"Why is that?"

"Well, you're the one with the dangerous job, aren't you? Kidnapped twice in the Congo. Now that's traumatic."

"I don't like to talk about that."

"I don't blame you." Grace picked up her glass again. "Let's toast again. To not talking about our pasts," she said.

There was a stage set up on the beach for the carnival and music fest. Grace searched the throngs of attendees, praying she would see the eagle costume sooner than later. The rest of the day and night with Stan had been torture. Grace told Stan she had a severe headache and after the roof deck she'd pretty much stayed curled up on the couch. Much to her surprise, when Grace left for the festival the next day, Stan had stayed back at the hotel and told her he would follow later. Of course it worried her, and she wondered what he was up to, but there wasn't any way she could find out. The desire to get away from him outweighed all curiosity. Besides, it would give her a chance to find Jake and Carrie Ann and get the heck out of Dodge.

It was too bad she wasn't here just to enjoy; the sun was warm on her shoulders and a band was already playing on stage. It was a block party–like atmosphere, and Grace wasn't going to be able to enjoy any of it. She had just worked her way to the middle of the crowd, when suddenly a hand clapped over her eyes from behind. Whoever it was had a tight grip, and he or she was tall. She knew, even before she put her own hands over the one that covered her eyes, that it was Carrie Ann.

"Let go or else," Grace said. She could feel Carrie Ann behind her, shaking with laughter. All doubts at what she was going to do flew out of Grace's head. She lifted her boot and brought it down on Carrie Ann's foot. She made contact. Carrie Ann screamed, and her hand immediately sprung off. Grace whipped around to find Carrie Ann doubled over in pain. When Carrie Ann's eyes met Grace's eyes, Carrie Ann smiled through her pain, threw open her arms, and said, "I forgive you. Surprise! Happy birthday!"

Grace stood still as Carrie Ann enveloped her in a hug. Grace placed her hands on Carrie Ann's shoulders and pushed her back. She made sure to make eye contact.

"I'm furious with you, Carrie Ann, but now is not the time to hash it out."

"I know," Carrie Ann said. "Jake wanted me to hit Rafael over the head with something, but I just couldn't. But I did handcuff him to the bedposts. As soon as Jake gets here, I'll have to go and set Rafael free."

"Where is Jake? We have to get out of here before Stan gets here."

"Aw, you figured it out! Stan was right."

"What did you just say?"

"Stan thought you were on to him."

"Look at me, Carrie Ann. When did Stan say that?"

"Why are you freaking out? The drugs and kidnapping

weren't my idea, okay? I was supposed to disappear. But I have to admit, it was rather dramatic."

Grace grabbed Carrie Ann's shoulders. "When did Stan tell you he thought I knew?"

"I don't know. Right before you came back from Cadaqués."

"Oh, God." So that's why he had been quiet in the car. If he suspected she knew, why had he let her come here alone? Worse, what was he planning next?

"What is the matter with you? It's over!"

"I don't have time to explain. Where is Jake?"

"Probably getting into costume—"

"Where?"

"At Rafael's apartment. He'll be here soon. Let's dance, or get a drink."

"He's in serious danger, Carrie Ann. We all are. We've got to get to the apartment."

Carrie Ann grabbed Grace's arms. "I really just wanted us to have an adventure. Like old times."

"We have to go, Carrie Ann. Now."

"Aren't you going to sing? Haven't we at least cured your phobia of facing scary things?"

"Stan wasn't pulling a prank, Carrie Ann. Stan is unhinged."

"Well, he's always been a bit off."

"No. He killed—"

"There he is!" Carrie Ann pointed past Grace. Grace turned around to see the giant eagle coming toward her.

"Jake." Grace ran to him, threw herself at him, nearly knocking them both to the ground. He squeezed her back, then lifted her off the ground and twirled her around. His face was covered with white paint, and he was even wearing the eye mask.

"You went all out," Carrie Ann said.

"There's no time," Grace said. "We have to find a safe place now." She grabbed Jake's hand, and then Carrie Ann's, and began to pull them as quickly as she could through the crowd. She found a taxi and ushered them in. Stan knew where the apartment building was, so that was out.

"Carrie Ann, where can we go that's out of the way?"

"I don't understand what's going on."

"Where?"

"I don't know. Old Barcelona?"

"Tell the driver," Grace said. "I'll explain everything when I feel we're safe." Carrie Ann repeated Grace's request to the driver, and they pulled out into traffic.

"Grace, it was a joke," Carrie Ann said.

"Not for Stan," Grace said. "He's a true psychopath." She dug into her purse and brought out the sketches. She showed them to Carrie Ann. She turned to Jake. "I wish you could take that makeup off." Jake reached up with his hand and rubbed. Only a little came off his cheek. "It's okay. As soon as we're safe we can get to a sink."

"What is this?" Carrie Ann shrieked. "What is this?"

Jake leaned forward, trying to have a look. The taxi pulled up to a small alley. The driver pointed down the length of it and spoke.

"He said there is a private little courtyard down there," Carrie Ann said. Her voice was shaking. Thank God she understood the seriousness of the sketches.

"Perfecto," Grace said. She paid the driver, and they piled out. They headed down the alley and reached the courtyard. It consisted of a few trees and a couple of benches. It was tiny— postage stamp–size.

"Let's help Jake get this off," she said. They unzipped the back of his costume and helped pull the sleeves down. "Can you get the rest?" Jake nodded.

"Stan killed Brady?" Carrie Ann said.

"With my pink scarf," Grace said. "My mother thought you had killed him. That's why she sent you away."

Carrie Ann's hand flew over her mouth. "Oh my God. Oh my God." Jake had stopped undressing and was standing still, listening.

"You saw the rest of the drawings. I think he killed his dad."

"His dad hanged himself."

"Stan left me a note to come to the hayloft. I thought it was from you. When I got there—when I saw Lionel—his shoes had just been polished. They were pristine. The leather bag where I found these sketches was filled with tins of shoe polish."

"He has a picture of me being stabbed, and of Jake being beaten—"

"I know. We have to get to the police."

"Why? Why would he kill his father?"

"I've been thinking about that. I think his father found out what Stan was doing."

"What do you mean?"

"Really, Carrie Ann? After all this time, you still won't tell the truth?"

Carrie Ann's face paled. "What?" Her voice cracked.

"It was Stan, wasn't it? He was the one coming into your room at night." Carrie Ann's face said it all.

"Why did you lie?" Grace said.

"Because I was mortified! You already hated Stan's guts. I didn't want anyone to know. I just wanted to get out of there. I thought if I told you . . . I swear. I had no idea anyone else was going to find out. I had no idea Lionel would kill himself—"

"He didn't. But I didn't spread those rumors."

"I didn't either."

"I know. I'm pretty sure Stan did."

"My God."

"His dad must have threatened him with something when he found out—so Stan turned it around on him."

"This is sick, just sick. You were right about him all along."

"Jake—what's taking you so long—" Grace started to say. She was interrupted by the sound of clapping. They turned around to find Jake standing with his back to them, applauding. "Jake?" Grace said. He turned around. Half the white paint was gone. It was Stan. "No," Grace said. "Where's Jake?" She screamed. "What have you done with him?"

"It's true, isn't it?" Carrie Ann said. "Everything Grace just said." Grace grabbed Carrie Ann's hand.

"Hey, girls," Stan said. He threw open his arms. "Just like old times."

"Let's not do anything crazy," Carrie Ann said.

"What did you do to Jake?" Grace said.

"I kept my promise," Stan said. "He's not dead. Yet. I'll even let Carrie Ann go take care of him. But only if you come with me, Grace." Stan still had the costume half on, pooled around his ankles. It didn't look like he was wearing the knives either. If they had any sort of chance of getting away, it was right now.

"Run," Grace said to Carrie Ann. "Run!"

CHAPTER 43

Stan's brilliant plan was unraveling. The costume was too cumbersome. He'd thought the Universe was on his side when Rafael finally broke down and confessed that Jake was going to show up at the festival in his eagle costume. That's when Stan knew it had all been meant to be. He would get into the costume instead, assuring that Grace would come to him as long as she thought he was Jake. It was easy enough to knock lover boy out, and with a little luck, he'd be dead by the time anyone got to him. It would all be for nothing if Grace and Carrie Ann got away. He could hear their heels clacking in the alley as he struggled to get free of the godforsaken feathers. He had to kick his damn shoes off to get the costume all the way off, and by the time he shoved his feet back into the sneakers, they had made it through the alley and hopped into a cab. He thought about chasing the cab, but it screeched away and was soon all the way to the end of the street. There wasn't another cab in sight. They were heading to the apartment to find Jake. He knew some shortcuts. He'd head over on foot, and hop in a cab if he saw one. If he was lucky, their cab would get stuck in traffic, and he might even beat them there. He liked this. All of their fates now depended on luck. Just like his father's life had ended because of a streak of bad luck.

It had changed him, killing a person. He hadn't meant to do it. Not like he'd meant to strangle that hideous cat. It was always hissing at him when he came at night to climb up in Grace's tree house. With binoculars, he could see into her room. See her cute little body in her shorts and tank tops. Once he had seen her naked. But that damn cat's yowling had spooked her, and she had pulled the shades.

Then, his father had come to him in the middle of that crisis, and told him he knew it was Stan going into Carrie Ann's room with his flashlight. Lionel had said he wasn't going to let Stan get away with it. Lionel was going to send him to one of those military-type detention schools. Stan had lost it. His father had made the mistake of coming up into the hayloft to confront him. Stan had seen an opportunity when his father had turned to go back down the ladder. In order to back down the ladder, he had to get on his hands and knees. When his father had assumed that position, Stan hadn't thought; he had just pounced.

Before his father could even turn his head, Stan had jumped on Lionel's back, grabbed him around the neck, and squeezed. His father had been in a crawling position, supporting himself as he had been about to step onto the ladder, and with the weight of Stan on top of his back, Lionel hadn't been able to bring his hands up to fight for his life. Stan hadn't planned it, but once his hands had been wrapped around his father's neck, rage had just seemed to funnel through his hands. His father had not had Stan's bulk; he had been just as tall, but skinny. It had all happened so fast. When Stan had finally let go, his father had slumped to the floor of the hayloft. Stan had been hit with a wave of terror and nausea. He couldn't go to jail for murder. His dad had been the one everyone thought of as the pervert. Child molester. That's when Stan had looked out and seen his tire swing, swaying in the breeze. His eye had followed up the long, thick rope. And the rest, as they say, was history. It had been easy enough to make a noose and attach one end to the rafters. Then all he had to do was attach Lionel to the noose and push him into a hanging position from the hayloft. Out of respect, Stan had shined Lionel's shoes. His dad would have liked that.

Stan had waited to get caught. He had been terrified for a long time that the medical examiner might have caught something. He had done his best to fit the rope exactly over the strangulation marks. And they had bought it. Or maybe they just didn't want to investigate the suicide death of a child molester. Either way. They had bought the suicide and closed the case as quickly as possible.

That was Stan's history. That's who Grace Sawyer was messing with.

She hadn't changed. She had thought he was a nobody back then; he'd never forget the look on her face when she had first climbed up to her tree house to find him sitting there next to Carrie Ann. The look she had given him had made his palms slick with sweat, made him want to instantly apologize, as if it were a crime to be sitting in her precious tree house. Carrie Ann had been twelve times more popular than little Miss Grace Sawyer, and he still liked—no, loved—her more than he had ever liked or loved Carrie Ann. He'd really hoped Grace had changed. No such luck.

Damn it. He shouldn't have whispered to her. That was probably when she realized that nobody else could have been in that tiny house without her knowing. Or maybe she had recognized his voice. It was possible. Again, he couldn't help himself. She looked so sweet, sitting there with her pretty eyes closed. She was so dainty! Carrie Ann had a voluptuous figure that most guys went for, T&A and all that. But Grace was so tantalizing, so petite. Her ankles alone were enough to whip him into a frenzy. How could he not whisper to her?

The leather bag in the bathroom. He'd forgotten all about it. And even if he had remembered, he certainly hadn't taken Grace for a snoop. What had she been doing in his bag? This wasn't the way it was supposed to go. He was supposed to be on a train to Rome with Grace.

He was halfway to the apartment now. If he ran the rest of the way, he could be there in ten minutes. Grace and Carrie Ann were surely at the apartment by now. But all was not lost. He didn't have to beat the girls there—just the police.

And then it would be too late. For all of them. Stan knew what had to happen. If he found them all in the apartment, that was going to be it. The end. Not one of them was going to make it out alive. Not even him. It was too bad. He'd been telling the truth about wanting to take his last breath while lying in a rowboat and bobbing out to sea.

CHAPTER 44

Something was ringing. At first Jake thought it was coming from inside his head. He tried to move his head and pain shot through it. He was lying on the floor. Rafael was shouting from the bedroom. Why couldn't he just come out? Jake's phone was in his back pocket. Stan had knocked him over the head, but hadn't taken the phone. He'd been in too much of a hurry. To get into the eagle costume. To find Grace. Oh, God, how long had Jake been knocked out? Doing his best not to move his head at all, after three tries, Jake finally reached his phone. He couldn't even say hello; he just let out a groan.

"Hello? Hello?" It was Grace's father. Jake groaned again, louder this time. He heard a woman's voice in the background.

"Is it her?" Jody Sawyer could be heard saying. "Is it Grace?"

"I think it's a wrong number," Jim said.

"Help," Jake said. At least tried to say. It was the best he could do to form the word. Did Grace's parents know the address of their flat? He couldn't remember. And even if they did—why would they think to look in the apartment above? And why couldn't he talk?

Because before Stan had hit Jake over the head, Stan had tried to strangle him. Came awfully close too. But Jake had been able to get in a good kick to the shins, and that's when suddenly Stan had some sort of heavy vase in his hands, and the next and last thing Jake remembered was it crashing down on his head. It was no joke, the blood on the floor was all too real. "Help," Jake said again. Not for him. But for Grace. Somebody had to get to Grace.

"What's wrong?" Jody said when Jim hung up the phone. They were in a cab from the airport. The driver had assured them that any minute now they would be in the center of Barcelona.

"I think that was Jake. I think he's hurt."

"Oh, God. Should we tell the driver to go faster?"

"No," Jim said. "We should ask him where to find the nearest police station."

The taxi was taking too long. *Please let Jake be okay,* Grace prayed. She'd do anything. "You should get out," Grace said. Carrie Ann was still holding her hand.

"What?" Carrie Ann said.

"Stan will figure out we're on our way to the apartment. He may even beat us there. But you could get out now. He'd never find you."

"I'm staying," Carrie Ann said. "It's my fault you're in this mess."

"It's Stan's fault," Grace said.

"I'm so sorry," Carrie Ann said.

"Let's just focus on Jake right now." When the taxi pulled up, Grace flew out of it and ran into the building. She took the stairs two at a time and burst through the door to the apartment. "Jake. Jake. Jake." He wasn't here. She heard Carrie Ann continuing up a flight. Grace raced after her. By the time Grace got into the room, Carrie Ann was already kneeling down by Jake. There was blood on the floor. Carrie Ann just looked up at Grace.

"I forgive you," Grace said. "Just tell me this is part of the prank, and I forgive you for everything."

Carrie Ann reached for a phone near Jake. "It's dead," she said.

Grace frantically searched her purse. "My cell is gone," she said. "Stan must have it." She ran to Jake and knelt next to him. "Is he breathing?"

"Help," Rafael called from the bedroom. "Let me out!"

"Yes," Carrie Ann said. "But it's shallow, Grace. He doesn't sound good." Grace went to cradle his head.

"Don't touch his head," Carrie Ann said. "Here. Hold his hand." She took Grace's hand and placed it on Jake's. At the feel of his hand, Grace burst into tears. Carrie Ann put her arms around Grace.

"Shh," Carrie Ann said. "I'm going to run and get help, okay?" Grace nodded. "I'm sorry, Grace. I never meant—"

"What's going on out there?" Rafael yelled. "Will somebody let me out?"

"Just go," Grace said. "Please. Hurry." Carrie Ann nodded, and then she was up and running to the door. Just as she reached it, she screamed. Grace didn't even have to look up; she knew it was Stan.

Grace bent down and whispered in Jake's ear, "You're going to be okay. You hear me? You stay right here. Don't you go anywhere. Stay here, Jake. With me."

"Hello, Grace." Stan's voice was deep; his accent long gone. Grace looked up. He had Carrie Ann's back pressed against him, and his arm was around her throat. Carrie Ann's eyes were wide and pleading, and even through the panic, Grace found herself thinking that there was something wrong about seeing Carrie Ann so vulnerable. As if the entire universe were upside down, and maybe it was.

"I'm in here," Rafael yelled. "I'm chained to the bed."

"Let her go, Stan," Grace said. "Let them go and you can have me."

"You had your chance, Grace. You didn't take it," Stan said.

Grace stood slowly, put her hands in the air. "I mean it. Let me call an ambulance, and then you and I will run out of here."

"You think I'm letting Carrie Ann get away? After what she made me do?"

"What did she make you do, Stan?"

"Always talking about how she slept in the nude. She wanted me to come into her room. She planned it." Carrie Ann tried to shake her head. Stan gripped her tighter. "Then she ruined my father's life with her lies."

"They were your lies, Stan. You spread the rumors," Grace said.

"Because of her! I had no choice. She wanted me in her room. It's all her fault. Ruined my mother's life. My life."

"Did you kill Brady, Stan?"

"That stupid cat? You want to talk about that stupid cat now?" Grace just wanted to keep him talking, period. Jake's foot suddenly tapped her. She made sure not to react, but slowly looked down. There, kicked underneath a small table, was a leather cuff. She had no idea what it was, but she bent down as if groaning over Jake. Once she was eye level, she saw what it was. Rafael's knives. It was time to find out if they were real. She prayed harder than she'd ever prayed in her life, even though she didn't want to have to do it.

"Please. Tell me what I can do," Grace said. She wailed, hoping the noise would distract Stan as she fell to the ground in front of Jake. She reached her arm out and found the cuff. She whipped it behind her back and stood. Her heart hammered as she waited to see if Stan had noticed.

"I'm going to kill Carrie Ann, and then I'm going to beat your boyfriend until he stops breathing, and then if you still want to go with me, we can leave."

"No," Grace said. "I won't go with you. If you kill Carrie Ann, or Jake, I won't go with you."

"Then all four of us leave here in body bags. That's the way it was going to be anyway. We all knew that."

"It was a Tuesday night, he was a working man, he had a son named Stan." Grace stomped her foot.

"Stop that," Stan said.

"Stan had a tire swing, he liked everything, he was a boy with hope." Grace stared at Carrie Ann until she made eye contact. Grace raised her eyebrows and stomped her foot again.

"Stop singing," Stan said.

"His feet could touch the sky, he could really fly, it was a long, thick rope."

"Enough!" Stan roared.

Carrie Ann wasn't getting it. This time, Grace mimed stomping on her own foot. The light finally came into Carrie Ann's eyes, and she pulled up her foot and stomped as hard as she could on Stan's foot with her heel. Stan let go for the briefest second as he yelled out. Grace didn't have time to think. He was going to kill them all; she'd seen it in his eyes.

"I'm sorry," she screamed. She rushed Stan and aimed the knives at his shoulder. He twisted the wrong way, and she had no choice. She plunged the knives straight into his chest. He screamed. The loudest Grace had ever heard. It almost didn't even sound human. Then, clutching his chest, he slumped to the ground.

Stan was alive, but barely. Carrie Ann immediately searched Stan's pockets for a cell phone, but just then, they heard sirens. A ton of them. Getting closer. Carrie Ann ran to the window as Grace ran back to Jake. "Hang on, hang on, hang on," she kept repeating. "Please hang on." She had no idea who had called the police and the ambulance, but whoever it was had just given Jake and Stan a fighting chance.

Because Grace felt as if her heart were in her throat, the wait felt like forever, but eventually they heard footsteps pounding up the stairs, and seconds later the police swarmed in. They were followed by Jim and Jody Sawyer. Grace was so thrown, for a minute she thought she was dead and seeing things.

"Mom?" Grace said. "Dad?"

"Gracie," her mother said. She clasped her hands under her chin and grinned at Grace. "Spain is so exciting," she said.

"Dad?" Grace said.

"Jake called us," Jim said. "He said you were in trouble."

"How did you know where to find us?" Grace asked.

"Jake," her father said. "We were meant to be here from the beginning. To surprise you for your birthday. Thank God or I never would have known where to send the police."

Grace looked down at Jake, and another sob tore from her. She clung to him until they physically pulled her away so they could place him on a stretcher. Others attended to Stan, although Grace could not have cared less right now. Carrie Ann was speaking to the police in Spanish. Hopefully, she was telling the whole truth and nothing but the truth. Although Grace realized now that not everything Carrie Ann had said back then had been a lie. Just the truth as she believed it to be. That was the thing about truths; they were all subjective. Being true to yourself simply meant telling the truth as you knew it. Singing from the heart meant singing whatever the hell you wanted, as long as you really wanted it. She was so lost in her thoughts that she didn't know her mother was beside her until Jody was squeezing her hand.

"I like this play," she said to Grace. "It's very exciting."

"I'm glad you like it, Mom." Grace leaned over and put her head on her mother's shoulder.

"Is that stud muffin going to be in it?"

Grace looked at her father. He gave a little smile. "I'm right here, darling," he said with a wink. Then he smiled at Grace and shrugged. "At least she's in Spain," he said. "At least we're all here in Spain."

A scream tore from the bedroom. Her parents jumped. "Oh, shit," Carrie Ann said. "I forgot about Rafael." Jake was on the stretcher now. Grace followed him out. For all she cared, Rafael could stay in there forever. All that mattered now was Jake.

CHAPTER 45

Carrie Ann slowly approached Grace. "You must hate me. You must wish I was never born." Grace and Carrie Ann were on Rambla el Raval. Raval was one of the most ethnically diverse neighborhoods in all of Barcelona. Once one of the seediest spots in the city, it was now a destination in and of itself, not only for its colorful characters and red-light-district past, but also for its great selection of restaurants and bars. They had stopped in front of a giant cat sculpture, made by the artist Fernando Botero. Carrie Ann glanced at the cat. It was chunky, and primitive, and smiling. Unlike Grace. Except maybe the primitive part, that part was a little like her, given that she wanted to rip Carrie Ann's hair out by the roots.

"This neighborhood has redeemed itself," Carrie Ann said, looking up the street.

"Yet it still holds on to its seedy past," Grace said, looking at Carrie Ann.

Carrie Ann nodded and held her hands up as if surrendering. "Are we here for a cat fight?"

"It certainly seems like the perfect spot."

"Don't forget. Cats have nine lives. Any chance you'd be willing to give me another?"

Jake was still in the hospital; he was going to need some recovery time, but he was going to be okay. He'd already been given a blood transfusion. Carrie Ann had donated the blood. To everyone's surprise, they were the same type. Carrie Ann had joked that maybe she and Jake were long-lost siblings. That wasn't funny at all, but given that Carrie Ann had done something to help Jake, Grace had agreed to let Carrie Ann speak with her privately.

"No more games, Carrie Ann. No more jokes. If we're going to talk, we're going to talk."

"You're right," Carrie Ann said. "Let me have it."

"Why? Why did you do this?"

"I just wanted us to have an adventure—"

"We haven't spoken in almost fifteen years."

"But I've thought of you and your parents every day. Every single day."

"Look. I didn't answer your letters. I'll give you that."

"You sent them *back*."

"I sent them back."

"You. Not your mother. You wrote 'return to sender' across every single one and sent them back."

"Yes. To your PO box in Tennessee. Have you lived there all this time?"

"No."

"I'm not going to pry words out of your mouth."

"I'll tell you anything you want to know."

"If you were so desperate to talk to me, why didn't you just show up in person?"

"I did. I came to several of your shows. You're so good, Gracie. You really are."

Grace started to pace in front of the cat. It was early in the morning, too early to draw the stares of passersby. Across the street there was a man sleeping in a doorway, folded up into a brown blanket. From a distance he looked like a giant, rotten banana. Otherwise they had the block to themselves. Grace was not embarrassed to raise her voice. "This is what I'm talking about! You were at my shows and then what? You just snuck out without saying anything? That's not normal, Carrie Ann. That's diabolical behavior!"

"I was trying to respect you! After getting every single letter back, I kind of figured—hey, this chick wants zero to do with me anymore. I'm scum to her."

"Oh. So you kidnap me and my boyfriend instead?"

"That wasn't the original intent. It started out as a prank of sorts. Really it was the only way I felt brave enough to confront you."

"I don't think that was normal, Carrie Ann. I think maybe you still need help."

"Well, believe it or not, I did this for you."

"Forgive me if I don't see it that way."

"Grace. I saw what you were going through—that nasty review you posted on Facebook. I hated that guy. I fantasized about ripping his throat out for making you feel bad. You're gifted, Grace. I swear to God. I thought maybe I could help you. I could feel the pain you were in—"

"No, Carrie Ann. You couldn't. You don't know me. Not anymore."

"Maybe you're right. And maybe you never really wanted to be my sister. But in my head and in my heart, you were mine. I didn't know your mother thought I killed your cat, Grace. Think about it. Think about how I felt to be kicked out of the only place where I felt I had a home. The only place I had ever lived where I could actually exhale. Where I felt safe. And loved. By you. Do you have any idea what that did to me? Do you even care?"

"Of course I care."

"Don't say it if you don't mean it."

"I do mean it. But at the time—I thought maybe you did kill Brady. You were always so jealous."

"I know. I know I was. I can't change that now. But you of all people should have known that my bark was way worse than my bite."

"Well, your bark was pretty fucking bad."

"Touché. So is this how it ends? We're going to let a series of misunderstandings ruin everything?"

"You didn't kill Brady, and I'm sorry we thought you did. But you can't say that living with you was easy sailing."

"I was a wreck. Okay? I was the *Titanic.*"

"I wouldn't go that far."

"I would. But I loved you, Grace. I still do. You have to know that. I don't care how much time has gone by for you. No time has gone by for me. Not when it comes to you. You gave me something I'd never ever had before. You were the only person who made me feel as if I was worth something. I've spent the past fifteen years determined to prove to you that you were right."

"Where have you even been all this time? I don't know a single thing about your life. Where you live, what you do—if you've ever been in love. I don't know you at all."

"At the psych ward, I had a great therapist. Karen. When I turned eighteen and was about to get out, well, I actually was going to come find you then. Karen talked me out of it. She said I was too angry, hadn't processed enough of the trauma. She encouraged me to look at things from your point of view. But then she up and told me she was moving to Sarasota, Florida, to set up a private practice. I thought she was abandoning me like everyone else. To my surprise, she suggested I move with her. So I did. I didn't live with her or anything. Got my own apartment. I stripped at first to make ends meet, but eventually Karen got me to see it wasn't the best use of my assets. So I switched to waitressing. Even took some classes at a community college. I slept around a lot, but I could never get really close to anyone. That was because of Stan, of course. And in some ways—you."

"Me?"

"You really hurt me, Grace. I guess I was stupid to think you really loved me—"

"I did love you, Carrie Ann. But I was a kid. I couldn't handle—"

"Me," Carrie Ann said. "You couldn't handle me."

Grace and Carrie Ann locked eyes. Finally, Grace nodded. "I'm sorry."

"I understand that now, Grace. I'm telling you. I worked through a lot of stuff. Karen was there when I was working through everything that happened with Stan, and Lionel. She was the one who encouraged me to confront Stan."

"That sounds like really bad advice," Grace said. She leaned against the cat.

"We certainly didn't know he was a murderer," Carrie Ann said. "Mental case, I was fine with."

"And so you went to see Stan."

"And so I went to see Stan. I'd been in Florida for eleven years. Eleven years of therapy. I even have a college degree, believe it or not."

"That's great," Grace said. "I mean it. I'm proud of you. In what?"

"Theater."

"Perfect." Grace laughed despite herself.

Carrie Ann moved to the other side of the cat. "So, back to confronting Stan."

"That must have been difficult," Grace said.

"Well. It certainly didn't go the way I thought it would. I thought he'd still be overweight and completely bumbling. I thought I'd intimidate the hell out of him—yell at him—hit him, even—anything to make myself feel better. Imagine my surprise when I saw his transformation. I didn't believe it was him at first. Except of course he was still living at home. I mean—the door opens and here is this drop dead gorgeous man. At first I thought Lydia had bagged herself a younger man—I was like, way to go, Mrs. Robinson. Then he starts telling me how happy he is to see me, and how sorry he is for everything. I'm like, holy shit. That's Stan? That's Stan?"

"Add a French accent and no one would ever suspect," Grace said.

Carrie Ann looked sheepish, but continued. "He said he'd

been to therapy too. He said he was on medication, that he'd had severe psychological problems and that all these years he'd hated himself for what he had done to me—he even said he blamed himself for his father's death."

"That's ironic."

"Right? Slowly but surely, we started to talk. I moved back to Tennessee. Against Karen's wishes, I might add. She thought I still had a long way to go." Grace arched an eyebrow. "I know, I know. Anyway. It wasn't long after I moved back and started hanging out with Stan that he started talking about you. How miserable you seemed on Facebook. And how—if he and I could heal the rift between us, then why couldn't we do it with you? I'd told him all about our tree house promise of our thirtieth birthday and how we always said we'd celebrate it in Europe. That's when he came up with the idea for the surprise. I have to admit. I couldn't resist the idea of seeing your face when you found out what Stan looked like now. Especially since you were always so grossed out by him."

"With good reason," Grace said.

"He made the plan sound so good, Grace. I got so involved with it that for a time I thought it was really my idea—after all, I was the one who came up with it as a kid. And then it just snowballed. I wanted to see you. I wanted the three of us to heal our past. I wanted to celebrate in Europe. Especially if Stan was paying for it. I guess I thought we deserved it. All of us. In my mind, you were the last piece of the puzzle I needed to heal. And maybe I wanted to hurt you a little bit too. For rejecting me. But never—never, ever, ever, did I think you were going to be in any real danger. I swear on my life, Grace. You're my sister." Carrie Ann let out a sob. "I was supposed to disappear. It was so childish, but I was supposed to disappear and I was going to leave you little clues all around Spain—like a scavenger hunt, and I had no idea Stan was a psychopath. This is my fault. This is all my fault. Jake is lying in the hospital because of me."

"Jake is going to be fine. Thanks to you."

"Somebody else would have donated blood."

"Somebody else didn't have to. You stuck around. You could have left when I found out what you did. But you didn't. You stayed. That means something to me. It means a lot."

"If anything had happened to you—"

"Shhh," Grace said. "You know how much cats hate water."

Carrie Ann looked at her tears, dripping onto the sculpture. "Sorry, kitty," she said, wiping them off. Then, she laughed. "You could always make me laugh, Gracie Ann. Every time." Carrie Ann sobbed again, tears that had been buried too deep for too long. Grace's heart broke open too. She bridged the distance between them and enveloped Carrie Ann in a hug.

"It's going to be okay."

"Is it?" Carrie Ann asked.

"I want to know you again. I want to start over. As equals."

"I want that too."

"Nashville is a great place to live."

"Maybe a town over, so you don't think I'm stalking you."

"Or maybe next door. Where I can keep an eye on you."

They linked arms and began to walk down the street. "Happy birthday, Grace," Carrie Ann said.

"Happy birthday, Carrie Ann."

"I think I finally decided what I want to be when I grow up," Carrie Ann said.

"What's that?"

"Grown up." They held eye contact until Carrie Ann laughed. Then Grace shook her head and laughed with her. Soon, they were laughing uncontrollably, tears streaming down their faces. And they walked.

Four days following the scene in the apartment, Jake was out of the hospital, and they were in the square near the apartment. It was warm and peaceful. Jake had a bandage wrapped around his head, and was warned to take it easy, but otherwise he was going to be all right. Stan was still in the hospital, but he was also expected to make a full recovery. That is, when he recovered, he would still be a psychopath. But this time he would be on his way to a Spanish jail. Lydia was on her way to see him. Grace wondered if she had ever suspected the truth about what happened to Lionel, and she couldn't help but feel sorry for Lydia. So much pain for such a wonderful woman.

Jody was weak, and her memory was coming and going again, but in her more lucid moments, her eyes lit up at her surroundings. Earlier in the day Jody and Grace had sat in the middle of the square watching tango dancers. Her mother's eyes had filled with tears, and she had grasped Grace's hand. Now that they knew the truth about who really killed Brady, they had all made their apologies to Carrie Ann, and Grace didn't tell them how far Carrie Ann had gone to pull off this birthday prank. And even though it was just a small audience this morning—Jody and Jim, Carrie Ann, and Jake; in other words, family—this was the perfect place for Grace to face her one last fear. It seemed like nothing compared to what had happened the past few days.

Her little audience sat on benches, and Grace stood in front of them, took a deep breath, and sang from the heart.

> *"It was a Tuesday night,*
> *He was a working man,*
> *He had a son named Stan. . . ."*

The groove opened, that welcoming space where the music flowed through Grace as if she were the instrument and not the guitar. She was no longer afraid.

> *"She was a foster child*
> *She was a girl gone wild*
> *Her name was Carrie Ann. . . .*
>
> *"We shared my tree house,*
> *She was a friend in need,*
> *But not a friend in deed*
>
> *"It was a Tuesday night,*
> *He was a working man,*

He had a son named Stan
Stan had a tire swing,
He liked everything,
He was a boy with hope
His feet could touch the sky,
He could really fly
It was a long, thick rope. . . .

"That was a long time ago
And what I didn't know
Was what to believe
But what I didn't see
Through all her smoke screens
Was that she needed me
She was my sister then
She is my sister now
And we'll forgive somehow. . . ."

She looked up to find tears in Carrie Ann's eyes. Carrie Ann looked at Grace and nodded.

"It was a Tuesday night,
He was a working man,
He had a son named Stan
I'm just a Nashville girl,
And I've been on a whirl
And now I've got what I need
My family is here and my love is near,
And I'm lucky indeed
Marsh can go to hell because I can tell
There's only one thing to do
He is my everything, and he's there
When I sing and he loves TV—"

Jake snorted on that line—not a sound he meant to make, but he'd tried to disguise his laughter. Grace was thrilled to hear the sound.

"Jake, I love you, you're my hero to be,
Jake, will you marry me?"

Grace finished the song on her knee. Jake rushed up. "Careful, careful," she cried. Jake got on his knees too and gently touched her face.

"I forgot the ring," she said.

"Shut up," he said.

"I've loved you ever since we met and you cried over that little kitten."

"A little louder. I don't think they heard you in France."

"I never want to lose you again."

"You never lost me at all."

"Will you, Jake? Will you marry me?"

"Of course I'll marry you," he said.

"Your partner Dan is not invited to the wedding."

"In his defense—he thought he was helping us get a free trip. And he has been taking care of our sweet Stella."

"Fine. Dan can come too."

"You're a pushover."

"Damn," Grace said. "Marsh Everett is right. Everything in my life always ends on a happy note." And before she could complain anymore, Jake wrapped his arms around her and shut her up with his beautiful lips. When they parted, her mother clapped. Her father took her mother's hand and held it. Grace took Jake's hand, and pulled him up. Then she stretched out with her other hand, and waited for Carrie Ann to take it.

MEET ME IN BARCELONA

Mary Carter

ABOUT THIS GUIDE

The suggested questions are included to enhance
your group's reading of Mary Carter's
Meet Me in Barcelona.

DISCUSSION QUESTIONS

1. Grace Sawyer is leery when she and her boyfriend, Jake, "win" a trip to Spain. Should she have followed her initial reservations and remained at home?

2. If Grace had remained at home, do you think Carrie Ann would have showed up in Nashville instead?

3. Grace's mother isn't well and may not have long to live. How does that influence Grace's decisions throughout? Had her mother been well, do you think Grace would have told her that Carrie Ann had come back from the past? Would it have changed any of the outcomes if she had?

4. In the beginning, Grace is obsessed with a bad review from Marsh Everett. Does her perspective change by the end? In what way?

5. What influence does the setting of Barcelona play in the events as they unfold? Could the story have just as easily taken place in Paris, or Rome?

6. Do you think that confronting her past changes Grace as an artist? If no, why not? If yes, in what way?

7. If Carrie Ann had never showed up in Barcelona, do you think Grace would have ever tried to find her? Why or why not? Do you think it was ultimately a positive thing for Grace that she was forced to confront Carrie Ann and the past? Please discuss.

8. Along those lines, do you think Grace would have eventually told Jake the truth about Carrie Ann and Stan? Why or why not?

9. Carrie Ann and Grace had a complex love/hate relationship. Was Carrie Ann all to blame? Did Grace let Carrie Ann down after she went to live with the Gales?

10. Do the events in Barcelona make Jake and Grace stronger as a couple, weaker, or not changed at all?

11. Marsh Everett thinks Grace should "sing her pain." Yet while in Barcelona, she finds joy in Gaudí's and Miró's works. Does the best art come from joy or pain?

12. Grace finds herself attracted to Jean Sebastian and leans on him when Carrie Ann and Jake disappear. In retrospect, you might say she had "blinders" on when it comes to him. She doesn't see him for who he really is. Is there anyone else in her life she's ever applied these same "blinders" to? Carrie Ann? Stan? What about Jake?

13. Do you think Grace and Carrie Ann will remain in each other's lives, or will they drift apart?

14. People always ask, "Were there any warning signs?" What about Stan and the revelations in the end? Were there any warning signs? Could he have been "helped" if someone had noticed the warning signs and intervened?

15. Magicians, costumes, identity, and denial—please discuss how these symbols and themes are interwoven throughout the story.

16. Was Carrie Ann an evil girl, or just a product of abandonment and neglect? Has she changed? Can she change? Does Carrie Ann really love Grace?

Thank you for taking the time to read and discuss *Meet Me in Barcelona*. Please feel free to contact me via my Web site if any questions linger. I love to interact with readers.